SCENT *of* TRIUMPH

Jan Moran

SCENT of TRIUMPH

ST. MARTIN'S GRIFFIN

NEW YORK

SCENT OF TRIUMPH. Copyright © 2015 by Jan Moran. All rights reserved.
Printed in the United States of America. For information,
address St. Martin's Press, 175 Fifth Avenue, New York, N.Y. 10010.

www.stmartins.com

The Library of Congress Cataloging-in-Publication Data is available upon request.

ISBN 978-1-250-04890-5 (trade paperback)
ISBN 978-1-250-06607-7 (hardcover)
ISBN 978-1-4668-5002-6 (e-book)

St. Martin's Griffin books may be purchased for educational, business, or promotional use.
For information on bulk purchases, please contact the Macmillan Corporate and Premium
Sales Department at 1-800-221-7945, extension 5442, or write to specialmarkets@macmillan.com.

First Edition: April 2015

10 9 8 7 6 5 4 3 2 1

For my mother, Jeanne Hollenbeck,
who contributed her memories of life during
World War II, and instilled in me a love of perfume
and all things beautiful. My deep
appreciation and love.

Acknowledgments

My deep appreciation and love goes to my mother, Jeanne Hollenbeck, who contributed her memories of her life during the World War II era. And to my grandmother Eva Hammons, who taught me how to sew and appreciate perfume.

Great love and appreciation to my husband, Steven Fish. Thank you for believing in me.

Much love to our children: my son, Eric Moran, and to his wife and my beautiful daughter-in-law, Ginna, who proofread this manuscript and is a wonderful writer in her own right—and their little daughter, Zoë. And to the brothers Fish: Daniel, Brian, and Eric, who brighten our family moments with humor and laughter, as well as Rachel, Daniel's wife and the newest member of our family. Plus, a shout-out to the Hollenbeck clan: Mike, Amy, Mitch, Justin, and their families.

Deep gratitude to my agent, the amazing Jenny Bent, as well as the incredible team at St. Martin's Press: my editor, Jennifer Weis, and editorial assistants Sylvan Creekmore and Molly Traver.

Warm appreciation to friends in Paris and perfumery: Karen Marin, and Celeste and Francois Duquesne, and many others at Sephora, DFS, and LVMH, as well as friends Josette Banzet and Tommy Roe, and Twila and Gary Rosonet. Sending hugs to Aly Spencer, Vana Margolese, Deborah Ritchken, Francesca Daniels, Karen Marin, Alicia Past, Suzie Yazzie, Heidi Powers, and Sandy Williams for their enduring friendship.

Kudos to all my beta readers, especially Judy Gutman, Jeffrey Past, and Judy Schwartz. And special thanks to my writing pals: Rebecca Forster (and her mom!), Melissa Foster, Anita Hughes, Belinda Jones, Michelle Gable, Gill Paul, Liz Trenow, and so many, many others that listing them all would fill several pages.

Sincere thanks to my beloved readers, bloggers, and media partners. Without you, I would have no reason to dream life into fleeting ideas.

Finally, Dad and Frank and Lane, sure wish you could've stayed around for this—but like Sofia, maybe, in a way, you are.

SCENT *of* TRIUMPH

I

A rose, the symbol of love, the queen of the perfumer's palette.
How then, does the perfume of war intoxicate even the most
reasonable of men?

— DB (*From the perfume journal of Danielle Bretancourt*)

3 SEPTEMBER, 1939 — ATLANTIC OCEAN

Danielle Bretancourt von Hoffman braced herself against the
mahogany-paneled stateroom wall, striving for balance as she flung
open a brass porthole, seeking a moment of respite she knew would
never be. A damp, kelp-scented wind—a harbinger of the storm
ahead—whistled through the cabin, assaulting her nose with its raw
intensity, but the sting of salty spray did little to assuage the fear she
had for her little boy.

Nicky was only six years old. *Why, oh why did I agree to leave him
behind?* She had wanted to bring him, but her husband had dis-
agreed, saying he was far too young for such an arduous journey. As
a trained scientist, his arguments were always so logical, so sensible.
Against her instinct, she had given in to Max. It was settled; in their
absence her mother-in-law, Sofia, would care for Nicky on their
old family estate in Poland.

Danielle kept her eyes focused on the horizon as the *Newell-Grey
Explorer* slanted upward, slicing through the peak of a cresting
wave. The ocean liner creaked and pitched as it heaved through the
turbulent gray waters of the Atlantic on its voyage from New York

to England. Silently, Danielle urged it onward, anxious to return home.

Her usually sturdy stomach churned in rhythm with the sea. Was it morning sickness, anxiety, or the ravaging motion of the sea? Probably all three, she decided. Just last week she'd been so wretchedly ill that she'd seen a doctor, who confirmed her pregnancy. The timing couldn't be worse.

She blinked against the stiff breeze, her mind reeling. When they'd heard reports of the new agreement between Germany and Russia, they'd cut their business short to hurry home. Had it been just two days since they'd learned the devastating news that Nazi forces had invaded Poland?

Someone knocked sharply on the door. Gingerly crossing the room, Danielle opened the door to Jonathan Newell-Grey, heir apparent to the British shipping line that bore his family name. His tie hung from his collar and his sleeves were rolled up, exposing muscular forearms taut from years of sailing. A rumpled wool jacket hung over one shoulder.

Danielle and Max had met Jon on their outbound voyage to New York several weeks ago. They had become good friends, dining together regularly on the ship, and later in the city. Well-traveled and physically fit, Jon loved to explore and dine on fine food, and insisted on taking them to the best restaurants in New York, as well as little-known nooks that served authentic French and German fare, assuring Max and Danielle of a salve for their homesickness after their relocation. During their time in New York, Max worked tirelessly, tending to details for their pending cross-Atlantic move, so they both appreciated having a knowledgeable friend to call on for help.

With his gregarious yet gracious manner, Jon had helped them find a good neighborhood for their family, introduced them to his banker, and even explained some of the odd American colloquialisms they couldn't understand, as they all laughed together over well-aged bottles of his favorite Bordeaux. They had all climbed the Empire State Building together, and one night they saw a play on Broadway, and even danced to Benny Goodman's big band into the late evening hours. Jon also went to the World's Fair with them, where their crystal perfume bottles were featured in a potential business partner's display. Danielle and Max were both glad they'd met Jon, a man who embraced life with spirit and joie de vivre, and they looked forward to their new life in America far from the threat of Hitler's forces.

But now, with news of the invasion, Max and Danielle's guarded optimism for their future had turned to distress over their family's safety.

"*Bonjour,*" she said, glad to see Jon. "Any news yet?"

"None." He pushed a hand through his unruly chestnut hair, droplets of water spray glistening on his tanned face. "The captain has called a meeting at fifteen hundred hours for all passengers traveling on Polish and German passports."

"But I still hold a French passport."

"You'll need to attend, Danielle." His hoarse voice held the wind of the sea.

"Of course, but—" As another sharp pitch jerked through the ship, Jon caught her by the shoulders and kept her from falling. He moved intuitively with the ship's motion, a testament to his years at sea.

"Steady now, lass," Jon said, a small smile playing on his lips. He stared past her out the porthole, his dark eyes riveted on the ocean's whitecapped expanse. Blackened, heavily laden clouds crossed the sun, casting angled shadows across his face.

Embarrassed, Danielle touched the wall for support. She recalled the strange sense of foreboding she'd had upon waking. She was blessed—or cursed—with an unusually keen prescience. Frowning, she asked, "Can the ship withstand this storm?"

"Sure, she's a fine, seaworthy vessel, one of the finest in the world. This weather's no match for her." He turned back to her, his jaw set. His usual jovial nature had turned solemn. "Might even be rougher seas ahead, but we'll make England by morning."

Danielle nodded, but still, *she knew.* Anxiety coursed through her; something seemed terribly wrong. Her intuition came in quiet flashes of pure knowledge. She couldn't force it, couldn't direct it, and knew better than to discuss it with anyone, especially her husband. She was only twenty-six; Max was older, wiser, and told her that her insights were rubbish. Max wasn't really insulting her; he had studied science at the university in Germany, and he simply didn't believe anything that couldn't be scientifically proven.

Jon touched her arm in a small, sympathetic movement. "Anything I can do to help?"

"Not unless you perform miracles." Jon's rough fingers were warm against her skin, and an ill-timed memory from a few days ago shot through her mind. Danielle loved to dance, and with Max's encouragement, she and Jon had shared a dance while Max spoke to the captain at length after dinner. Danielle remembered Jon's soft breath, his musky skin, his hair curling just above his collar. He'd been interested in all she had to say, from her little boy to her work at Parfums Bretancourt, her family's perfumery in the south of France. But when she'd rested her head against his chest, it was his skin, his natural scent, which was utterly unique and intriguingly virile, that mesmerized her.

A third-generation perfumer, Danielle had an acute sense of smell. Her olfactory skills were paramount in the laboratory, but at times this acuity proved socially awkward. Jon's scent still tingled in her nose, taunting her dreams, its musky animal appeal relentless in the recesses of her mind. His memory crept into her mind more than she knew it should. *After all,* she told herself firmly, *I am a happily married woman.*

Danielle forced the scene from her mind, took a step back out of modesty. She caught sight of herself in the mirror, her thick auburn hair in disarray, her lip rouge smeared. She smoothed her celadon green silk day dress—one of her own designs her dressmaker had made—and drew her fingers across her pale skin. "I've been apprehensive about this trip from the beginning."

"Have you heard anything else from your mother-in-law?"

"Not since we spoke in New York. And my mother's last cable said they haven't arrived." When she and Max had heard the news, they called Max's mother, Sofia, and told her to leave immediately with Nicky for Paris, where Danielle's parents had a spacious apartment in the sixteenth arrondissement, a fine neighborhood in the heart of Paris. Sofia's voice had sounded dreadful; they hadn't realized she was so sick. *What if she isn't well enough to travel?* Wincing with remorse, Danielle fought the panic that rose in her throat, fearful for her mother-in-law.

"They have to get out of Poland." Jon touched her cheek.

Reflexively, she turned into the comfort of his hand, inhaling, her heart aching, his scent—at once both calming and unsettling—edged with the smell of the sea and a spiced wood blend she normally could have recognized in an instant. But now, Nicky was ever present in her mind. Danielle pressed her eyes closed and stifled a sob.

"Max is resourceful," Jon said, trailing his hand along her face. "He'll manage."

But can he? she wondered. Max had planned everything, from organizing their move to New York, to returning to Poland to close their home. He'd arranged their immigration to the United States, and he was also trying to bring their most valued employees with them for the business. *He'd made everything sound so sensible.*

Max was German, born in Berlin to an aristocratic family. When Max was young, his mother had inherited her family's estate and crystal and glass factory in Poland. Sofia and her husband, Karl, along with Karl's orphaned nephew, Heinrich, moved into the castle, which had originally been built as a wedding gift in 1820 for Sofia's ancestors. While the men set about rebuilding the factory and the business, Sofia tended to the home, a masterpiece of romantic English neo-Gothic style. After Max and Danielle married, Danielle had thrown her considerable energy into helping Sofia restore the grand salons and chambers, the arboretum, the gardens and ponds. And yet, Danielle missed her craft, retreating whenever she could to the perfumery organ—a curved workbench with rows that held essential oils and other perfumery materials—she had installed in their quarters, to conjure her aromatic artistry in solitude. Perfumery fed her soul; her urge to create could not be repressed.

The ship pitched again, sending the porthole door banging against the paneled wall. Shifting easily with the vessel's sharp motions, Jon caught it, secured the latch.

He moved toward her, and she could almost sense the adrenaline surging through his muscular frame. Leaning closer, he lifted a strand of hair limp with sea mist from her forehead. "If I don't see Max, you'll tell him about the captain's meeting?"

"We'll be there." She caught another whiff of his sea air–tinged skin, and this time a vivid sensory image flashed across her mind. A leather accord, patchouli, a heart of rose melding with the natural scent of his skin, warm, intriguing . . . then she recognized it— Spanish Leather. *An English composition. Trumper.* But the way he wore it was incredible; the *parfum* blended with his own natural aroma in such a fascinating manner. She was drawn in, aching to be swept farther into his scent, but she quickly retreated half a step. *This is not the time.*

His expression softened and he let her hair fall from his fingers as he studied her, his dark-browed, hazel-flecked eyes taking in every feature of her face.

Danielle stepped back, and Jon's gaze trailed back to the sea, his eyes narrowed against the sun's thinning rays, scanning the surface.

She matched his dark gaze. "Something unusual out there?"

"Might be German U-boats. *Unterseeboots.* The most treacherous of submarines. Bloody hell, they are. But don't worry, Danielle, the Newell-Greys always look after their passengers." He left, closing the door behind him.

U-boats? So it was possible. She touched a trembling finger to her lips. But that wasn't the only thought that made her uncomfortable. Jon's friendly, casual way with her increasingly struck a chord within her. Fortunately, Max was too much the aristocrat to make a fuss over nothing. *And it* is *nothing,* she thought. She loved her husband. *But that scent . . .* her mind whirred. *Fresh, spicy, woodsy . . . I can re-create sea freshness, blend it with patchouli . . . .*

Abruptly, the ship lurched. Cutlery clattered across a rimmed burl wood table, her books tumbled against a wall. She braced herself through the crashing swell, one hand on the doorjamb, another shielding her womb. There were so many urgent matters at hand. *Our son, our family, our home.* She pulled her mind back to the present.

When the ship leveled, she spied on the floor a navy blue cap she'd knitted for Nicky. He'd dropped it at the train station, and she'd forgotten to give it to Sofia. She cradled it in her hand and stroked it, missing him and the sound of his voice, then pressed the cap to her nose, drinking in his little boy smell that still clung to the woolen fibers. Redolent of milk and grass and straw and chocolates, it also called to mind sweet perspiration droplets glistening on his flushed cheeks. They often played tag in the estate's lush, sprawling gardens, laughing and frolicking, feeding the migratory ducks that visited their ponds, or strolling beneath the protective leafy boughs of ancient, towering trees. She brushed away tears that spilled onto her cheeks.

She picked up her purse to put his cap inside, and then paused to look at the photograph of Nicky she carried. His eyes crinkled with laughter, he'd posed with his favorite stuffed toy, a red-striped monkey with black button eyes she'd sewn for him. Nicky was an adorable bundle of blond-headed energy. A streak of fear sliced through her. She stuffed the cap into her purse and snapped it shut.

The door opened and Max strode into the stateroom, his proud face ashen, his lean, angular body rigid with what Danielle knew was stress.

"Jon just left," she said. "There's a meeting—"

"I know, he is behind me," Max said, clipping the words in his formal, German-accented English. He smacked his onyx pipe against his hand, releasing the sweet smoky scent of his favorite vanilla tobacco.

Jon appeared at the door. "Shall we go?"

The muscles in Max's jaw tightened. He slipped his pipe into the pocket of his tailored wool jacket. "I need a drink first. You, Jon?"

"Not now, mate."

Max moved past Danielle to the liquor cabinet, staggering slightly as the ship pitched. He brushed against her vanity and sent her red leather traveling case crashing to the floor.

Danielle gasped. Bottles smashed against one another inside as the case tumbled. The lid burst open, and scents of jasmine, rose, orange blossom, bergamot, berries, vanilla, cedar, and sandalwood exploded like brilliant fireworks.

"Oh, Max, my perfumes." She gathered the hem of her silk dress and sank to her knees, heartsick. These were all the perfumes she had with her; she could hardly remember a day when she hadn't worn one of her *parfum* creations. She knew Max hadn't meant to destroy her precious potions, but now there was nothing she could do but gather the pieces. With two fingers, she fished a crystal shard and a carnelian cap from the jagged mess. "Max, would you hand me the wastebasket?"

"I, I didn't mean to . . ." Looking worried, Max turned away and reached for the vodka, sighing in resignation. "Just leave it, Danielle. The cabin boy will see to it."

Jon knelt beside her. "Did you make all these?"

"Yes, I did. And the case was Max's wedding gift to me."

"These are beautiful works of art, Danielle. Max told me you were once regarded as the child prodigy of perfumery." He took a sharp piece from her. "Don't hurt yourself, I'll send someone to clean this up while you're gone."

She caught his eye and mouthed a silent thank-you, then rose and opened the porthole. A gust caught her long hair and slapped it across her face, stinging her flushed cheeks. Staring at the ocean, a quiet intuitive knowledge crept into her consciousness. *It's true,* she thought, and spun around. "Jon said there might be U-boats out there."

She watched Max pour a shot, then pause with his glass in mid-air, his intellectual mind whirring, weighing the probabilities. She knew her husband well; she saw his eyes flash with a moment of intensity, then clear into twin pools of lucid blue as he decided the odds were against it. "Impossible," he said.

"Anything is possible." Jon brushed broken crystal into the waste-basket and straightened.

Danielle's thoughts reeled back over the morning. "Is that why we've been zigzagging?"

Jon shot a look at Max. "Smart one, your wife. Not just an artist, I see." One side of his mouth tugged to a reassuring grin, shifting the deep cleft in his chin. "I'll grant you that, Danielle, but it's just a safety measure. U-boats aren't a threat to passenger liners."

Pressure built in her head. "Like the *Lusitania*?"

"A disaster like that couldn't happen today," Jon said, rubbing the indentation in his chin. "Every captain checks Lloyd's Register. It's clear that we're a passenger ship. Even so, there are rules of war;

an initial shot across the bow must be fired in warning. And England is not at war."

"Not yet." Max tossed the vodka down his throat and gave a wry, thin-lipped grin. "So is that why you have been holding court in the stern, Jon?"

"I confess, you're on to me, old boy. But seriously, we'd have time to signal to a vessel that we're not armed. Even a submarine must abide by these rules of war. Even the Nazis."

Nazis. The word filled Danielle with dread. What the Nazis were doing to Jews in Germany was unconscionable. New laws required that yellow stars for identification be sewn onto clothing. *Imagine.* Jewish businesses were being destroyed, entire families beaten or killed. These were *German* citizens, many of whom had lived in Germany for generations. It didn't matter how educated they were, whether they were young or old, wealthy or poor. A chill crept along her spine. "We've taken too long, Max. We have to get Nicky and your mother out now."

"The Polish army is not yet defeated, my dear," Max said quietly, pouring another shot. "Try to have patience."

"How can you be so calm?" Her voice hitched in despair. Her father was from an old French family, long recognized in French society. Danielle's mother was Jewish, so by German law Nicky was one-quarter Jewish. "You know what could happen to Nicky."

"We've been over this. Nicky is just a child." Max looked weary, the prominent veins in his high forehead throbbing as he spoke. "You were raised in your father's faith, you are Catholic. Nicky was also baptized. How would the Nazis find out anything different?"

But she knew they had ways. She pressed her hand to her mouth, consumed with worry and guilt. *Why did I agree to leave Nicky?*

Max gulped his drink, and then glanced at Jon. "We should go now." Max walked to the door. Without turning he paused, his voice thick. "I am sorry for your perfumes, Danielle. I am sorry for everything."

Danielle sucked in her breath. Max only drank when he was frustrated, when he had no clear answers. *And he seldom offers an apology.* To him, it was a sign of defeat, a sign that his scientific mind, or measured actions, had betrayed him. Max took pride in providing financially for his family, their well-being was his constant concern, especially that of Nicky, his beloved son. Danielle was the heart of their marriage, and she always felt safe with him. *Except today,* she thought, fear gripping her body like a vine. *Today is different.*

Jon opened the door, held it for them. She snatched her purse and followed Max.

Passengers jostled past in the crowded corridor and Danielle could feel anxiety rising in the air like a heat wave, smell the sour perspiration—like coddled milk left in the sun—emanating from panicked, angry passengers. Ordinary perspiration smelled different when tainted with fear. "Rotten Krauts," they heard people say. She saw Max stiffen against the verbal assaults.

When they came to the open-air promenade deck, Danielle glanced out over the sea, but she could see little in the gathering mist.

Jon followed her gaze. "We've got a heavy fog rolling in."

The air held the ozone-scented promise of rain. "It's so dim," she said. "Jon, why aren't the running lights on?"

"We're blacked out for security."

There's more to it, she thought, her neck tightening with trepidation.

They arrived at the first-class lounge, where tense passengers crowded shoulder to shoulder. Jon excused himself to take his place near the front as the owner representative. A hush spread when the grim-faced captain approached the podium.

"Thank you for your attention," the captain began. "Two days ago, Hitler's Nazi Germany violated a European peace agreement. Now, on the wireless we have a reply from the Prime Minister of the United Kingdom."

He nodded to a crew member. The loudspeakers crackled to life and a nervous murmur rippled across the room.

England was on the airwaves.

The radio announcer was speaking about Poland. "*Blitzkrieg,*" he called the German attack on the country.

"Lightning war," Max translated, shaking his head. He flexed his jaw, and Danielle could see veins bulging from his temples as he sought to control unfamiliar emotions.

"Oh, no." Danielle turned her face against Max's chest, the tentacles of terror slithering into her brain. *It has begun,* she thought, *and so horribly.* She trembled. *My poor Nicky, dear Sofia. Mon Dieu, what's happening to them? How frightened they must be.*

Max slid a finger under her chin and lifted her face to his, wiping tears from her eyes with an awkward gesture. "It's my fault, I should have already relocated our family. I didn't realize this would happen so quickly."

The tortured guilt in his expression tore at her soul. *He has failed. All his plans, all his actions, were to protect our family.* She averted her eyes from his pain, trying to calm her breathing as people wailed around her.

The radio crackled again. "*And now, Prime Minister Chamberlain.*"

"*This morning the British ambassador in Berlin handed the German government a final note stating that, unless we heard from them by eleven o'clock that they were prepared at once to withdraw their troops from Poland, a state of war would exist between us.*"

Chamberlain's voice sounded burdened, yet resolute. "*I have to tell you now that no such undertaking has been received, and that consequently, this country is at war with Germany.*"

A collective gasp filled the room, and Danielle sank against Max for support. He wrapped his arms around her, murmuring in her ear. "We'll find them, they'll soon be safe." *But is he reassuring me or himself?*

At the end of the broadcast, the captain stepped aside and Jon strode to the podium. Jon's baritone voice boomed over the murmuring tide. "Tomorrow, when we arrive, Newell-Grey agents will be available to assist and accommodate you. We shall keep you informed as we receive additional information."

Danielle pressed a hand to her mouth. *Who knew it would come to this?* A sudden clamminess overtook her, and her nausea returned with unbridled force. Tearing herself from Max, she bolted through the crowd, bumping against other passengers as she raced to the outer deck. She reached the railing, leaned over, gulped for air. Her stomach convulsed in a dry heave as the wind whipped the celadon scarf from her neck.

"Danielle," Max called, following her. Jon rushed after them.

I can't stand this, she thought, anguish ripping through her as images of Nicky and Sofia filled her mind. Max and Jon reached her side, and the three of them stood gazing through the shifting fog into the bleak waters below as Danielle clung to the railing, one arm clutching her abdomen, pressing her fevered cheek against the cold metal railing for relief.

Max draped an arm across her shoulders, rubbing her back, and looked across at Jon. "Her morning sickness is much worse with this pregnancy."

But Jon's eyes were fixed on the ocean. His face froze.

A sleek, narrow wake rippled the broken surface.

"What the—" began Max.

"Good God, get down," Jon bellowed. He leapt across Max and Danielle, his powerful body crashing them to the deck.

Danielle hit the wooden boards with such force that her shoulder cracked and her eyes blurred. *My baby,* she thought frantically, curling instinctively around her midsection, wrapping her arms around her torso and drawing up her knees to shield her unborn child.

In the next instant, a violent impact shot them across the deck. An explosion ripped into the bowels of the great ship. Screams pierced the haze, and the ship's massive framework buckled with a roar.

"Torpedoes," Jon shouted. He crushed his hand over Danielle's head and cursed under his breath. "Stay down."

An icy burst enveloped them like a sheet and soaked them to the flesh. Danielle gasped in terror. *Mon Dieu!* She could hear Max scrambling behind her, sliding on the slippery deck. *Protect us,* she prayed, keeping her head down and pressing her chin against her chest.

Another explosion rocked the ship. Wood and metal twisted with a grating screech as the ship listed to the starboard side, rolling like a wounded whale. The ship groaned and folded under her own weight, frigid salt water pouring into her open wounds.

Jon struggled to his feet. "Take my hand, Danielle, we must reach the lifeboats. This way, Max." Jon dragged Danielle behind him. "Nazi bastards." He stopped, and pulled his shoulders back. He turned to face the dazed crowd behind him.

"Attention." Jon's voice rang with urgent authority. "We must proceed quickly and calmly to the lifeboats."

Amid the chaos, people turned to follow.

Danielle reached for Jon's hand again, stumbling on something in her haste. She wiped stinging water from her eyes and blinked. A woman she'd met yesterday lay bloodied at her feet. She smothered a scream, and then reached down to help the woman.

Jon caught her arm. "Don't, it's no use. She's gone."

"No, she can't be," Danielle cried. She'd never seen a dead person before. Except for the blood soaking the deck beneath her, the woman appeared merely unconscious. *This can't be happening.* Then she saw that the back of the woman's skull was gone and she started to retch.

Jon shoved his handkerchief into her hand to wipe her mouth. "Keep going," he yelled.

Soon they came upon a lifeboat that dangled above them like a toy.

"Max, give us a hand, we haven't much time. Danielle, wrap your arms around the rail." Jon slicked his wet hair back from his eyes and grabbed a line. Max fought for balance, staggering to the lifeboat.

Water poured over the rail and mixed with the dead woman's blood, sloshing across the deck and staining it a deep crimson. All around them people slid across the tilting deck, screaming in hysteria. Danielle lost her balance, along with one leather pump that tumbled into the pandemonium. She kicked off her other shoe and clung to the railing.

Jon and Max began to toss life vests from the boat into the crowd.

Danielle's heart raced at the sight of the life vests. "Are we . . . are we going to sink?"

Jon's jaw twitched. "Just put on one of these."

"But I can't swim," she cried, her voice rising with fright.

"You won't have to if you're wearing this."

Despite her panic, Danielle fumbled with the strings on the vest. Jon and Max worked feverishly to free the lifeboats. Within moments, several crew members arrived and began to herd women and children into the boats.

Max checked her vest, tugged her knots to strengthen them, and kissed Danielle while the first boat was lowered. "Go now, I'll see you soon."

She peered at the lifeboat and terror gripped her chest. *No, not this.* She'd never liked small crafts, had nearly drowned off one when she was a child. Danielle stood rooted in horror at the thought of climbing into a boat.

Jon waved his arm at her. "Get in," he roared, his voice gravelly.

She turned to Max, her eyes pleading with him. "Max, I can't."

"Yes, you can. I'll be right behind you, my love." Despite the bulky life vest, Max pressed her to him and kissed her again, reassuring her.

Jon grabbed her arm with such force that Danielle yelped with pain. "Danielle, people are waiting."

"No, Jon, I—I can't get into that boat. I'll stay with Max."

"Bloody hell, you will." Jon's eyes flamed with urgency, startling her. "For God's sake, woman, get your wits about you. What happened to your famous French courage?"

Max threw Jon a wary glance, and then nodded to her. "He's right, you must go now."

Indignant, Danielle jerked her arm from Jon. "I'll show you courage." She stepped into the boat, barefoot, still clutching her purse.

As she settled unsteadily into the boat, a man with a sobbing young child rushed toward them. "Please, will someone take my boy?"

Danielle thought of her own little boy, shot a glare at Jon. "I will." She reached for the frightened child.

"His name is Joshua. You will take care of my boy?"

"I give you my word." She prayed someone would do the same for her Nicky, if need be. She hugged the tearful child, sweet with a milky smell, to her breast. Joshua was the same size as Nicky and it was all she could do to keep from calling his name.

Jon gave the signal and the lifeboat plunged into the choppy ocean. Danielle squeezed her eyes shut and bent over the boy to protect him as a wave hurtled toward the boat and broke against the wooden bow, blasting them with an icy shock and plastering their hair and clothes to their skin.

Her teeth chattering, Danielle looked back at the great ship. She was taking on water fast. All around them lifeboats crashed into the sea amid the most heart-wrenching cries she'd ever heard.

She strained to see through the fog and the frantic crowd, but couldn't spot Max or Jon. The *Newell-Grey Explorer*, the fine ship that bore Jon's family name, was giving way, slipping to her death. For a moment, the ship heaved against the crushing weight of her watery grave.

Danielle's eyes were glued to the horrific scene. Then, she remembered something she'd once heard. *We've got to act.* Alarmed, she turned to the young crew member with them. "When a ship goes down, the force can suck others down with it. We've got to get out of here."

Dazed with shock, he made no reply.

Frustrated, she turned to the elderly woman next to her. "Here, take little Joshua, hold him tightly." She gave the woman her purse, too.

Another woman let out a cry. "But what will we do?"

"We've got to row," Danielle shouted. "Who'll help me?" She had watched her brother Jean-Claude row often enough. *Surely I can manage this,* she thought desperately.

A stout Irishwoman with coppery red hair spoke up. "I might be third class, but I'm a first-class rower."

"Good." Danielle's resolve hardened and she moved into position. She tucked her soggy silk dress between her legs, its dye trailing green across the white deck, and grabbed an oar.

"Together, now stroke, and—no, wait." When she lifted her arms to row, the life vest bunched up around her neck, inhibiting her movement. She glanced at little Joshua and realized he had no life vest. She tore the vest strings open, shrugged out of it, and gave it to the elderly woman. "Put it on him."

"All right, now stroke," the Irishwoman called. "Steady, and stroke, and stroke."

Danielle pulled hard against the oars, struggling for rhythm, though splinters dug into her hands and her thin sleeves ripped from the strain.

They were some distance out when she looked up. The immense ship, the jewel of the fleet, gave one last, mournful wail as she conceded defeat. The ship disappeared into the Atlantic blackness, leaving only a burgeoning swell of water and a spiral of smoke in her wake.

Where's Max? And Jon? Did they make it off the ship? She couldn't watch anymore; she turned her back to the ship, numb to the cold.

And there, in the distance, she saw it. A strange vessel was breaking the surface. As it crested, she saw on its side in block print the letter *U* and a series of numbers. *A U-boat.* Treacherous, Jon had said. *And deadly.*

Danielle narrowed her eyes. *So, this is the enemy, this is who holds Poland—and my family—captive.*

A scorching rage exploded within her and sent her to the boat's edge, her hands fisted white, shaking with fury. *Look at them, surveying their handiwork, the bastards.* Steadying herself on the bow, she cried in a hoarse voice into the gathering nightfall, "Someday, there will be a day of reckoning for this. *C'est la guerre.* And I'll never, never surrender."

"You tell 'em, dearie," yelled the Irishwoman. As Danielle and the other lifeboat occupants stared at the U-boat, a mighty force began to gather below them. Silent as a thief, a swift undersea current drew water from beneath the bobbing craft.

Danielle sensed an eerie calm.

She turned and gasped.

A wall of water, born of the wake of the *Newell-Grey Explorer*, rose high behind them.

The wave crashed down, flipping the lifeboat like a leaf. Grappling for a handhold, Danielle screamed, and then plunged into the swirling current. The lifeboat completed its airborne arch, and an oar hurtled toward her. She tried to twist away, but it cracked her on her head, stunning her to the core.

Her moans for help were muffled as she sank into the frigid depths. She flailed about, desperate to swim the short distance to the surface, but her efforts only sucked her farther into the unrelenting sea. At last, she felt nothing but the icy claws of the Atlantic. Her breath gave way and she slipped into darkness.

2

In the seventeenth century, Turkish concubines devised a secret method of communication with flowers by attaching a meaning to each blossom or plant. The fascination swept Europe and reached its zenith of popularity in Victorian England. In the language of flowers, the red rose symbolizes love, while the calla lily signifies a magnificent beauty. Together, a stunning marriage to the perfumer.

—DB

3 SEPTEMBER, 1939 — POLAND

Sofia von Hoffman had scant time to prepare her escape. Despite her illness, the aggressive carcinoma that invaded her body with tumors, she'd worked without a break since the predawn invasion the day before. With the help of Jacob, her chauffeur, her large ancestral home had been cleared of much of its personal effects, what valuables and artwork they could gather locked in the cellar.

Now it was almost midnight. She stood in the stone doorway, gasping for breath, the dust from their work aggravating her lungs. Her body shook as she coughed, a violent hacking cough, her lungs aching. When she recovered, she drew herself up, her posture impeccable, and turned to Jacob. "This is all we have time to do. You must bring your family here. Together we'll find safety. Take the car, there isn't much time."

"I'll be back for you before daybreak." Jacob paused at the door and rested his broad hand on her arm. His eyes rose to an oil painting in the foyer behind her.

Sofia followed his gaze to the fine painting, illuminated with a glimmer of moonlight, a portrait of her in a fluid white gown, creamy calla lilies in ivory hands, on the eve of her marriage fifty years ago.

Jacob's eyes brimmed with admiration. "I remember when that was done."

Sofia tilted her head. "You were just a boy."

"Tending the horses and carriages. Still I knew, even then, that you were an unparalleled beauty," he said, his voice thick.

She averted her eyes and glanced down at her thin, frail hands, spidery with veins. Her illness had reduced her to a ghost of the force she had once been. But she didn't mourn the loss of her youth, only the loss of her energy.

"I'm sorry," Jacob said softly. "I didn't mean that you aren't still beautiful."

"We have more important matters to speak about." Her heart quickened. Nazi troops were advancing, and she knew his family was right in their path.

Jacob hesitated on the doorstep. Beneath his dark bushy brows, his eyes were moist. "If I don't return, I want you to know that I've always—"

"I know." She gave him a sad smile. "And I want you to know that I haven't long."

"No, you'll be better soon. You should see a different doctor."

She shook her head, and then raised her eyes to the west, where a faint, eerie light glowed orange on the horizon like a distant fireball. "You must hurry. And please, be careful."

On his return, they would travel into the nearby forest, hide until danger passed. At best, they could return home. At worst . . . She shuddered.

I'm so glad Jacob was here. Heinrich, her husband's nephew who lived with them, had disappeared after the invasion.

Sofia and Karl had taken Heinrich into their home the day his parents had died, when he was just a boy. From that moment on, she had taken care to treat him as her own son, just as she did Max. After Karl's death, there was no question that Heinrich would remain with her. Sofia loved Heinrich like a son, but he'd always had a fierce temperament and an explosive temper.

Where was Heinrich now that she needed him?

Another round of coughing gripped her like a vise. If only she'd been well enough to travel to Paris with young Nicky, as she'd promised Max and Danielle.

She pressed her hand against her chest. The doctor had told her she'd have more time. But even he hadn't realized her illness would be so aggressive.

In her dignified way, she'd kept it from her family. She didn't want to worry Max and Danielle.

Sofia gasped for breath slowly, her coughing subsiding. What would Max and Danielle return to? In the last few days, unbelievable stories from the front lines had filtered into town. Thousands of innocent people had been killed in ground and air strikes. People were running for their lives. And their village, Klukowski, was dead center in the Nazi path.

She thought of her precious grandson, Nicky, and regret flooded her mind. Danielle had been so anxious about leaving him. Sofia had assured her the boy would be fine, that they would meet them in Paris. How wrong she had been.

Once the news about the agreement between Germany and Russia was broadcast, people had mobbed the petrol and train stations. She'd tried to board a train to Paris, but she was too weak to fight the frantic swarm of humanity desperate to escape.

She heard the rear door slam and heavy footsteps raced up the rear servants' stairs. She knew the sound of those boots. "Heinrich?"

Sofia met him in the hall. Heinrich's blond hair was sticking up like thorns, his clothes soggy with perspiration. He held a small bag in his hand.

"Aunt Sofia. I—I thought you'd left already."

Sofia pulled herself up. "You saw the car leave and you assumed I was in it. You did not want to face me?"

"No, I—"

"Where have you been?"

He lowered his pale blue eyes and studied his feet, then threw his head back and puffed out his chest. "I am going to join in the glory of the New Germany. I've enlisted."

Shocked, Sofia reached out to the wall for support. She struggled to speak, her breath rattling in her chest. "But you've lived here since you were ten. You're more Polish than German."

"No, *you* are Polish. My uncle was not. I had no choice after my parents died, did I?" His lip curled in a sneer. "My blood is German and I'm proud of it. *Mein Führer* needs me."

She knew Heinrich idolized everything German. As a child he'd played soldier games, staged battles and studied strategy. He yearned for the uniform, the comradeship, the imagined glory—but there was no honor in the Nazi ideology. *How can I stop him?* She touched his arm. "Heinrich, I've always loved you like my own son."

"That's a lie, and you know it." He jerked away. "Your precious son, Max, betrayed his race by marrying a little half-breed French Jew who passes herself off as Catholic. And you welcomed her into this home. You spent more time with her and that brat than you ever did with me."

"Is that what's behind this? You're jealous of Danielle and little Nicky?" She shook her head in disbelief. True, Heinrich had been moody after Danielle arrived, but Sofia had assumed it was just adolescent behavior.

"Jealous? No, they're beneath me, Aunt Sofia. And so are you." He spun on his heel and pounded down the stairs.

Sofia heard the door slam. She ached for Heinrich; her heart burned with rage against the Nazis. She leaned against the wall and tried to catch her breath.

She recalled how he'd been a frightened young boy, missing his Berlin friends, when he came to live with them. She thought that was the reason for his surly demeanor. But how he must have resented her.

He has joined the enemy. He has betrayed the family.

A chill crept over her. Heinrich knew the secret of Nicky's heritage. He wouldn't inform on little Nicky, would he?

She heard feet padding behind her.

Nicky flung his arms around her knees. "Grand-mère, why is Heinrich mad?"

"It's complicated, Nicky. But he's gone now. He won't be back."

Nicky appeared thoughtful. "He says awful mean things to me."

Sofia's heart clutched. So it was true.

He looked up at her with rounded eyes of innocence. "I'm glad he's gone."

Sofia knelt and hugged Nicky, even as her heart broke for Heinrich. "Go back to bed, Nicky, my dear. You need your rest." She took his hand and walked him to the nursery.

After she tucked him into bed and kissed him, she went to her bedroom. Her mantle clock read after midnight, yet she had little time to indulge her aches and anxieties. Her maid had already fled in hysterics and there was still much to do.

She selected a simple black wool traveling dress and sewed her finest jewelry into the hem. Photographs, money, and real estate deeds went into a large bag, along with a change of clothing, eyeglasses, medical supplies, and food.

Exhausted, she collapsed at her desk in the study. She tried once more to call Danielle's parents in France. "Hello, hello?" But the line was thick with silence.

And then she thought, *Why isn't Jacob here yet?*

4 SEPTEMBER, 1939 — ATLANTIC OCEAN

Hours after the sinking of the *Newell-Grey Explorer*, Danielle sat shivering on the quiet darkened deck of the British destroyer that had come to their rescue. She drew a damp woolen blanket, heavy with its animal aroma, around her shoulders, but it offered little warmth.

Danielle owed her life to the Irishwoman in the lifeboat whose strong arms had lifted her to the surface, yanking her from the brink of crossing over, of leaving her loved ones behind. *I wasn't ready to die,* she thought, anxiety crawling through her skin as she recalled the surreal moments she'd experienced, the sense that she was being thrust through a passage from the life she'd known. She pursed her trembling lips and blinked back fear. *Nicky needs his mother, and I will find him.*

Thankfully, everyone in her lifeboat had survived, including Joshua, the little boy she'd promised to look after. When Danielle regained consciousness, she was worried about Joshua. The Irishwoman assured her that Joshua was well; the captain had personally made sure the boy was being cared for. On his request, several teachers had gathered children who'd been on lifeboats alone to comfort them, look after them, and try to reunite them with family after they disembarked. Danielle was relieved to learn that Joshua wasn't hurt, and hoped his father had survived, too.

Danielle was unharmed, except for a few bruises and a throbbing welt on the back of her head. But other passengers weren't as fortunate. The sight of stiff, discolored bodies adrift in the sea, the scent of death rising from the waves—these memories would plague her forever.

One thought revolved endlessly through Danielle's mind: *Where are we?* She had seen neither Max nor Jon since she'd boarded the lifeboat. She could only pray they were aboard the ship that trailed them, a Norwegian vessel that had also aided in the rescue. Both ships were observing radio silence, so survivors could not be confirmed.

She drew her hands into fists and crushed Nicky's woolen cap to her cheek, inhaling his memory. As a perfumer, Danielle knew the sense of smell was a strong memory trigger, but it was more than that, too. The olfactory sense was a key to the door of human emotions, to emotions often barred from the surface of consciousness. She drank in the unique aroma of her son, the intimate scent that any parent knows.

With another breath, the aroma of wet wool conjured the last moments she'd been with Max, the fibers of his jacket drenched with salt water. Inevitably, the vision of the U-boat appeared in her mind. Her breath quickened as anger grew within her. She recalled the horrible stories that had filtered in from Germany and realized now, with a sinking feeling, that the stories must be true.

Muted sobs reverberated in the thick fog of the salted midnight air, but Danielle remained dry-eyed, resistant now to any emotion but rage, her breath coming in short rasps.

She clasped her knees and rocked in the biting cold, trying to keep her body, and her baby, warm. It was far too soon to feel any movement, but she prayed the child was unharmed by her ordeal.

Her husband might well be among the dead, yet she dared not think of mourning. She fixed her gaze toward England.

No doubt, Nazi U–boats tracked the ships' movements. Would they even reach England? *And then what?*

At least Heinrich was with Nicky and Sofia. Although in truth, she'd always been wary of Max's cousin. Heinrich acted distant, but Max only laughed and said it was his Prussian background. Yet she sensed he viewed her as an interloper.

Danielle turned to concentrate on the blackened form of the Norwegian vessel. As she did, she imagined that she could feel the presence of Max and Jon. *They must be there.* Finally, exhaustion set in and she drifted into a troubled slumber.

When Danielle woke, the English shore was in full view. *Where am I? What's happening, where's Max?* Then the memory of the night before rushed through her mind, and she stumbled to her feet.

She drew herself farther into her soggy blanket and crinkled her nose against the sour smell of damp wool. The air held an ominous chill, and the charcoal sky reflected the somber mood of the morning.

The stout, red–haired Irishwoman from the lifeboat stood near her at the rail, worry lines on her face. "Morning, dearie," the woman said. She pointed ahead at the docks. "We're pulling into Southampton. How're you doing?"

"I've been better, but glad to be alive. I can't tell you how much I appreciate what you did for me," Danielle said. "If it weren't for you, I would've drowned."

"Don't mention it, dearie, but sure'n you should learn to swim." The woman patted her on the back.

From the deck of the British destroyer that had rescued them, the two women watched as the Norwegian ship docked. Then the destroyer maneuvered into port.

Solemn passengers lined the rail of each vessel. Danielle strained to see Max or Jon. She peered out over the throng of people who'd gathered to greet the ships, heard them call out names in hope. Then the heavens burst with a crack of thunder and far below, clusters of umbrellas unfurled against the sudden rain.

The Irishwoman left her, marching ahead to look for her family. Danielle shuffled off the ship with the ragged mass of survivors, following the queue into a large, rectangular brick building. Once in the processing area, she continued to search the crowd for Max and Jon. But all she found were dry blankets and bland soup, and volunteers who could do little more than offer condolences.

"Refugees," she heard them called. Her face burned with renewed anger. *That's what we are now.* Barefoot and clutching her purse, Danielle gave a volunteer her information. With her heart in her throat, she asked about Max.

The woman consulted a list, frowned, and then excused herself.

Danielle licked her raw lips, tasting salt water. The smell of perspiration and dampness infiltrated her nose. Not far away, she noticed a trim man with a press credential tucked into his hatband.

"How many people were aboard?" he asked an official. He sounded American.

"Twelve hundred ninety-four," came the reply.

"Survivors?"

Danielle strained to hear.

"At last count, nine hundred seventy-six."

Her head throbbed as she calculated. *More than three hundred dead.*

The reporter scribbled in his notebook. "And what can you tell me about the SS *Athenia*?"

The official shook his head. "She was bound for Montreal but suffered a U-boat attack north of Ireland. More than a hundred civilians and crew died."

No, not another ship. Danielle's head swam. *So this is war.*

3

What a shame the lilac flower jealously guards its aroma,
refusing to share its magic. Relying on alchemy, a perfumer
recalls its impression with a blend. Together, the essences of
jasmine, ylang-ylang, neroli, and vanilla plot to mimic the fair
lilac flower.

—DB

4 September, 1939 — Southampton, England

Across the spartan brick-lined immigration center through which
visitors to England passed on their way into the country, Jon searched
the crowded winding queues of hundreds of weary souls. *Where the
devil is she?* He ran a hand through his hair, praying she hadn't been
on the lifeboat that sank. He and Max had been up all night, desperate to find her. She wasn't on board his vessel, and even he couldn't
get a message through to the British destroyer.

After being approved by Immigration, Max was taken in for questioning by the British authorities. Jon had promised him that he'd
continue searching for Danielle.

It had been more than twenty-four hours since the ship had gone
down. *Did she make it?* He'd never forgive himself if she hadn't. He
couldn't imagine Danielle not fighting like hell to safety, but then,
he'd known many strong sailors who'd been bested by the frigid
waters of the North Atlantic.

Then he saw her and relief surged through him. She stood with a blanket wrapped around her willowy frame, her auburn hair slicked from her forehead and hanging in a tangled rope down her back.

He caught his breath, not because of her bedraggled appearance, but rather because of the way she stood, so straight and tall. *Courageous.*

She looked regal in her woolen blanket, her face set with determination. Her chin lifted defiantly. No other woman had ever made his pulse quicken like her.

When he moved closer, he saw the intensity of her gaze as she looked about the room. Her eyes were the color of Colombian emeralds, with fiery sparks that would make any man think twice about crossing her.

If only I'd met her before she married Max. Heat prickled his neck. He stopped, and checked his thoughts. *Don't be a fool.* He was practically engaged to Victoria. But what was the harm in looking?

Against a bright overhead light, Danielle saw Jon. Her eyes snagged on his height, the broad span of his shoulders. She waved and pressed through the crowd, her heart surging.

Jon wrapped his arms around her, his lips brushed her forehead. Relieved, she clung to him, felt the steady sureness of his heartbeat. She drew away to put a proper distance between them. "They can't find Max's name on the list. Have you seen him?"

Jon looked down at her, his bleary eyes bloodshot and damp.

She sucked in her breath. *Not Max.* "No, no," she murmured.

"Max is fine, Danielle. He was incredible, helping so many people to safety. Along with the captain, we were the last off the ship."

"Where is he?" Danielle gripped his jacket lapel. "I must see him."

"He's being questioned." Jon chuckled. "He gave the investigators quite a start. They think he looks like Edward, the Duke of Windsor. But I assured them, he's not a Nazi sympathizer."

4 September, 1939 — Poland

Gasping for breath, Sofia's eyes fell on the silver-framed family photographs on her desk. She remembered how hard Max had worked to restore the crystal and glass factory he had inherited from his father, her Karl—that handsome, lovable rascal.

She and Karl were married in Germany, and it wasn't long before she discovered Karl's gambling debts. All that remained was Sofia's family estate in Klukowski, Poland, in the village named after her ancestors. Several generations of her family had lived on this land, descendants of a valiant Polish knight and his striking wife, a Silesian countess. Years later, after Karl's heart finally gave out, Max inherited the floundering firm.

Sofia touched a wedding photograph of Max and Danielle. Max had been lucky to meet Danielle at a perfume conference in Paris.

She shook her head, the furrow between her brow deepening as she wondered if news of the invasion had reached Max and Danielle aboard the ship. *If it has, how worried they must be.* She removed the cherished photographs from their frames and stashed the pictures in her bag, then checked her watch pin. Five-thirty. Threads of light crept into the room. *Jacob should be here.*

She woke Nicky to dress him.

The little boy rubbed his eyes. "Where are we going?"

"We're taking a short trip." Sofia pulled a warm sweater over his head.

"Will Maman and Papa be there?"

"As soon as they return from New York." She kissed his cheek. "Until then, we must carry on and have courage."

He hugged his favorite stuffed animal, a red-striped monkey. "I want to take him."

"As long as you promise to carry him." Danielle had made it for him.

At last, they were ready. Sofia held Nicky's hand and waited in the rear doorway for Jacob to return. A distant church bell chimed seven times. *What was keeping Jacob?*

"Look over there," Nicky said. The light summer breeze ruffled his fine, golden hair as he pointed to the west. Smudges of gray smoke drifted on the horizon.

Sofia sniffed. A faint burning odor permeated the morning air. She hugged Nicky to her breast, but he grew restless.

"Let's walk through the garden." Sofia took his hand and he tried to run, but she refused to let go. "My, you're energetic this morning."

They knelt on the carpet of grass, damp with dew. Sofia glanced around, taking solace in her garden. Realizing she might never see it again, she closed her eyes and inhaled the delicate aromas of her luscious red roses, the creamy white honeysuckle, and her favorite, mounds of lilac bushes that blazed purple every spring.

She heard her car turn into their lane. Nicky scrambled from her lap. She smoothed her chignon and straightened, bone thin but regal, and strode to meet the car.

Jacob's wife, Irma, and three small children were crowded in with Jacob's brother, Oscar.

Sofia walked to the front of the chateau, removed a large skeleton key from her pocket, and locked the pair of intricately carved entry doors. She hesitated on the stone steps.

Her family had endured much; they would weather this, too. She gazed up at the great house and hoped it, too, would survive. For her son, Max, for Danielle, and for Nicky, the next generation.

Jacob appeared at her side. "I'm sorry," he said, his tone soft and respectful. "It's time to go."

Sofia rested her hand in the crook of his elbow, grateful for his support. She walked to the car, trying to appear stronger than she felt, and slid into the front seat. She took Nicky in her arms.

As they drove away, she turned to watch her grand home disappear behind the hill. Silent tears slipped from her eyes, splashing onto Nicky's fine hair.

A high thin whistle sounded overhead. Sofia clutched Jacob's arm. "What's that?" Before he could answer, a thundering roar shook the car.

Sofia craned her neck to see. Black smoke billowed behind them. A silvery glint in the sky caught her eye, then another, and another. "Airplanes. Good Lord, they're dropping bombs."

Jacob pressed the accelerator to the floor.

4 SEPTEMBER, 1939 — SOUTHAMPTON, ENGLAND

At the processing area, Danielle went through a debriefing, gave their address in Poland, her parents' address in France, and tried to assure officials that Max was not working against British interests.

Minutes later, Danielle felt a hand on her shoulder. She whirled around, and at the sight of Max, a rush of pent-up anxiety surged through her. "Oh, darling, I've been so worried about you," she said, choking out her words.

"Thank God you're here," he said, swaying her in his arms and peppering her with kisses. He drew his brows together. "And the baby?"

"Fine, I think." She caressed her slight belly. "I should see a doctor to make sure."

"Right away, dear." Max turned to Jon, who stood next to Danielle. "If it weren't for you and your father speaking on my behalf, I don't know what they would have done to me. I could be on my way to Germany, back to certain disaster."

"It was nothing, really. Father has friends who understand the situation. You've both been granted temporary asylum." Jon gave them a smile that didn't quite reach his eyes.

Max turned back to Danielle, thick blue veins protruding from his temples. "They arranged a call to Paris, too." He struggled with his words. "I spoke to your mother, Danielle. But there's been no word from Nicky and my mother."

She heard a child cry in the distance, and it fueled her anger. "I should *never* have left Nicky."

Max looked shocked, and it was only then that Danielle saw the anguish etched on his face. He put his arms around her. "I'm sorry, I never dreamed it would come to this."

Danielle steadied herself. *Two apologies in two days. It was unlike him.* "Max, we have to find a way home."

"Soon, I promise," he said softly.

Jon traded a look with Max, and then placed a comforting hand on Danielle's shoulder. "Herb and Libby Leibowitz are family friends, they have room for you in their home." He glanced at his wrinkled, soiled clothes. "We could all use a hot bath and a change of clothing. Here she is now."

A small, dark-haired woman dressed in a nubby tweed suit approached them. "You must be the von Hoffmans." She turned a lined, birdlike face up to them. "I'm Libby Leibowitz," she said, an Eastern European accent clearly evident. "You'll stay with me and my family in London until it's safe to travel again."

Danielle replied, "We appreciate it, we're exhausted."

Max and Danielle followed Libby to her car. When Danielle saw the shiny black, chauffeur-driven Rolls-Royce, she glanced down at her tattered clothes in embarrassment. *But I am so grateful.* They stepped into the car and Danielle breathed in the rich scent of the leather upholstery.

During the long drive from Southampton to London, Libby turned to them. "My husband is an advisor to the Crown. He's been in meetings all day, but will be pleased to meet you." She sighed. "I have lived through one war, that's what brought me here. Hitler must be stopped at any cost."

"May I ask where you're from?" Danielle couldn't place the woman's accent.

"I'm from Lithuania," Libby replied with obvious pride. "Although I haven't been back since the war. My life is here now, with my husband." Her eyes darted from Max to Danielle. "Do you have family?"

Danielle fought back panic.

"Our son, Nicky, is at home with my mother in Poland," Max said.

Libby's face clouded. "This is not good, not good at all. You must get your family."

"As soon as we can," Danielle said, her jaw set.

The Leibowitz home was in Belgravia, an exclusive area of London. Danielle caught her breath when she entered the gracious foyer, brimming with flowers. The wood parquet floors and Aubusson rugs reminded Danielle of her parents' home in Paris. She thought of her parents, her brother and his wife, and their little daughter, who was nearly the same age as Nicky, and felt a pang of longing to see them again. She leaned in, peering at silver-framed photographs of smiling people—much like the photographs that filled their home in Poland.

Danielle and Max followed Libby up a mahogany staircase, its rail polished to a smooth sheen, sleek beneath Danielle's hand. She caught the faint aroma of lemon oil. A crystal chandelier sparkled overhead, as fine as their factory produced. She frowned as she thought of their employees' fate.

They reached the second floor and Libby turned. "I want to reiterate that you're welcome here for as long as you wish."

"You are too kind," Max said.

"Not at all. It's a little selfish on my part, really. You see, we weren't blessed with children. We tried to claim Jonathan and his sister, Abigail, as our own, but their parents wouldn't hear of it." She smiled wistfully. "I only wish the circumstances were more favorable."

Libby showed them into the guest room, where a fireplace crackled, filling the room with a comforting scent of wood smoke. Once Libby had gone, Danielle noticed a delicate Chippendale writing desk overlooking a manicured garden mew. She gazed at a green maze of clipped hedges woven among colorful strands of well-tended roses, and recognized that it was beautiful. But she couldn't feel it.

Max left early the next morning before Danielle woke. Libby asked their family doctor to come to the house to check on Danielle. Mother and baby were pronounced healthy and the doctor ordered ample food and rest.

After the doctor had gone, Danielle sorted through clothing that Libby's maid had brought to them. Libby collected clothes for the London Women's Society. Danielle selected a dark wool suit, zipped the skirt closed, pinned the waist's fullness to fit, and folded under the jacket sleeves to shorten them. She brushed her hair and wound it into a simple chignon.

But something was missing. She realized that it was the first time she could remember not applying perfume as she dressed, and she felt exposed. Losing her perfumes was like losing a friend, a piece of her past. *But that's the least of our worries.*

The door opened behind her. "You look lovely, Danielle," Max said.

"Where have you been today? The doctor came this morning."

"I spoke to him, and I'm relieved that you're well. But I had something to attend to." He gave her a peck on the cheek, then went to light his pipe.

"What are you not telling me?" Her intuition prickled on the back of her neck. "And how are we going to return to find Nicky and Sofia?"

He sighed. "Danielle, what I'm about to say requires absolute secrecy. It involves your brother. I think maybe he can help us."

"Jean-Claude? But he's in medical school, what can he do?"

Max dropped his voice. "He has connections. Do you remember his friendship with my secretary's niece? Jean-Claude helped her family escape from occupied Czechoslovakia and cross into Portugal, where they sailed to America. He works with underground networks across Europe to free innocent people from Hitler's regime."

"I–I had no idea." She thought she and her brother shared everything. What else didn't she know?

Max took her hand. "Europe is connected by cells of people like your brother who have the courage to help others in need. You should be proud of Jean-Claude, but this is confidential. His life depends on it. Not even his wife or your parents know about this, especially not your father. I swore on my life to keep his secret."

"Hélène doesn't know?" Danielle frowned. "And Papa—"

Max cut her off. "As long as your father's bank continues to finance Germany's industrial expansion, he must never know about Jean-Claude's activities."

Her heart sank at the realization and she pressed a hand to her mouth, remembering. "Jean-Claude thinks Papa's job is a betrayal. But how could Papa know that the bank's funds would be used for munitions, to advance against other European countries?"

Max's lips formed a thin line. "Jean-Claude is right."

Hitler's evil tore at the very fabric of her family. She lifted her eyes to Max. "Are you involved with this secret organization?"

"We have no choice now. Perhaps Jean-Claude can get a message to my mother."

"I just want to know that they're all right, and if we can get them out of Poland. If we can, oh, darling, I'd never ask for another thing as long as I live. Let's wire Jean-Claude right away."

She hugged him, warm tears spilling onto her cheeks, and prayed it was not too late.

Max buried his face in her hair. They held each other for a long time, exhausted, listening to the clock's measured rhythm, the minutes marching on.

Still, something gnawed at her. A strange sense of terror gathered within her. *Max is still keeping something from me. What is it?*

10 OCTOBER, 1939 — POLAND

As sunlight filtered through the trees, the ragged group shrank into the shadows of the forest. "Split up," Jacob whispered, motioning Irma and the children away.

Sofia followed them, holding Nicky by the hand. "Run as fast as you can," she told the little boy, her heart throbbing in terror.

Eyes wide, Nicky seemed to grasp the magnitude of the situation as they scrambled through the thicket, their clothes and hair snagging on overgrown bushes. Sofia craned her neck to glimpse a patch of sky, wishing they could soar with the ease of the birds above them. How far could their feet carry them?

The petrol in the car had only taken them this far. For weeks they had been camping in the forest with other families who had also fled from the advancing troops, moving as troops fanned out in search. When gunfire pierced the stillness of the night, Sofia would cover Nicky's ears and send up a silent prayer for the victims.

Wordlessly, Nicky stopped and pointed toward several soldiers advancing toward them. Sofia pulled him farther into the brush.

"Let's clean out this area," Sofia heard one of the soldiers say. *They sound young,* she thought, barely older than boys. Sofia peered out at them. Their skinny necks protruded from green uniforms, their smooth hands clutched weapons. Sweat beaded their fear-lined faces. But they had their orders. *Three, no, four of them. Now five.* Sofia crossed herself and pressed Nicky to her chest. *Dear God, protect us.*

A few more steps and the soldiers would discover the children. She saw Jacob give a series of hand signals to Oscar and some other men, who began to creep forward, then pounced from behind. Wild shots rang out, ricocheting off trees. Sofia crouched, sheltering Nicky with her body. He was shaking, and it broke her heart. *He should not know this horror.*

Suddenly, Irma leapt up from behind her, wild-eyed, and hurled herself onto the back of a soldier who, with another step, would have stumbled upon her three children. Sofia covered Nicky's eyes. She heard a scuffle, followed by a thud.

"Run," Irma cried in a hoarse whisper. She pulled Sofia from the ground and tore Nicky from her arms.

"I can't keep up," Sofia cried, huffing, branches slapping her face and leaving stings of blood on her thin skin.

Irma was persistent; when Sofa tripped, Irma helped her along, the children racing ahead of them.

"Stay together, children," Sofia cried.

She could hear the skirmish behind her, and knew that Jacob and Oscar and the other men were fighting back the soldiers.

A gunshot exploded in front of them, and the children raced back. Sofia grabbed Nicky and pushed him behind her. The little group turned to run in another direction when another, larger soldier appeared, blocking their path.

"*Halt.*" He snapped a gun to his beefy shoulder and Sofia found herself staring at a barrel trained on her head. Irma crushed the frightened children to her, while Nicky clung to Sofia's legs. "Shh, don't cry," Sofia whispered, trying to remain calm, but her hands were shaking. *Will he kill us or spare us?*

4

Native to the Molucca Islands, the seeds of the nutmeg tree produce a spicy, sweet, aromatic essence. History holds that nutmeg enhances women's fertility and aids intellectual stimulation.

—DB

29 OCTOBER, 1939 — LONDON, ENGLAND

Danielle pulled up the blackout shades in their suite, exhausted from another night of ear-piercing air raid sirens, during which everyone in the house trooped into the cellar for two hours. However, no enemy aircraft were spotted, and people began to suspect that these were merely drills. Outside, leaves had fallen from the autumn trees. Raindrops began to dot the windowpane; in another minute heavy rain sluiced across the glass. Danielle adjusted a quilted robe Libby had given her over her expanding waist. *What an awful world to bring an innocent child into.*

Max had insisted that they remain in London. "We can obtain more information here about our family's situation than in Paris," he told her, and he didn't want her to leave him. Fortunately, the Leibowitzes seemed glad to have them.

She'd been up the rest of the night thinking about Nicky and Sofia, her heart laden with memories. Every spring Max had gone to Paris to visit boutiques, stores, and couturiers to showcase the finest perfume bottles their factory produced. Their luxury designs featured weighted crystal, hand-polished flacons, acid-etched frosting, and ground stoppers. Styles ranged from the classic squares and round apothecary bottles to strong-shouldered Art Deco shapes and curved Art Nouveau whimsy.

Their business was flourishing, and while Max met with important clients in Paris, Danielle travelled with Nicky and Sofia to her family's chateau near Grasse in the south of France, called Bellerose, and the perfumery. Her uncle, Philippe, oversaw the farm, where undulating rows of flowers above the main chateau were transformed into precious oils for perfumery. Her mother often joined them from Paris; Marie was stylish and cheerful, and adored Nicky.

With two grandmothers to watch Nicky, Danielle often slipped away to her perfumer's organ, the semicircular, multitiered desk where she explored innovative ideas to blend beautiful, soul-touching perfume formulas.

After Max concluded his business in Paris he would join them at Bellerose. On mild evenings they would gather with friends to dine al fresco on the season's freshest fare, usually under an ivory canopy of climbing roses spilling forth sweet scent on cool Mediterranean breezes.

Her memories were so vivid she could actually smell Nicky's silky hair, as well as the buttery scent of the *boulangerie* in Grasse where they bought croissants, and the bountiful aromas in the perfume laboratory, where she'd already begun to train Nicky's nose. His laughter tinkled in her ears; she could feel his soft cheek against hers. *If only we had brought him with us,* she thought, tortured.

How can we find them? Why does everything take so long?

She knew Max had visited British officials to ask for help, but he had been acting strangely, rushing off to meetings but refusing to tell her why or what was discussed.

Now, he was insisting they go to a dinner party at Jon's family home tonight. It was the last thing she wanted to do, but Max contended the diversion would be good for her and the baby. She could think of little else besides Nicky.

Libby had once described the Newell-Grey's Art Nouveau–styled home as an ocean liner. It loomed ahead on a corner, sleek and cur-vaceous, with long lines and rounded corners. Porthole windows framed the front door and a shiny brass railing lined a balcony.

A carnelian red entry door flew open and light flooded the stoop like a beacon.

Jon greeted Max with a hearty handshake and kissed Danielle on both cheeks. Danielle's pulse quickened, though his gesture meant nothing more than friendship—it *was* her native custom, after all. A flurry of thoughts exploded in her mind, and before she could con-trol her reaction her face grew warm. *Don't,* she admonished her-self, averting her eyes.

"It's wonderful to see you again," he said to her, a broad smile crinkling his eyes. "I'd like you to meet my younger sister, Abigail, and an old friend from Los Angeles, Cameron Murphy. Cameron's a popular singer in the States; he's working on a Red Cross charity project for Abigail."

"I promised Abigail I'd call when I came to London." Every-thing about Cameron resonated sensuality, from his melodic voice to his dark-lashed eyes, to his muscular frame beneath a perfectly tailored evening suit. "And I never break a promise to a beautiful woman."

Abigail laughed. Wearing a shimmering bronze silk evening dress that framed her alabaster complexion and chestnut hair, she shared her brother's good looks and friendly manner. "Don't believe him," she said. "He's such a star, he's left a string of broken hearts and promises in his wake. Thank goodness we're just friends."

Cameron turned to Danielle and bowed, his black eyes dancing. "She lies, *madame*. Do I look like a slimy swain?" He gave her an alluring smile, took her hand in his strong palm and kissed it. "I am but a noble knight, at the bidding of damsels in distress."

Max cleared his throat. Danielle noticed Cameron's manicured nails; she withdrew her hand and wrinkled her nose as she caught a whiff of Irish whiskey. *Northern Ireland whiskey,* she noted, instantly recalling the aroma. *Bushmills.* Nevertheless, he *was* charming. An involuntary thought flashed across her mind: *So is Jon . . . in a more genuine way.*

"Come on, Cam, she's taken." Jon glanced pointedly at Max. "Careful with your wife around this one. He's been known to melt the will of nuns."

Abigail arched a brow. "Oh, Jon, you're just jealous because Cameron always steals your girlfriends. Speaking of which, where's Victoria?"

"On holiday in Ireland with friends," Jon said with a shrug.

Danielle glanced at him from the corner of her eye. He had never mentioned a girlfriend to her. *But why should I be surprised?*

Jon was glaring at Cameron. "How's Erica?" he asked. "Is she making any new films?"

"You're behind on the headlines, old man." Cameron grinned. "Erica Evans is a single woman now, which makes me a free man. Ain't divorce a grand thing?" He brushed his hands together. "As if it never happened. Can't do that in Ireland. That's why America is the place to be."

"Why, Cam, you don't mean that," Abigail said. "I'm truly sorry to hear it." She took Cameron's elbow, guiding him into the next room for cocktails. The conversation turned to the sinking of the *Newell-Grey Explorer* and Germany's advances. Danielle detected a tense undercurrent in the room. She listened as Max spoke first in defense of the German people, then against Hitler. He'd always taken pride in his homeland. His father's family was an old and distinguished line.

"We're converting our ocean liners for military service," Jon said. "Even the *Queen Mary* will be pressed into service."

Danielle realized that was why they hadn't heard much from him in the past weeks. *It's just as well,* she thought, though she missed his company. They'd grown so close in New York, dining and dancing, and sharing their dreams and goals. *Perhaps too close.* Max had always been there, but she and Jon seemed to communicate on an exclusive wavelength. *Had Max noticed?* She swallowed hard. *No.* She quelled the inappropriate thoughts and smiled at Abigail, who, she realized, was saying something to her.

"How are you feeling with the baby, Danielle?"

"Much better now, *merci.* What a lovely dress you're wearing, Abigail," she added, admiring the bronze silk bias-cut, empire-styled evening dress that skimmed Abigail's svelte figure, and the creamy pearls that encircled her slender throat. Danielle wore a burgundy brocade dinner suit from Libby's charity collection that she'd altered, enlarging it for her thickening waist. She looked presentable, but Abigail was spectacular.

While the women chatted, Jon threw a look at Max.

Max tapped his pipe. "Let's have a smoke outside, shall we?" The men excused themselves.

Are Max and Jon up to something?

"Come," Abigail said to Danielle, "let's sit by the fireplace until dinner."

Walking behind Abigail, Danielle sniffed the air. "Smells delicious. I love nutmeg, it always reminds me of home."

Abigail looked surprised. "You *are* good. That's the secret ingredient in my pheasant recipe. You'd make a great chef."

Danielle smiled. "I prefer perfumery, it's the language of love."

"So is cooking," Abigail replied with a wink, tossing her glossy hair over a bare shoulder. Danielle noticed that Abigail's arms were lean and muscular, and she moved with easy confidence. *She must be a sportswoman,* Danielle thought, recalling the feminine styles that Jean Patou and Gabrielle Chanel had designed for sports. Danielle loved fashion; she'd been designing and sewing many of her own clothes since she was young.

"This is a wonderful room." Danielle sank into a black leather club chair near the brightly burning blaze. The sitting room was decorated with teakwood paneling and brass fixtures. She spied a Turner seascape above the fireplace, with the artist's signature light reflected on a turbulent sea. It brought to mind their ill-fated Atlantic crossing, the memory of kelp and salt rushing into her nose. The Turner painting was eerily realistic.

Abigail leaned forward. "I'm returning to Los Angeles soon for a Red Cross fund-raiser. What do you plan to do?"

Danielle said, "Our priority is to find our family."

"People are fleeing Europe in droves. What if the Germans reach France?"

"I pray it never comes to that." *France?* The Maginot Line ensured protection; everyone knew that. France was virtually impenetrable.

"It could happen." Abigail looked concerned. "You and Max should come to the States."

"Until we find Nicky and Sofia, we can't think of anything else." Danielle gazed into the fire.

Abigail leaned in conspiratorially and lowered her voice. "America is a land of opportunity. Look at Cameron Murphy. Imagine, he was one of eleven children in a family from County Cork, Ireland. Had a terrible childhood, poor as beggars. He said his father beat him so badly that he ran away and worked his way to America, then to Los Angeles. He was only fifteen at the time."

"How did he become such a success?" Danielle rubbed her hands in front of the fire.

"He worked at our Long Beach shipping dock, which is where

he and Jon met. Then he found a job as a bartender in a private club. Whilst he tended bar, he also sang a little; a record producer heard him. The rest, as they say, is history. Cameron's a rascal sometimes, but he always helps the Red Cross raise money."

"That's admirable." She hadn't imagined such a generous, hardworking side to the flirtatious charmer.

"He's a good man, despite the gossip. Of course, he and Jon don't always see eye to eye. Cameron always gets the girl, I suppose. It's an old rivalry." Abigail inched her chair near the fire and cradled her glass of sherry. "The Cameron Murphy I know is sweet and kind, though he seems rather lost. I'd like to see him marry again."

Danielle lifted a brow. "Do I detect some interest on your part?"

Abigail laughed. "He's hardly my type. And my parents would simply die. No, I'm resigned to being an old maid, Danielle. I'll probably never have children, and a virile man like that, well, I'm sure he wants scads of children."

Danielle heard a twinge of sadness in her voice. "Why did he and that actress divorce?"

"I'm not sure. But I've heard Erica is still crazy about him."

Outside on the balcony, when Cameron excused himself, Jon extracted an envelope from his dinner jacket. "Max, my father asked me to give this to you."

"I hope this is what I've been waiting for."

Jon hesitated. "You know how dangerous this is, my friend. You've got to think of Danielle. What if—"

"I don't return?" Max cut in, distress deepening the lines on his lean face. "My son and my mother are missing, Jon. What would *you* do?"

Blowing a breath out, Jon shook his head.

"Exactly. I don't have a choice." Max slipped the envelope into his pocket. "Neither do any of the poor souls still there."

Cameron rejoined them, now staggering under the effect of the alcohol he had consumed. He began to ramble on about being on the lookout for enemy airplanes.

"Ah, nary a one tonight," Cameron slurred, his Irish brogue evident. "Scared they are, of havin' to contend w'me."

Jon winced at Cameron's thoughtless humor.

Cameron wavered over the brass railing, his black dinner jacket flapping in the breeze, his starched white shirt open at the collar. "An' a fine night 'tis, too. Fit for the saints in heaven, it is."

Max seemed unruffled. He placed his hand on Cameron's shoulder. "Cameron, we should join the ladies. Abigail and Danielle probably miss us."

Cameron glared at Max's hand, and then gave him a sarcastic grin. "The fair Danielle, the beauty with the cinnamon hair. What a lucky man y'are, Max. Far too lucky fer y'own good, I'd say." As he spoke, he pulled a flask from his jacket and refilled his tumbler, pouring Irish whiskey to the brim.

Jon's skin prickled at his mention of Danielle. "Cam, old boy, don't you think you've had enough?"

Cameron shot him a wicked grin and turned back to Max. "Sure, an' she's just the type o' woman I'd like to know better."

Jon saw Max stiffen at Cameron's comment, but he knew his friend's logical, scientific mind would process the remark, before tossing it aside as irrelevant. Max's eyes clouded, and then cleared as he maintained control.

And yet, shame blazed on the back of Jon's neck. "I'm sorry," he whispered to Max. "I didn't realize he'd gotten so bloody sodded."

"Jon, I heard that," Cameron said. "C'mon, be a sport. The good Max doesn't mind, d'you, Max? Why, I bet he might even be willing to share the lil' lady with a few good friends, for the right sort o' trade, I mean." He waved the whiskey bottle toward Max. "Marriage can get mighty dull, I can tell you that. One woman, day in, day out. Bor-rrr-ing." He winked at Max. "I could introduce you to some starlets, then we could—"

"That's quite enough," Jon sputtered, incensed. *If she were my wife, I would not stand idle while Cam sullied her reputation.* "You're insulting Max."

Cameron gave a snort. "C'mon, Max, you goin' to keep her to yerself?"

Max stared straight ahead, obviously trying to ignore Cameron.

"That's it." Jon grabbed Cameron by the arm. "Time to go, Cam."

Cameron lashed out at Jon with his fist, but Jon ducked his punch with ease. Whiskey sloshed across Jon's face from the open flask before Max snatched it.

"Come on, sailor." Jon wiped alcohol from his stinging eyes, then deftly grabbed Cameron and pulled him from the balcony. Though Cameron tried to give fight, Jon easily overcame him; he'd had plenty of experience quelling drunken sailors.

With the help of the family's broad-shouldered driver, Jon disposed of Cameron, sending him back to his hotel in their car. Still seething, Jon went to his room to straighten his dinner suit and splash water on his whiskey-drenched face. What Cameron had said about Danielle had rattled him, and more than it should have. He still couldn't understand why his sister adored the slosh. Cameron was a rude, self-centered imbecile. They were at war now, but he was still playing games. *I'm through with him.*

Jon was accustomed to crude language among the men with whom he sailed. Not that Max couldn't handle an idiot like Cameron—in fact, to find his family, he was going right into the heart of the beast. No, Max had treated Cameron with incredible grace. *But if she were my wife, I wouldn't tolerate Cameron's remarks.*

But she isn't, he thought, reprimanding himself. He enjoyed Max's company, but in New York he had realized that he was calling on the couple for dinner and sightseeing just to be near Danielle. His growing feelings for her were completely inappropriate, but he couldn't control them. Guilt washed over him. He found himself thinking more about Danielle every day, and less about Victoria. He and Victoria had known one another so many years. Their families assumed they would marry someday, although he hadn't yet proposed to her. But this attraction he had for Danielle was new to him, and it was growing more and more addictive by the day. He couldn't stop thinking about her.

Toweling his face dry, he thought about the stories his father had shared with him about the last war. The enormous effort, the relentless pressure, the haunting tragedies. Most of his friends truly had no idea of the magnitude of what lay ahead for them or their country. He and his father had been working around the clock already. *And we are just beginning.*

Jon rejoined the party, nodding to Max, who was making excuses for Cameron.

As they dined on the pheasant that Jon had shot last season, Danielle asked Abigail about her work in Los Angeles.

Abigail's face lit up, and Jon smiled, his eyes on Danielle. "Here she goes. You had to ask, didn't you?" But he was proud of his sister's work.

Abigail ignored him. "The Red Cross renders aid to needy people everywhere, especially children. Even though America isn't at war, there is still so much that can be done for the effort through private funding." Her brown eyes danced. "Did you know the Red Cross traces its roots to Byzantine battlefields, where volunteers aided fallen knights?" Abigail smiled wistfully. "I wish I could persuade you two to move to Los Angeles."

"Someday, perhaps." Danielle traded a worried look with Max. "But not without our family."

Jon stared at Danielle's graceful hand, her slender fingers, the touch that he yearned for, and desire flamed within him. He flexed his jaw and raised his wine goblet to Max. "Here's to your success, Max. I hope you and Danielle reunite with your family soon."

Danielle and Max barely spoke during their return to the Leibowitzes' home, each of them lost in their own thoughts as they drove into a gathering rainstorm.

When they returned to their room, Danielle asked, "Why did Jon wish you success?"

"It's time you knew," Max said, sighing. "Do you feel well enough to travel?"

Danielle reached for a chair and leaned into it, her heart racing. "Are we going home?"

"Not you, my darling. I want you to go to France. In your state, you should be with your family."

She started to protest, but realized he was right, and nodded in numb acquiescence. A flutter of knowledge filled her. "Then you're going home."

Max nodded. "Through Germany. The British government has asked me to work for them."

"You mean, as a spy?" She fought the urge to scream. Outside, the rain grew harder, pelting against the roof like pebbles. "How can you even consider this?" she snapped. "Is it not enough that our family is in danger?"

"I have no choice," he said, his voice weary. "From Germany, I can travel into Poland to find Mother and Nicky. Then Jean-Claude will help us send them on to France."

"Without you? Why wouldn't you come with them?"

"I'll continue working for the British Secret Service. They need me, Danielle. My skills and language are critical in this fight."

"It's *their* fight, Max. All I want is my family."

"This is the only way. We must all commit ourselves to maintaining liberty on the European continent. And there's more . . . Heinrich has enlisted with the Nazis. One of my assignments is to find him and extract military information."

Danielle stared at him, her eyes welling.

"Trust me, darling." Max cradled her face, and drew her into his arms.

"You don't *have* to do work for them. Don't do this; as your wife, I beg of you, it's too dangerous. Please, just bring Nicky and Sofia to safety."

"I've weighed the risks, Danielle. And I've given my word." A shadow crossed Max's face, illuminating the deepening lines in his forehead.

Danielle let out a breath. *So it's done.* An eerie sense of foreboding spread through her mind like a charcoal fog, but no matter how she pleaded, she knew that her husband would not renege on a promise.

Max stroked her hair and they held each other, listening to the deluge outside as the rain intensified, pounding the windows in portent.

She buried her head into his shoulder. Somehow, she knew disaster awaited him, yet she refused to acknowledge it. *Not this time,* she decided. *This time will be different. Max will return with Nicky. God help him, he will.*

12 NOVEMBER, 1939 — POLAND

Sofia lay on a scrawny mattress that had been abandoned in a storage closet, staring at the wall with unseeing eyes as light from the setting sun filtered in from a window above. Outside the barricaded warehouse she heard soldiers barking gruff commands, their boots crunching on packed snow. Through the thin wall, she heard the incessant wails of a woman brought in last night. She wished she could tell her not to waste her strength crying, but she was too weak. She had to conserve her energy.

No child should ever be forced to suffer in a prison, Sofia thought, her heart aching for the children, who were too young to understand the horrors they witnessed, but not too young to feel distress.

Since their capture five weeks ago, Jacob had been determined to escape. Tonight was the night, he'd told her this morning.

"I'll call for you after sunset," he told her.

Sofia shook her head. "Go without me, Jacob. I'm dying."

"No, we'll find a doctor. You'll get better."

"But I'd only slow your escape."

"Sofia, you must come with us. For Nicky's sake."

At last, she agreed. But it was only for Nicky. She had promised Max and Danielle she'd look after their son.

Now she rested, waiting for Jacob to arrive. With a herculean effort, she turned onto her side, gasping for breath. She thought about all she had left—her family, her friends, her home, her possessions.

Nothing mattered now but the safety of those she loved. She would do what she could to protect them, use whatever means she still had at her disposal. She thought of the beautiful jewelry that she had once planned to leave to Danielle. At least her precious stones had served their purpose. She had given Jacob the gems she had stitched into her clothing to bribe the prison guards.

Dear, sweet Jacob. How kind he had been to her and her family all these years. *All these years.* There had been good ones, even great ones, as well as years she would rather forget.

The light from the tiny window grew dim, and she knew twilight was upon her, too. Shadows of snowflakes played against the barren wall like the puppet shows of her youth. Her breathing became more labored. The pressure crushed her chest.

She had always prayed that God would take her in her sleep

when her time to go arrived. She had imagined that her final days would be peaceful, that her loving family would surround her. But this was not to be. She thought of her family now, and prayed for each of them. She wondered, as she did every day, *where are they?*

As much as she missed Max and Danielle, she would not have wanted them to share this horror. She hoped they'd made it to France. If only Nicky had gone with them, if only she'd been strong enough to make the journey to France with him. Would her actions ruin poor Nicky? No, she decided, drawing strength from her convictions. *God will provide.*

The room darkened as the sun slipped beneath the horizon. Sofia closed her eyes and strained to draw another breath. The sounds from outside and the room next door grew muffled, as if they were miles away.

The door opened and Jacob crossed to her bed.

"Where's Nicky?" she asked.

"He's with Oscar and Irma." He pressed three tablets into her hand. "Take these for your pain," he whispered, handing her a cup of water. "It's time to go."

She swallowed the tablets, and swung her legs off the bed, summoning her reserve of strength.

They crept through a dim corridor to the rear of the warehouse and came to a locked door, which Jacob opened with a key. Through a crack in the door, they could see a guard with his back turned to them, but Jacob urged Sofia on.

"Go on," Jacob whispered. "He knows." After Jacob slipped through the door, the guard stopped him with the butt of a gun, and Jacob returned the key to him.

The air was bitter cold, their breath trailing moist clouds. Under the cloak of night, they scrambled to a spot in the soldiers' makeshift fence where the snow was packed hard and their footsteps wouldn't be noticed.

Jacob's wife, Irma, their children, his younger brother, Oscar, and Nicky waited by the fence.

The bribed guards turned away. Jacob and Oscar lifted a loosened section of the fence.

"Hurry," Jacob said. "Children first, quickly. Nicky, Irma, good. Sofia?"

Nicky reached under the fence. "Take my hand, Grand-mère."

"Go with the others, Nicky," Sofia whispered.

Oscar knelt and slithered under the fence, then stretched to grasp her hand. She grimaced as she slid under on the cold, hard earth; barbed wire clawed at her clothes and hair. Placing a strong arm around her thin waist, Oscar lifted and half-carried her, clambering to the edge of the forest, where they took refuge in the dense undergrowth.

Jacob was last out. As he dove for the brush, a searchlight flashed across his legs. "Run," he said hoarsely, cursing under his breath. "Don't wait for me, run!"

Sofia's heart was in her throat as they scurried through the frigid night, oblivious to the thickets that tore at their clothes and skin as they raced for their lives.

19 NOVEMBER, 1939 — DOVER, ENGLAND

The port of Dover was dreary and gray this morning, as it had been the day Danielle and Max arrived in England more than two months ago. High above on a cliff loomed a castle, ominous in the gathering fog.

As they waited in the passenger queue for the ferry to France, Danielle framed Max's lean face in her hands to memorize his features—his strong jaw, his aquiline nose, the eyes that could be so determined one moment, so loving the next.

"I nearly forgot." Max pressed a small, felt-wrapped bundle into her hand. "Take these with you."

Danielle opened the cloth. In it was his favorite pipe and the platinum Art Deco lighter that she'd had made for him in France as a wedding gift. The velvety aroma of his favorite vanilla tobacco drifted to her nose, and she ran her fingers across the ribbed case, touching the tiny emerald and sapphire baguettes with reverence.

"To be safe, I can't take anything with me unless it was made in Germany."

"I'll keep them for you." Her words felt thick on her tongue.

Max slid his arms around her and Danielle did the same, tightening their embrace, burying her head against his chest.

"All ashore that's going ashore!"

Max trailed a finger along her chin and heat gathered along her neck. "I hope to see you before the baby is born, darling. Until then, you'll be safe with your family."

"Max—" she began, but choked on her words, her sense of foreboding deepening. She lifted her face and their lips met in a kiss that united them and filled her with longing—for their family, their lives, the way they had once been . . . so in love, unencumbered by the world's turmoil. *How odd that when life is happy,* she thought, *you don't notice it. You can't imagine that the peaceful, bucolic state might not last forever.* She resolved never to take happiness for granted again.

She ran her hands over Max's clean-shaven face, smoothed the worry lines around his eyes, and feathered kisses on the crevice between his brows. She willed her love and strength to form protective armor around him, shielding him from harm.

Max cradled her face in his hands. "You'll have your son again soon. I'll find Nicky for you. I promise."

Danielle stifled a sob. "And your mother."

"I'll send them to Paris. Soon as I can." He began to pull away.

She knew it was time. "Max—"

"I love you, my dearest," he whispered, his voice raw. He crushed her head to his chest, and she could feel his heart pounding beneath his coat. "Always remember that. Be safe, and pray for me."

"I will . . . I love you, Max," she said, choking on her words. *My darling Max.* Loneliness engulfed her as she stepped aside, her fingers sliding from his face to his woolen coat, lingering in his capable hands. He squeezed her hand, and she saw him struggle to hold back tears.

As the ferry eased from the harbor, she stood trembling at the rail, waving until her husband dimmed to a tiny speck on the dock.

After Max disappeared from sight, Danielle gathered her woolen muffler higher around her ears, catching a prong on her wedding ring in the fabric. Max had insisted she keep the magnificent emerald and diamond ring that once belonged to his grandmother, even after they had sold his gold pocket watch to raise money for her passage. "No matter what happens, never sell our ring," he had made her promise, but she would trade it in a heartbeat for the safety of her family. A sob burst from her as she thought of his dangerous mission.

She gazed ahead, her eyes transfixed on the whitecapped waves surrounding her, separating her from her husband and her son and all those she loved. The scent of the sea filled her nostrils, reminding her of her last voyage across the Atlantic. She steeled herself against the memory, but a lash of fear struck her neck, spiraling down her spine, and her teeth began to chatter. Her old fear of drowning— now all too real—usurped her courage.

At the same time, a puzzling thought filled her mind. She'd had the same feeling once before, as a tiny girl, the last time she'd seen her grandfather. Somehow, she'd known she'd never see him again. She even told her mother. That was when her intuitive sense had first emerged, and ever since that incident, it filled her with dread.

The thought that she had not allowed to enter her consciousness now formed into clear, terrifying words in her mind.

Will I ever see Max again?

5

Consider the relationship of odors, one to another. A perfume is a symphony, the sum of the parts, where the whole is far greater than the individual. And yet, excellence stems from individualism. The artist intuitively understands this circular relationship, and therefore selects only the best ingredients.

—DB

19 November, 1939 — Paris, France

Danielle's parents and Jean-Claude met her at the Gare du Nord train station in Paris in the family motorcar. As they drove, sunlight danced on the river Seine, glancing off the gilded dome of Les Invalides. She craned her neck to see the spires of Sainte-Chapelle reaching skyward above the Île de la Cité. She never ceased to be amazed by the bustling verve of life that wove Paris together like a fine, rich tapestry.

But the visit was bittersweet. According to their original plan, Max and Nicky and Sofia should have been with her. And now she could smell the dread that permeated the city, sense the threat of war looming in the air like a great gray ghost, stretching its menacing fingers toward the prized city.

When they arrived at the family home, a Haussmann-era apartment on the street level, memories flooded her mind. Underfoot were the worn parquet floors she and her brother had slid across in stocking feet as children; overhead soared a high ceiling with ornate moldings where a pigeon had once floundered in distress after flying in through the front door, sending the staff into a panic before her parents' dinner party as she and Jean-Claude screamed with glee. Finally, the poor bird fractured its wing. Jean-Claude had created a splint and nursed the creature back to health. And there, on the carved mantel, sat the ormolu clock that had marked time in her father's family for generations.

Lean of build but as strong as ever, Jean-Claude carried her suitcase with ease to her old bedroom. They passed her mother's boudoir, where Danielle spied an antique étagère laden with Marie's perfume bottles, the aromas wafting through the air. She was home.

When they entered Danielle's musty bedroom, she wrinkled her nose. She opened the window, then collapsed into a stuffed chair, whose cheerful red print had faded in the years since she'd left. She studied her brother's strong profile, his dark shaggy hair, the wool trousers and slightly wrinkled shirt that looked like he'd studied all night in them. He seemed worried. "Any news from your sources?"

"No, nothing from Poland." He knelt in front of her chair, sunlight shadowing lines on his forehead that she didn't remember. "But that doesn't mean Nicky and Sofia aren't all right."

"Is there anything we can do?"

Jean-Claude's dark eyes flashed with passion. "There's an enormous amount to be done," he said with force.

His intensity scared her. *I don't know this side of my brother,* she realized. *So much has changed.*

Jean-Claude stood and strode to the door. He paused with his hand on the knob and glanced over his shoulder. "You'll soon see what we're up against, Danielle."

Later that week, Danielle realized Jean-Claude's admonition was well founded. Terrifying tales from Germany about surveillance appeared in newspapers. Employees were informing on employers, neighbor on neighbor—even family members on their own. She'd seen underground leaflets with photos of businesses burned, windows smashed. Jews were required to display yellow stars on their clothing. Nazi troops crossed borders, invading neighboring countries. People disappeared. Death became commonplace.

The stories sickened Danielle; she grew more desperate to reunite her family. How could she help?

"When can I go with you to your meetings?" she asked Jean-Claude one day, feeling restless.

Jean-Claude's expression darkened. "How do you know about that?"

She shrugged. "You must meet with others to make your plans."

He stood abruptly. "It's too dangerous."

"My son is in danger. What would *you* do?" Surely there was something she could do to help Max find Nicky and Sofia.

"You're pregnant, Danielle. I can't put you in jeopardy."

"I'm pregnant, not dead. Besides, who would suspect a pregnant woman?"

He expressed a puff of air in exasperation. "Absolutely not."

After more than two weeks of rambling around her parents' home and feeling useless, Danielle finally decided to go to Grasse and the family home there. The timing was perfect, because her father had started renovations on their apartment that he had been planning for years, seemingly in protest to the chaos threatening Europe.

Danielle sat in a Louis XV gilded chair in her mother's boudoir, construction dust already layering the fine antiques. She admired her mother, Marie, her dear *maman*, with her silvery blond hair and trim suit, who always seemed to handle everything in her life with grace and ease.

Marie turned to regard Danielle. "Just look at you," she said. "Your skin is pale, your eyes are dull, even your beautiful auburn hair has lost its luster. My darling, I wish you'd join us at the Hôtel Ritz. I feel like I'm turning you out, just when you need us most."

Marie ran her manicured hands over Danielle's long hair and drew her from her chair, kissing her on both cheeks. "I know you love the perfumery and your uncle, but I wish you'd stay in Paris. Why, we haven't even shopped for clothing for you."

Danielle sank into her mother's warm embrace, her familiar *parfum* comforting. *I have missed her so much,* she realized. "I love seeing you and Papa, but I need to occupy my time." Waiting for news that seldom came was torturous. Bellerose had always been her creative sanctuary, where she worked alongside Philippe in the family's perfume business.

"Business is slow," Marie said, "but I'm sure Philippe will welcome your company." She stroked Danielle's cheek. "Do you know how proud I am of you? You've earned your place among the rarefied clique of the world's top perfumers."

Danielle smiled to herself. It was true. There was Ernest Beaux, who blended Chanel No. 5, Jacques Guerlain of the Guerlain dynasty, Ernest Daltroff, who created Nuit de Noël for Caron, and the prolific François Coty. Her skills had helped establish La Maison de Bretancourt as a modern, world-class perfumery.

Marie kissed her on her forehead. Danielle truly appreciated her mother's recognition, for her mother was also a leader in the industry. Marie handled marketing, while her brother, Philippe, oversaw production. Their clients included scores of wealthy patrons and members of royal houses across Europe, and even as far away as Shanghai and Buenos Aires.

"Until Max returns with Nicky and Sofia, Bellerose and its fresh air will be good for you in your condition," her mother continued.

She had told her parents that as a German, Max could persuade the government to release Sofia and Nicky for travel. But she hadn't told her parents everything. *Why worry them?*

Danielle glanced at the ormolu clock and started for the door. "We should go soon. My train leaves in an hour."

"Of course, and remember, we'll visit soon for Christmas." Marie's voice carried its customary melodic lilt; Danielle knew it was to mask her worry.

8 DECEMBER, 1939 — GRASSE, FRANCE

Danielle stepped off the train at the small Grasse station, her nose twitching, thirstily drinking in the rustic aromas of the countryside. The sun warmed her shoulders, melting some of the tenseness she'd felt in Paris.

She spied her uncle, a wiry, bespectacled white-haired man standing on the platform. "Philippe," she called, waving.

"*Bonjour,* Danielle, how good to see you." A large, broad-chested man, Philippe had the weathered face of a Gallic farmer, and it creased into a welcoming, genuine smile. He kissed her on both cheeks, and she warmed to the remembrance of his familiar aroma, a subtle veil of jasmine, lavender, and rose, the natural perfume oils he worked with every day.

"I've missed you," she said. She had a special bond with Philippe. Besides farming the land, he was a well-traveled man of great intelligence, high morals, and artistic talents. "How is everything at Bellerose?"

"Needing a woman's touch. I'm glad you decided to come."

"I couldn't wait. How was the flower harvest?"

"It went very well this year, so we have a surplus of essential oils. But the business is slow. This damned war." He stooped to pick up her small suitcase.

"I'll get that, *mon oncle.*"

"Nonsense, I'm still strong as an ox. Is this all you have?"

She nodded, despondent. "All I have in the world."

"No, my little one," he said, his ivy green eyes twinkling behind his wire-rimmed glasses. "All you have is within you, and that is all you will ever need."

In Philippe's battered farm truck, they wound through Grasse on narrow cobblestone streets lined with lace-curtained shops. The aroma of garlic and saffron wafted through the air from a corner *café*. When they approached the *boulangerie*, Danielle detected the sweet scent of *calissons d'Aix*, the almond cookies she had loved as a girl. "Let's stop."

In the bakery Philippe selected fresh breads, including *brioche* and Danielle's favorite, *fougassette*, a flat bread made with orange blossom water.

While he shopped, Danielle wandered around the shop. She wished she were in Poland, helping Max. *This is the worst time to be pregnant.* Instantly, she regretted her thought. She and Max had been trying to have another baby.

They continued their drive through the foothills. Danielle spied the lavender fields she'd once traversed on horseback. When she mentioned it to Philippe, he smiled.

"Well, since you can't ride in your condition, you'll have to learn to drive."

She beamed. "Would you teach me? Max never thought it important for me to learn."

"You're a modern woman, Danielle. Someday all this will be yours." He waved his hand. "It's easier to oversee the operation by truck than on horseback. Especially with my old bones."

Danielle gazed out the window. She shook her hair in the cool breeze and inhaled, the scents of lavender and rose and jasmine sweet in the lucent air. They passed fields where delicately scented *rosa centifolia* bushes grew. "How was the rose crop this year?"

"Excellent. We had a mild spring and a generous rainfall. Twenty to twenty-five blossoms on every branch. Our rose was indeed the

'queen of the flowers' this year, to quote the Greek poet Sappho."
He lifted his chin and peered at her down his nose. "Our *rose de mai*
is expensive, Danielle, but far superior to others."

Laughter bubbled in her throat. "Your Gallic pride is showing,
Philippe."

He expressed a puff of air between pursed lips. "Bulgaria? Mo-
rocco? You can't tell me their roses are better than mine."

"Just different," she said with patience. "Moroccan roses have a
rich perfume, and Bulgaria's Valley of the Roses produces lovely
damascena roses scented with a brilliant tinge of pear." She glanced at
him from the corner of her eye. "But you know that."

Philippe returned her sidelong glance with a grin. "I see you
haven't forgotten my training."

"I had the best teacher, didn't I?" She gazed out over a rowed
field, dormant after harvest, undulating like ribbons over the hillside. Dread surged through her. *What if the Nazis took France? What
would happen to all this?*

Her grandfather had founded the business after apprenticing with
Pierre-François-Pascal Guerlain at his Rue de la Paix shop in Paris.
Like the Guerlain family, Danielle's family was also steeped in
the tradition of perfumery. They grew and supplied raw materials,
but they also created perfumes for private clients and couturiers, a
relatively new trend popularized by Paul Poiret and Gabrielle Chanel,
who augmented their couture business with *parfum*.

Someday the perfumery would be her responsibility. The Bretancourt family chateau, Bellerose, would pass to Jean-Claude, but Marie
planned to bequeath the perfumery and the flower farm to Danielle.

Danielle wanted to preserve this heritage for her children. But if
France fell . . . . *All this—our ancestors' labor, our birthright—would be
stripped from us.*

Her grandparents had died of influenza and consumption when
she was so young that she barely remembered them, and her father's

beloved younger twin brothers had died in the Great War the same year she was born. Her father had also fought in the war, though he refused to speak of it; Danielle understood that his pain was too deep.

She looked more closely at her uncle; something seemed different about him. Was it the deep cut of lines on his brow, the sag of age in the stoop of his shoulders, or the contemplative silence as he drove? Or was it just loneliness? Philippe's wife—the only love of his life—had been a nurse during the war. The day after she'd told Philippe she was pregnant with their first child, she was killed in a battlefield explosion. Philippe was in the army, and he returned to the farm after the war. Danielle believed the *parfums d'amour* he spent sleepless nights creating were dedicated to his wife's memory.

Philippe's wife had been Marie's dearest friend since childhood. Danielle's father told her once that Marie had been inconsolable, that only her children had kept her sane.

Rolling hills of meticulously rowed land sped past Danielle's window. After the Great War, her parents and Philippe had toiled to rebuild the farm, to maintain their homes, to provide for her and her brother's welfare and education.

Compared to them, Danielle's life had been tranquil, but now she wondered if her family's tragic history would be repeated. Had she taken her life for granted?

The destruction she had witnessed on the Atlantic Ocean haunted her dreams. *I must fight for my family,* she decided, *as my parents and Philippe did.*

Over the rise loomed their perfume factory, where rose and jasmine and lavender were processed after harvest. The building was quiet today, but she could envision in vivid detail the busy summer harvests, when workers began before sunrise to pick and process flowers. The roses and jasmine were sweetest when picked by dawn.

The work was demanding. A good worker could pick twenty-one hundred rose blossoms an hour, about twenty-five kilos. Eight hundred kilos produced just one kilo of absolute, which was a concentrated product. Their lavender was harvested by hand using a sickle, and then tied into clumps to dry. The process was labor-intensive, but the end result—the perfumer's alchemy—was pure magic.

A thought crossed her mind. *What's happened to our factory in Poland?* But in that same moment, she knew, and her heart sank at the realization. The Nazis would assume control. Glass was important to the war effort.

The road curved, and they turned onto the lane leading to the stately chateau. She and her family had spent summers there, with their father visiting on weekends from Paris and taking holiday for the entire month of August. Philippe preferred the two-story cottage on the grounds, claiming the chateau was too large for him.

They arrived at the stone cottage. When she spied the attached laboratory, she recalled the hours she'd spent there, happily immersed in aromas that still danced in her imagination. Philippe had been her first tutor in perfumery; when most little girls were playing dress-up or learning to play the piano, she had been tagging along after her uncle—then a man in the prime of life, passionate about growing the finest flowers that yielded the most fragrant, sought-after aromatic materials. She remembered how he had patiently trained her nose, making a game of quizzing her on the memorization of aromas. He taught her how to blend the basic formulas, how to unleash her creativity.

"Do you still have my old journals?" she asked, referring to her records of trials and formulations. The moleskin journals held his teachings, as well as her thoughts and observations.

"They're still in your work area," he said, grinning.

Danielle walked in. A mélange of aromas permeated the stone walls of the cottage, burnishing it with omnipresent scent. Essential oils produced from their own fields jostled with aromas of other exotic raw materials that Philippe imported. The smell lay imbedded in

Danielle's memory. "Would you mind if I go to the laboratory first?"

"Go on." Philippe laughed. "You're a true perfumer."

Danielle opened the laboratory door and inhaled deeply. Beyond the vats, across the worn stone floor, in the far corner beneath a window framed with pink bougainvillea, sat her workbench, or, in the lexicon of perfumery, the organ.

Several tiers rose above the horseshoe-shaped desk. Labeled apothecary bottles filled with raw material oils lined the risers: flowers, resins, leaves, woods, mosses, spices, herbs, seeds, grains, roots, bark, and fruit. From the animal kingdom came fixatives: civet, musk, and ambergris. The absolutes, the resinoids, the essential oils. Here she had learned to identify hundreds of aromas, committing each to memory.

Philippe had taught her how to weigh and blend a formula, and which materials complemented others, such as orange blossom and rose with a dash of vanilla, her first attempt when she was six years old. Her eyes glistened at the memory. *Someday, my children will follow in my path.* A lump formed in her throat as she thought of Nicky, and then she touched the curve of her developing child.

Lovingly she trailed her fingers across the worn wooden table and drank in the aromas until she was dizzy with excitement. Here, only here, did she dare to release completely her intuitive sense, to rely on it to the fullest. Ideas swirled in her mind.

But do I still have the power to harness the magic?

In her mind's ear she could hear Philippe, saying, "simplify, simplify," and indeed, she sought beauty in simplicity. She was known for perfumes that spoke to the soul. Harmony and grace; these were the hallmarks of her creations.

When she was very young, one of her favorite Guerlain perfumes, Mitsouko, inspired her. A simple ten-line formula, Mitsouko was a perfume of incredible depth, a miracle of achievement. Not unlike her subsequent creations, designed to transcend time. Like a Monet canvas, she hoped her work would also live on, far beyond her years.

For like an artist, the true test of a perfumer lay not in the skill with which she blended her materials, but in the imagination. To create an original *parfum* was a natural talent, just as one might have a natural talent for music or art. Danielle understood she had been blessed with a rare gift, and for this, she was thankful.

But a gift had to be used, constantly honed to perfection. Without use, rust would set in. Perfumers had been known to lose their abilities. And it had been a very long time for Danielle.

The next morning Danielle awoke with the sun. She started for the kitchen, hoping to find her uncle, who was also an early riser, when she heard a noise coming from Philippe's office.

She pushed open the door, peering into the room that hadn't changed since his wife had decorated it years ago. Morning rays filtered through lace curtains she had made, and a faded family crest hung over a rectangular antique farm table her uncle used as a desk. Philippe sat in a cracked leather chair, his head on the table, eyeglasses off, snoring softly, as a short-wave radio emitted a low signal. She started to wake him, but something caught her eye beneath his hand.

It was a perfume formula.

Curiosity overtook her, and she slid the paper from under his fingers. He shifted, but didn't wake.

Holding it near the light she began to read, intrigued, imagining the composition in her mind. *Bergamot, yes, rose, yes.* Then the ingredients began to jumble together in a shocking riot of scent that made no sense. It couldn't even be called avant-garde; the measurements were all wrong. *This is dreadful,* she thought, glancing at Philippe. *Has he lost his mind?*

She suppressed a sneeze, and Philippe woke at the sound. "Who's there?" he demanded, grabbing a wooden club next to his chair in his broad hands.

"It's me," she replied.

"*Mon Dieu,* don't sneak up on an old man, *ma chère*." He dropped the club with a thud. "What do you have there?"

"Your formula." She shrugged. "It's . . . not bad, but . . ." How could she tell him that it was horrible? That it looked like the work of a madman? *He must have dementia.*

"It's not what you think." He grabbed the paper from her. "This is a cipher. It's used to encode messages."

"*You're* working with Jean-Claude?"

"Actually, he's working for me. When he told me that you want to return to Poland, I wasn't surprised."

"Why didn't you say something yesterday?"

"I had to see your state of mind, Danielle."

"*My* state of mind? You sound just like Max. I'm ready to do whatever I have to do to reunite my family."

"I see that now. And you should see this." He picked up a perfume bottle from the desk. With a swift tug, he pulled off the base, exposing a cavity that held a small dial. With a flick of his wrist, he removed a metal trinket from a silk cord around the neck of the bottle. He joined the two pieces and held it out for her to see.

Danielle watched in awe as the metal piece swung around.

"North," Philippe said. "Very important to know if you're a courier or a pilot shot down in a strange country."

"It's a compass?"

He twisted the tall cap, and it fell into two pieces. "With a map," he said, extracting a tiny roll of paper. "We've improved since the first war."

6

A breakthrough in chemical research led to the creation of aldehydes. Paul Vacher and André Fraysse employed them for Arpège, Ernest Beaux for Chanel No. 5. Aldehydes add a vivid, quick quality to top notes; variations can be powdery, fruity, green, citrusy, floral, or woody. Utterly magical with rose and jasmine absolute, adds sparkle and brilliance.

—DB

24 DECEMBER, 1939 — GRASSE, FRANCE

With a white starched apron tied around her thickening waist, Danielle stood at the kitchen counter beating eggs with a whisk into a meringue, sadly reminiscing about last Christmas, when she had made this recipe for Max and Nicky. Today was Christmas Eve, and her mother and father had arrived at Bellerose bundled in sweaters and scarves the day before, along with Jean-Claude, his wife, Hélène, and their little daughter, Liliana, who was the same age as Nicky.

As Danielle worked she prayed for the safety of her missing family, and even hoped that they might appear on the doorstep, calling her name. A lump formed in her throat; the truth was immutable. Driven by heartache, she beat the eggs even more vigorously until the glossy meringue quickly formed into stiff, bird's beak peaks.

"Philippe, do you have any orange liqueur?" Marie asked, rummaging through her brother's pantry.

"Here it is," Philippe said, handing a corked bottle to her. "What are you making?"

"A *bûche de Noël*," Danielle said, concentrating on her task. Carefully measuring each rationed ingredient, she combined sugar and flour in another bowl, grated orange zest, added the liqueur, and folded the meringue into the mixture.

"It's not Christmas without a traditional Yuletide log." Marie ran a finger down a page of an old recipe book, reading directions for the sponge cake, or *biscuit*. " 'Spread into a shallow pan and bake for ten minutes.' "

"I wouldn't know about that," Philippe said. "I don't celebrate your husband's holiday," he said pointedly to Marie.

"Let's not dredge up that old argument, *mon frère*," Marie said, softening her words with a smile. "I converted for love."

A knock sounded at the front door. Danielle threw a look of concern toward Philippe, who hurried to answer it.

"Then we'll cool it," Danielle said, trying to stay calm. "And brush the surface with coffee liqueur and butter cream frosting, roll it like a log, and decorate." She thought about the meringue mushrooms she had made with Nicky last year, and how he had helped score the frosting to mimic wood grains. She remembered how his luminous green eyes had lit with joy when she gave him the first swirled slice. She swallowed against the tautness in her throat and met her mother's eyes. "Liliana will love it, won't she?"

Her mother nodded with understanding, just as the little girl wandered into the kitchen. "Is it ready yet?" Liliana asked.

"We'll have it tomorrow at dinner, but we'll have a little taste for you soon," Marie said, hugging Liliana and brushing her silky hair from her forehead. "Where is your papa?"

"With Grand-père." Liliana cast her eyes down. "They're arguing again."

"Men and their politics," Marie said, rolling her eyes.

Philippe rushed into the kitchen clutching a piece of paper. "Danielle, we have a message from Max."

Danielle pressed her hand to her mouth, stifling a cry. "What does it say?" She hurried to him, wiping her hands on her apron. The folded note was written in German. "What is this?" she demanded. "It looks like a grocery shopping list."

"Yes, it should, it's encoded," he explained, putting on his glasses. "Come with me." They hurried to his office. Her heart pounding, Danielle leaned over his shoulder as he decoded it.

My dear D, I am fine, it read. *Looking for family. Some leads. Don't worry. Take care of our baby. I love you.*

Danielle slumped into a chair and sank her head into her hands, sobbing as relief and despair coursed through her. She was grateful for the message, but it was not what she had hoped for.

31 DECEMBER, 1939 — PARIS, FRANCE

Despite the unrest in Europe, Parisians flocked to the venerable Hôtel Ritz on New Year's Eve to celebrate the birth of a new year.

Upstairs, Marie sat at her vanity in an ivory silk-and-lace dressing gown and thought about how quickly the year had passed, and how their family troubles had coiled as tight as a corkscrew. Last week, Christmas at Bellerose had been a bittersweet holiday filled with sadness, despair, and angry tirades.

Marie had wanted to stay in Grasse, but Danielle had urged her to return to Paris with her father. "I'll be working in the laboratory every day," Danielle had told her.

Marie chose a *parfum* and touched her neck with its crystal stopper, trailing it along the length of her neck. She breathed in one of Danielle's finest aldehydic *parfums* blended of Bulgarian rose and jasmine absolute. It was a masterpiece, with a mysterious, warm *sillage* of amber and vanillin, extracted from the seed pods of a vining orchid. The result was modern, stylish, and sensual—Danielle's aromatic hallmark.

Was the brief happiness they had known lost forever? Were the horrors of the last war destined to repeat?

Marie gazed into the mirror, aching for Danielle's distress, wishing there was something she could do to help her daughter and her family, and her poor little grandson, Nicky. It was so tragic, but what could she do? What could any of them do? She sent up a prayer for Max, that he would return soon with Nicky and his mother.

She dressed in a slim camel-colored wool dress, and set about tidying their airy salon while she awaited the arrival of Jean-Claude, Hélène, and Liliana. Marie had a special evening planned for her granddaughter. She arranged a silver tray of petit-fours and canapés from room service on an inlaid table.

"Oh, Edouard," Marie called to her husband, conscious of making her musical voice lively. "They'll soon be here."

From the bedroom, he grunted in reply.

Exasperation swiftly darkened her mood like a rain cloud. The argument between Edouard and Jean-Claude on Christmas Day still rang in her ears. In recent months, her son had grown flagrantly antagonistic toward his father, blaming him in part for Hitler's advancement. Marie paused, her hand over a crystal figurine. *Could Jean-Claude be right?*

Edouard was a partner in one of the foremost banks in Paris. For years the bank had lent money to European businesses, many of which were based in Germany. As it turned out, some were involved in munitions manufacturing, and Jean-Claude did *not* approve. He had unleashed an angry tirade during Christmas dinner.

"The Nazi party and its members are prospering," Jean-Claude argued, "and at the expense of everyone else, especially the Jews, a category which includes your own wife, if you recall, as well as your children, even if we were baptized."

Edouard roared his defense. "A man does not have to justify his business to his family. You've profited, too. How else could you afford to complete your medical studies, with a wife and child?"

"I could manage," Jean-Claude retorted.

Edouard snorted. "This prosperity benefits all Europeans. Besides, I'm outnumbered on the board."

"Then you must stand alone for what is right."

"You're an idealistic idiot. I refuse to continue this discussion."

Heartsick over their argument, Marie had tried to mediate, but to no avail. Now, she feared another quarrel, another ruined holiday.

Marie had surprised Hélène and Jean-Claude with a special treat for New Year's Eve. She promised to look after Liliana while they rang in the new year with dinner and dancing at the hotel. Hélène had been thrilled, saying that Jean-Claude had been away studying every evening.

Marie pressed her fingers to her lips. *Why was he out every night of the week?* She hoped Jean-Claude hadn't succumbed to the thralls of another woman. She adored Hélène.

There, she thought, surveying the room. *All is ready. New Year's Eve will be perfect, as long as the men behave themselves.*

How are you, my little one?" Marie took Liliana from her son, laughing and cooing over the child who so favored Danielle. "We're going to have such fun this evening."

"May I play with your perfumes, Grand-mère?"

"But of course, *ma chérie*, I have one your aunt Danielle made for little girls like you." She turned to Jean-Claude, noting the fatigue that clouded her son's dark eyes. "Won't you come in? Have a canapé, say hello to your father."

Jean-Claude threw a glance at Hélène. "No, we haven't time, Maman."

Hélène shot him a reprimanding look.

"Maybe when we pick up Liliana tomorrow," he muttered.

Edouard's voice boomed from the next room, "Jean-Claude, is that you and Hélène?" His commanding frame filled the doorway, his smooth silver hair impeccable. He moved with the assurance of a general, hugging Hélène and Liliana, then turning to his son. "Jean-Claude." He leaned toward him to kiss him on the cheeks.

Jean-Claude shoved his hands in his pockets and acknowledged him with a curt nod. "Papa."

Marie rolled her eyes and disappointment settled heavily on her shoulders. *There goes a lovely evening.*

"I've heard you've been busy, son," Edouard said, his voice even. "I'd like to speak with you." He turned to Marie and Hélène. "Will you excuse us for a moment?"

Hélène took Liliana into the bedroom and Marie followed, but left the door cracked open. She wanted to hear what Edouard had to say.

Edouard cleared his throat. "Jean-Claude, I've heard that some of your friends are underground activists, supplying false papers and passports to Jews and 'undesirables,' smuggling out citizens. Is this true?"

"I have no idea what you're talking about," Jean-Claude answered.

A chill ran down Marie's spine like a serpent's tongue, while Hélène looked terror-stricken. Marie touched her hand.

"Jean-Claude, why would you become so entangled, with your family responsibilities and a bright future before you? These are dangerous, irresponsible activities."

Jean-Claude's voice rose, "My responsibility is to humanity, Papa, and I'm not alone in my beliefs. You, too, could make a difference. Use your position and power at the bank to benefit mankind. Call the loans, turn off the financial spigot."

"That's not the way we conduct business," Edouard replied.

"Papa, if men like you take a stand, we'll halt Hitler's war."

Marie strained to listen, motioning to Liliana with one finger to be quiet. A long silence ensued. Edouard had survived childhood poverty, the Great War, the deaths of his twin brothers, and near financial ruin during the depression. She knew he would not endanger his family's financial stability. But she, too, had begun to wonder about her husband's business activities.

Something slammed, startling Marie. *Probably Jean-Claude's fist on the desk.*

"Then think of your family, Papa. For God's sake, look what's happening to Danielle."

"She should never have left France," Edouard stormed. "I never approved of her marriage. But this I can promise, Jews in France will never be harmed."

"If you believe that," Jean-Claude roared, "you're delusional. Paris is the prize Nazis covet above all others."

Marie flung open the door, incensed. "Keep your voices down. You're scaring Liliana."

"It's all right, Maman. I have nothing left to say to him." Jean-Claude pivoted hard on his heel and called to his wife. "Hélène, let's go. We're late for dinner."

Hélène murmured her apologies to Marie and Edouard, kissed Liliana, and followed her husband.

Marie folded her arms. "Well, I'm glad the two of you tried to make up."

Edouard huffed from the room.

Marie held Liliana and the little girl clung to her, her sweet face saddened by the angry exchange between her father and grandfather. "They mean no harm," Marie whispered, rocking her.

Despite what Edouard said, if Nazi troops broke through the

barricades, she feared French citizens of Jewish heritage would be treated no differently than those in Germany. She hugged her granddaughter to her chest.

Can France hold her own against the Nazi machine? she wondered. Her friends in Austria lived in fear under the new regime. What fate awaited her family if the Nazis occupied France? What if the battle for France was lost? She pressed a hand to her mouth, horrified that Nazi occupation might be near.

She began to piece together a puzzle: Jean-Claude's late nights, his confrontations with Edouard, Danielle's plan to return to Poland. When she had asked Danielle how she thought she could return to Poland, Danielle hadn't answered.

Marie's skin crawled with unease. Jean-Claude must be involved with some freedom organization. She had heard about such groups, and that members often would not, or could not, speak about it, even to their families.

Marie tightened her arms around Liliana. *Perhaps the time has come for us to leave France.*

15 JANUARY, 1940 — GRASSE, FRANCE

Danielle pushed back from her perfumery workbench and rotated her neck, which was tense from the detailed work of measuring ingredients in precise quantities and testing results. She was also anxious about Max and finding it difficult to maintain her focus. Shivering, she removed her lab smock and replaced it with a pearl gray wool sweater she'd embellished with white lace and tiny rose embroidery.

Every day she hoped that a message from Max would arrive saying that he'd found Nicky and Sofia and they would soon return to her. She gazed numbly at the barren trees outside the window, her head throbbing from the incessant strain.

Far too infrequently Philippe received a message over his shortwave radio, or he would return home with a message smuggled through the underground network. She would nearly faint from anxiety until the message was decoded. *I love you,* he always wrote. *Still searching. Working hard.*

She pressed her fingers to her temples. *I've got to get out of here.*

Danielle did most of the cooking, housekeeping, and laundry for Philippe. Her uncle had kept his promise about teaching her to drive, and over the past few weeks Danielle had learned to handle the truck under his patient tutelage. One day he laughed when she ran off the road, the vehicle mired in a field of lavender, but he dug out the tires while Danielle maneuvered out of the rut. "You must learn how to get out of trouble, too," Philippe told her. She practiced often, driving into the nearby village center of Grasse for supplies.

Hugging her sweater around her midsection, Danielle decided to shop early for supper. She stepped outside, drinking in the cool air to clear her mind. She cranked Philippe's old truck to life, and was soon steering past dormant fields along narrow roads toward the village.

She hadn't gone far when she spied another truck rambling toward her, and recognized the local postal courier. She waved her down and both vehicles slowed to a stop.

"*Bonjour,* Danielle, you're out early today," the portly woman said.

"Needed some fresh air. Any mail for us?"

The woman reached into a bin on the seat beside her and handed Danielle a small bundle of letters. "Here you are."

On top of the stack was a letter that bore a London postmark. She and Abigail had been corresponding, but the handwriting wasn't Abigail's feminine, lacy style. The writing was bold, masculine. Anxiously, she eased the truck to the side of the road, turned off the engine, and ripped open the letter.

It was from Jon.

My dear Danielle, it began. *I promised Max I would check on you, make sure you were safe. Abigail sends her love, and we both worry about you. I must tell you, I received word from my father that Max was reassigned into more sensitive areas, so you might not hear from him for a while. Try not to worry; he is highly skilled and entirely capable. I trust he'll find your son and his mother soon as well. Have faith, Danielle. Please write, let me know how you're doing. Thinking of you always.*

She lowered the letter and rested her head against the steering wheel, trembling with apprehension. *What does this mean?*

2 FEBRUARY, 1940 — POLAND

Threads of daylight filtered through the cracks between the wooden planks overhead, which had been quickly covered with a thick mound of straw. None of the children made a sound, and for this Sofia was thankful. Along with Jacob, Irma, and Oscar, she lay in a shallow pit hastily dug beneath the barn, the children huddled between them on the frozen dirt.

Yesterday an icy blast of winter had barreled through the country-side. Their footsteps left telltale imprints in the soft snow, rendering safe travel nearly impossible. They'd tried to cover their tracks, and found refuge with a kind young woman whose husband had been killed in the war.

Now thick-soled boots stamped across the structure above them, shaking the floorboards with their authoritative march. A pitchfork stabbed through the straw, scraping the planks above them.

Sofia managed to contain her coughing until after the barn door was closed. They dared not move until their young benefactor came to them several hours later, carrying with her a jug of water, a loaf of fresh-baked bread, and a stack of old wool blankets.

Sofia sat up, her stiff joints creaking. She shook dirt from her hair and clothes, and wiped smudges from Nicky's face. Seeing the brave expression he wore, she wondered how long they would be safe here.

Danielle sat at her workbench in the laboratory testing several perfume compositions, dipping blotter strips into small amber-colored bottles. She waved them under her nose, but her mind strayed, thinking about the past few weeks at Bellerose.

The wait for Max was agonizing, and she could barely contain her worry over Nicky and Sofia. In the last month she had written to Jon several times, pleading for any information he might have. Jon wrote back, always reassuring her. He also wrote about his military training and included news about the war. She responded, sharing details about her work and life in Grasse.

Philippe had also revealed stories she had never heard about his intelligence missions during the Great War. She watched him craft special perfume bottles, hollow out their large, fanciful crowns and insert tiny papers that held codes or maps. Using code, he prepared formula lists that held no meaning other than to a special operative.

She had spent most of her time in the laboratory immersed in her perfume work, trying to divert her thoughts from constant worry.

Working with aromatic materials improved her concentration and provided a measure of relaxation, but her family was never far from her mind.

Regaining her focus, she waved another formulation under her nose, inhaling. She was working on a new perfume with a base accord similar to one she had created for her wedding day. But this perfume was more mature, deeper and richer—a reflection, she realized, of her life and recent trials. Every artist revealed himself in his art.

She made notes in her perfume journal, where she logged

formulas, impressions, and thoughts. *Too much bergamot in this one, too tart; no depth in this one; bring forward the orange blossom.* Measuring out drops from several vials, she blended another variation, leaning heavily on her keen intuition. Inhaling, she let her mind wander, visualizing the aromatic impression. She was on the verge of discovery. *An ethereal freshness with subtle spiciness, like the voluptuous scent of orange blossoms on a sunny spring morning.* The hair on her arms bristled with anticipation.

She inhaled again, going farther, detecting the bouquet of jasmine absolute and rose attar, rich and silky, entwined with a spicy note of carnation, adding verve and vitality, robust brilliance. *It needs a splash of complexity here, a sprig of basil there, an accent of clove.* Images of lovers danced in her mind, a soaring sonata thrilled in her soul.

A vision intruded, no, a memory—she was dancing with Jon, resting her head on his shoulder, a salty hint of ocean, breathing in his scent, intoxicated with the musky, virile smell of his skin . . .

Another breath and she dragged her thoughts back, delving deeper into the essence. *The mystery of amber to balance the soul; the silky smoothness of sandalwood; the delicious lure of vanilla, like a lover's midnight embrace.* An ache grew within her at the core of her being. And in her mind's eye, veiled visions of a moonlit night, a couple dancing barefoot on the beach, swirling silks of scarlet and gold, the sultry caress of a whisper, so vivid she trailed her fingers along the nape of her neck, remembering . . . Seductive, sensual, the essence of *amour.*

Remembering Jon . . .

She shook her head, dispelling the thought.

Go back . . . back to the impression, inhaling, back to the vision, his breath on her skin . . .

And yet, something was missing.

The deepest satisfaction of the soul, the complete connection to the spirit, the psyche. Almost, but not quite.

Have I lost my touch? Danielle opened her eyes. She couldn't focus. She bowed her head to make notes in her journal. The remembrance of Jon disturbed her.

She cradled her belly with one hand and rocked, wondering where Max was. Losing her concentration, she put her pencil down and drew her hands over her face, thoughts racing through her mind.

I can do this, she thought, trying to quell her memories, strengthen her resolve.

Philippe opened the door and walked in. "Are you all right?" he asked.

She shook her head. "Difficult morning." She held out a bottle. "Here's what I have for Chimère so far."

He closed his eyes and inhaled, then opened them. "Excellent progress, with a unique, clear motif. Entirely new, radically different from anything else today. Still needs work, but you know that. So, why do you call it Chimère?"

"It's a lovely word, don't you think?" A wistful smile tugged at her mouth and she took the sample back. "It's full of imagery; it's my fanciful folly, that's what Max thinks of my work. But this will be a grand perfume, once it's complete. It's our future," she added firmly. "Of that I'm certain."

Philippe crinkled his brow. "Doesn't Max admire your work?"

"He'd rather I tend to our children." She chewed her lip at the thought of Nicky.

"Even so, you must not deny your art." Philippe stroked his stubbled chin. "Why can't you do both? Marie always has."

"I will when the children are older." Danielle put the vial away. "Max is a proud man; he wants to provide for our family." After mentioning his name, she grew quiet.

"You may have your differences, Danielle, but Max is an honorable man." Philippe's voice sounded thick. "And brave. To go back into occupied Poland, well, you know how dangerous it is. Many men would not have done that."

19 MARCH. 1940 — GRASSE, FRANCE

"This must have been written six weeks ago," Danielle said, her voice rising as she clutched Max's note. Since his reassignment, she'd been praying for a message from him. Despite her busy daily routine of perfume blending, cooking and cleaning, handling the laundry and shopping, it was growing increasingly difficult to retain her faith in Max's safety. *He should be here by now, with Nicky and Sofia.*

Philippe sat at the kitchen table with a meager plate of cheese before him, his shirtsleeves rolled up, and refilled his wineglass with a deep, ruby-colored Bordeaux he'd put in the cellar several years ago. He sipped the wine and said thoughtfully, "He might have written it later."

She paced the length of the kitchen, one hand on her burgeoning belly, inspecting Max's familiar scrawl, which was barely legible now after the paper had been folded and secreted away for so long. "No, there's a date on the other side. It's a receipt." Max had scribbled a list on the reverse.

Danielle stared at the wine glimmering in the low overhead light. The message had been delivered right after supper. She had sworn off alcohol during her pregnancy, but tonight, more than ever, she longed for a glass of wine to calm her nerves. "I have a terrible feeling, Philippe. What if he can't find our family?"

As soon as the words left her mouth, Danielle shivered, and fear flared within her. Too much time had passed. Something was terribly wrong.

She just knew it.

7

Leathery and sensual, labdanum is a resin derived from the rockrose herb, its impression as black and shadowy as the crevices of the human heart.

—DB

4 APRIL, 1940 — POLAND

After a few weeks the snow dissipated and the small, shadowy party pressed on in a southerly direction through the countryside. During the coldest part of winter they had taken refuge in a barn on a farm. With the snow beginning to melt, Jacob decided it was time to move on, even though the Nazi territorial expansion challenged their progress.

Jacob and Oscar took turns supporting Sofia while Irma led the way, their youngest son in her arms. Next came Nicky, with his dirty stuffed monkey strapped to his back. Following him were Jacob and Irma's two other children—a girl of Nicky's age and her younger brother. All the children held hands, catching one another when they tripped on vines or stumbled on rocks.

Traveling only at night, they'd been living off the land and the kindness of strangers, desperate to escape the horrors of their homeland.

They trudged on by moonlight until Sofia could go no farther.

"Over the ridge," Jacob panted, "there should be a shed where we can sleep for a few hours."

"You go on," she wheezed. "I'll catch up." In truth, she had lasted longer than she had ever thought she would, but she had promised Max and Danielle she would protect Nicky.

"No. Here, put your arm around my shoulder." Jacob whisked her up with one swift movement and continued.

At sunrise, they spied the small wooden shed their underground contact had promised. The door swung open, revealing two canvas cots and a three-legged table crowded into the weather-worn structure.

"Sofia, you and the children must rest." Jacob turned to his brother. "Oscar, you can move more stealthily without us. Go on ahead, see what we're facing."

Oscar took his leave and, while the others slept, Jacob and his wife took turns on watch during the day.

Through the gathering dusk, Jacob spied a soldier at the top of the ridge they had come across. They had been tracked. He woke his family and Sofia, and told them to hurry. They could leave through a rear window.

Sofia woke coughing. When she took her hand from her mouth, she saw blood in her palm. Her heart sank, though she knew this was inevitable.

Irma hurried to her with a handkerchief and a jar of water. Sofia wiped her hand and mouth, and took a sip. Jacob came to her side; she raised her eyes to him. "I haven't long now," she whispered, not wanting to alarm the children. "You should go without me."

"We can't leave you here."

Sofia glanced at the children. They looked like waifs, with worn shoes and hollowed cheeks—and yet, determination shone in their expressions. *How I love them all.* She closed her eyes for a moment, feeling their love, drawing its warmth into her cold, aching bones. She knew her incapacity would only endanger them, hinder their escape. "I have an idea," she said slowly. "Perhaps I can stall for time so that you can get away."

Jacob looked horrified. "Absolutely not," he said, shaking his head.

She reached out and squeezed his roughened hand in her own frail hand. "Jacob, my time has come. My cancer will not go away, no matter how many pills you manage to find for me. A day, maybe two, is all I have. This I know. At least I will die a free woman, here with the fresh air and the tall trees and the birds singing to me. My soul will be free to soar high, high above with them. What better place to die?"

Jacob knelt and stroked her forehead, speaking softly. "My dear Sofia, we love you, and I will do anything for you. This can't be the only solution—"

"It's what I want, Jacob. Soon I'll be at peace, all my pain will be gone." She turned her head. "Nicky, come here, my darling."

Pushing a shaggy blond lock from his dirty face, Nicky stepped forward, eyes wide, clutching his stuffed monkey. "Grand-mère?"

Sofia could hear the fear in his voice, and it saddened her. She pulled herself up and hugged him to her breast, willing what strength she had to flow into his slender body. "Go with Jacob, my dear little one. Someday soon, you'll be reunited with your mother and father. I'm going to heaven, where I'll watch over you, and your little monkey here, forever and ever." She kissed him on his warm, smudged cheek.

"I love you, Grand-mère," Nicky said, flinging his arms around her. Tears filled his brilliant green eyes, twin pools that mirrored his mother's eyes. "I want to go to heaven with you."

She held him tightly, willing her love to protect him like an invisible shield. "You will someday, and I'll be waiting for you. But not now, it's too soon for you. You must go with Jacob and Irma."

Nicky nuzzled her neck, sobbing. "Don't leave me."

"I'll always be with you, and you'll know this, I promise." She pressed her lips to his fine hair and kissed him again. "Be strong for me, and remember that I'll always love you."

Nicky stepped back, sniffed, and drew his sleeve across his eyes. He lifted his head, and in his expression, Sofia saw the frightened little boy waning, and the fresh vigor of courage flaring in his eyes. *He's strong now,* she thought, smiling. *Like his parents.*

Sofia turned to Jacob, Irma, and the children. She gazed at each beloved one. "Go now, my dearests," Sofia said, then added urgently, "and run like the wind."

Jacob opened the rear window and held it as the others passed by Sofia, each one hugging her and kissing her cheek in good-bye.

Gently, Irma took Nicky's hand and kissed Sofia. "I'll look after him for you."

Jacob touched his lips to Sofia's forehead. "Good-bye, my beautiful lady." He pulled back, his eyes brimming with tears.

"Don't cry for me," Sofia murmured. "I am soon free."

Jacob forced a smile through his tears. Within seconds, he was gone.

Now that she was alone, Sofia gathered her strength. She had one more vital task to accomplish.

4 APRIL, 1940 — GRASSE, FRANCE

Danielle glanced outside the laboratory window. Beyond the bougainvillea's ruby flush, she could see wisteria vines laden with violet-hued blossoms. Like the wisteria, she had also grown heavy with the springtime's promise. According to her calculations, the baby was due in two weeks.

The farm was in full operation and Philippe rose early to oversee the work, even though he worked late every evening, relaying vital information over his shortwave radio. Danielle often listened, learning all that she could. If she didn't hear from Max soon, she had a plan of her own in mind.

This morning, she sat at her perfumer's workbench and scribbled furiously in her journal, checking numbers. Waving a strip of blotter paper under her nose, she felt a frisson of excitement. She still had a great deal to do, but she was finally on the right track with an incredible, intoxicating blend of rose, tuberose, and jasmine, sandalwood and an amber blend. Inhaling, the romantic scent conjured exquisite joy.

The path had come to her in a dream, the melding of sandalwood and patchouli with amber notes of vanillin and labdanum absolute in a manner that was nothing short of exquisite. And now her masterpiece, Chimère, was nearing completion. But could she go the distance with it? The thought disturbed her; she'd never had such difficulty in her work.

Danielle put her pencil down, rubbed her eyes, and stretched. As she did, her baby turned and kicked. She traced a circle on her stomach and tried to imagine Max's delight with the new baby, but it was hard to conjure such thoughts. It had been so long since she'd heard from him. She drew a deep breath to quell her nerves.

Philippe entered the laboratory and Danielle looked up. His demeanor was subdued; he pressed a hand to his forehead. Alarmed, she rose from her chair and put her arm around him. "What is it, Philippe? Don't you feel well?"

He paused, strangely awkward. "A British gentleman is here to see you."

A chill coursed down her spine.

"It's Jonathan Newell-Grey."

Danielle spun around and rushed through the hallway, her heart racing. Philippe followed her as quickly as he could. When she saw

Jon, he caught her in his arms. Her heart was beating so fast she could hardly breathe.

"Jon, what brings you here?" A sense of dread settled over her, even as she pressed her face against his neck, breathing in the scent that haunted her.

"Danielle." Jon's voice was grave. As he took in her enlarged belly, his dark, impassioned eyes grew even more troubled.

Jon seemed leaner, older. She didn't remember the gray hair that glistened at his temples.

She clutched her throat. "Is it Nicky?"

He shook his head and clenched his jaw.

And then she knew, though her mind refused to accept it. Her breathing accelerated in short, sharp breaths. "No, oh, no—"

He wrapped his arms around her, cradling her head against his chest. "I'm so sorry, Danielle. Max is dead."

"No," she whispered. She began to shiver and tears sprang to her eyes. *It can't be.* Blood pounded in her ears. The room swirled and her legs began to give way beneath her.

Jon helped her to the sofa, then held her, rocking her as she moaned, his tears mixing with hers. Philippe put his broad arms around the two of them, stroking her hair to comfort her as he had when she was a child.

After several minutes, she leaned back, her grief momentarily spent. Her mouth felt dry, her tongue thick. She tried her voice and heard it come to her, eerily flat. "When?"

"Last week." Jon dabbed her face with his handkerchief.

"What happened?" she asked, choking on her words.

Jon smoothed his knuckles across her cheek. "He was shot. I'm told it was probably very quick. Always remember that he was brave; he acquired valuable information for England. His actions saved many people." He hesitated, his eyes glistening. "We believe Max discovered the whereabouts of his mother and your son."

Danielle gasped.

Jon glanced at Philippe. "We don't think he actually saw them, but we have reason to believe they're still alive. However, before he could reach them, he spoke to his cousin."

"Heinrich?" A chill overtook her.

"Heinrich was promoted to the SS, the *Schutzstaffel*, or special security force, but it seems Max still thought he could trust him." Jon's face reddened. "My father told me Heinrich betrayed Max, his own flesh and blood. Our sources told us Max was going to meet with Heinrich. Max was found later, at their designated meeting place, shot through the heart. He died a hero, Danielle."

"I don't want a hero, I want my husband," she snapped, anger rising within her. "So, Heinrich shot him?"

"We don't know for certain. At the least, he deceived Max."

Danielle began to reel. "And Nicky?"

"We don't know anything more about Nicky or Sofia. I'm so, so sorry."

White spots sparkled in front of her eyes; the room wavered and grew dark. Danielle could hear her uncle and Jon say something, far, far away, and then, everything went black.

Outside, the moon hung high above like a silent sentinel. Danielle shifted in bed. The sheets were warm beneath her. She shoved her hand under the duvet cover, and then removed it. Her hand glistened bloodred in the moonlight.

She began to scream.

Jon burst into her room and raced to her side. "Danielle, it's all right, I'm here."

"No, no, no, something is wrong." A pain sharp as a dagger sliced through her. "It's my baby."

Philippe was at the door. "*Mais non!* It's coming early. I'll get the midwife."

"I'll stay with Danielle." Jon rolled up his sleeves and took charge. He stroked Danielle's face. "Don't push, just breathe."

She slipped half out of consciousness, but through the haze she heard Jon's voice, sure and commanding, like the last minutes on the ship. She turned from the darkness toward him.

"Stay with me," he said, grabbing her hands. "Grip my hands and squeeze, Danielle, come on, do this for Max,"

8

Perfume is my memory, the chronicle of my life.

—DB

4 APRIL, 1940 — PARIS, FRANCE

Jean-Claude pushed his cap back on his head and studied the diagram on the rickety chalkboard. A colleague was scratching out a complicated plan to disable the financial mechanism behind the Third Reich. Overhead the raucous sounds from a Parisian bar filtered down, in stark contrast to the seriousness of the clandestine group in the cellar.

Jean-Claude thought of his sister's predicament, of Max's death and Heinrich's duplicity, of Danielle's child and her mother-in-law now at the mercy of Nazi forces. It sickened him to the core. Since his uncle Philippe had radioed him with the news, he swore to himself that he would liberate them, and as many as he could, or die trying.

His wiry frame shook with anger. This was for them, he vowed, for all those who suffered cruel injustices from the actions of this madman.

4 APRIL, 1940 — POLAND

After Jacob and Nicky and the others had left, Sofia rose from the canvas cot, coughing blood, and limped to the front of the shed. She stepped outside.

A black raven flew from the shed's roof and perched in a nearby tree. Sofia blinked. Soldiers were charging over the hilltop. *I need to stall them as long as I can.* Six, seven, eight of them now.

I am tired, so very tired. My pain will be over in a moment.

Shouts erupted when they saw her. She stood perfectly still, her posture erect.

"There's one," a soldier called out.

The voice sounded strangely familiar.

"Only one?" An older voice now.

"*Ja,* only one."

Sofia tilted her head toward the hill. *That voice. Why, it couldn't possibly be.* She squinted, but the waning light played tricks on her old eyes.

"Look around. Jews and Poles and queers, they hide like rats."

Sofia cleared her throat. "There is no one else. They're hours from here, across the border by now. Don't waste your effort. I'm tired, take me back." But she knew they wouldn't take her back. She was an insignificant old woman.

A silence ensued, broken by the raven's screech.

"Let's get rid of her, then we can go."

That voice. Sofia pressed a hand to her throbbing temple. She knew that voice. "Coward, show your face."

A soldier stepped forward. The last ray of sun slanted across his face, illuminating his steely blue eyes.

Sofia grasped the doorjamb for support and suppressed a gasp. It was Heinrich, her husband's nephew, whom she had loved as her own child.

Heinrich pointed his gun at her, and though a flicker of recognition crossed his face, he did not waver.

The older voice rang out, "She's old. Hardly worth our effort."

Sofia pushed aside her despair and disappointment. "Then they'll think you didn't find me." Only the safety of Nicky, and Jacob and his family, mattered now. Nothing else. And every second would help them.

Laughter rolled down the hillside. "Then we'll take your head back."

The raven screeched again, calling a passing flock into the barren trees as if to witness the drama. A straggling bird flew low over Heinrich and left a chalky splotch on his gun.

Heinrich cursed under his breath, but held his gun level. His gut churned. *Why did it have to be her?* he thought with a grimace. Taking care of Max was one thing. He'd always hated Max for his superior attitude. But when Max had married Danielle, why, that was the ultimate betrayal. Aunt Sofia had catered to her. Nothing had been the same since Danielle had arrived on the scene, and then their bratty boy, Nicky. Why did Aunt Sofia make a fuss over such inferior beings? He couldn't understand it. But he'd decided long ago that she had lost her mind.

The older voice bellowed, "Let's get on with it."

Heinrich shifted uncomfortably. He was expected to act. He could not disobey. Squinting, he brought Sofia into his sight and steadied his wavering hand. *She's a sick, crazy old woman, ready to die anyway.*

Sofia stared at Heinrich. All emotion had drained from his handsome young face, replaced by calculating ambition and a cool evil that sent a chill through her. Sofia had no doubt as to what he would do. But he would have to live with that.

"I surrender," she said, stretching out her words, stalling for time. In slow motion, she raised her arms straight out to her side, her palms and face turned upward toward the birds and the sweet towering trees and the endless canopy of sky. To heaven.

The command rang out.

Another moment of hesitation—a piercing silence—then gunfire ripped through the murky dusk.

A cacophony of cries and the flapping of wings erupted in the trees overhead as the flock took flight, a dark mass lifting to the sky.

The first shot burned into her, robbing her breath and shattering her ribs with the force of steel, and yet, she felt strangely little pain. It must be shock, she thought, as the sweet, smoky smell of gunpowder rose to her nostrils. Then she felt her own warm blood flowing onto her freezing skin. *Run, Jacob, run,* she screamed in her mind.

Another shot buckled her legs and she sank to her knees.

Her arms were still stretched wide, hovering against the pain seizing her body. The longer she took to die, the farther away Nicky and Jacob and the others could be. *Run, run, run.*

With Heinrich at the forefront, the soldiers advanced on her. They seemed perplexed by her, a dying woman, whose curious, proud actions stalled them for another moment.

Sofia closed her eyes as they came closer. A metal barrel jammed against her skull. She knew to whom it belonged. *God forgive him.*

The noise was deafening.

A bright, opalescent light flooded her being. As she soared high above the treetops she could see Jacob racing through the forest below with Nicky by his side, the little boy's expression fierce . . . running far, far away.

An indescribable peace set in, covering her like a whisper-soft cashmere blanket, coddling her frail limbs. Warmth spread throughout her body for the first time in these frigid winter months. The iridescent glow spread from her limbs to encompass her, bathing her very being in a shimmering white light that shone with such clarity. So beautiful, so transparent, so ethereal.

Her pain dissolved and fell to earth, like chains cast aside. She could breathe without effort, sweetly perfumed air refreshed and revived.

Through the pearly white haze, she could see Danielle, who

seemed to be writhing in pain. *Such pain.* Sofia went to her and tried to comfort her, but only briefly, for she knew it was time to go.

Sofia felt a loving presence surround her; she raised her eyes. Max appeared above her, his serene face wreathed with love, his hands outstretched. She grasped his hands, strength returning to her grip, as the satisfaction of knowing that her work was complete flooded her with joy.

9

The empress of the perfumer's palette, jasmine must be harvested before the rising sun to retain the full force of its delicate fragrance. Fragile and fleeting, jasmine is a fair nymph of a flower with a potent perfume. A world without jasmine? Simply unimaginable.

—DB

5 APRIL, 1940 — GRASSE, FRANCE

"I can't bear it," Danielle cried, panting through a contraction.

"Yes, you can. Breathe, Danielle, breathe." Jon pushed her sweaty hair aside, kissed her forehead, and gripped her hands. He and the midwife sat by the bed in her room, one on either side of her. "Squeeze my hands—harder." His face was grim with determination, his dark eyes bloodshot, urging her on.

Danielle gritted her teeth through the pain, and then flopped against the damp, linen-covered pillows, her energy spent. She gazed up at him, so thankful he had stayed with her. *If he hadn't* . . .

"We've got to keep your strength up," he said, adjusting her pillows and gently covering her bare arms with the sheet. "You're a strong woman, and this little baby is depending on you. I'm here for you, Danielle, as long as it takes. I won't leave you." He kissed her forehead again.

"Can't go on . . . much longer," she said faintly.

"Yes, you *can*, I know you can do this. Remember, I've seen your famous French courage in action."

At that comment, Danielle managed a small smile.

His hands felt cool and sure on her fevered brow. She glanced at the clock next to her bed. *Twenty-seven hours in labor.* The first tendrils of dawn crept into the room where Jon had kept vigil with her through the sleepless night, as Max had when Nicky was born. *Max, my poor, poor Max . . .*

She shifted and caught a glimpse of herself in the mirror. Perspiration beaded on her brow, her hair hung in strands, and her eyes were glazed with exhaustion. *What would I do without Jon?*

She cried out again, the spasms mounting, tightening like a vise across her belly and back.

Jon braced her. "That's it, breathe. Won't be much longer."

Reaching deep within, Danielle panted through the contraction. Her agony crested and then subsided, like a tide sweeping out to sea. Her body shook involuntarily. She fell limp against the stack of pillows, sticky with her perspiration. The iron bed creaked beneath her movements. She was losing control of her limbs, losing her grasp of consciousness. Could she continue?

Jon lifted a glass of water to her parched lips, helped her drink, and wiped her face with a cool washcloth.

A look passed between them, and in that instant, Danielle knew he would fight for her, even if she was too weak to fight for herself.

The midwife pressed her fingers to Danielle's wrist to monitor her pulse rate. Danielle's eyes fluttered and the midwife shot a worried look at Jon.

Gray specks clouded her vision. "I can't go on," Danielle mumbled.

The midwife beckoned Jon away.

Danielle could hear them speaking in hushed tones. The past day had been a blur, shocked as she was by Max's death, the news that had sent her into premature labor. Now, besides her memories, this child was all that remained of her dear Max. Danielle pressed her dry lips together, determined. *I will not let him down.*

Danielle watched Jon's expression grow graver. "She was delirious last night," he said, "calling for Max and saying that she'd seen Sofia. Where is Philippe with that brew he promised?"

Weary, Danielle closed her eyes. Her body was giving out. During the night, she'd imagined Sofia sitting with her. She'd always loved and admired her mother-in-law, and her unearthly presence had comforted and strengthened her. Sofia assured her that she would look out for Max. The vision had been incredibly vivid. *Did Sofia die, too?*

Or was I delirious?

In her dream, Sofia had looked well, without the gray pallor she'd had. Danielle had felt Sofia's soothing touch upon her brow and detected the rose perfume Danielle had blended for her. She'd even heard her speak, her words ringing out as clear and vibrant as a well-toned bell.

Take up the reins, Sofia had told her. *In all ways be strong. You are the new matriarch of my family.*

I must hold on, Danielle thought, though she felt her body slipping away with every breath she drew.

Philippe entered with a mug in his broad hands. "Have her drink this." He passed a mug to the midwife. "It's an herbal tea blend, should help her dilate."

The midwife smelled the concoction. "This might work. Now, both of you must leave. I have work to do."

Jon knelt by Danielle, smoothing hair from her feverish forehead, his lips brushing her hot cheek. Too weak to speak now, Danielle's eyes were pleading.

"I'm not leaving her," he said, clutching her hand.

12 APRIL, 1940 — GRASSE, FRANCE

A week later, Danielle sat alone on her bed in her whitewashed bedroom. The sun warmed her shoulders through her white cotton dress, and a spring breeze drifted through the open window.

After all that had happened, now she had an infant to care for. A bittersweet blessing, she thought, blinking hard. She had so many decisions to make. *How can I find Nicky? Where will we live? And how will I manage it all with this new baby?* She brushed away tears of frustration. Her mother had promised to help, but she was so sick with influenza that she couldn't come to visit yet.

Jon tapped on the door and pushed it open. That morning he'd volunteered to bathe the baby. This offer alone had endeared him to her even more. He held her now, tiny and pink and clean, swaddled in soft cloth.

Her daughter was small but well formed, a real fighter. Jon had helped bring her baby into the world; he'd fought for her. *Without him, I might not have survived her birth.*

She sniffed and pushed her hair from her face. Her face tingled with embarrassment. "What a mess I am." She repositioned herself against the stack of pillows and reached for her child.

Jon sat beside her and handed the baby to her. He leaned forward and smoothed a wayward strand of hair from her face.

"Thank you," she murmured, acutely aware of his closeness. *He looks tired,* she thought, noticing the circles under his eyes and the furrow of his brow. She blinked, turning her attention to her daughter. *My darling baby, how full of life she is. How will I manage on my own?*

"Have you thought of a name yet?" He draped his arm around her shoulder; it was a natural movement. Being close to him eased her mind a little.

"Our family has a tradition. We always name girls after flowers. My niece is Liliana, my mother is Marie Mignonette, and I'm Danielle

Rose. I've decided to name her Jasmin, after one of the most precious flowers in the perfumer's palette."

Jon reached out to touch the baby's tiny fingers. "Jasmin is a beautiful name for this precious bundle." He watched the baby for a moment. "Danielle, I've been thinking . . . you shouldn't be alone now. What would you think about . . ." Jon ran a hand through his wavy hair.

Why is he so nervous? "About what?"

The midwife opened the door to her room. "How is my valiant patient?"

Danielle glanced up at her. "Much better. Thank you, you delivered a lovely, healthy baby for me."

"Couldn't have done it without Jon's assistance and your tenacity."

Danielle could swear that Jon actually blushed at the remark, but before she could say anything, the midwife shooed him from the room in order to examine her.

"You're healing well." A peculiar expression crossed the woman's wrinkled face. "In all ways be strong," she said. With a sympathetic glance, she picked up her bag and shut the door swiftly behind her.

Danielle's lips parted. *In all ways be strong.* She had heard those words in her dream with Sofia. Was she going crazy? Then Sofia's rose perfume filled the air and she sensed her mother-in-law's peaceful presence again.

She gazed at the spot on the bed where she had seen Sofia. "Have you come to visit your new granddaughter?"

Danielle looked down at her daughter, her little Jasmin. She looked content in the moment.

Danielle lifted her eyes. "She's perfect," she said to the spot, which fairly vibrated with energy. As though in reply, an indescribable peace enveloped her.

———

Downstairs, Jon pressed freshly ground coffee and placed a steaming cup on a wooden tray. He started upstairs with the coffee and brioche, and sprigs of fresh jasmine that he had plopped into a little vase for Danielle, amazed that such tiny blossoms gave off such an intense, sweet aroma.

Climbing the stairs, he thought of the tragedy that had brought him to Danielle. Max had been a good friend, and he grieved for him. Other friends had enlisted, and some had already met with the same calamity. Now, the war was personal.

He pushed Danielle's door open with his foot. She sat with Jasmin in her arms, the sunlight glinting off her burnished hair, framing them in a wash of soft light. Jon paused, fixing the scene in his mind.

He poured milk into the large coffee cup and handed it to her, noting her small, slender hand as she took the cup. "Be careful around the little one," he said, smiling.

"Thank you, *mon ami.*"

He placed a plate before her and stifled a yawn. He'd been awake half the night wondering what to do about Danielle. What would Max have wanted him to do? *But I know what I want.* "I'll take Jasmin while you eat." He took the baby in his muscular arms, cradling her and cooing to her. She could almost be his own child, and would be, if Danielle would have him. "How's my tender flower?" He picked up the vase and waved the sprigs of white jasmine under Jasmin's nose. "I wanted to be the first to bring you the flowers of your namesake."

"I think she likes them," Danielle said, laughing as Jasmin made a small moue. "How thoughtful of you," she added, a heartrending expression on her face. She sipped the coffee, curling one slim leg over the other.

Jon stole a glance at Danielle. *Is it too soon for her?* He started to say something again, but his courage failed him, something he was unaccustomed to. *Of course it's too soon, you idiot.*

His shoulders tensed. His inclination told him to take up where

Max had left off. To ask Danielle to come to England, where he could look after her and the baby. But Jon wasn't smooth with women. *Not like Cameron.* Oh sure, he knew everyone thought of him as gregarious. But those were friendships, not the deep relationship he craved with Danielle. Except for Victoria, who always commanded the center of attention, he hadn't dated much. His father had high expectations of him; and then, there was the war—his patriotic duty. A leader he might be, but when it came to expressing his innermost feelings to women, he often faltered.

Danielle put her coffee on the nightstand, pushed aside her brioche. "Jon, what's bothering you?"

Her voice sounded so gentle that he wanted to take her in his arms and never let her go. *She's the one who needs comfort, after what she's been through.* And yet, she was concerned about *him.* This was another of the comparisons between her and Victoria that had kept him awake last night. Victoria was charming and beautiful, but could be so demanding—*"compassionate" isn't even in her vocabulary.* Confusion roared through his mind and he pressed a hand to his forehead.

When he didn't answer, Danielle said, "You can tell me anything, you know."

Could he? Could he tell her that he'd loved her from the moment he'd seen her on the ship? *Is that what you say to a woman who's just lost her husband?* It was a fantasy to think she would come to him now, and he was wrong for even imagining it. He brought Jasmin to his chest, her sweet baby smell tugging his heartstrings. *If only things were different.* He longed to ask Danielle to return to England with him. A terrible thought crossed his mind. *If I die in service to my country, Danielle will be widowed again.* He raised his eyes, saw the raw pain etched on her face.

I couldn't do that to her.

Finally, he made up his mind and cleared his throat. "What I want to tell you is that I came to say good-bye."

Disappointment filled her eyes. "You're leaving?"

"I'm returning to enlist."

"Oh, Jon," she murmured, her shoulders drooping, her voice filled with sadness. "Promise you'll be careful. I'll miss you so much."

Jasmin had drifted to sleep, so Jon placed her in a makeshift bassinet, and kissed her cheek. Danielle and Jon moved across the room into an alcove, where a pair of slip-covered chairs flanked a brick fireplace. They sat down, and Danielle leaned forward, elbows on her knees. "When do you have to go?"

He wished again that he never had to leave her. "Today. Now."

"So soon?"

He could hear distress in her voice, and he ached to reach out to her. But instead he said, "My country needs me. Norway and Denmark have just fallen to the Third Reich, so there's no doubt that Hitler's gunning for England."

"I wish you could stay."

A simple statement, but her eyes seemed to say so much more. "You're my only regret, Danielle." His heart pounding, he touched her cheek, drawing the backs of his fingers along her jawline.

Danielle leaned into his hand. "I'm leaving for Paris soon, to see my family."

That's where she belongs, he realized. He could feel the warmth of her skin, her heart beating below the surface.

"Jon, I want to share something with you."

He took her hand in his, tracing her slender fingers. "What is it?"

"It's about Nicky. I know he's still alive, I can feel it." She hesitated. "Max never really believed me, but I have a strong intuitive sense. I *know* Nicky is still there."

"I believe you," he said simply. "I believe every word you say, Danielle." Then he added, "Promise you'll call if you need anything." Jon leaned forward, touching her forehead with his own head. His lips brushed her cheek, and finally, he had to push himself from the chair. "I have to be off," he said, resigned. "You don't need to see me downstairs."

"Take care of yourself, sailor." She slipped her arms around him, burying her face into the crook of his neck.

Tentatively, he put his arms around her, drawing her to him until their bodies were tightly entwined. He could feel her strength, and matched it in his embrace.

She gazed up at him, her green eyes luminous.

He could feel her heart beating wildly, in perfect synchronization with his. He let his finger trail her cheek. *This is it, will I ever see her again?* With great reluctance, he turned to go.

"Wa . . . wait."

As Danielle's single word cracked with emotion, he hesitated, then whirled around, cupped her face in his hands, and kissed her fully, deeply, on the lips. She twined her arms around him; her mouth was warm and pliable, opening to him, yearning for him, and he returned her need with his own desire. They drank one another in, until finally, Jon released her, gazed at her to memorize every feature of her face, then turned and closed the door behind him.

He made his way down the stairs, his eyes misty and his thoughts in turmoil. *What happens now?* he wondered.

IO

The rose: though its petals are easily bruised, it blooms with exuberance. What power the rose possesses; the merest hint of a blossom conjures the deepest memory. At dawn, roses must be picked quickly, for they lose half their essence—the perfumer's treasure—by the high sun of noon.

—DB

28 APRIL, 1940 — PARIS, FRANCE

From her vantage point on the bridge over the Seine, Danielle gazed out wistfully across the city she loved, the Eiffel Tower looming in the distance. She tucked a light blanket around Jasmin, making sure that she was warm in her pram. She started for the Tuileries, where she and Jean-Claude had played as children.

As she walked, sadness settled over her like a damp cloak. She and Max had also spent part of their honeymoon in Paris, and every land-mark held a memory of their idyllic time together.

She entered the park, where the sound of fountains and the sweet smell of spring blossoms filled the air. Lovers strolled arm-in-arm, some pausing to kiss. Danielle pressed her fingers to her lips in re-membrance. What came to mind was not the taste of Max's tender kiss, but Jon's fiercely passionate kiss. At night, she lay in bed bewil-dered, not by Jon's sudden action, but by her reaction. She savored the memory of his touch, reveling in the reminiscence. And then there were his letters. She chewed her lip and glanced down at her black dress. She was in mourning for Max, but the world seemed to be spinning faster; traditions were changing.

The sound of children's laughter filled the air. She paused, dizzy with thoughts of Nicky. In her mind's eye she imagined him running and playing. She would bring him here for a visit, with Jasmin, along with their cousin, Liliana. *Yes, that's exactly what I will do.* A small sigh escaped her lips.

But how?

Denmark and Norway had been invaded. France could be next, no matter how the government assured the people.

I must go to Nicky.

She thought about Jean-Paul and Philippe, their efforts, and what she had learned from Philippe in Grasse.

There was one plan she had considered, though it was dangerous.

Jasmin began to fuss. "Oh, my poor baby," Danielle murmured, picking her up and pressing her against her chest. She patted her back and soothed her cries. As she rocked the tiny baby, who depended on her, she felt torn between her children. Both of them needed her, and she needed them, now more than ever. What if something happened to her in Poland? *What if I'm killed?*

What if Nicky were killed?

She gasped, choking on the thought.

If anything happened to her, she knew that her mother, or Jean-Claude and Hélène, would look after Jasmin. Danielle gazed at her baby, who turned her head and began suckling on Danielle's blouse. She touched her fingertips to Jasmin's mouth, and the baby sucked her finger, temporarily satisfied. She'd have to wean her baby before she left, introduce a bottle. A rush of guilt consumed her. *Am I a terrible mother?*

But then she thought about Nicky.

What choice do I have?

She sat on a stone bench near a fountain, swaying with Jasmin in her arms. She loved this little one with all her heart, but she couldn't bear the thought of Nicky wondering about his Maman and Papa. She thought of the dream she'd had, the tinge of rose that had appeared in her room after Jasmin's birth. *If something has happened to Sofia . . .* She couldn't finish the thought. *Dear God, I would never forgive myself if Nicky were harmed.*

"*Bonjour, ma chère,*" Marie said, kissing her in greeting. "Ah, how could one not love Paris on such a beautiful day?" She sat next to Danielle and took Jasmin from her, cooing at her granddaughter. As she did, she cast a sideways glance at Danielle from under her spring hat. "You look like you have a great deal on your mind."

"Maman, what if France were to fall to the Nazis?"

Marie threw a sharp look at Danielle. "The Maginot Line, with its underground fortifications, is supposed to protect us. Still, I admit, I'm worried. Your father and I have discussed leaving, but you know your father. It's the bank that keeps him here. I'm trying to persuade him. But we won't leave without you."

Danielle nodded. "I have to find Nicky."

Marie blinked, sadness filling her eyes. "I know."

Danielle glanced down and realized she was fidgeting; she had frayed the edge of Jasmin's blanket. "I'm going back to Poland." She looked up and saw tears in her mother's eyes, which mirrored her own. "Will you look after Jasmin?"

"You don't have to ask, *ma chère.*"

Later that day, ensconced in the guest bedroom of Jean-Claude's crowded flat, Danielle began to change for dinner. She shrugged out of her black dress and changed into a royal blue dress that Hélène had given her. *To hell with traditional widow's wear,* she decided, *Max always liked me in color.* A soft knock sounded at her door. "Come in."

Jean-Claude shut the door behind him and deposited a brown leather cosmetics train case on the bed. "We haven't much time.

Hélène will be ready in a moment, and we're due at dinner in half an hour." He extracted a small package from his leather bomber jacket and handed it to her. "Here, open this first."

The package held a rose made of yellow silk, and a brilliant scarf of canary and chartreuse.

"You must wear these items on your trip. There are more clothes in the closet for you to wear. Everything is from Germany. Don't take any items from France. Wait, there's more." He fished out an envelope from a pocket. "These are your official papers, your passport, and your travel visa."

Jean-Claude explained each document. She was impressed with his efficiency, and made a mental note to emulate his tone and manner on her trip.

"You'll be traveling as Frau Werner, the wife of a high-ranking Nazi party member."

"Did you have to be so bold about my cover?"

"Trust me, this way you won't be questioned much. No underling wants to incur the wrath of your husband."

Danielle grimaced. "A devil, is he?"

"One of the worst." His expression darkened. "*D'accord,* here's the plan. Pin the flower to your hat, wear the scarf around your neck. These will identify you to people who will look after you if, and only if, you need it."

Danielle nodded, fully aware of the consequences. "If I'm caught, I won't reveal anything."

"I'm not saying you would." He crossed to the window; he pulled the shade ajar and peered outside. "These people are only there to save you from disaster, if possible."

Danielle watched Jean-Claude at the window, wondering who or what he was looking for.

Jean-Claude turned back to her. "Now, when someone says to you, 'Your flower is the color of the daffodils in my garden,' they can be trusted. Do precisely as they say. Speak to no one else." He wrapped his arms around her, hugging her to him. Danielle could feel his heart beating as rapidly as hers. "After dinner, study these documents well. Know your address, your husband's name and rank, every number in there."

Sounds of Hélène bustling around the apartment filtered through the door.

Danielle opened the passport. "Is there really a Frau Werner?"

"Yes, she sympathizes with us, and she's happy to spend a few weeks with her lover. As Frau Werner, you're going ahead to sort out living arrangements at her husband's new post, or that's the story. You'll have to work quickly, before he arrives."

Danielle nodded, striving to commit every detail to memory.

"Now, open the cosmetics case."

She flicked the latches and lifted the lid. "These are our designs," she said, running her fingers over the makeup brushes with hollow handles, the perfume bottle that converted to a compass, caps that contained tiny tools, and the clothing brushes that concealed documents.

"Everything has been outfitted for a female operative's special mission. When you arrive, you'll receive instructions about the case."

Jean-Claude tugged on the bottom of the case. It swung open, revealing a false bottom containing row upon row of minuscule electrical devices. "Make sure it's secure, like so." He snapped it back in place.

"Every morning your driver will meet you, supposedly for you to shop for suitable accommodations during the day. This is when you can search for Nicky and Sofia. As Frau Werner, only speak German. If someone speaks to you in French, or Polish, or English, do not answer. Do not even appear to understand. Keep your answers short and mind your pronunciation."

The hair on Danielle's neck prickled. "And if I need help?"

He handed her a slip of folded paper. "Your driver will arrange everything. If for any reason he does not appear one day, you must call this number and wait for instructions." He paused to wipe perspiration from his forehead. "Memorize the number, destroy this paper."

"One more thing." His eyes roved over her hair. "Frau Werner is a blonde. That auburn mane of yours is like a beacon." He jerked a thumb toward the case. "You'll find a bottle of hair dye in there."

Danielle touched her hair, twirled a strand tightly around her finger. "I'll tell Maman that blondes are all the rage."

"Good. The rest is up to you, Danielle."

Hélène's voice floated through the door, "Jean-Claude, Danielle. We're ready to go."

Jean-Claude hugged her again. "Max was a good man, Danielle. He died a hero. I pray Nicky will be spared in return."

His breath was warm against her hair and she remembered how, when she was a child, Jean-Claude had protected her from the neighborhood bullies. But she was soon to be on her own. *And I must succeed.*

"When can I go?" she asked.

"Soon, a week or two. I'll receive a signal." Jean-Claude looked at her with somber eyes. "You are one of us now. For the rest of your life."

29 April, 1940 — Poland

Nicky belly-crawled through the bushes on this moonless night, inching his way across a field, dirt clogging his nose and eyes. He suppressed his coughs for fear of being discovered.

After they had left Sofia, Oscar had not returned to their group. Jacob and Irma had hurried to lead them farther away to the next hiding place. They had stopped to rest, and Nicky had been drinking water from a stream with the three children of Jacob and Irma behind a cluster of trees when they heard an argument erupt between the adults and soldiers. They had been discovered.

Nicky winced at the memory. The children had hidden and covered their eyes, but they would never forget the sound of the shots, or the complete silence that ensued. The other children were frightened, so Nicky had gone to check on Jacob and Irma. The horrific sight was seared into his brain. It was so awful he wouldn't let the kids see their parents.

Insects scampered across his hands and legs. He was old enough not to be scared of bugs anymore. That's what he kept telling himself, gritting his teeth. He blinked hard to dispel the prickly sensation behind his eyelids. He must lead the children to safety.

Nicky shimmied past a soldier on the roadside to safety and hid himself under the brush. He gave a series of birdcalls he and the others had practiced so they could begin their escape. He shivered, brushing insects from his limbs. He peered across the field toward another barn where they could hide. *Would they make it?*

11

A thought on Tabac de Bretancourt. Imagine a smoky quality, reminiscent of Max's vanilla tobacco curling around the open deck—consider vetiver—smoky, green, slight anise aroma . . . flank with sandalwood and teak, finish with amber of a subtle hand.

—DB

30 APRIL, 1940 — PARIS, FRANCE

Hélène adjusted her brown felt beret, on which she had strategically fastened a faux cameo pin to hide the moth holes. She stood by the table in the tiny kitchen of their flat sorting through mail, waiting for her mother-in-law.

She'd arranged for Liliana to stay with a neighbor, because she had something terribly important to discuss with Marie. Since her mother died, Hélène had no one to confide in—no one whom she trusted enough to divulge her suspicions about Jean-Claude.

At the sound of the knock, Hélène opened the door.

"*Bonjour,* am I too early for lunch?" Marie asked.

"No, I'm ready." She picked up her gloves and purse.

Hélène glanced at Marie's spring suit with a matching hat and purse. She felt dowdy in comparison. Maybe she should try to dress better. Could that be why her husband had lost interest in her? She was only twenty-six. "Marie, how do you manage to always look so chic?"

Marie laughed. "I haven't thrown anything out in decades. Over time, one develops a wardrobe to accent one's personal style. But when my children were young, they were my priority."

"I'm proof of that," Hélène said, feeling self-conscious. Maybe she spent *too* much time on her daughter. Could that be the reason Jean-Claude was out late every night?

Marie patted Hélène's arm. "Don't worry about your clothes, I'll take you shopping. I wish I were as pretty as you are. That's why your artist friends love to paint your portrait." She smiled at her. "We have important things to discuss today. Shall we start walking?"

Uneasy about raising the subject of her husband's possible infidelity, Hélène asked, "How soon will your home be ready?"

Marie clucked her tongue. "The renovation is far behind schedule. It's been delayed because so many craftsmen have joined the war effort. *As they should.*" She shrugged. "Of course, Edouard is livid. Men want instant gratification, don't you think?"

Hélène felt like bursting into tears, but instead, she swallowed hard against the knot in her throat.

Marie continued. "Edouard's birthday is coming soon and I'm planning a short trip to Bellerose—but I'd like to have a surprise luncheon for him before we leave."

The day was sunny, so they chose an outdoor café and ordered their food. Marie went on, "I know Edouard would like to celebrate his birthday with you and Liliana. Naturally, Jean-Claude is welcome, too, but I doubt if he'll want to join us."

"Jean-Claude is incredibly stubborn." Hélène was losing her nerve to broach the subject of her marital woes.

"Time will heal their differences, though Jean-Claude's words have had a tremendous impact on Edouard."

"Really?" Hélène didn't think Edouard even listened to Jean-Claude. He seemed more stubborn than his son, if that were possible. "Two hardheaded men, that's what they are."

Marie lowered her voice. "Some people overlook grave injustices when money is at stake, especially bankers." Marie sniffed. "Men and their politics."

Hélène stared at her. She thought Marie had sensed her concern about Jean-Claude. *What is she talking about?*

A waiter brought a carafe of Beaujolais to their table and poured two glasses for them.

Marie sipped the red wine. "It's precisely Jean-Claude's stance, as well as Danielle's situation," she said, "which has caused Edouard to reexamine the impact of the banking community's actions. He's thinking hard about the political ramifications of the bank's lending practices, which he never would have done had Jean-Claude not been so steadfast in his argument."

"Because of Jean-Claude?"

"You should be very proud of your husband, for his courage of conviction."

Hélène took several sips of wine. Now her concern over her husband's fidelity paled in comparison.

"The bank has been Edouard's life, hasn't it?"

"He cannot disregard Hitler's actions." As Marie spoke, she grew unsettled. "And although he doesn't believe it, I fear our fortifications may not be adequate to stand against Hitler."

A chill coursed through Hélène. *Hitler, in France?* She reached for her wine.

Marie went on. "My children were raised in the Catholic Church, at my husband's behest. This was a condition of our marriage, and I was in love." She blew air between her lips. "But according to Jewish law, my children—and according to Hitler's laws, your Liliana, too—have Jewish blood in their veins. Nazi laws would strip us of our rights. You know this, Hélène."

Hélène shifted uncomfortably. Liliana yanked from her arms?

Impossible, this is France. Or so she wanted to believe. "What should we do?"

Marie's voice dropped to an urgent whisper. "We must leave France. Consider your daughter. Look at poor Danielle and Max, her son, Nicky, and Max's mother, Sofia. *Tragic.* Hélène, I implore you to persuade Jean-Claude. He won't listen to me. This is why I had to speak to you today."

Hélène's head was spinning. She had been counting the days until her husband graduated from medical school. To leave France was unimaginable.

"Edouard has old friends in Montreal," Marie said. "We can stay with them until we find an apartment. We can travel after Edouard's birthday. Danielle won't leave without Nicky, but she shouldn't be gone long."

"I can't imagine living in Canada," Hélène said, then thought about Danielle's catastrophe.

"You must think of Liliana and your husband. Your father could join us, too."

After lunch, they walked back to Hélène's flat. Though birds sang above and the sun was shining, anxiety filled Hélène. *Montreal . . . has it really come to that?*

In front of Hélène's building, Marie turned to her daughter-in-law, clasping her hands. "Think about what I've said. Jean-Claude is committed to France, he won't want to leave, but he needs to protect you and his daughter. Make him come with us, Hélène. *You can do this.*"

Marie reached into her purse, withdrew a few francs, and pressed them into Hélène's hand. "Tell Jean-Claude to take you out to dinner this weekend. Have a bottle of wine, speak to him. You must insist."

"I'll try." Hélène shook her head. "But he studies so much."

"He has time for his—his political interests, doesn't he?"

Hélène averted her eyes. "It's another woman, I think."

"My dear girl, Jean-Claude only has eyes for you." Marie tilted her head. "Is that what you thought?"

Hélène could only nod; her heart was breaking.

"Oh no, believe me, Hélène." Marie's voice sounded thick. "His passion is not another woman."

Hélène saw a strange expression cross Marie's face, a fleeting combination of pride and sadness. She grasped Hélène's face in her hands and kissed her on both cheeks.

"Why, Marie, you're shaking," Hélène said.

Marie drew back, her eyes meeting Hélène's. "That's because there's a chill in the air."

After Marie left Hélène, she thought about Danielle. *Jean-Claude must be helping her.* Did Hélène know?

Marie walked to the square of the Place Vendôme. Winded from her recent illness, she pressed her hand to her chest. She couldn't stand the thought of losing either of her children. The tragedy of little Nicky, and now Max's death, was horrible enough. Marie wasn't certain she could endure the calamities her daughter had. *But Danielle is strong.* Stronger than she was in many ways.

My children are on dangerous paths. As a mother, she had dedicated herself to her children; there was nothing she wouldn't do for them. Now she realized she must allow Danielle the same privilege of responsibility, and put aside her own motherly concerns.

Dear God, bless my children in their efforts.

If she could trade places with Danielle, she would. Marie sighed, nodding to the doorman as she entered the Ritz.

Dressed in dark clothes with his cap pulled low, Jean-Claude scurried through the darkened alley on silent feet, glancing furtively behind him. Tonight he was to learn of one of his most important assignments. The moon cast eerie shadows on the cobblestones. A sharp noise rang out above. Instinctively, he flattened himself against a rough brick wall. Was it a door, or a gunshot? His heart pounded as he waited, listening.

After a moment, satisfied that he was unobserved, he slipped into a shadowed doorway and knocked two times, paused, then repeated the sequence. The door swung open.

A barrel-chested man greeted him. "We're just beginning."

Jean-Claude acknowledged the small group in the dimly lit room. He removed his cap, ruffled his thick brown hair, and perched on a wooden milk crate at the table. He listened intently as their leader began to outline a complex plan on a chalkboard.

"If we can cripple the flow of money into Hitler's coffers," the man said, "the result will be unpaid salaries, low morale and dissent, scarce ammunition, and eventually, the demise of his expansionary activities. Rats flee a sinking ship." The man went on to explain details of the operation.

"These are the assignments," the man announced, holding up three envelopes. "Any volunteers?"

A slender blond woman raised her hand. "For which targets?"

"Vienna, Berlin." He paused. "And Paris."

She whispered to her male companion. "We'll take Vienna."

"Good. Each of the three operations must occur at precisely the same time. Berlin?"

Three men looked at each other, raised their hands.

"Paris?"

Jean-Claude met the steady gaze of the red-haired woman who sat opposite him.

"We'll handle Paris," she said, nodding to Jean-Claude.

The leader stared at him. "Jean-Claude?"

"*Oui,* Paris." Jean-Claude returned his partner's nod. "With Yvette."

The leader observed the teams. "Divide into groups and work out the details." He placed an envelope before each team.

Jean-Claude looked at Yvette Baudin. At twenty-eight, she sported a short cap of henna-red hair, a firm, buxom body, and an iron will to match. She was an attractive woman, though hardly his type. He reached across the table and slid a cigarette from her open pack.

Yvette grinned. "Thought you didn't smoke, Doctor."

"I don't." He tore open the envelope. He smoked half the cigarette, and then ground it out. Tossing the note to Yvette, he stood and paced the length of the cellar while she read.

When she finished, she looked up, her mouth agape. "This man works at your father's bank. Do you know Louis LeBlanc?"

"He sits on the bank's board of directors." Jean-Claude placed his hands on the table and leaned forward. "He's been my father's best friend for thirty years."

Yvette lifted a shoulder. "I don't have a problem, but can you do this?"

"Who better than I?" Jean-Claude balled a fist and struck his palm. He thought of the disastrous situation with Danielle and thousands, no, *millions* of other innocent people. His gut wrenched, but his eyes didn't flinch. "LeBlanc is a Nazi sympathizer. One of the worst," he snapped with contempt. "Of course I can do it."

He was less confident than he sounded, but he couldn't let on that he had reservations. It was not their way.

He and Yvette coordinated the time, and then talked about the placement of the bomb.

Jean-Claude stroked his chin. "Last summer, Hitler's Swiss spy, Didier Steiger, who also serves on the bank's board, gave LeBlanc a new Bentley motorcar. LeBlanc likes to take it to the club for lunch, show it off."

Yvette shook a cigarette from her pack, struck a match, and lit it. "How do you propose we plant the bomb?"

Jean-Claude thought for a moment. "We have to get onto the property. I could pose as a mechanic making an emergency repair."

"Like what?" Yvette blew smoke toward the ceiling. "A flat tire?"

"Sure. You can distract the parking attendant while I tend to business, and then alert him to the flat. He'll call LeBlanc, who will have his secretary phone the garage for an immediate repair."

"Could you be recognized?"

It was possible, he knew. "I'll wear a disguise."

"Better be a good one." Yvette leaned forward and flicked an ash. "I'll take care of the secretary and the parking attendant. There will be a mix-up. You'll have time."

"*Bon.* LeBlanc won't care who makes the repair, so long as it's done." As he spoke, dread washed over him. He looked down at his hands, his long slender fingers. Surgeon's hands, precise and exacting, were ideally suited for intricate explosives work.

And yet, as he thought about the mission, his hands began to tremble.

12

A fungus grips the continent, infecting its very soul. Like oud wood, the diseased heartwood grows dark and odorous, resistant to cure.

—DB

19 MAY, 1940 — POLAND

A hush fell over the train car as they crossed into the ravaged landscape of occupied Poland. A blur of images flashed past the window as Danielle's train sped near its destination. Her convoluted journey had taken her from the graceful civility of France, across neutral Switzerland, and through occupied Austria and Czechoslovakia.

Danielle passed through several checkpoints without incident, though her pulse raced during every encounter. Each time officials checked her identity papers her heart thudded so loudly that she was certain it would give her away. Yet the documents Jean-Claude provided so far had withstood scrutiny. Danielle gave silent thanks; she had no doubt what fate awaited her if she were found to be an impostor.

As Jean-Claude predicted, the soldiers who inspected her papers treated her with deference. A couple tried to strike up a conversation with her. But Danielle waved them away, feigning a sore throat.

One person who didn't speak to her was a woman who now sat across from her in the compartment. About forty years old, Danielle guessed, she had jet black hair slicked into a bun and piercing blue eyes behind heavy tortoiseshell glasses. A bulky knitted shawl lay next to her. Other passengers came and went, but this woman stayed and spoke to no one. She held an open book in her lap, but Danielle caught her snatching glances her way.

Was this woman following her? If so, was she a comrade? Or a Nazi informer?

Danielle pressed her fingers against the cold pane. Dirty faces peered from bushes as they sped past ghostly villages strewn with skeletons of charred homes, the acrid smell of smoke still in the air. She had entered another world, a world gone mad.

Poland had been her adopted home, and Danielle shared the palpable grief of its people. She lowered her eyes, and as she did, she caught the eye of her compartment companion.

"What a pretty flower on your hat," the woman said in German.

"*Danke,*" Danielle replied softly. Her brother's words echoed in her mind: *Don't say any more than you must.*

The raven-haired woman started to say something more, when the compartment door opened and a large man with an unwieldy package came in.

Danielle sniffed. An unusual aroma filled her nose. She recognized it instantly. Startled, Danielle stared at the man, but she didn't recognize him. The essence of oud wood was common in the Middle East and India, but it was rare here. She'd once given Heinrich a small bottle of oud wood. She ran her fingers over the smooth brown leather of the cosmetics tote, moving it closer to her.

The sound of steel wheels clacking in staccato rhythm on the rails was the only thing that kept the deafening silence at bay.

Danielle stared out the window, her thoughts centered on her son. She tried to imagine what Nicky looked like now. They'd last seen him before their journey to New York. He was surely taller and probably thinner. She counted the months and her mouth went dry. *We have missed nearly a year of our lives together.*

The rhythm of the train slowed. She held her breath while her documents were reviewed before the station came into view.

A small clutch of people waited on the platform. She hooked the cosmetics case over her arm and gathered her bags, stalling until the dark-haired woman gathered her knitted shawl and left.

Emerging from the compartment, she checked the yellow rose pinned to her hat and adjusted her scarf. The crowd moved at a snail's pace, impeded by a pregnant woman with four small children. Nervously, Danielle glanced outside.

She stepped from the train. *Did Max walk here, in my very steps?* She shivered from the thought, and from the dampness that hung in the chill air. With trepidation, she scanned the blur of faces. She hesitated, and then made her way into the terminal.

From behind, someone tugged her jacket sleeve. Danielle nearly leapt from the ground. "Excuse me, *Fräulein*."

She turned expectantly. *Was this her contact?* There stood an efficient-looking young man, who asked, "Do you need transportation?"

She waited for him to deliver the coded line.

He said nothing.

She glanced around. The small crowd was thinning. *Perhaps he'll say the code word once I'm in the car.*

She thought fast. "Can you take me to the hotel?"

He picked up her bag. He led her outside to his car, deposited her bag in the trunk, and turned to her. "Which hotel?"

At that, Danielle's heart raced so fast she thought it would explode. *He should know where to take me. Something is terribly wrong.* An almost uncontrollable urge to flee gripped her. She noticed a Nazi soldier standing guard nearby. *What should I do? This man is not my driver.*

"Which hotel, *Fräulein*?" The man was growing impatient. The soldier glanced in her direction, taking interest in her.

Danielle dabbed perspiration from her upper lip. As she opened her mouth to speak, she heard a commotion behind her.

A woman's voice rang out, "Frau Werner, Frau Werner."

Werner. That's me, Danielle realized with a jolt.

A woman's heels tapped toward her. Danielle froze.

The woman grabbed her shoulder and spun her around. It was the dark-haired woman from the train. Her steely blue eyes bored into Danielle's.

"Frau Werner, we almost missed you." The woman had a smile plastered on her face. She motioned to a short stocky man behind her. "Here's my driver."

Sweat trickled through Danielle's hairline as she waited for the woman to deliver the code phrase. But the woman said nothing. *Which way to go?* Her heart hammered so hard she thought it could be seen beneath her jacket.

Then, from the corner of her eye, Danielle saw another Nazi soldier striding in their direction. He stopped in front of her, his face stern.

"Your passport," he demanded.

She handed it to him. *Just breathe.*

"Frau Werner."

"*Ja,*" Danielle said. She lifted her eyes and stared directly into his.

"You will stay here." He spun on his heel and walked toward a group of soldiers. They examined her passport, conferring for several minutes.

Now I can't leave, she thought. *They'd shoot me.*

The woman and the two other men stood motionless, each of them staring at Danielle. She tightened her grip on the cosmetics tote.

The soldier began walking back toward them, his heels clicking sharply. He rapped her passport against the palm of his hand.

Danielle hardly dared to breathe.

He stopped. With a quick movement, he snapped the passport toward her. "Please give your husband our regards, *Fräulein*."

Unable to speak, Danielle gave a polite bow of her head.

The man clicked his heels, spun around, and left.

Faint with relief, she dabbed the sweat from her face.

The short man behind the woman from the train stepped forward. After a furtive glance at Danielle, he bowed his head and tugged his cap over his face. "If you don't mind my saying so," he said quickly, "the flower on your hat is very pretty. Your flower is the color of the daffodils in my garden."

Danielle almost cried and hugged him. She did neither, but struggled to retain her composure. Instead, she choked her words to the woman, "Thank you for meeting me," then turned to the first driver. "I won't need your services."

The second driver scurried to retrieve her bag, and led them to his car. Her train companion grabbed her arm and they walked to the car, arm in arm. "It's been so good to see you," the woman said, then she whispered, "When you get in the car, leave the door open and slide your cosmetics case over my arm, under my shawl. Do it smoothly, so no one will notice."

Danielle slid into the backseat, and the woman leaned over to kiss Danielle on the cheek, letting her shawl fall over their arms. Danielle transferred the case to the woman, their movements hidden from view.

"Good-bye," the woman said brightly.

Danielle sank into the threadbare backseat of the rusted car. *There, I've done it.* The driver stashed her bag, slammed the trunk, and took the wheel.

They drove for what seemed an eternity before he spoke again. "I must stop the car. Something under the hood sounds bad." He veered onto a dusty country lane. He got out, raised the hood, looked around, and then walked to her side of the car. Pressing his finger to his lips, he motioned for her to follow him. She complied, trailing him to the front of the car, where he stooped to peer under the hood.

"You don't recognize me, do you?" He had switched from German to Polish. He pushed his hat back. "I didn't recognize you at first with blond hair."

"Oscar? Why, you've lost so much weight, I wouldn't have known you." Oscar had worked for her as a handyman.

"At your service."

She started to hug him, but he stopped her with his hand. "You never know who is watching." He motioned for her to lean over the engine. "I didn't know it would be you until we found you at the station."

"Are you going to help me find Nicky and Sofia?"

"This is my assignment?" He leaned heavily against the car. "You should know that Sofia saved us all. Right after the invasion, Jacob came for us—Irma and the children—in her car. Sofia refused to leave until we joined her. We hid for a while, and then the Nazis caught us."

"Oh, no." Danielle touched the hood for balance.

"Sofia's jewels bought our escape. We traveled together for a while, and then I went on to see what lay ahead. Sofia wasn't well, and Nicky and the other children were tired. We got separated, I never saw any of them again."

Oscar glanced nervously around. "We should leave, we might raise suspicion. Shouldn't talk in the car, though I check it every morning for listening devices."

They wound their way through the rubble to the hotel. When they arrived, Danielle glanced around the sparsely furnished lobby. The innkeeper told her that during the invasion, the hotel had been looted.

That night, she slept fitfully, but she was ready the next morning when Oscar arrived.

On Danielle's insistence, Oscar drove her to the village where her family had lived. What Danielle saw on the way made her heart ache. Gone were the pretty villages that lined the country roads. In their place stood piles of rubble, rats scampering among the remains. She saw weary, downtrodden people queued for food and medicine, both of which were in short supply.

As they cleared the rise to her village, she bristled at a Nazi flag flying boldly over their glass and crystal factory. Soldiers guarded the iron gates. "They're producing windshields there," Oscar told her, careful in his choice of words. Danielle dared not reply. Nor could she speak when they passed the family estate—her home— where a slew of army vehicles were parked on the trampled lawn and soldiers stood smoking by the stately front door. A woman's coarse laughter drifted from her bedroom window.

Danielle bowed her head. Silent tears burned her lids, pouring over her cheeks. She pressed a gloved hand to her mouth to suppress her sobs, her body shuddering.

When Oscar stopped for petrol, they overheard Nazi soldiers belittling the new British prime minister, Winston Churchill. "We shall never surrender," Churchill had said. Danielle shielded her face, but was determined to cleave to Churchill's words with renewed vigor.

13

Steam distillation of the starlight white blossoms of the Seville bitter orange tree produces a brilliant green material—neroli. (Solvent extraction yields the subtly spicy orange blossom.) Named after a duchess of Nerola, neroli was favored by Grasse glove makers, who used it to scent their finest gloves, masking the stench of animal urine in which the leather was cured. Oh, that neroli could cure the stench that blows across our country today.

—DB

22 MAY, 1940. — PARIS, FRANCE

Jean-Claude eased himself under LeBlanc's pristine Bentley automobile and removed the cap and glasses he'd worn as a disguise. He slipped out the package concealed in his shirt. Gritting his teeth, he began to attach the explosive device to the underside of the Bentley.

Done. He checked his wristwatch. *Right on schedule.* He slid out from under the Bentley and tugged his cap low over his forehead, glancing around the parking garage. *Good,* he thought with relief. No sign of his father's car. His mother, Hélène, and Liliana planned to take his father out for a birthday luncheon. *They should be at the restaurant by now.* His father always ate precisely at noon. He didn't want them anywhere near the bank now.

His job complete, Jean-Claude stood up and waved at the attendant, who signaled to him. Jean-Claude hurried away.

He was on his way to the café to meet Yvette, when he realized he'd forgotten to put his glasses back on. *Had he been recognized?*

Marie sat in front of the mirror in her hotel suite and brushed her platinum blond hair, securing it in a chignon. At her ears she fastened discreet pearl earrings that Edouard had given her, and touched a filigreed crystal perfume stopper to her neck, releasing sweet harbingers of spring, neroli and orange blossom.

As she slipped on her white linen jacket, she thought of her baby granddaughter. Jasmin was with a trusted nanny in the hotel, but Marie didn't want to leave her alone too long. She arranged a silk print scarf around her neck and as she finished the knot, the phone rang.

"Hello?" She listened for a moment. "Don't worry, Hélène, Edouard will understand, though he will miss his granddaughter. Forty minutes? Don't rush, dear, how about an hour?"

She dialed Edouard's office number. "Liliana has a fever," she explained to his secretary. "One of Hélène's neighbors will stay with the child, but Hélène will be late. Tell Edouard we'll have to have lunch at one o'clock instead of noon."

With extra time, Marie decided to walk to the bank. Edouard had taken the car that morning, as he usually did. She thought about Edouard's recent decision. "Danielle's situation clarifies the issues," he had told them at dinner the night before. Even Jean-Claude had acquiesced and attended on Marie's urging, in an attempt at a truce.

"I've decided to retire," Edouard had announced. The partnership agreement he had signed years ago restricted partners who left early. Their only investment was the equity of their home, but unbeknownst to her at the time, Edouard had been borrowing against it during the economic depression.

Edouard had finally done the right thing, but Jean-Claude had exploded, calling Edouard's actions cowardly. Whatever his father did, it was never enough. Jean-Claude couldn't understand the courage it had taken his father to walk away from a lifetime of labor.

Though it would be difficult to start over at their age, Marie was glad that Edouard had decided to leave France. Would Jean-Claude and Hélène come with them? Would Philippe? Her thoughts turned to Danielle, and she said a little prayer that her daughter would soon return safely with Nicky and Sofia.

Marie arrived at the bank. "*Bonjour*," she called to the clerks in the marbled lobby, and then made her way to Edouard's office. "Happy birthday, my dear."

Edouard's face lit up when he saw her. She deposited her purse on his desk and embraced him as he kissed her. "You look beautiful today. White always suits you well."

Marie smiled at the compliment—they were rare coming from her rigid husband, and therefore always managed to take her by surprise. "Has Hélène arrived yet?"

"Not yet." He shrugged. "Nothing is going according to schedule today. The car overheated on the way in, so I left it at the garage. We can take a taxi to lunch, and I thought I'd spend the rest of the afternoon with my beautiful lady."

Louis LeBlanc, a precise, arrogant man, appeared in the hallway. "Nice to see you again, Marie. I understand you're taking Edouard to lunch."

Marie greeted her husband's old friend and business partner. "Are you certain you don't need my husband today?"

"No, but we shall miss him in the future."

"Thank you," she murmured. Marie knew that there had been contention about his resignation. She turned to Edouard. "Hélène should be here soon. We could arrange a taxi and meet her downstairs."

"Nonsense," declared LeBlanc. "Come with me to the club. I had a flat tire this morning, but the attendant tells me the man from the garage is changing it now. Should be ready by the time Hélène arrives."

"Are you sure it's no imposition?"

"Not at all." LeBlanc waved his hand. "Besides, I think you'll find my new Bentley much more comfortable than a taxi."

Edouard tipped his head in appreciation. "And here's Hélène now."

Hélène rushed in. "Sorry I'm so late."

"Relax," Marie said. "These things happen with children—and cars. Monsieur LeBlanc has offered to take us to lunch in his new motorcar. Isn't that lovely?"

They walked out to the Bentley. The two men sat in the front seat, discussing business, while Marie and Hélène slid into the backseat. But just before LeBlanc started the car, Marie noticed she'd left her purse in Edouard's office.

Yvette sat in a dark café nursing a cup of coffee, a cigarette dangling between her fingers. She raised her eyes as Jean-Claude approached. "How'd everything go?"

"Smooth as silk. Now we wait."

"Cigarette?"

"Yeah." Jean-Claude took a cigarette, struck a match to it, and inhaled deeply to calm his jittery nerves. A waiter poured coffee into a cup and pushed it toward Jean-Claude.

Yvette dabbed perspiration from her face and took another drag from her cigarette.

They waited.

Jean-Claude drank his coffee. He thought about his father's inevitable grief for his friend and partner. He tried not to think of LeBlanc's family, imagining instead the suffering that LeBlanc had inflicted upon millions of innocents by his actions. At least his father had tendered his resignation.

Jean-Claude thought of all his father was giving up—his career, his income, and, probably, his home. *Perhaps I was too hard on him.* He gulped his coffee. He resolved to speak to his father, to apologize for his harsh judgment.

The minutes crawled and the ticking of their watches seemed thunderous. Smoke curled around their table. Jean-Claude bowed his head, studying his grimy hands. *Healing hands, hands that kill. A surgeon's hands, steady and sure, so well suited for planting bombs.* His father had accused him of acts of terror. Had he become what he despised?

Yvette reached across the table and grasped his hand. "Justice comes to us all."

"Justice—" he began.

All at once, a jolt as sharp as an earthquake shook them. The sound of an explosion ripped through the air, rattling windows. The coffee in his cup vibrated from the impact, and he and Yvette stared at each other.

"God forgive us," he whispered, clutching the table.

14

Thyme crushed beneath a boot, the bowed head of a wilted flower, the acrid smell of smoke—this is the perfume of destruction. The sacrilegious scent of annihilation cloys the air like cheap perfume. What sort of aromas are these?

—DB

15 JUNE, 1940 — POLAND

Today is the day, Danielle thought, trying to appear calm as she stepped into the car with Oscar. She thought about her new plan as they drove. Time was running out and she had exhausted all leads, all possibilities, save one. Heinrich. She'd finally found a lead on Max's cousin, who was now part of the SS. A few days ago she'd heard that Heinrich would be attending a party at the old Czapenski estate. She found the caterer, a café owner, and discovered she needed help. Luckily, the caterer hired her. Today was her first day on the job, and tonight she hoped to confront Heinrich.

As he drove, Oscar turned on the radio to the morning news report: *"We are proud to announce that France has been added to our expanding empire, with Paris its crown jewel."*

"No," Danielle cried. *France—captured—it can't be.*

Oscar whirled around, reached across the seat, and clamped his hand over Danielle's mouth. "Another victory for the Third Reich!" he exclaimed.

With horror, Danielle remembered the possibility of listening devices. She fell back against the seat, panic-stricken. Not Paris. *Not again. Her family, her baby.* She had wept last week when she'd heard that 340,000 French and English forces had been evacuated by the Royal Navy and other ships from the beaches of Dunkirk in northern France to escape the advancing Nazi line. In shock, she thought of Jon. *Was he there?* And then she thought of her family in Paris, and she grew frantic.

She drew a ragged breath. "That's very good news, driver," she said, trying not to choke on her words.

Oscar slowed to a stop at the end of the street near the café. "Here we are," he said, frowning and shaking his head. Oscar didn't like her plan, but what else could she do?

Danielle walked to the café and by noon she found herself elbow deep in hot soapy water with towers of greasy, food-encrusted dishes piled around her. *How will I approach Heinrich?* He hated her, but he was her only hope. Maybe he would slip, divulge a clue that would lead to Nicky. She had to try.

Danielle changed into a serving uniform as the caterer directed, then followed the woman's orders to load a paneled truck with racks of lamb, vegetables, golden fruit pastries, fresh-baked breads, and serving dishes.

They cleared the guarded checkpoint to the once grand estate and continued on a gravel lane. The land was unkempt; weeds swayed in the wind and flower gardens had been crushed under military wheels. Like her home, this estate had also been overrun with soldiers barking orders.

The butler met them at the rear entrance. "There now, pretty one, pick up your step," he called out, slapping Danielle's behind. She shot him an icy look and ducked her head under the white bonnet she wore. By the time she'd completed her task, perspiration dampened her black dress and white apron.

Once the dinner began, Danielle took her post at the sink, her hands submerged in dishwater. A young man in service at the estate whisked through the door carrying a stack of dirty china plates. When she turned to relieve him of his armload, she saw Heinrich through the doorway.

Danielle caught her breath, but she quickly registered every detail. *He so resembles Max.* Her heart ached for what Max must have endured. Heinrich bore the family's trademark chiseled features, though the tilt of his strong jaw was arrogant, whereas Max's fine bone structure had appeared aristocratic. Fair-skinned, muscular, blond, and blue-eyed, Heinrich favored the German side of the family.

She could hear him speaking with a superior officer, who sounded pleased with Heinrich's reports.

The dinner droned on as Danielle scrubbed pots and dishes. *How can I see him alone?*

She glanced around the kitchen. Her eyes fell on the butler's desk. Walking by it, she slid a notepad and pencil into her apron. Inside the bathroom, she scribbled a note.

After she emerged, she gave the note to a footman. "One of the ladies passed this to me for a gentleman. Take it to him, please," she said, indicating Heinrich. When the dinner ended, she hurried outside.

Heinrich waited on the darkened porch. He turned expectantly, but his face fell at the sight of a servant girl.

"Who the devil are you?" A shaft of moonlight illuminated her face. His face paled and his transparent blue eyes narrowed. "What are *you* doing here?"

"How lovely to see you again, too," she replied. "I have news for you."

A malicious grin played on his thin mouth. "You've come all this way to tell me Max is dead."

"I *know* he was on his way to meet you. Did *you* shoot him?"

"He deserved what he got. Our family was fine until he married you."

"I suspected you didn't like me, Heinrich." She squared her shoulders. "As for Max, I'm shocked at your lack of remorse."

"Max was a fool," he muttered. "He could have done so much better than you."

She ignored his contemptuous remark. "Max was an honorable man; he died a hero."

"He couldn't even save his own child." His eyes gleamed with spite. "Couldn't even find his precious little Nicky."

Hatred flared within her. She advanced, her hand flying to his face, savoring the sting as she slapped him. "Where are Nicky and Sofia?"

Heinrich's features twisted into a salacious grin. "Wouldn't we both like to know?" He extracted a pack of cigarettes from his pocket.

Danielle slapped it from his hand, sending cigarettes flying. "Where are they?" she demanded, grabbing his hand. *Damn him to hell*. Her nails dug into his skin, drawing blood.

"You don't scare me." He jerked a thumb toward the door. "You're a little outnumbered. Besides, Nicky and Sofia are *dead*."

His words rushed in her ears. "I—I don't believe you." She stared at him, but he didn't flinch. "It can't be."

Hatred spread across Heinrich's face; his eyes glowed with morbid satisfaction.

No, it can't be. She saw him clench and unclench his hands as he always did when he was lying. "How do you *know* they're dead?"

A sardonic grin contorted his face. "I killed them, Danielle. *I did it,* I shot them both." He pointed a finger, like a gun, to his temple. "And you're next."

As he started toward her, fury coursed through her veins like hot molten lava. Danielle balled her fist and struck him in the face as hard as she could.

He reeled, then caught her arm, twisted it, and shoved her to the floor. She hit with a thud, her hands scraping the rough wooden planks. She rolled over, her hands burning and bloodied. Heinrich lunged; straddling her, he pressed onto her throat with his forearm. She struggled for breath as his face warped into a gruesome mask; in a few more seconds, she knew she'd be dead.

Terrified, she tried to kick him off her, but his weight pinned her to the floor. She saw he was enjoying it, watching her flail as he pressed down harder. "Good-bye, Danielle," he whispered in her ear, and then started laughing. "Now it's your turn to die."

The pain escalated, horrific now; she couldn't breathe, and blackness crowded her vision.

This is it, she thought, *one last chance.*

She worked her free hand inside of his arm and up by his chest. Summoning her strength, she shoved the heel of her palm up into the base of his nose.

He yelled and reared back, blood spurting from his nose. Choking and gasping, Danielle rolled to her side, drew up her knee, and landed a solid kick to his groin.

Heinrich erupted with a string of expletives. Danielle clawed her way out from under him, stumbled to her feet, and ran.

"I'll kill you, you French Jew bitch. You're dead, you hear? *Dead.*"

As she flew from him, she could hear him screaming, and knew he was writhing in agony.

"Go ahead, run, but you'll never get away from me. *I'll track you down, no matter where you go.*"

Danielle raced around to the back of the estate. The caterer pushed open the door. "My God, girl, what happened?"

Before she could speak, the butler appeared behind her employer. "He's going to kill her, and there are more of them coming."

Danielle grabbed him by the collar. "Hide me," she cried, her voice hoarse.

Acting quickly, the butler pointed to a door. "Cellar," he said. "I'll tell them we saw you run away. They'll believe us; we don't know you, and we don't have any reason to protect you."

Danielle flew downstairs and hid in the musty darkness, her heart pounding.

Her throat burned, and she tried not to cough. She listened to the commotion and threats upstairs. *Will the staff give me up?*

Finally, the only sound remaining was the normal clatter of dishes and silverware. She curled into a corner behind a stack of boxes that smelled of onions and garlic, wrapped her bloody hands in her apron, and waited.

The door above her creaked open and a slit of light illuminated the cellar. The butler crept down the stairs, calling softly to her.

"Over here," Danielle managed to say.

He hurried to her, knelt, and pressed a glass of water to her lips. "They're gone."

She drank tentatively; every swallow was an effort. He helped her up the stairs.

The truck was near the rear door. The kitchen staff stood on lookout, shielding her from sight as the butler lifted her into the back of the truck.

"Why are you helping me?" she asked them.

"Nazis killed my father," the butler said.

"Nazis raped my daughter," the caterer added. Other solemn faces nodded. Each had a story, she realized. She was not alone.

She looked from one face to another, each of them a fighter, each a survivor. "Why do you stay?"

"This is still our home," was the simple answer.

The butler drew a blanket over her head. She heard the engine fire and the gravel crunch beneath the wheels. And then she thought, *Is this what Nicky and Sofia endured?*

Danielle huddled beneath the blanket, praying that the guards wouldn't search the truck on its way out.

15

In Greek mythology, the goddess Iris sped messages to the gods on the rainbow's arc. Her flower bears no perfume, but steam distillation of the root, or rhizome, yields orris, a precious essence that smells of candle wax, but its impression in perfume is powdery, silvery green, violet-like—a prize of the perfumer's palette. How I wish I could summon the goddess to carry my message to those I love.

—DB

8 JULY, 1940 — PARIS, FRANCE

The voice behind her was a mere whisper. "Pardon, Madame von Hoffman?"

Danielle nearly jumped with fright, but she'd learned to contain her reactions in Poland. It had taken weeks to return to France. Travel routes were circuitous, as many border crossings were closed. The web of Resistance fighters had led her by foot over moonlit trails for much of her return journey.

She had just entered the wide expanse of the Place Vendôme in Paris. Nazi soldiers were guarding the entry of the Hôtel Ritz, where occupying German forces had taken up residence. Were her parents still there? Her heart beat wildly. She swung around, her face expressionless. She recognized the Ritz hotelier's uniform.

"I'll get someone who can help you," the dark-haired man said. "Wait here." He disappeared into the hotel.

Danielle watched as Nazis paraded in and out of the hotel, many with German wives, and others with slender young Frenchwomen extravagantly clothed.

Danielle tried to look nonchalant. The Ritz had been requisitioned and was now under Nazi control, as were many of the grand palace hotels in Paris, including the George V, Le Meurice, Lutetia, and Crillon. Only the Ritz allowed civilians to stay, and only with *Luftwaffe* commander-in-chief Hermann Goering's approval.

Paris was a mess of fear and confusion and armed soldiers, but at least it had been spared the *Luftwaffe* air attack that had decimated Poland. She prayed her parents were safe.

She noticed an elegant woman attired in a couture suit, layers of pearls, and a chic black hat. It was Mademoiselle Chanel, who was known as Coco, the couturiere who lived at the Ritz near her rue Cambon atelier, which was now closed. She was so close she could smell her perfume, No. 5.

She sucked in her breath. Marie knew her quite well. *Do I dare approach her?* Averting her face, she decided to wait as she'd been told. After she passed by, Danielle saw a German officer greet her with a kiss.

Another man brushed past Danielle, his hat angled low. "Follow me," he said, nodding slightly to the Ritz employee. "We've been waiting for you," he added, his accent that of an aristocrat.

He darted into an alley beside a brasserie and she caught up with him.

"Who are you, and where are my parents?"

Instead of answering her, the man withdrew a handful of letters from his jacket, with the address of her brother clipped to the top. "The concierge, a friend of your parents, managed to keep these for you."

"Where are they?" she demanded, concern rising in her voice.

Evading her question again, he motioned to a delivery truck that had slowed to an idle at the end of the alley. "Get in the truck, you must go to your brother's apartment."

She climbed in, relieved but still worried, and the young man behind the wheel gave her a sharp nod. "Better we don't talk," he mumbled.

Danielle glanced at the letters. One was from Abigail and two were from Jon, all received before Paris had been occupied. His first letter was confident, but in his second letter he wrote that he had watched a close friend die. *What can you say to ease their suffering?* he wrote. Her heart went out to him. Abigail's letter stated that she had returned to Los Angeles, and she shared news of her charity work. She was glad Abigail was doing what she could; Danielle had seen firsthand the scope of devastation, the extent of aid needed. *Maybe somehow it will help Nicky.*

As they drove, she heard shouts in German from the street outside. *How strange to hear this in Paris.* A sliver of fear sliced through her. Still, Paris was intact.

Rubbing her temples, she closed her eyes, thankful to be so close to the comfort of her parents and Jean-Claude, even though Paris was occupied, and she dreaded what that meant. She was so anxious to hold Jasmin; her arms ached for her. When Nicky was born, Danielle had been both elated and nervous about motherhood. She'd once asked her mother what his cries meant. "How will I understand what he wants? How will I know when he's ill?"

"A mother knows," Marie assured her. "Sometimes he'll be cranky, but if something is truly wrong, you'll know."

When they were young, Danielle and Jean-Claude always thought their mother had a sixth sense, that she could read their minds at times. After Nicky was born, Danielle came to understand.

Was it motherly intuition, or was it her gift of prescience? She didn't know, but a flicker of knowledge flamed within her, illuminating her mind.

Nicky is alive.

Despite what Heinrich had said, she knew it was true, just as she knew that Sofia was dead. *But how am I going to find him now?* She chewed her lip. *Jean-Claude or Philippe will know.*

After arriving at her brother's building, she rushed upstairs to his flat, eager to see Jasmin, speak to Jean-Claude, and see her family. The door swung open. A neighbor greeted her, a Spanish nurse named Christina who often watched Liliana when Jean-Claude and Hélène went out. "Danielle? Why, your hair is so light, I almost didn't recognize you," she said, embracing her.

Glancing over Christina's shoulder, Danielle noticed the apartment was brimming with flowers. *A special celebration, perhaps.* "Where is everyone?"

Christina lifted her hand to her mouth and stared at her.

"Where is Jasmin?" Danielle asked.

Christina hesitated. "In Liliana's room."

Danielle hurried to see Jasmin, who was sleeping in Liliana's old bassinet. Relief coursed through her. *My baby is safe.* Stroking Jasmin's fine hair, she kissed her cheek. She smelled like sweet milk. She would never know her father. But she *will* know her brother, Danielle vowed.

She tiptoed out and walked past the small kitchen. Flower arrangements were everywhere. *Everything seems so odd,* she thought. *Or is it me?*

Christina joined her on the sofa, placing two etched crystal glasses and a bottle of sherry on the coffee table. "I thought you might like a drink," she said, pouring sherry. She still wore her nursing uniform.

Danielle glanced at her own brown wool suit, now dirty from her extended travels. She removed the jacket and pushed up her sleeves. "Why all the flowers, Christina? There are so many irises it looks as if someone—" Danielle stopped. *Died,* she started to say. *Irises were funeral flowers.* "Did Maman and Papa have a party?"

Christina spilled the sherry as she lifted it to her lips. "Didn't you receive my telegram in Grasse?"

"No, I must have missed it." Danielle swallowed, hoping Christina wouldn't detect her subterfuge. Outside their family, no one knew where she had been. "What's wrong?"

"*Dios mio.* It's about your family," she began, grasping Danielle's hand. She spoke gently, explaining that there had been an accident, a car explosion, on the day Marie and Hélène had met her father for his birthday lunch.

Danielle listened; it was as if she were watching herself through a shadowy haze in a horrible play. The flowers overwhelmed her with their putrid stench of sympathy.

Christina drained her glass. "The police think the bomb was intended for your father's partner, Monsieur LeBlanc, a supposed Nazi sympathizer."

Danielle gripped the arm of the sofa.

"Your father and Hélène were killed immediately."

Danielle gasped, and found it hard to breathe. *No,* she screamed in her mind. "My mother?"

"She survived, *gracias a Dios.* It was a miracle; she had just gotten out of the car when the bomb exploded. She's in the bedroom resting, though she's not really with us. The shock was too much."

The room swirled, closing in on her. Her mind was a torment of emotion. *Where will it all end?*

Danielle pressed the sherry to her lips, her hands shaking.

"I'm sorry, Danielle, but there's more," Christina said. "When your mother was in the hospital recovering, I asked to be the nurse assigned to her. The day after the accident, Jean-Claude appeared at the hospital with Liliana and Jasmin. He looked half-crazed," she said, her eyes widening. "He visited with your mother, and then begged me to look after the girls, saying he had something urgent to attend to."

Christina shook her head, her distress escalating. "Jean-Claude returned to the apartment, and left a note asking us to care for Marie and the girls until you returned. He told us you were ill and couldn't travel. He said if you hadn't returned by the end of the month to wire your uncle Philippe."

"Oh, no." Danielle sank her head into her hands. "Where is Jean-Claude?"

Christina wrung her hands. "I'm so sorry to tell you this," she sobbed. "We found him in the basement. He put a bullet through his head."

"Suicide?" The word tasted strange on her tongue.

"He left a letter for you," Christina added, motioning toward a stack of envelopes on the étagère. "He made all the burial arrangements before he took his life. There's also a letter marked 'Urgent.' It just came for you, hand-delivered."

Danielle fought the urge to scream, to snatch Jasmin and race from the flat. She tried to think clearly. "My poor *maman*. I wish I'd been here."

"Amazingly, her injuries were minor." Christina dabbed her eyes. "She's under sedation, but I'm afraid the natural defenses of the mind have taken over. She seems oblivious to the tragedy. She's quiet, but occasionally she chatters pleasantly about you and Jean-Claude, or new decorations for the house. And she keeps asking for her purse. It's hard to predict the outcome for patients who've had a nervous breakdown."

Danielle struggled to assimilate the details. *How can it be?* She blinked back tears. First Nicky and Sofia, then Max. Now her father and Jean-Claude and Hélène. *Malheur ne vient jamais seul.* Misfortune never comes alone.

After Christina had gone, Danielle tore open the letter marked "Urgent."

You don't know me, but I was a friend of your brother. If you see F.W., tell her someone is looking for her in Paris. She must leave the city without delay. The letter was signed: *Y.*

F.W., Frau Werner. Tiny hairs on her neck bristled. The Nazis were on her trail.

She lowered the note, then ripped open another letter bearing Jean-Claude's hasty scrawl.

My dear sister, it began. *Forgive me, I can't live with what I've done. I was responsible for this horrible accident. Philippe will tell you everything. Please look after Liliana, tell her I'll always love her. May God protect you, Jean-Claude.*

His words didn't make sense. *How could he have been responsible?* Danielle wiped her eyes, her mind swirling with questions.

But she knew one thing. The Nazis had traced her. Courtesy of Heinrich, no doubt. She prayed that Oscar had been spared.

Not only was she in danger, but also her family. *We must leave now.* But where could they go? Her head pounded with terror.

She gnawed her lip and thought. *Philippe.* If they hurried, they could make the last train. But would they be allowed on it?

Danielle glanced through the window. There, in the street below, stood young, skinny German soldiers in their green uniforms, shouldering guns. The *haricots verts*, the French disparagingly called them. The string beans. *Are they waiting for us?* She yanked the curtains shut.

Danielle hurried to her mother and Liliana. Her mother's hair, normally in a neat coiffure, lay tangled on the pillow; her face had a grayish pallor and looked drawn and lined. Danielle sighed; she hardly recognized her.

Liliana stirred. On silent feet, the waif-like six-year-old scrambled off the bed and ran to Danielle. Marie didn't move.

Liliana hugged her tightly. "Maman and Papa went away. You won't leave us, will you?" Liliana asked. Her vivid green Bretancourt eyes, the mirror image of Danielle's, were wide and desperate.

"Never," Danielle whispered, smoothing the little girl's fine blond hair. Fighting back her own tears, she kissed Liliana on the forehead. "We're going to Grasse to see Uncle Philippe. I need your help now with my mother and Jasmin. You'll have to be a big girl. Can you do that?"

Liliana nodded, her face pale and serious.

"Good. I thought we'd go tonight." Danielle spied her mother's jewelry box on the dresser and emptied its contents into her purse, including her wedding ring and Max's lighter that she had left with her mother. She packed a small satchel with essential clothing for all of them. When she was done, she woke Jasmin and her mother. They were groggy, but complied.

When she opened the front door to leave, she saw a note pinned to it. *Go to the rear entrance.* With Jasmin in her arms, she quickly herded Liliana and Marie down the stairs, where the young boy in the delivery truck met them in the dark.

"We're taking the train," she began to say.

"You can't. But I have permission for deliveries to and from Paris." He lifted a false floor in the back of the truck and motioned for them to get into a shallow compartment made of fresh-cut pine and covered with old, distressed wood. Marie and Liliana climbed in, and then Danielle squeezed in with Jasmin.

Was this to be their rolling coffin? Thankfully, Marie was catatonic. Next to her was Liliana. Her whines almost imperceptible. Jasmin was in her arms, falling mercifully asleep. Could she remain quiet?

The truck careened over roads so pitted that splinters scraped Danielle's cheek, drawing blood. As the truck slowed, Danielle caught her breath, hardly daring to breathe, and heard Liliana do the same. The truck halted; outside, boots crunched gravel. She heard a rap on the truck, and a command. "Open it."

The doors were unlatched, swung open. Danielle curled her hand around Jasmin's mouth. Beams of light shone through the cracks, a set of boots thudded on the floor above them and paced the length of the interior, the truck shuddering with each footfall. Liliana trembled beside her, and Danielle prayed fervently as the light beam raced around, seeping into their dungeon. Perspiration trickled into her hair.

And then, it was over; the boots crashed onto the gravel, the doors were latched, and the engine rumbled to life. Liliana sobbed quietly as Danielle exhaled, murmuring reassurances.

Early the next morning, Danielle found Philippe at the kitchen table drinking coffee.

"I heard you on your shortwave radio last night," she said, pouring a cup.

"Danielle, we need to talk. I called the midwife who delivered Jasmin, and she agreed to look after the girls and Marie. Let's saddle the horses, go for a ride. I have your old riding gear. Are you feeling up for it?"

She gulped her coffee. "Is it safe?"

"For now, the Nazis have no immediate plans to occupy the south of France."

The summer sky was crystalline blue, but Danielle felt an ill wind blowing. As they rode, they passed fields of rose and lavender, their aromas jostling in the breeze.

On a knoll above Bellerose, Philippe pulled on the reins of his old bay gelding. "Let's stop here."

Danielle slowed her dappled gray horse to a trot. She told Philippe about Heinrich and his threats. "I don't believe Sofia survived, Philippe, but I *know* Nicky is still alive."

Philippe's keen eyes regarded her with interest. "Your insight tells you this?"

She nodded. "Maybe you don't believe me, but—"

"No, I do. You've always had the gift."

"I *must* find him, I've got to go back."

He scratched his chin. "I'll make inquiries again through my contacts."

She stroked her horse's mane, thinking. "Jean-Claude left a letter. He said you had something to tell me."

He cleared his throat. "It's about the accident."

"What more is there to say?" Danielle's words tasted bitter in her mouth. "Nothing can bring them back."

"Your brother set the bomb."

Danielle's mouth opened, and at first, no words came out.

"I want you to know what happened and why Jean-Claude took his life."

"Does it really matter now?"

"Someday it will matter to Liliana, and you must tell her that her parents died for a noble cause." He touched Danielle on the shoulder. "I share your pain . . . their blood is on my hands. If I have the courage to live with this, then you must have the courage to listen and try to understand."

Danielle steadied her horse. "Go on."

"He saved many lives before his last mission went awry. Yvette, his partner, told me Marie, Edouard, and Hélène were not supposed to have been in that car." His eyes grew moist. "Jean-Claude could not live with the knowledge of what he had done to his beloved wife and parents."

"Why do you tell me this now, Philippe?"

"Because Yvette wanted to give you her condolences." He motioned to a woman with short henna-red hair walking toward them. "She sent the note yesterday."

"You're Yvette?" Danielle's tone was clipped.

The woman nodded. "I wanted to tell you how sorry I am. Your brother and I often worked together, and he would never have endangered your family. He was a man of high principles." She placed a hand over her heart. "We all miss him. I wanted you to know that if you need help again, I'm here."

"Yvette arranged your traveling documents to Poland," Philippe said. "And arranged your passage here."

"Come closer." Danielle's voice softened and she reached down to shake Yvette's hand. "Then you've already helped me. Thank you for the warning."

"And thank you for delivering the cosmetics case," Yvette said. "Because of you, a key operative made her escape from behind enemy lines."

"Yvette is a brave warrior," Philippe said. "But we always need more people, more money, more arms." His steady gaze held Danielle's. "We must all fight this war, each of us in our own way. My place is here. For now, we'll endure the Vichy government. We're helping people flee through Cannes, Marseilles, and Toulon. Eventually we'll weaken their forces and reclaim our country."

Yvette spoke quietly. "We're committed to freedom, as was your brother."

"Well, he's free now, isn't he?" Danielle bit her lip. "I'm sorry, I didn't mean that the way it sounded. First my husband, then my family. And my mother—I fear she's not long for this world, either . . ." Her voice trailed off and she frowned, her gaze transfixed on the neat rows of flowers that stretched beneath them toward the horizon.

Philippe removed his glasses and drew his sleeve across his eyes. "They're not going to stop looking for you, Danielle."

"But I still have to find Nicky."

"You must make a choice," Philippe said.

"Your mother and the children aren't safe," Yvette added. "Neither are you, Philippe."

He shrugged. "I can take care of myself. We could hide you, Danielle, but is that any way for Marie or the little girls to live? And there's no guarantee they'll survive. You should leave France."

"We can help you escape," Yvette said.

Danielle bowed her head, overcome with anguish. *Save them or save Nicky?* She didn't believe Heinrich, she *couldn't* believe him. In her heart she knew he was lying. She *knew* Nicky was alive. *But to make such a choice, oh Lord, how can I?*

"You have to make your decision now," Philippe said.

Blinking hard, she tilted her head back, searching the endless canopy of sky for answers she knew would never come.

"We'll try to find Nicky for you," Philippe said gently, nodding to Yvette. "Danielle, leave while you can, save Marie and the girls."

She swung her gaze between Philippe and Yvette, saw quiet courage in the depth of their eyes, in the lines of their mouths. "We'll go," Danielle said, and felt her soul splinter. Tears on her lashes, she drew her shirtsleeve across her eyes and straightened in her saddle.

"You're a brave woman," Philippe said. Yvette nodded her approval.

"I have seen the destruction in Poland," Danielle said, gaining strength from them. "I will not allow Hitler's racist henchmen to terrorize what's left of my family."

After Yvette left, Danielle and Philippe turned the horses toward home. As they rode, they shared their grief over their loved ones. Danielle confessed, "The sound of Max's voice is growing dim in my ears. How did you cope after your wife died?"

Philippe slowed his horse. "I grieved for a long time before I decided that my wife was still with me in spirit. Now I feel her presence in the first rays of the morning sun and in the last sliver of every moon. Her love lives in every drop of perfume I blend, and always in my heart."

But Danielle felt raw inside, as if her heart had been hollowed out. "Papa, Jean-Claude, Hélène," she choked out their names.

Her uncle cleared his throat, struggling to find words. "They died pursuing their dreams and ideals. They died for liberty, for equality. They died so that others might live."

"Is that really what you believe?"

He grimaced. "Evil killed them, Danielle. But believe my other words."

Tears wet her cheeks again, and she rubbed a hand over them. "I wish I could have said good-bye."

"They'll always be in your heart. And if your thoughts spill over into words, speak aloud to them. You're never alone."

Two days later, Danielle thought of Philippe's words as she stood by the rail at the bow of the ship bound from Lisbon to New York, holding Liliana's hand and Jasmin in her other arm, the smell of the sea filling her nose. Marie sat behind them, rocking, a vague expression on her face and a blanket around her shoulders.

The sea churned under turbulent skies as the great ship cast off. The wind howled and whipped Danielle's hair wildly about her shoulders, while a sharp prick of salty spray spattered across her brow. She tried to shake the trepidation she had about their crossing.

She wept for the lives and the life they had lost. She thought of Max and Jon, and her confused feelings. She said a prayer for Nicky, and gave thanks for Philippe's promise to help find him. Memories of Heinrich and his heinous crimes and threats sprang to mind. *Have we managed to escape him?* she wondered.

Jasmin squirmed and Danielle tightened her grip on the baby. *My uncle and Yvette, they applauded the bravery of my decision, but inside, I am ashamed, for I have no bravery. I have only the responsibility of my family.*

The loved ones she had lost were casualties of war, all of them. She glanced at her mother and the girls. *Especially the living.*

16

Stanislaus Jean, chevalier de Boufflers, once wrote: "Pleasure is the flower that passes; remembrance, the lasting perfume." How can it be that our pleasure is as fleeting as the flower?

—DB

12 AUGUST, 1940 — LOS ANGELES, CALIFORNIA

Danielle stood in the middle of a squalid one-room apartment near downtown Los Angeles. The smell of rancid grease and human feces hung in the air. She wrinkled her nose. Fried food and diapers, Danielle thought, pinpointing the aromas. Only the price of the room was right.

She'd exchanged French francs that morning and received few U.S. dollars in return. Philippe had given her what money he could spare and she had taken her mother's jewelry from Paris, but her funds wouldn't last long. She turned to the landlord of the Bradley Arms building. "It will do."

The landlord chomped on a cheap-smelling cigar and held out a beefy hand. "Cash," he said in a loud voice. "In real money, American. The green stuff."

Does he think I'm an idiot because I have an accent? She opened her purse, counted the bills, and handed him exact change.

He raised his bushy brows, scratched his belly through his undershirt, and counted the money out loud. "The rent is due weekly, paid in advance." He raised his voice again. "If you're more'n one day late, you're out. Understand?"

"Perfectly." *And does he think I can't understand English unless spoken at high volume?* She held out her gloved hand. "The key, please."

He fished into his pocket and produced two grimy keys. A smirk spread across his face as he handed her a key. "I'll keep the other one."

Danielle sniffed. *Note, change the lock.* She dropped the key in her purse and snapped it shut.

The landlord shuffled out the door.

Danielle bolted the door after him. She removed her black beret, peeled off her white cotton gloves, and rolled up the sleeves of her black-and-white-checked blouse. "A good cleaning and airing is all this place needs," she said to herself, though she had her doubts.

She forced open a warped window. The sounds and smells of the busy street two floors below wafted in. A cacophony of foreign languages rose on the wind, some Asian, some Eastern European. Pungent spices Danielle recognized as dominant in Indian cooking punctuated the breeze as it lifted the faded gingham curtains from the wooden sill.

She had chosen this place because it could accommodate all of them. The space wasn't an apartment really, but a large single room. Sparsely furnished, it contained only the bare necessities: a bureau, three lumpy beds, and four rickety chairs. A single sink, and an old icebox marked one corner as the kitchen. She found a rusted can of soap powder and rags in a cabinet. Her mother and the girls were at Abigail's home. *I must clean this room before they see it,* she decided.

Tackling the sink, she scrubbed until the battered porcelain approached an acceptable shade of white. She fashioned a kitchenette in the corner with a table for food preparation and dining.

As she worked alone, intent on abolishing the filth, she thought of their dire predicament. Even though Abigail's home was comfortable, she'd hardly slept. They couldn't stay with Abigail, her bungalow simply wasn't large enough, and Danielle wouldn't impose on her friend.

She thought about the past few weeks, and the magnitude of events overwhelmed her. *I fear I can't maintain the brave face I wear for the girls and my mother, who depend on me for their existence. I have no family to turn to here, not my mother, father, husband, or brother.*

The emotions she'd tried to suppress overpowered her at last. There were days she wished to die. Sometimes she dreamed that she was whisked away on the wind to peaceful fields of wildflowers, the sun warm on her face.

Tears streamed down her cheeks as she worked alone on her hands and knees, scrubbing the floor of every speck of dirt like a woman possessed. *Why was I spared? So that I might experience more heartache, even the loss of my son? That if my grief was not enough, more should be added?*

Breaking down, she collapsed onto the floor, sobbing, drawing her knees to her chest, her body heaving in agony. *But I must live, if only to give Liliana and Jasmin a better life, a life where they will never know the pain I've endured. My mother—physically she's with us, but emotionally her mind is elsewhere. Am I selfish to want her back? To ask her to feel, to experience the relentless pain that blackens my heart? Or shall I leave her in her prison of oblivion? I have no answers, no guidance on this horrific path. Only Philippe understands my loss.*

She lay on the floor until shadows formed through the windows. Her emotions spent, she rose to her feet, surveying her handiwork with grim determination. *And now we're imprisoned in poverty,* she thought. *Dear God, how am I to manage this?*

Here we are." Danielle stepped out of Abigail's Packard in front of the Bradley Arms building. With Jasmin in her arms, and Liliana and Marie trailing her, she started bravely up the steps. Her face and eyes felt puffy from yesterday; today, with her family, she had to control her emotions.

Abigail's mouth dropped open as she stared at the peeling eaves, the dirty white brick. A radio blared from an open window. "Danielle, you can't be serious."

Danielle's neck grew warm and she swung around, acutely embarrassed. "It's what we can afford."

"Good Lord, had I known—"

"We'll be fine, Abigail." Danielle reached for the front door and went in. "Our room is on the second floor." The carpet underfoot was threadbare, the banister rickety, the walls smudged with dirty handprints. Danielle shuddered. "Liliana, don't touch anything."

Abigail picked up a bundle of linens she'd brought for them and started up the stairs.

Danielle swung open the door to their room. "This is it, our new home."

Liliana sniffed and made a face. "What's that smell?"

Danielle flung open a window. "We'll take care of that odor soon enough."

Abigail glanced behind her. "Danielle, where's Marie going?"

"*Mon Dieu!*" Danielle whisked past Abigail into the hallway, Jasmin still in her arms. Her mother had taken to wandering away on board the ship. She spotted her at the end of the hall. "Maman, come this way, this is our room."

Marie turned slowly, her eyes vacant. Danielle led her back. "Here, sit down and rest."

Abigail put down her bundle and reached for the baby, a wistful look crossing her face. "I'll take Jasmin while you see to your mother. Danielle, I wish you'd let me help you. Jon said to make sure you were comfortable. Why, this place—"

"Abigail, I don't want to discuss it." And she didn't want to hear about Jon. She was so conflicted about her feelings for him, while she was still grieving for Max, and now, for her family. Danielle's heart sank. She'd snapped at Abigail, who was only trying to help. But after a few days at Abigail's small though posh home in Beverly Hills, she knew she'd have to find other lodgings. "Forgive me, Abigail."

"You've had a long journey. Crossing the Atlantic, the train across the States, moving your family. I know it hasn't been easy. If it's money you need, I can help."

"No, I can manage, thank you." As soon as the words left her mouth, Danielle was sorry. A rush of guilt tore through her.

Abigail was right, the journey had been exhausting. *But I've no time to rest.* Her funds were running out fast. Reaching across the table, she touched Abigail's hand. "Maybe you can help me find a job."

Abigail's eyes lit up. "As a matter of fact, maybe I can."

The next morning Danielle awoke with the sun. She bathed and dressed in a secondhand brown tweed suit from London. She wished she could have brought some of her mother's chic couture clothes from Lanvin and Lucien Lelong, but they'd left Paris so quickly. She was thankful they'd managed to escape at all. Her family was safe here; Heinrich couldn't harm them in America. She peered into an old mirror. *Or could he?* His threats echoed in her mind. She thought of the underground resistance in Europe—did the Nazis have a similar spy network in America?

She trailed a fresh floral perfume she'd created—one she'd taken from Philippe's before they'd fled—along her neck and wrists. *Honeysuckle and freesia with a touch of bergamot.* Then she hurried to prepare her family for the day.

She made breakfast, and Liliana helped her. The little girl had proven herself a calm, capable helpmate during their arduous journey.

"Make sure your *grand-mère* doesn't leave the apartment, Liliana." Danielle glanced at her mother, who sat smiling vaguely. She handed Liliana a piece of paper. "Here is our address, and the phone number of where I'll be. Keep it with you at all times."

A knock sounded on the door, and Danielle opened it to a petite Mexican woman in a brightly embroidered cotton dress, which Danielle instantly admired for its detailed handiwork. Her dark hair gleamed in a tight glossy bun, and the most delicious aroma of roasted peppers and maize surrounded her like an exotic culinary aura. "I hope I'm not too late," the woman said, smiling. "I had to get my children off to school."

"You're right on time, Anna." She had met the woman yesterday and had instantly liked her. Anna agreed to look after her mother and the girls while she was out. *After all,* she thought wistfully, *Maman is in no condition to be left alone.*

As Danielle opened the door to leave, Marie called out to her, "Are you and Jean-Claude going to school, Danielle?"

Danielle shared a poignant look with Liliana. "I'll be back soon. You must not go out today. Stay here with Anna and rest."

Half an hour later, Danielle stepped off the bus outside an exclusive boutique owned by Abigail's friend. Her nerves on edge, she opened the beveled glass door to the shop.

Abigail had mentioned that Clara had once lived in Paris. *Quite evident,* Danielle thought. The shop was a replica of a fine Parisian boutique, from the Savonnerie rugs and crystal chandeliers, to the Louis XV marquetry reception desk. Extravagant clothes and precious accessories were displayed like fine art.

Clara appeared at the top of the curved staircase. *"Bonjour."*

Danielle stared, momentarily awestruck.

Clara was tall and tanned. Her platinum hair curved over one eye and fell in soft waves to her shoulders. Her gold bracelets clinked with each step; amethyst chandelier earrings sparkled against her neck. "You must be Danielle," she said, descending the stairs.

Feeling self-conscious, Danielle glanced at the mirror. Her tweed suit was hopelessly outdated. Her dyed blond hair clashed with auburn roots, and her face, devoid of makeup, was alarmingly pale.

Danielle drew herself up. Clara cleared the last step and held out a manicured hand, a smile curving her lips.

"*Bonjour,*" Danielle said, shaking her hand.

They spoke first in French, then in English. "You speak English beautifully," Clara said. "I know you're a perfumer, but do you think you can sell clothing and accessories?"

"I'm quite familiar with fabrics and silhouettes; I've designed and made many of my own clothes—but certainly not what I'm wearing today," Danielle explained, acutely embarrassed.

Clara tilted her head. "Abigail said you've just immigrated."

Danielle nodded and continued. "Fashion, like perfume, is more than an indulgence, it's a reflection of a woman, or the woman she aspires to be."

"Well said." Clara smiled, then outlined the hours, work, and wages. "You're hired, but first, you must see Esmeralda, my head seamstress. She'll have something more appropriate for you to wear."

Danielle's face grew warm. "But I have no money to pay for clothes."

Clara dismissed her concern with a wave of her hand. "I don't expect you to. Follow me." She introduced her to Esmeralda and spoke a little Spanish to the stout Mexican woman. Clara turned to Danielle. "Be here tomorrow morning at nine o'clock."

After Clara left, Esmeralda brought out three dresses for Danielle to try on. One was a chic black silk sheath, the other two were made of wool crepe fabric, one in royal blue, the other in emerald green.

Esmeralda put a hand on Danielle's shoulder, her lined face crinkling into a warm smile. "Clara knows clients trust stylish salespersons. These dresses were worn before they were returned. We can't sell them, so you might as well have them. Choose some shoes, too."

Danielle murmured her thanks. She left Clara's filled with a mixture of relief and elation.

The next morning, she dressed in the blue wool crepe dress, and after Anna arrived to look after her family, she hurried to Clara's, eager to begin.

Clara unlocked the door. "You're early, I like that. Say, that's a good color on you." She put a finger to her chin. "You need accessories." She plucked a scarf from a display, and then scooped up a strand of costume pearls and a pair of pearl earrings. "Your color is striking." She draped the scarf around Danielle's neck. "You must accent it."

"It's lovely, Clara. But how about this?" Danielle turned to the mirror and rearranged the scarf, nestling the pearls within its folds.

"Much better. You have a good eye."

"Clara, thank you for everything."

Clara held up a hand. "No need to thank me." She brushed her platinum hair over her shoulder. "I have a business to run, and with that accent, I'm betting you can charm my customers into buying vulgar amounts of clothing and jewelry. Now, let's get started."

Danielle paid close attention to Clara's manner with customers. By noon, Danielle was making sales.

That afternoon, Clara showed her the customer book, which outlined each client's purchase history, size, and preferences. Clara had saved photos and articles clipped from the society news pages. "You must remember and greet each person by name." The clientele included established Los Angelenos, wealthy Europeans and Latin Americans, and a host of movie stars.

At the end of the day, Clara called Danielle to her office. "You have an excellent sense of style, and you're good with customers." She peered at Danielle over the rim of her rhinestone glasses. "But you need a good hairstyling. What in heaven's name is wrong with your hair color?"

Danielle's face grew hot. "It's growing out. I dyed it."

"Whatever for? Well, never mind." Clara scribbled a number on a piece of paper. "Call Mr. Roberto's salon right now. And don't thank me again. Mrs. Groves spent a fortune following your advice."

You must be Danielle Bretancourt," the young woman at the front desk said as her eyes roved to Danielle's hair. "Madame Clara shared your, ah, problem."

Danielle surveyed the Beverly Hills salon with its sleek modern divans, fresh lilies, and ornate mirrors. Two fashionable women were chatting in a corner, elegant leather purses on their arms, and peep-toe platform pumps on their feet.

"Darling!" A man in an immaculately cut white linen suit with a crimson silk pocket handkerchief and matching ascot approached her, his arms held wide in welcome. Glossy black hair waved from Mr. Roberto's tanned temples with casual precision. But his broad smile dissipated when he saw her hair.

Mr. Roberto clucked his disapproval as he examined Danielle's hair. "Can you repair it?" she asked.

"Darling, I'm not the hairstylist to the stars for nothing." He clapped his hands for his assistant, and Danielle found herself whisked away.

Marie has been roaming away from the apartment," Anna said to Danielle when she returned. "She says she's going to her bedroom, then wanders through the hallway. It's hard to stop Marie when I'm changing Jasmin's diaper or feeding her."

"I realize we have a problem," Danielle said, depositing a grocery bag with fresh milk, butter, and eggs on the table. The Bradley Arms was no place for Marie, no place to raise her girls. If only she could earn enough for a little home in a safe neighborhood where the children could play safely. Marie could have a companion nurse. A home where the girls could have their own bedroom. *And one for Nicky, too.*

"I'll put another latch on the door," Danielle said. As Anna let herself out, Danielle removed her gloves and the chic black hat she'd styled from a few remnants of felt and netting and an antique brooch. Two of Clara's customers had asked to see one like it. She smoothed her hair; luckily Mr. Roberto had managed to restore her hair to its former shade. Now she had a new American style, parted on one side with an auburn cascade of natural waves around her shoulders.

Danielle quickly fed Jasmin, changed her diaper, and then warmed a supper of vegetable soup and bread that she'd made over the weekend. Liliana and Marie ate hungrily.

Danielle sipped her soup thoughtfully. A few days ago she had mentioned to Anna that they had lived in Poland. "Then you should try the Polish restaurant in the neighborhood," Anna exclaimed, and gave her directions.

"Such a warm evening," Danielle said. "After we eat, let's go for a walk."

The evening was balmy, with a high wispy breeze rustling the palm trees that lined the street. The scent of sun-warmed grass caressed the night air. "This is fun," Liliana said, clutching Marie's hand. Danielle had put Liliana in charge of Marie—a tiny little blond-haired girl guiding her grandmother along the sidewalk. Danielle pressed the sleeping Jasmin against her shoulder.

They came to small restaurant with a sign that announced: *Poslaniec's Fine Polish Food.*

They walked in and Danielle spotted a large man who wore a long apron over shirtsleeves and trousers. "Are you the owner?"

He bowed with a flourish. "At your service. You sound French."

"*Oui,* but I lived in Poland until last year. In fact, I was just there."

His eyes lit with keen interest. "Come, sit down, we must talk." Liliana's eyes grew wide at the desserts being served at nearby tables. "Would you like to eat?" he asked.

"No, we've had our supper, thank you," Danielle replied. "Do you have family or know people there now?"

The man nodded gravely, and then smiled at Liliana. "Dessert? It's on the house, as they say here." Marie looked quizzical, while Danielle quickly explained the unfamiliar saying to her. Liliana giggled at the expression and looked up, as if expecting to see a cake on the ceiling. "Now, I have many questions."

Danielle had questions, too. A waiter brought coffee and a warm chocolate roll, which the owner proceeded to slice and serve as they spoke.

"My son is still there," she told him, explaining her story. "I have a photo of him, maybe you know someone who has seen him. I can leave it here with you."

The restaurant owner shook his head. "I'm so sorry to hear this. I'll pin it on the community board, where people post notes for friends and relatives who might have arrived here. Have you contacted the embassy?"

"Yes, I have." They continued talking, and she told him what she had witnessed in Poland, while he shared information about other Poles in the neighborhood.

The next day she found more Polish immigrants through an aid service at a church. Others she found working in restaurants or taking in mending. She showed them Nicky's picture, told them her story, and asked if they had seen him. No one had, but she left her address and the telephone number at Clara's. She wrote Philippe, but no news was forthcoming. Even so, she clung to her belief that her son was alive.

Her first week's small paycheck didn't go far and she realized she would never get ahead. Food, clothing, medical services, transportation—her small family needed so much. She'd had such hope for their new life in America, but now despair set in.

One evening, after Danielle had made potato soup for dinner, bathed Liliana and Jasmin, and put everyone to bed, she picked up a pencil, a pad of paper, and a small amber-colored bottle of perfume she'd been working on in Philippe's laboratory, one of a handful she had hastily stuffed into her purse with her journal before leaving Grasse. She went outside onto the front porch of the apartment building, settling on the creaky wooden steps under a dim overhead light. She gazed up at the clear night sky, deep in thought.

She had an idea.

Danielle chewed on the tip of her pencil. If Philippe could send aromatic materials, she could start to blend again.

She held the bottle to the light. This was Chimère, the *parfum* she had been working on in Grasse. It still needed work, but it *could* be a masterpiece . . . if only she could capture the magic again.

Danielle had never started a business. *But if others can do it, so can I.*

She recalled how her mother had often assisted clients, suggesting bottle designs, color schemes, and even names. "Our clients appreciate our insight," Marie once said. "They are experienced in fashion and retailing, but we know the perfume business."

She would also need to create the packaging, image, and business plan. Although she had never delved into these aspects before, she had often observed her mother and uncle and their clients at work.

Where to begin? She decided to work backward, first projecting the number of bottles she thought she could sell. She frowned. Surely Clara would agree to sell it at the boutique.

Next, Danielle estimated supplies and the time she thought it might take to sell her inventory. She calculated the cost of the fragrance compound, or ingredients, from Philippe, but with the Vichy government in place, she knew trade would be impacted; she'd have to find other sources soon. She could manage the rest of the processing and filling in the States, but she would need bottles. The beautiful bottles Max had produced sprang to mind, along with memories.

He would want me to be strong. She drew a ragged breath. *Where was I?* Bottles. She recalled the people she and Max had met in New York, and made a note to call them. She frowned, considering the money she would need, which she didn't have. *But I will find a way.*

While she worked, crickets chirped their evening serenade. The night air grew cool and Danielle pulled her sweater around her, oblivious to the late hour. She hunched over her notepad. Once she had completed her cost, wholesale, and profit calculations, based on her projected sales, she turned her mind to the creative aspects of the project, the bottle design and packaging.

Danielle picked up the work-in-progress she called Chimère. Opening it, she inhaled deeply. A fresh, uplifting mélange of Italian bergamot, mandarin, and raspberry that comprised the opening accord filled her nostrils with the carefree scents of spring. Her imagination soared with memories. The gardens of Bellerose, picnic baskets bursting with summer fruits on sunny Mediterranean beaches, summers spent on the Riviera, yacht parties, and the casino in Monte Carlo. The plain little bottle held the essence of the happy life she had known.

She inhaled again, closed her eyes, and allowed her mind to wander, to visualize the images the aroma evoked. Excitement coursed through her veins. She imagined a glamorous, luxurious lifestyle of exotic locales, mysterious lovers, sandy beaches, glittering parties, elegant gowns, and precious jewels.

And amid it all, sumptuous bouquets of fabulous flowers, enchanting and romantic, intense aromas of pure, bridal white jasmine and sultry tuberose, and the heady, evocative aroma of rose. Seductive spices, clove with musk and patchouli, smoothed with sandalwood and vanilla, elegant and sensual, like a lover in the night.

And finally, she realized what was missing. A strong, smooth core, a warm amber blend that would provide a deep connection to the soul. *Love.*

In her mind, she could smell her vision; it filled her with serenity and misted her eyes.

This was Chimère.

Her eyes still closed, she breathed in the magical scent and let herself slip farther into her dream world, where her creativity and imagination swirled and became one with the provocative aroma.

She moistened her lips. In her mind's eye she saw vibrant colors, she heard a soaring symphony, she saw the colors of the music, and the shapes took form. Visions of Max, then Jon, floated before her.

Her eyes fluttered open. As if in a trance, Danielle picked up her pencil and began to make notes to complete the formula. She sketched what she had seen and felt and recalled. She let her heart guide her pencil as she drew fluid, graceful lines of the bottle she envisioned, along with the elegant imagery for her perfume. Golden brocades, silken pouches, exquisite bottles.

Finally, when the moon was high in the midnight sky, she sat back, sated, and studied her sketches. Chimère was taking shape. It was beautiful, but where would she find the money?

She glanced at her wedding ring, the nearly flawless emerald and diamond ring that had belonged to Sofia's mother, the ring Danielle had promised Max she'd never sell. She extended her hand. *How it sparkles, even in the moonlight.* Sadness trickled through her, and guilt tugged at her conscience.

A taut lump formed in her throat. *Do I have the strength to do what I must?*

17

Deep within the stench of despair blooms the perfume of hope.

—DB

28 August, 1940 — London, England

As soon as Jon's train eased into the station, he saw his father. The trim figure of Nathan Newell-Grey towered above the crowd. Jon hoisted his bag, wincing from a recent shoulder injury. Like so many other brave men, he had joined England's effort full of hope and patriotic pride, only to discover the gruesome realities of war. He'd been granted forty-eight hours leave, a mere salve for the wounds to his soul. He stepped from the train.

"Hello, Father, Mother." Jon greeted them with warm embraces.

Nathan frowned. "How's the shoulder, son?"

"Not too bad, it'll mend."

"We're so glad you're home," his mother said. "Everyone is looking forward to seeing you. A few people might call by this afternoon. Victoria is quite anxious to see you."

"Actually, I'd hoped for some rest." Jon was exhausted, his usual ebullience subdued. The Dunkirk evacuation and ongoing defense of British shores had tested him to the brink, and there was more to come.

They got into the car and started for home. Although he wanted to avoid company, Jon had always had a soft spot in his heart for

Victoria, despite her stormy personality. Their parents were close friends, and he had fond childhood memories of country weekends, of horseback riding together. They had dated, but when he returned from Grasse to enlist, he told Victoria that she shouldn't wait for him; she was free to date other men. After seeing Danielle, he knew he couldn't commit to Victoria.

His mother's cheery voice intruded, "So what do you think, Jon? Will there be an engagement announcement this evening? Many couples are getting married now."

Jon leaned forward. "Sorry, what was that?"

"Didn't you hear a word? I said it would be a perfect time to announce your engagement." She blew out a breath in exasperation. "Why are you denying us grandchildren?"

"Harriet, leave him alone," his father said. "Can't you see he's worn out?"

His mother's words startled Jon, but also struck him to the core. It was true; the continuation of the family line was his responsibility. On Abigail's thirteenth birthday, they had gone horseback riding, and his horse had crossed over into hers. It was a wonder she lived, but her injuries were so severe she had been rendered infertile. When the doctor told her, she had wept, heartbroken. She loved children, but wouldn't even think of getting married now. It was his fault. And instead of diminishing, his guilt had only increased.

His duty to his parents was more important than ever. And his mother wasn't giving up on the idea of his marriage to Victoria.

Victoria was charming, but he wondered if she would develop the dignity, grace, and determination he found so attractive in Danielle. Further, he couldn't imagine getting married right now, not with the war at hand.

When they arrived home, Jon excused himself to freshen up.

Upstairs, he tore off his shirt and found a fresh one in his closet.

Marriage. Grandchildren. Nothing would make his parents happier. He understood the advantages of marriage to Victoria, particularly in view of Abigail's condition. He owed it to his family.

But he couldn't get Danielle out of his mind. If she lived in London, they could be together when he had leave. Was it such a crazy thought? He'd almost mentioned it in his last letter to her, and then she had written to tell him about her visit to Poland, and to say she was living in Los Angeles. At least she was near Abigail. *But oh, how I miss her.*

In the mirror, he saw more gray in his bleached chestnut hair and new lines on his ruddy forehead. He didn't recognize the aged expression in his eyes. Victoria and his family would never understand the horrors he'd witnessed. Danielle did; she knew firsthand, she understood him.

He went downstairs and spotted his parents in the drawing room, standing by the mantle, Victoria beside them.

Victoria flew to meet him, her blond hair cascading behind her. "Welcome home, Jon darling." She flung her arms around him.

"Victoria, what a surprise." He gave her a friendly hug. Despite his reticence, her silvery, ethereal beauty was astounding. Her eyes were the shimmering blue of a sunlit sea, her figure undeniably superb.

"Harriett, let's give them a moment." Nathan left the room with Harriett reluctantly following, craning to hear what she was missing.

Victoria lowered her lashes and gave Jon a coy look. "I've been waiting for you. But I can't wait forever, you know."

Jon touched her gently on the cheek. "Victoria, we've talked about this. I'm not ready to get married. You really shouldn't wait for me through this war; it could take years, and I might not return."

"I know you said I could see others," Victoria pouted. "But I only want to be with you."

He shook his head. "We've known each other a long time, but times have changed. *I've* changed."

"That's just war talk, Jon. I'm not giving up on you."

"Victoria, you really should."

"Why?" She narrowed her eyes. "Is there someone else?"

Jon lifted his shoulders, let them fall. How could he lessen the sting? "As a matter of fact, there is—"

"There, I *knew* it, oh, how could you?" she cried indignantly, her eyes blazing. Before he could stop her, she spun around and stormed out of the house, slamming the door behind her.

His mother appeared in the doorway. "Good heavens, what happened?"

Jon raised outstretched arms. "I told her the truth."

Harriet's eyes flashed with annoyance. "I don't know what transpired between you and Victoria, but we're at war, for heaven's sake. Anything could happen."

Jon put his arm around his mother. Under her facade, he knew how scared she was for him. He gave her a kiss on the cheek. "I want nothing more than for you to spoil and show off your grandchildren someday, but I'm not ready to marry. And when I am, I'd like to be there for my children, not away fighting a war."

The next morning Jon walked to see Libby, making good on his promise to visit her before he had to go.

The afternoon sun cast a golden glow, warming his aching shoulder. It was the same time of day, the same golden glow, when he had witnessed his first war casualty, an old friend dying in his arms, his broad chest slashed open by a mortar shell. Jon, awash in his friend's blood, felt utterly powerless as his friend choked out his final words. *Tell my family I love them.*

Before the war, he had taken so much for granted. Family, friends, love. Now that he'd witnessed how quickly one could lose those most dear to them, he valued his relationships even more.

With swift steps, he covered the distance to the Leibowitz home.

Libby greeted him with a warm hug. "I'm so glad to see you," she said.

They passed a crystal vase of luscious yellow roses, which burst from tight salmon buds into golden, creamy yellow blossoms tinged with delicate strokes of subtle peach. Libby waved her hand. "My roses were voted Best of Show this year," she announced. Their intoxicating aroma filled the atrium, reminding Jon of his visit to Grasse—and Danielle.

Danielle. Loneliness tore at him again.

"So good of you to visit," Libby said as they sat down. She motioned to Hadley for tea service. "Tell me, how are you? Really?"

"It's been rough." Jon blew a breath out. "I suspect this war will last longer than we'd originally anticipated."

"We have to see it through." Her face darkened, and she looked down at her hands, neatly folded in her lap. "My sister was killed when Holland was invaded. Carted off like cattle, murdered."

He took her tiny hands and stroked them tenderly, concerned for her. "Mother wrote me; I was so sorry to hear it, Aunt Libby. What can I do for you?"

"Your visit is enough," she said. "You're not here for long, so let's talk about something else. How is Abigail?"

"Busy with her Red Cross work in Los Angeles. She's also starting a new charity for war orphans."

"Good for her. Your mother must be proud. And happy to see you, I daresay."

"I know she only wants the best for me, but you've got to hear this." He told her about Harriet and Victoria.

"Your mother meant well, but she did overstep her boundaries, indeed." She hesitated. "Victoria's a fine girl. You've known one another for many years, your families are close."

Guilt coursed through him. How well did he really know Danielle? And, if he had never met Danielle, how would he feel about Victoria now?

Libby went on. "Forgive me if I'm speaking out of turn, but I simply don't see the two of you together. She's so . . . spirited. But the pressure from your family must be immense." Libby inclined her head. "After all these years, I love my husband more today than the day we met. If it's the real thing, you will know. Listen to your heart." She traced Jon's scarred knuckles. "Have the courage you show in battle to make decisions for the rest of your life."

He grew quiet, thinking of his devotion to his family. Someday he hoped to have a son to follow him in the business his father had built. His conscience gnawed at him. He had always been a dutiful son, and now he was a man of honor.

Was there some truth in his mother's words?

Libby regarded him for a moment. She lifted the teapot and poured tea. "It wouldn't be fair of you to marry Victoria if you're in love with another woman." A smile flitted across Libby's face. "What about Danielle?"

Am I that transparent? Danielle was everything Victoria was not. "I don't know, the timing is all wrong. And I don't know if it will ever be right."

"I received a letter yesterday from her. Danielle is a woman of immense character. She sounded quite burdened, but determined."

"Max was a good man. They were in love. For Danielle to lose him and most of her family is unfathomable. How can someone possibly survive so much loss?" He rubbed the dimpled cleft in his chin, thinking. "How could I ever help her overcome the pain she has been through?"

Libby sipped her tea thoughtfully. "I was devastated after I lost my parents in the Great War. I thought I would never recover. Survivor's guilt, it's called. But life goes on, and I came to be grateful for that which others had lost. And now, my sister . . ." She shook her head, put her tea down, and took his hand in hers again. "Life is short, Jon. Given time, Danielle will overcome her grief. She has an inexorable will to survive. The war can't last forever."

"But we're separated by an ocean. I don't know how to express what I feel. Is it truly love? Or just these crazy times?" A feeling of helplessness washed over him.

"Have you told her how you feel?"

"No, but I think she knows." He hesitated, remembering their embrace, their kiss. He had held her in his arms for but a moment, yet he had relived that moment a thousand times as he lay in his bunk at sea.

"Be honest with her." Libby smiled.

After he'd kissed her cheek and promised he'd write, he paused on the front step, thinking. The continuation of their family line depended on him, and it weighed heavily on his conscience.

But marry a woman he might not love in order to please his family? Marriage was forever, and the only forever he wanted was with Danielle.

He had to see her. *But how?*

18

John Dryden once wrote: "The sweetest essences are always contained in the smallest glasses." Perfume: the tiniest drop slays the most hardened heart.

—DB

28 SEPTEMBER, 1940 — LOS ANGELES, CALIFORNIA

Danielle sat in Clara's office, waiting for her to arrive. She had worked through the night finalizing the exquisite pouches for her perfume. She clipped a thread here, straightened a bow there. Everything had to be perfect.

Philippe had sent perfume supplies from Grasse, and after countless attempts to create the perfect formula for Chimère, she had finally discovered it. She knew in her heart that it was her masterpiece. Perhaps it was her intense longing for Nicky, her undying love for Max, the despair over her family's tragedy, or the growing attraction she had for Jon—feelings she didn't fully understand, but could no longer pretend weren't in her heart. The power she'd harnessed from her raw emotions had inspired a perfume of incomparable beauty.

She sat now, thinking about what to say, nervous about Clara's response.

Clara breezed into her office. She was a startling vision in a shocking pink suit, her platinum hair swinging about her shoulders. With a deft motion she tugged off her kid gloves and tossed them onto her inlaid marquetry desk. "What's this?" she blurted, waving at the perfume bottles that sat next to the outline of her upcoming speech.

Danielle heard the annoyance in Clara's voice. "It's my new perfume," she began. "I call it Chimère, which means—"

"I don't have time to look at anything today. The fashion show starts in an hour, and we have more than a hundred ladies and members of the press arriving. Even Lou Silverman, the studio head, is coming to personally scout designs for the new Erica Evans film."

"Exactly. That's why I thought today would be the perfect time to introduce it. All your best customers will be here." Danielle had spent the night filling crystal bottles and sewing golden brocade pouches by a dim light as her family slept.

"We've discussed this, I don't sell perfume here."

"But, Clara—"

Clara raised a finely arched brow. "I'm running very late, Danielle." She kicked off her flat shoes. "Now where did I put my platform pumps? And where is Esmeralda?"

She emerged from the armoire with the missing platform shoes and a fuchsia and violet scarf. "Esmeralda, I need you," she shrieked.

Danielle chewed her lip in thought. *Today is the perfect opportunity.* "I can set up in the foyer and demonstrate after the show."

Clara scowled at her. "Danielle, I've got my hands full. I need to know if my models are ready, if the champagne is on ice, if the valet attendants and photographers are here. I haven't time to discuss your perfume." She called again, "Esmeralda, where are you?"

"Everything is ready. Here, won't you at least try it?" Danielle picked up a crystal bottle and spritzed the air with its gold-tasseled bulb atomizer.

Clara put her hands on her hips, her silver bracelets clinking. "American women don't understand perfume yet, they don't pamper themselves the way French women do. They wait for their husbands or lovers to buy it for them. I tried it once; it didn't sell. This isn't Paris."

Esmeralda appeared at the door.

"Where in the world were you?" Clara huffed. "Oh, never mind, fix this hem. I stepped on it when I put my skirt on this morning."

Danielle pressed on. "But if you can make a good profit—"

"Danielle, I have work to do. And so do you," she added with a piercing glare.

Worried, she gathered her perfumes and left Clara's office. She had spent so much time preparing, and she desperately needed the money for her family. *How can I convince Clara?*

She thought about fellow perfumer François Coty and his creative marketing decades ago. As she made her way down the sweeping staircase, her eyes fell on the marble foyer floor.

She thought of the red leather traveling case that Max had knocked from the dresser in their stateroom, before everything went down with the ship. *How the fragrance had filled the air.* She knew it was a risk—she could lose her job—but it was a risk she had to take for her family.

While the other sales clerks busied themselves with the fashion show, Danielle commandeered a round display table by the front door in the foyer and quickly arranged her crystal bottles and brocade pouches.

She stepped back to admire her work, then anxiously glanced outside. Through the beveled glass door she could see Cameron Murphy and Abigail Newell-Grey, and behind them, a woman in an extravagant wide-brimmed hat, whom Danielle recognized as Hedda Hopper, the Hollywood gossip columnist. *This is my chance.*

She drew a nervous breath. Glancing around to make sure no one was watching her, she picked up one of her crystal perfume bottles. She hesitated, thinking about how furious Clara would be, before smashing it onto the marble floor.

In an instant, the rich aroma of Chimère exploded.

Cameron opened the door for Abigail and Hedda Hopper. When he caught sight of Danielle, his dark eyes sparkled. "Why, it's the beautiful Danielle. It's been a long time since London," he added. His deep voice was rich and silky, and seemed to imply much more than Danielle recalled. But that's what had made Cameron an international singing sensation, Danielle reminded herself. That voice, and his charm.

Abigail greeted Danielle with cheek kisses. "Danielle, darling, you look lovely." She shot a reprimanding look at Cameron. "Don't mind him, he's in rare form today. I'd like you to meet Hedda Hopper. May I present Danielle von Hoffman."

"Danielle Bretancourt, please, my family name." Danielle took Hedda's proffered hand. In the present political climate, she was no longer using Max's German surname.

Hedda sniffed the air and her face lit with pleasure. "What is that marvelous aroma?"

Danielle could hardly contain herself. "Oh, I'm terribly sorry, I knocked over a bottle of perfume. Please watch your step."

Hedda held on to her hand. "But, what is it? I can't quite place it."

"No?" Danielle smiled and waved her slender hand for emphasis. "Well, I suppose not. It's exclusive to Clara's." Danielle could see Abigail standing behind Hedda, a smile playing on her lips. "It's called Chimère, *madame.*"

"Chimère? You say it so beautifully." Hedda finally released her hand. "You're French, aren't you?"

"*Mais oui.*" Danielle picked up a bottle and sprayed a veil of scent across Hedda's eagerly offered wrist.

Abigail leaned over to whisper in Hedda's ear, "I happen to know it's one of Lana Turner's favorites."

"Ginger Rogers, too," Cameron added with a wink. He stooped to pick up a shard of crystal. Danielle reached out to take it from him, and as she did, he caught her wrist with his other hand. He gazed deeply into her eyes as he spoke, his smoky voice mellowing every word. "You know, it's a fragrance to make love by."

Hedda waved her wrist under her nose. "A fragrance to make love by," she intoned, her eyes fluttering. "And how would you know, Cameron?"

Cameron pulled Danielle close, encircling her with one arm. "I know the creator, Hedda. I know exactly what this woman is capable of."

Danielle gave him a coy smile. "Do you, now?" she said, gracefully extricating herself.

Hedda shot Abigail a knowing look. "I suppose there's no better judge of aphrodisiacs than Cameron Murphy." She gave Cameron a long, appraising look, and then turned back to Danielle. "I'll take a bottle of this, and I want to talk to you after the show. I want to know all about you, my dear." Then she waved to a distinguished man in a fine Savile Row suit entering the store. "Why, there's Louis Silverman. Lou, darling." She sailed away, leaving a fragrant wake behind her.

Danielle breathed a sigh of relief and Abigail nudged her in the ribs. "I suppose this concoction is yours, Danielle?"

"That's right."

"It's gorgeous." Abigail gave Cameron a playful punch in the arm. "And you—what a line. *A fragrance to make love by.* I can already see it in Hedda's column tomorrow."

Cameron shrugged. "Why not? That's how the game is played, Abby."

"And what game are you playing, Cam?"

"Game?" He glanced at Danielle. "No games. Just dinner. How about it, Danielle? I'm free tonight."

"Well, I'm not, not if Hedda Hopper is going to write about my perfume." Her head was spinning, and it wasn't from Cameron

Murphy's advances. Danielle was already making a list in her mind of things to do. *I've got to buy more bottles, sew more pouches, tend to the children and my mother, shop for groceries, make dinner, wash clothes, write to Philippe about Nicky.* Her list was endless. Though she was already exhausted, she smiled to herself with a sense of satisfaction as she thought of Hedda and Cameron, and their response.

After they moved on, Danielle cleaned up the broken crystal, but the magical aroma lingered in the air, drawing people to her table.

The show began on schedule. Clara welcomed guests and acknowledged celebrities in the crowd, including Katharine Hepburn and Marlene Dietrich. Danielle knew most of the stars, had created chic ensembles for them. She had also helped Clara create new looks for the runway, and couldn't wait to hear how her work was received.

Clara cued the jazz quartet, and an upbeat, provocative melody quickly set the mood. Danielle stood to one side where she could see the models and watch the audience response. She twirled a lock of hair in nervous anticipation.

The first model appeared wearing a casual, asymmetrically designed cashmere sweater and wool trousers, inspired by menswear, with a felt hat dipped at a low angle above full ruby red lips. Aviator glasses completed the modern look. It was daring—most women wore skirts and dresses, but Danielle had suggested they open with an unconventional ensemble. Danielle saw Hepburn and Dietrich applaud with honest enthusiasm, then make notes on their programs.

Models paraded on the runway, showcasing fashions ranging from casual sporting clothes to smart luncheon suits. The evening wear segment, in a sensational rainbow of colors, was greeted with zealous applause, which reached a crescendo for the finale: a glamorous halter-neck evening gown in shimmering gold lamé, glittering bangle bracelets, and platform pumps. Danielle had selected and styled the entire outfit.

The show was a clear success, and Danielle had gained valuable insights. She knew which styles had drawn the most applause, the most photographs, and the most notes.

Furthermore, by the end of the show, she had a waiting list for her new perfume. "And I personally heard Cameron Murphy says it's 'a fragrance to make love by,'" she heard Hedda say. She was elated.

Lou Silverman, head of Silverman Studios, added his name to the list, too. "Hedda told me you dropped a bottle just before she arrived."

"An accident," Danielle murmured.

"A brilliant accident." Lou's eyes shone with a knowing intelligence. "Clara has a gold mine in you."

After he left, Danielle did a mental tally, pleased with her numbers. But she knew Clara would be livid, and might still fire her.

As the crowd was thinning, Cameron approached Lou. "Mr. Silverman, may I have a word with you?"

Lou swung around. "Cameron. What's on your mind?"

"That movie you're planning on producing with Erica, did Conrad mention to you that I'd like the part of Jack?"

"Yes, your agent called. I'll consider it. Of course, you'd have to read for the part."

"I haven't read for a part in years." Cameron flexed his jaw.

Lou shot him a look. "We shoot on a tight schedule, Cameron. Delays cost money."

"Sure, and I know." Cameron glanced down. "Look, I'm sorry about the last movie. It won't happen again."

"No, it won't."

"Listen, Erica and I were in a bad patch. I felt awful about everything. I've cut down on the booze, Mr. Silverman, and Erica and I are on good terms." He paused, his breath quickening. "She let me read her script, suggested I go out for the part of Jack. There's a couple of great songs in there I know I can make into hits for you."

Lou lowered his voice, "Look, Cameron, I don't know what Erica sees in you, but she's my number one star. I'll let you read for the part to keep her happy. But if you know what's good for you, you'll get your personal life sorted out and work on repairing your image. You want my advice? Get married, settle down."

Hedda Hopper brushed past them. "Well, look who's talking again," she cooed. "I heard you mention the 'M' word, Lou. Who's getting married? Anyone I know?" She turned to Cameron, threw a look at Danielle. "Well, if no one's talking, I'll have to keep my eyes open." With a theatrical sweep of her hat, she flounced away.

Lou followed Hedda's gaze. "Now there's an interesting thought, Cameron. Quite a lady, a woman of quality with a capital 'Q.'"

Cameron's mouth dropped open. "Hedda Hopper?"

"I meant Danielle Bretancourt." He arched a brow. "Not your type, though, is she? Pity. That's the type of woman you need. Smart, hardworking, respectable. A good woman, one who'd keep you out of trouble. You should be so lucky, Cameron."

"Ah, but remember," Cameron said, staring after Danielle and lapsing into an Irish brogue, "I've got the luck o' the Irish with me."

Later that evening, Danielle stepped off the bus. As she walked home in the dark, she had the distinct sensation that someone was watching her. It wasn't the first time she'd experienced this. It was almost as if she could still smell the scent of death in the air.

She'd read in the newspaper that Nazi spies had infiltrated American shores, and Heinrich's words echoed in her mind. *You're dead. You'll never get away from me. I'll track you down . . .* She quickened her step.

The day had been a success. Clara hadn't fired her, and her profits would allow her to have sketches of her photo of Nicky prepared to send to relief agencies in London. She stopped inside her building at the mailboxes. She withdrew a letter that bore a London postmark.

Her spirits soared. It was from Jon. She glanced up the stairwell. Her family would be fine with Anna for a few more minutes.

Danielle sank onto the first step of the stairs. She withdrew a thin sheet of writing paper dated August 31, nearly a month ago, and began to read.

My dearest Danielle, it began. *The seas were rough today, and now the night is so dark you can't see where the sea ends and the sky begins. Thoughts of you are ever present in my mind; I can't stop thinking about you.*

You must know that I hated leaving you in Grasse. And I have a confession to make.

Before we parted ways in England, Max asked me to look after you in the event he didn't return from his mission. The hardest thing I have ever had to do was to deliver the message to you that Max had been killed. How I hated hurting you; I would rather have taken a bullet myself. I want you to know that I will always be there for you, no matter how rocky our paths might be.

Ever since we met, I have wanted to take you in my arms and never let you go. But you were a married woman. I respected you and Max. What a fine man he was. I often wonder if I could ever measure up to him in your eyes. Did he know how I felt about you? Perhaps he knew there was nothing I wouldn't do for you. If he did, I hope it eases his mind, wherever he is now, to know that you are cared for.

Every night when I close my eyes to sleep, I replay our last moments in Grasse together. I can smell the sweet scent of your skin, feel your silky hair in my fingers, I can taste your lips on mine, feel your breath on my skin, hear your last whispered words. I knew you were grieving for Max, but I wanted to comfort you, to show you that you are still loved. I hope you didn't think my actions inappropriate, Danielle, but I simply couldn't conceal my feelings for you any longer.

I wish this war were over, and that I could turn this ship toward

America to see you. But I can't, I have a duty to do, and only God knows when this war will be over.

I have given this great thought. Will you come to London? I know my parents would welcome you and your family into our home, and we could see each other when I have leave. Please think about this, Danielle. I love you. Let me know when you can come. I'll make all the arrangements for you.

With all my love, Jon.

Slowly, Danielle folded his letter, her hands shaking. *How many times have I, too, replayed our days together in Grasse?* She moistened her lips and touched them, closing her eyes. *How many times have I tasted his kiss, conjured the smell of his skin?*

She looked at the date again, considering. The Nazis had commenced horrific night bombings of London after he'd written this letter. Nicky was still alive, somewhere, she knew it. Her family was settling well in Los Angeles; they were safe here.

When would London be safe again? And then, how would her family feel about moving to England?

19

Charismatic, magnetic, intoxicating—such is the enigmatic
perfume of success. What is this fine elixir? Confidence. And
so, too, in the perfumer's art.

—DB

7 October, 1940 — Los Angeles, California

The Silverman Motion Picture Studios lot stretched across 360
acres situated in the center of Los Angeles County. From a hilltop
perch at the farthest northern boundary of the studio, Abigail could
see clear out to sea. On the other side, beyond Hancock Park and
Boyle Heights, loomed downtown Los Angeles, the city lights twinkling beneath a fine mist of ocean haze. The view in the evening
was reputed to be one of the best shows in town.

Abigail stood at the full length, plate glass window, her fingertips
lightly touching the cool surface, while Louis V. Silverman concluded his telephone call. As she waited, she anxiously smoothed
the mahogany brown velvet suit Danielle had insisted would be
perfect for this meeting—it was, and so was the new perfume Danielle had created that she'd applied today.

She glanced nervously around his spacious office. In her fund-
raising efforts for the Red Cross, she had come to know many of
the Hollywood power brokers, but Lou Silverman was, by far, the
most curious of the studio bosses. He held himself above the Hollywood fray, donated vast sums to medical research, held nearly a

dozen patents, and published poetry under a pseudonym. Abigail smiled to herself. He was a true Renaissance man.

She had met countless stars and executives in the movie industry, had cajoled and flirted and bargained, even begged for the funding needed to ease suffering in far-flung corners of the world. She was proud of her success, passionate about her mission. Few people could resist her well-planned requests. But Lou Silverman was no pushover; he was one of the most formidable and respected members of the Hollywood club.

She stole a glance at him. With his silver hair, ruggedly creased bronze skin, and piercing blue eyes, he was an undeniably handsome man. He had already been exceedingly generous with her, having donated the princely sum of fifty thousand dollars to the Red Cross at her spring gala at the Beverly Hills Hotel. Yet, despite their favorable history, Abigail was nervous. Lou Silverman was the biggest of the big fish.

"Thanks, Erica," Lou said into the phone. "We'll talk more about the new movie later. You're perfect for it, and I know you'll love it. But think twice about Cameron's part, will you? *Ciao*, darling." He returned the phone to its cradle and rose to stand beside her.

Abigail took a small step away from him, so forceful was his presence. The faint aroma of a fine cigar, mingled with Bay Rum cologne, emanated from his skin.

Lou turned to her. "Now, where were we?"

"Such a beautiful view," she began. "From this distance, it's difficult to imagine suffering in other parts of the world."

He shook his head. "For anyone who's ever witnessed devastation, it's impossible to forget . . . Ah, it's cocktail time," he said, smoothly changing the subject. "What will you have?"

"Sorry, I don't mix business with pleasure," Abigail said.

"Pity." He inclined his head. "All right then, let's get down to business."

A lamp threw a shadow across his face, illuminating his deftly cut cheekbones. In his early fifties, Lou Silverman had a dignity and refinement that was rare in Hollywood, a remnant from his youth spent in part, Abigail knew, in the Russian court, where his father had served as a diplomat for the Romanov regime before the rebellion.

Abigail seated herself demurely in front of his imposing desk, shaking like a schoolgirl inside. "It's about displaced and orphaned children from Europe. If they are to survive this war and have decent opportunities, we must rescue them."

He listened, appraising her from his vantage point. "Tell me more."

"I've started my own charity, and I call it Operation Orphan Rescue." Abigail went on to plead her cause. She had crafted countless pitches in the course of her work, but this project touched her heart. She couldn't have children of her own, so she thought of these dear orphans as her responsibility. She wished she could take them all in, but at least she could find loving homes for them.

"So that's the story," she concluded. But hadn't she forgotten something? She paused. "You have children, don't you?"

"Someday I'll start a family with someone special." Lou met her gaze. "As noble as your idea sounds, I didn't hear a solid long-term financial plan." He remained standing, his arms crossed, his expression resolute. "I don't fling good money toward pie-in-the-sky plans, Abigail, no matter how attractive the messenger."

Abigail's mouth dropped in horrified embarrassment as she realized her mistake. How could she have left out the most important, salient points of her argument? "I do have a plan—"

"Abigail, I hate to cut you off, but I'm afraid our time is up." He strode to the door.

Taken aback, Abigail stood on wobbly knees. She couldn't believe she had mangled such an important pitch. *How can I salvage the meeting?* Her mind raced. "Please, can't we meet again? I'll show you a detailed business plan."

He waited by the door, his hand on the knob. "My schedule is full, Abigail."

"Haven't you any free time this week?"

"My only free time is in the evening after I've reviewed daily rushes. However, I certainly wouldn't want you to think I'm imposing on you." He opened the door. "Strictly a business meeting, over a brief dinner."

Abigail caught her breath. Lou Silverman was considered a catch, and he had just asked her to dinner. A *business meeting*, she corrected herself. She hadn't dated much; after all, no man would want a wife who couldn't have children.

Certainly not a man like Lou Silverman. He'd just said as much.

"I have next Wednesday evening available. Eight-thirty. Gladys will confirm the details."

She followed Gladys to her desk, where the woman consulted his schedule. She peered over her reading glasses at Abigail. "Here's the way it works. A car will pick you up and take you to the restaurant. This way, you won't get lost, forget, or leave him waiting. Besides, he seldom knows where he wants to eat until seven or eight o'clock. Fortunately, he has a standing table at most every restaurant in town. Though if I were you," Gladys added with a kind smile, "I'd dress for Chasen's. Something elegant. And be sure to order the Lobster Newburg or the Hobo Steak."

Abigail hurried from the office, nervous energy and excitement coursing through her. She was having dinner with Lou Silverman. He had the most beautiful women in Hollywood fawning over him. She was no match for them, nor could she offer him a family. *This is strictly about the orphans.*

But she couldn't get Lou out of her mind.

20

The thick, deep roots, or rhizome, of stately vetiver grass, native to India, yield rich oil upon distillation. Vetiver has a slightly green, woody, balsamic aroma, reminiscent of moist earth after a rain shower. An excellent, intriguing fixative, vetiver blends well with woods, lavender, and bergamot.

—DB

21 OCTOBER, 1940 — LOS ANGELES, CALIFORNIA

Shivering against the dampness, Danielle turned up her thin collar. As the bus lumbered through the streets of downtown Los Angeles, she watched rivulets of rain sputtering across the window.

The first rainstorm of the season had arrived, pummeling the California coastline and battering the piers that jutted out into the ocean like fingers beckoning to ships at sea. Danielle had witnessed the coastal destruction that morning during her visit to a Venice Beach boutique, another new account for her expanding perfume line.

Selling her line wasn't easy; she'd had to call on many stores and faced more rejection than acceptance.

At four o'clock in the afternoon, twilight was already encroaching. Ashen clouds were dense with the threat of a second, rapidly moving storm front. Her throat was raw, her nose was stuffy, and her forehead burned with fever. *But I've no time to be ill,* she thought.

She continued her search for Nicky. She'd heard nothing from Philippe's sources, but she refused to give up.

And then there was Jon. When she'd received his letter inviting her and her family to London, she'd been elated, but her rational mind soon took over. Marie had not improved, the girls had been displaced once already, and worse, England was under constant threat from the Nazis.

She blinked back regret. *What a burden we would be on Jon and his family.* She remembered how incredible it felt to be in his arms. But she couldn't endanger her family, no matter how much she loved Jon. Maybe, when the war was over, they would have their chance.

The bus reached her Boyle Heights neighborhood, and she gathered her bags and stepped gingerly from the bus, balancing a broken umbrella. She glanced down in dismay at the water sloshing over her shoes, hoping they would dry before morning.

She hurried through the rain, the scent of moist earth and grass reminding her vaguely of vetiver. Crossing the slippery street, she lost her footing. A man behind her grabbed her arm to keep her upright. When they reached the corner, she turned to thank him, but he rushed away. She noticed he was heavyset and walked with a slight limp.

Something about him unnerved her. But there were many down-on-their-luck people in her neighborhood. It didn't mean they were dangerous. Nevertheless, she was always wary. She continued to the market.

Her family's Christmas would be sparse this year. She had bought a little menorah for her mother to celebrate Hanukkah; it would be the first time since Marie had married and had to forgo her religious observance. She hoped it might give her mother a touchstone. Growing up, they had always celebrated Christmas, but Danielle often sensed her mother missed the faith she had been born into. And now, because Judaism was part of her heritage, Danielle wanted to learn more about its traditions.

She also planned to have a little tree for Christmas, especially for Liliana. If she waited until Christmas Eve, she could get a tree for a good price. She was making ornaments with scraps of fabric from her golden brocade pouches. She smiled as she imagined Liliana's delight.

She had recently left the boutique to form her own business. Clara wished her well, and advised her on how to create publicity. "Give it to the celebrities, and the press and customers will follow." Danielle had followed her advice assiduously, aware that Marie's improvement hinged on her ability to make money for medical care.

Crowds choked the streets as Danielle forged her way. Old men sat under awnings smoking and gossiping, observing the afternoon parade like sentinels on watch. Snippets of foreign tongues floated to her ears, melodious strains of Latin, Asian, and Eastern European dialects.

Extricating herself from the swarm of humanity, she stepped into the corner market. She opened her change purse and examined its meager contents. The boutiques wouldn't pay her until after Christmas. She pressed a hand to her throbbing temple. Their budget was beyond frugal. She was making a little more than she had at Clara's, but it still wasn't enough.

At the butcher counter, she gazed hungrily at the enticing array of pink salmon filets, fresh beef, and plump chickens. All she could afford was one small breast, limp vegetables from the half-price bin, and a loaf of stale bread from the markdown rack. After she paid, she counted every penny of change.

Dusk had given way to nightfall. Streetlights flickered to life, casting an iridescent glow on rain-slicked streets. As she started off to her apartment building, she noticed the man who had caught her earlier. When he saw her, he angled his hat and hurried away.

She would never forget Heinrich's threats to kill her, and often wondered about their safety in America. This man, whoever he was, had followed her. *Now he knows where I live, and my family.*

Or was it a coincidence? She blew a breath out, calming her nerves. *Have I become paranoid?*

Safely inside her building, she grabbed her mail, stuffed it into her pocket, and ran up the stairs. A bare, solitary lightbulb flickered overhead, threatening extinction. As she fumbled for her key, she heard a familiar police car radio squawk through an open window at the end of the hallway. The Hollenbeck precinct was a busy beat, but now the police presence was reassuring. She opened the door.

Liliana flung herself at Danielle in greeting.

Dropping her bags by the door, Danielle knelt to hug Liliana, but instead she gasped and her hands flew to the little girl's head. "What happened to your hair?" Liliana's long blond locks had been shorn into a choppy boyish bob.

"Grand-mère cut my hair." Her green eyes widened. "You like it, don't you?"

Danielle's heart sank as she surmised the situation. "I didn't recognize you." She hugged Liliana.

Her neighbor, Anna, hung back. "I was tending to the baby. I'm so sorry, it happened so quickly."

"It's okay, Anna. Go home, it's late." Danielle called out, "Maman, I'm home."

"*Oui, oui,* I'm coming," Marie answered from the bathroom.

Danielle put her groceries on the table, her teeth chattering. She checked on Jasmin, who slept soundly in her wicker bassinet. Fortunately, their desolate circumstances had little effect upon her. Jasmin communicated with gusto, laughed frequently, and was the only pure light in their dreary life.

"Maman, why did you cut Liliana's hair?"

Marie emerged from the bathroom. Her silver hair hung to her shoulders, she still wore her bathrobe, and her feet were bare. Her eyes were glazed with a feverish gleam. She smiled timidly. "Jean-Claude was beginning to look like a girl, his hair was so long. Didn't I do a nice job?"

Danielle bit back a reprimand. *What good will it do?* Her beautiful, capable mother was lost to them. "Sit down, Maman." She plucked a pair of woolen socks from a drawer. "Let's put these on."

With a sigh of resignation, Danielle tied on an apron to begin her evening duties. Liliana offered to wash the vegetables. Danielle smiled and handed them to her. "Look, Maman, isn't Liliana helpful?"

Marie peered at her as if she was trying to place her. "You're new here. What's for dinner, girl?"

"Chicken soup." Danielle filled a large pot with water and lifted it to the hot plate. "With garlic and onion, it's the best medicine for winter colds. That's what you always told us when we were little. Don't you remember?"

Danielle took the vegetables from Liliana and began to slice them. The doctor's warning came to mind: *Be gentle with Marie.* "You remember me, Maman, I'm your daughter, Danielle. And here's your granddaughter, Liliana. My sweet baby, Jasmin, is in the bassinet. You and Anna take such good care of her while I'm working."

Marie leaned over to kiss Jasmin's pink cheek. "My little Danielle is such a good baby."

Danielle sighed. Her heart ached for Marie, who had once been such a self-assured, confident woman. She returned to her well-worn recitation. "*I'm* your Danielle, Maman. I've grown up. That's my daughter, Jasmin. Your granddaughter. You'll remember soon."

Marie touched her temples, and Danielle could tell that she was trying to assimilate her words. She drew herself up. "Perhaps chicken soup is special to you, but my husband is accustomed to finer fare."

Danielle stopped slicing the vegetables, her knife in midair. *She is worse today.* Usually her mother came out of her fog quicker. Her heart pounded. *What if Marie never comes out of it?* Wiping her hands on her apron, she hastened to her mother, took her hand, and led her to the table. "Sit with me, you've had a long day." She searched for a flicker of understanding in Marie's face. She saw none.

Marie sank into the chair, glancing around in confusion.

Danielle handed Marie a glass of water. "Papa won't be joining us for dinner tonight."

"Oh?" Marie took the glass and drank. She blinked. "Danielle? Is that you?"

"*Oui,* Maman." Relief flooded Danielle. She took her mother's icy hand in hers and warmed it in her own.

"I'm so glad. And Edouard? Where is he?"

Danielle hesitated. "He's gone away with Jean-Claude."

Marie gazed into space. "They're on holiday together?"

"*Oui,* for a long time. I'll make a cup of hot tea for you while the soup simmers."

From the corner bassinet, Jasmin let out a piercing scream. Danielle hurried to put on a kettle, and then crossed to the bassinet. She cradled Jasmin in one arm and returned to the kitchen alcove, tending to her mother's tea with her free hand. Liliana watched with wide eyes.

Danielle smiled at her blond-haired pixie. She ruffled her newly shorn hair. "I do like your hair, it makes you look older. I was surprised, that was all." Liliana cuddled to her.

Thunder cracked outside the window and rain sluiced the pane. Danielle thought about her overwhelming responsibilities. Only her sheer force of will and perseverance kept her going.

She'd become increasingly alarmed at her mother's erratic behavior and her inability to emerge from her trauma. Marie appeared mired twenty years in the past, in the early years of her marriage, with her two young children.

A doctor had suggested a relatively inexpensive home where Marie could receive special care. One day Danielle visited the home and was appalled by the filth and neglect. The best care was expensive.

She turned her attention back to her family. The girls were content, her mother was placated with her tea, and the soup was gently simmering, releasing a soothing aroma. She sat at the table to finish bottle feeding Jasmin, and then put her to sleep.

She pulled out the letters. One was from her uncle Philippe, smuggled out and sent through an intermediary. Recognizing Jon's handwriting on another letter, she smiled. His frequent letters would sometimes arrive in bunches, or out of order. She would savor them tomorrow when she had time.

Danielle's thoughts drifted to her finances. The money she'd received for her wedding ring hadn't gone far. She'd worked hard to open new boutique accounts. Every store needed product for the holiday season, but wouldn't pay her until after Christmas. She was desperate for funds for medical bills, food, rent, and supplies.

How in the world will I manage?

Later that evening, Jasmin stirred and Danielle got up to check on her. After the baby went back to sleep, Danielle looked outside the window. She could see the liquor store's red electric sign blinking across the street. She peered through the foggy glass, and noticed that the man she'd seen earlier was standing beneath the sign. A sense of dread stirred within her. She watched him for a few minutes. *Three times is not a coincidence.*

She picked up the phone and called the police, who told her they would send a patrol car. She stood by the window watching, fighting a wave of panic. As soon as the police car turned onto the street, the man disappeared.

She watched for another hour, but he didn't return.

21

The stately tuberose is reluctant to share its effusive scent, yielding only to enfleurage—petals pressed into fat between glass, rinsed in alcohol. The carnal charisma of tuberose, one of the perfumer's most expensive essential oils, heightens the white floral bouquet, lifting it up on angels' wings.

—DB

23 OCTOBER, 1940 — LOS ANGELES, CALIFORNIA

Clara drummed her fingers on Danielle's business plan. She removed her rhinestone reading glasses and laid them on her desk. "Your perfume line is selling well. Your business plan is obviously well conceived."

"Thank you." Danielle's heart pounded as she sat in Clara's office, certain that Clara could hear it, see it through her thin black sheath dress that was too light for autumn weather.

"I know talent when I see it. But there are numbers that concern me. The bottle and packaging seem expensive. Can you reduce that cost?"

"The presentation must reflect the potion within," Danielle said. "A fine perfume is a blend of art and science. It can take months, even years, to develop a composition that sparkles with magic, captures the heart, and tantalizes the imagination. Fortunately, these development expenses have already been incurred."

"Well, it's beautiful, but—"

"Clara, this perfume has that magic, your customers and sales confirm it." Danielle perched nervously on the edge of her chair. "The weight of lead crystal bottles conveys luxury and quality. Fine design is absolutely crucial to success."

Danielle pushed a paper across the desk and tapped on the columns of numbers. "This is my inventory, here are sales to date, and these are my orders. The bottom figure is the amount of money I need, and here is my projected profit." She really needed funds now; her landlord had stopped her again this morning and given her an ultimatum.

Clara put her glasses on, frowned as she scanned the figures. "You could become a victim of your own success. If sales continue to double and triple, then your investment in inventory must rise, but can you get the money to fulfill the demand?"

"If you could refer me to a bank—"

"Forget it." Clara shook her head sharply, her platinum hair brushing her shoulders. "You haven't lived here long, or established credit. Your worst crime of all is that you're a woman in business, and an unmarried woman at that." She leaned across the desk, fiddling with her fountain pen. "Had it not been for private investors, I never could have opened my own shop. Now that I'm established, it's different. But it has taken forever, and the bank still asks for a man to co-sign my business loans." She rolled her eyes. "What we need are more women bankers."

"That's why I came to you for advice."

Clara leaned back. "It's not easy for a woman to be in business. Now we have the right to vote, and someday we'll own our own banks. Your girls will have a better shot at the brass ring than we do. Until then, we have to play the game."

"Yes, but by whose rules?"

Clara's expression hardened. "Your own. Only play by your own rules, Danielle." Clara studied her. "Are you sure you're ready?"

"American women adore French perfume and style. I know I can provide it. All I need is capital."

"Private capital, that's what you need. Someone who believes in you." She pursed her lips. "What's your vision for distribution?"

Danielle drew a deep breath. "First, Bullock's Wilshire, it's such a fashionable department store, and it's local. Next, to San Francisco for I. Magnin." She stopped, watching Clara's reaction.

Clara was making notes. "Go on."

"I'll take the train to the East Coast to call on Lord and Taylor in New York and Marshall Field in Chicago. In Texas, Houston is home to Sakowitz, Dallas to Neiman Marcus." That's enough, she thought, but later she planned to add fashion and accessories. Her field of vision expanded daily, despite the despondency she battled on the home front.

Sharing her plan with Clara imbued her with fresh determination. *I can do it,* she thought, envisioning an empire. *But I need this money now.*

Clara tapped her manicured nails, thinking. "Women need to help one another. I'll lend you the money you need." She stood, held her hand out. "Is it a deal?"

Vastly relieved, Danielle shook her hand. She was thrilled, but well aware of the financial risk to Clara. "I won't let you down, thank you," she said. "You have no idea what this means to me."

"I think I do." Clara smiled at her. "I'll have my attorney draw up a loan agreement. Your inventory can serve as collateral." She removed her glasses and leaned across the desk. "Remember, you need sales volume. Focus on volume and collections and publicity." She chuckled. "Actually, you have to focus on everything."

Danielle breathed a sigh of relief. Now she could pay her rent. And someday, move her family from their tired little hovel.

She left the boutique, her heart bursting with gratitude. She knew Clara loved tuberose; she made a note to bring the flowers to her tomorrow.

She was so happy that she didn't even notice the man across the busy street watching her intently.

Jon stood on the deck gazing at the edge of the sea where the waves stretched toward the horizon, as distant and elusive as his future. The moon cast an opalescent glow on the letter he held in his hand. From time to time he glanced at it, read it again, and thought about Danielle.

My dearest Jon, she wrote. *I am honored that you feel you can bare your heart to me, and want you to know that I share your feelings. You occupy a special place in my heart.*

Love is a deep commitment. If I were a woman without responsibilities, I would be on my way to England. But my life is full of other obligations. I have so much love for my daughter, my niece, and my mother. And with this comes a duty to protect them. Jon, we barely escaped the Nazi surge into France. And while I realize that England is strong, and will likely prevail against Germany, I cannot endanger my family again. I cannot accept your offer.

All that I can give you is the love in my heart, and prayers for your safety.

Frustrated, Jon lowered the letter, crumpled it, and flung it out to sea. Instantly he regretted his action. *She says she loves me. I should be happy with that.*

He had poured his heart out to her, had proposed an impetuous, unrealistic plan. *What did I expect?* He was glad that she'd had the sense to decline his offer. He wouldn't want to put her in the path of potential danger. But it didn't make it any easier to accept her decision.

Jon blinked against the stiff wind, his heart aching. He understood obligations. *I have duties, too,* he thought. *My duty to my country, and to my family.*

If Danielle would not come to England, he could go to her. He let his mind wander. *We could marry, have a home in Los Angeles. She'll be there waiting for me when the war is over. I could work from our Long Beach offices.*

But would she even want to have more children? This was imperative for him to fulfill his obligation to his family. And what if he didn't make it through? Should he be so quick to turn Danielle into a widow again? Hadn't she suffered enough?

For now, he would cherish their memories. The dances they'd shared in New York, the voyage on the ship, Jasmin's birth. He recalled the feel of Danielle's velvety skin, always incredibly scented—as if perfume had pigment, as mesmerizing as an Impressionist painting—like no other woman's he'd ever known. He loved everything about her—from the way she gazed at him with luminous eyes, to the tender way she held her baby, to the unwavering belief she had for her son.

Her capacity for love in the face of tragedy never ceased to amaze him. The way she'd fought for Jasmin to come into the world. How she cared for Liliana and Marie. Her courage and perseverance in searching for Nicky, the intelligence that marked her correspondence, her natural gift for perfumery. And yet, she made him laugh, too.

He'd never known a woman like her before.

In her letters she wrote that her business was successful, and assured him that she and her family were comfortable.

What could he possibly offer her now?

A sudden spray slapped across his face, jolting him. Wiping water from his face, he tasted salt on his lips. His father's words came to mind: *We Newell-Greys have salt water in our veins.* Jon knew that his commitment to Crown and country and the cause for which they fought took precedence over all else in his life.

He spat into the sea, expelling the taste of salt from his mouth.

Jon spun on his heel and strode inside. He still had a letter to write before turning in.

22

Beauty is revealed through the art of revision—whether one is revising a perfume, a dress . . . or life itself.

—DB

1 NOVEMBER, 1940 — LOS ANGELES, CALIFORNIA

"How do you know this man is following you? Maybe he lives around here."

"I just know it, I can feel it . . ." Danielle's voice trailed off. Even though it was dark in the hallway, the doubt in the police officer's eyes was evident. His pencil hovered above his writing pad. "Has he done anything to you?"

"No, but his behavior is menacing," she said. "Can't you arrest him?"

The police officer raised his eyebrows. "Ma'am, there's nothing we can do until a crime is committed. We'll patrol your street, but we need more to go on. Be careful, and have a good night."

Exasperated, she slammed the door. This was the second time the police had been dismissive of her. Or was she overreacting? But her intuition told her there was something truly ominous about the man. *How would she keep her family safe?*

The next morning, Danielle rose long before dawn, so anxious that she'd hardly slept. The first thing she did was look outside the window. The man who'd been watching her was no longer there.

Maybe the police picked him up for questioning. She'd be sure to warn Anna, who was coming to stay with her family, tell her to keep them inside all day and lock the door.

She had to calm down and gather her wits. Today was an important day; she was scheduled to launch her perfume line at Bullock's Wilshire department store.

Danielle loved working with people, but selling to a new store made her nervous. This opportunity had been hard won, but if her perfume sold well, she would receive compensation in time to remit her first loan payment to Clara.

I must finish the fashion collection I've been working on, too, she thought. Every day as Danielle rode the bus she propped a pad on her lap to sketch ideas, updated looks for clothes that she had made and worn in Europe. Marie had always had a marvelous sense of style; Danielle loved going with her to the couturiers in Paris for shows and fittings—and she had also created perfumes for several couturiers to sell with their seasonal lines. But Danielle had always preferred designing her own clothes; she took pride in wearing her creations.

Now, Danielle observed a new breed of women emerging— women who worked and bought their own clothes, who didn't have time, or the budget, for true couture. At Clara's, Danielle had helped women select the finest *prêt-à-porter* styles and fit them to their figures. These women liked the instant gratification of clothes that were ready to wear off the rack, and they spent lavish sums of money on their wardrobes. Actresses, heiresses, female professionals and entrepreneurs. They craved French style—the sublime, the glamorous, the unique. With the war under way, French couturiers and perfumers were struggling to survive, even shuttering their doors.

Danielle sensed a tremendous opportunity.

She borrowed more funds from Clara. With the money she bought dressmaker forms and fabric, and began creating samples. From sketches to pattern making, to cutting, draping, pinning, and sewing, she tried to do it all. Exhausted, she'd hired Anna's eldest daughter, a teenager who had excellent needlework skills, to help her with the workload.

She had shared fine techniques with Anna's daughter, instructing her on how to clip curved seams, how to cut fabric on the bias, and how to finish seams so that the inside of a garment was as smooth and finished as the outside.

Danielle couldn't afford to have a boutique, but she could take orders from stores and private clients with a sample collection. She'd shown a few sample pieces to Clara, and to Danielle's relief, Clara had placed a small initial order.

Today marked the beginning of another important retail relationship; she had to wear something with style. Frowning, she held up her black sheath dress. It had been worn so much the neckline had frayed. She clucked her tongue. This would never do.

Danielle grabbed a half-finished dress from a hook and rummaged through her sewing basket. She threaded a needle and bent over the ebony-colored garment, plucking steel pins from the slippery silk fabric and holding them between her lips as she quickly whip-stitched the final pattern pieces together.

"There, that should hold for today." Danielle bit the thread to snap it. She shimmied into the long-sleeved dress, which was nipped at the waist, straightened the seams on her hose, and turned to the mirror. A slow smile spread across her face. The stylish woman she had once been in Paris gazed back at her. *The right clothes have the power to transform.*

After Anna arrived, Danielle kissed her sleeping family. Jasmin had started to crawl, and Liliana liked her new school. But Marie was still a shadow of the self-assured woman she had been in Paris. And there had been no reports of Nicky. There was so much she had to do for her family.

A half hour later, Danielle stepped from the bus and swept inside, then rode the elevator to the executive offices. Her morning was jammed with meetings with the buyer, publicist, marketing director, and store manager. She shared her vision with them, her ideas for perfume, ready-to-wear, and accessories. Bullock's Wilshire had agreed to begin with the perfume line, and the buyer had made the terms quite clear: if the Bretancourt line didn't sell, it would be returned to her.

Later Danielle made her way to the first-floor cosmetics department, pausing to admire the soaring Art Deco architecture overhead, the finely detailed murals, the sparkling chandeliers. A tuxedoed pianist played at a black grand piano near the entrance. Nervously, she smoothed her hair, securing wayward tendrils.

She smiled through her fear, crossing to her appointed counter, where her product line was displayed against artfully draped scarlet satin. *Chimère, by Danielle Bretancourt.*

The cosmetics salesclerks greeted her laconically, and then returned to their gossip, spurning her efforts to engage them. Her mood sank. *What a difficult group.* Then she remembered what Jon had once said: *Where's your famous French courage?* Thinking about him gave her confidence. She stepped up to the perfume counter and introduced herself to the floor manager.

Several customers passed but ignored her. A stylish woman in a navy hat and fitted suit approached the counter.

"*Bonjour, madame.* Would you like to try a new French perfume today?"

The woman hesitated, sniffing the perfume, then admired the crystal flacons and satin brocade pouches. She glanced at Danielle, then back to the name on the display. Her face brightened. "Why, you're Danielle Bretancourt," she exclaimed. "I've read all about you in Hedda Hopper's column."

Danielle suppressed a laugh, recalling the scene at Clara's boutique. "Hedda Hopper adores my Chimère, too." Clara had been right about the press. "Louella Parsons also wears it," she added with a conspiratorial smile.

At the mention of the two Hollywood gossip queens, the salesclerks shifted their attention to Danielle.

The woman said, "I've heard all the movie stars wear it."

"*Oui, madame,*" Danielle said coyly. "Many do." She sprayed perfume in the air, creating a theater of scent. When the woman asked to try it, Danielle's mind raced. She remembered how Marie demonstrated the art of wearing perfume. "Allow me to help you discover the true heart of the perfume, *madame.*"

Danielle spritzed the fragrance on the back of the woman's hand with a flourish, and then placed her own hand over the spot, drawing strength from the connection. "The warmth of my hand brings out the true nature of the perfume. As it develops on your skin, it becomes unique to you."

"How fascinating," the woman said, smiling. "Tell me more."

This is my moment. Her heart pounding, she noticed the salesclerks were listening in rapt attention, too. "You see, a fine perfume usually passes through three phases, just as a symphony soars and glides through various movements. Yet, the phases are similar, like variations on a theme."

Danielle continued to hold the woman's hand, warming the perfume. "The initial phase, or opening accord, is evident on the first whiff from the flacon. It's designed to be enticing and engaging. In French, this is the *note de tête,* the head note.

"The floral heart," she went on, "or the *note de cœur,* develops within a few minutes, followed by the base accord, the *note de fond.* In this finale are found rich, long-lasting essential oils, including sandalwood, patchouli, and vanilla, which give the perfume staying power. These are superb fixatives. Naturally, the finer the oils, the longer perfume lasts on the skin, especially in perfume, or *parfum,* the richest, most concentrated version of fragrance." She removed her hand with a graceful flourish. "Try it, *madame*."

"Why, you're right, it's lovely."

The salesclerks were hovering with interest. One spoke up, her tone edged with sarcasm. "It sounds like perfume is related to music, what with all those notes and chords you're talking about. Are you sure you're in the right department?" A titter of laughter erupted.

Danielle swung around. *At last I have their attention,* she thought, *now I can teach them, help them learn.* "How perceptive of you. Years ago in France, in an attempt to bring order to the perfumer's art, a master perfumer created a system whereby every essence was assigned a note, based on a tonal scale of six and one half octaves. So yes, music and perfume are related," she finished, giving a dazzling smile.

A wave of murmured approvals swept across the crowd. "You really know what you're talking about," a saleswoman said.

The woman opened her purse. "Chimère is utterly magical. I simply must have it."

Excitement spiked the air. Danielle pushed on.

"*Merveilleux,*" she declared. "But for the most exquisite experience, you must use our perfumed soap and skin-softening bath oil for your *toilette*, then dust your skin with our silky talc, and finish with our *parfum, et voilà*. A cloud of fragrance, layers of sensual scent, will surround you. It will last all day and into the evening. But never, never will it be overpowering. *Mais non,* it will be subtle, in the French tradition. *Très chic.*"

The woman inhaled again, her eyelids fluttering. "I'll take one of everything. Put it on my house account."

Danielle wrapped her purchase. "*Merci, madame,* I'm sure you'll enjoy it."

After the woman left, Danielle turned to the salesclerks. "That's all there is to it," she said. "Show women how perfume can touch their deepest desires, teach them how to enjoy its artistry. Share the magic, the art of living well with them."

"But we can't present it like you do."

"I'll teach you the technique I demonstrated. Most of all, pamper your customers." She smiled warmly. "I believe in you, in your ability to make this a top-selling perfume. Here," she added, giving each of them a brochure. "This is my family story, of how the House of Bretancourt came to be. I wore an early version of Chimère on my wedding day; it was my husband's favorite perfume."

Whispers fluttered through the crowd. "Was he really a German aristocrat?"

Danielle's throat tightened at the thought of Max. "Yes, he was, God rest his soul. But like you, I'm an American now." And as the words left her lips, she realized for the first time that she truly felt like an American in her heart. It was a place to begin life anew, to prove her worth, to build her future. *And I will.*

She spent the rest of the day getting to know every salesclerk and assisting sales efforts, thrilled with their newfound enthusiasm.

After a quick mental calculation at the end of the day, she exhaled a breath of relief. She had just exceeded her goal for the day; she'd be able to pay Clara.

"So this is where you've disappeared to," a male voice said.

Danielle whirled around.

"Who're you hiding from, lass?" The handsome, dark-haired man lowered his sunglasses, and a wide grin spread across his face. Cameron Murphy looked every bit the glamorous star. He wore an evening suit that complemented his broad physique, complete with a sky blue silk ascot and diamond pinkie ring. Wavy black hair flowed from tanned temples, and his sparkling eyes were teasing.

"Cameron, what are you doing here?" Self-conscious, she smoothed her hair.

"Had a few things to pick up. Are you working here?"

"I launched my perfume line here today."

"Why, congratulations. Did you have a good day?"

Danielle grinned. "Thanks to you and Hedda Hopper." The gossip columnist had created quite a story about her and Cameron. It wasn't true, but people read the column, and publicity helped sales.

Cameron sniffed the air, glanced at the shimmering crystal bottles arranged on the counter. "Tell you what, I'll take ten of your largest perfumes. It's fine-smelling stuff, sure and it is. Real quality."

She laughed. "Really, Cameron, ten bottles?"

"You think I don't know ten beautiful ladies? Okay, here goes." He ticked off his fingers as he spoke. "Four sisters, my secretary, hairdresser, manicurist, a couple of waitresses, my housekeeper, and Silverman's secretary, Gladys, oops, I'm out of fingers, that's eleven. Give me a couple extra, say, thirteen, a baker's dozen."

"You're serious?" Danielle was amazed.

"Of course," he murmured. "Especially about you."

Danielle spun around, ecstatic. "Who can ring up Mr. Murphy?"

An impeccably attired, plump older woman stepped forward, surprisingly sprightly. "Aye, I will, ma'am." She smiled merrily, her cheeks like rosy apples. "I'm Mrs. Murphy."

"Sure, and I'm thinking we might be related," Cameron replied in a thick Irish brogue.

Just then, Danielle saw the same man who had been watching her lurking behind a display. When he saw her, he pulled his hat brim down and quickly turned away. A prickly sensation of fear crawled on the back of her neck.

She turned to the salesclerks. "Did anyone speak to that man?" she demanded.

One woman said, "I tried to, but he wasn't very friendly. He asked if you were here. Odd that he hasn't approached you."

"Did he give his name?"

She shook her head. "He had an accent, not like yours, but from Europe, I think."

Cameron turned to her, genuine concern on his face. "Which man is it, Danielle?"

She pointed to him, and Cameron strode off in his direction. *What's he going to do?* she thought, panicking. When the man saw Cameron, he hurried to the door. Cameron followed him out and grabbed him by the collar.

Danielle and the store clerks hurried to the entrance, where they could hear Cameron yelling. "And don't ever get near her again, or you'll have me to reckon with. You got that?" Cameron shoved him against the wall. Fumbling, the man picked himself up and rushed away.

When Cameron sauntered back inside, the clerks broke out in applause. "Why, it was like watching you at the movies," one of them said.

He grabbed Danielle by the waist. "Feel better now?"

"You were amazing," she said, relief surging through her. "Thank you. He's been following me, and the police haven't been able to do anything about it."

Cameron looked concerned. "What does he want with you, lass?"

"This is going to sound crazy, but I think he's been sent by my husband's cousin, Heinrich, who is an SS officer. He tried to kill me when I returned to Poland looking for Nicky. He threatened me, said he'd track me down." She paused. "He killed Sofia and Max."

"Leave it to me," he said gravely. "I've got friends on the force. I'll make some calls, and I'll make sure there's a squad car outside your home tonight, too."

"Could you? I'm always so worried about my mother and the girls."

"Let me take care of this for you." He hugged her. "You feel tense, you need to relax. Say, there's a party this evening at Lou Silverman's. Will you go with me?"

Danielle was startled at the invitation. Any other time it would have sounded like fun, but she wanted to return to her family. She also had to make dinner and balance her accounts. "I can't, I have work to do, Cameron."

"You need a break. Come on, no more work today. We'll call for Chinese take-out for the family, and then we'll head over to Silverman's party." He sidled close to her. "Come on, Dani," he whispered. "Say yes. I need a date tonight. Don't ruin my reputation in front of all these ladies," he said, feigning desperation. "Me very career depends on it, nay, I daresay, me very life."

She suppressed a smile. "You're impossible. And my name is Danielle." But then, how could she argue with him? After all, he had scared off the man who had been following her, *and* made her first day at Bullock's a resounding success. "All right, as long as my sitter can stay."

"Hallelujah, Dani!" he cried, ignoring her correction. By now, he had drawn a crowd, and the salesclerks applauded his shenanigans. "Put an extra bottle on there for yourself, Mrs. Murphy. You're the tops, you are." He signed the sales slip, hooked his arm in Danielle's, and marched her out the front door before she could change her mind.

Once outside, Danielle exploded into gales of laughter, releasing pent-up fear and anxiety, shaking from the adrenaline flooding her body. She couldn't remember the last time she had laughed so hard. *Was the man gone for good?* She didn't know, but at least tonight she was safe with Cameron.

"Here's my car." An attendant pulled a white convertible Rolls-Royce to the curb.

"Oh no, you can't drive this into my neighborhood." *This is crazy.* But she was glad to have a ride home.

"No one says no to Cameron Murphy, my dear Dani. Didn't you know that?" She slid in, admiring her unexpected surroundings. The burl wood dash and chrome dials gleamed in the sunlight, and the leather seats were smooth and supple beneath her touch.

Cameron tipped the attendant and hopped into the car. "Lead the way," he said, putting on his dark sunglasses.

She gave him directions and he turned onto Wilshire Boulevard. "Cameron, thank you for what you did back there."

"My pleasure, Dani. I'm really happy you're coming with me tonight. My ex-wife, Erica, is going to be there with her new boyfriend. Silverman expects me to be there, but I didn't want to go alone. And Silverman likes you." A twinkle came to his eyes. "Know what he calls you?"

"What, a poor waif?"

He laughed. "'A woman of quality,' that's what he says to me at Clara's fashion show. 'With a capital "Q,"' indeed he did."

Danielle was secretly pleased. And she was certain the store would be buzzing tomorrow with Cameron Murphy's purchase and their exit together. Fourteen one-ounce bottles of her best perfume. *Why, the money he must have.*

"You'll love it, Dani, Hollywood style, silver screen gowns, glitter galore." He glanced at her, a worried look crossing his face. "Ah, I'm an idiot, maybe you don't have—"

"I happen to have a few dresses." A smile curved on her lips. "I don't think you'll be disappointed."

23

Perfumers owe a debt to the civet cat, the musk deer, the beaver, and the sperm whale. Their secretions are pervasive, repugnant, but in the company of flowers, erotic. To achieve their superb fixative qualities, modern chemistry replicates these ancient ingredients from the animal kingdom.

—DB

1 NOVEMBER, 1940 — LOS ANGELES, CALIFORNIA

Cameron squinted out the window. "This is a tough neighborhood. Are we getting close?"

"We're almost there," Danielle answered quietly, watching him from the corner of her eye. "I warned you." She pointed to her building. "You can park in front."

He eased the Rolls-Royce into a space in front of the Bradley Arms apartment building. "Sorry, Dani, I just didn't picture you living here."

Her face grew warm in embarrassment. "Well," she began, looking up at the dingy building, "the price is right."

Danielle led him up the rickety stairs and through the grimy, malodorous hallway. A child's scream pierced the dark, and scratchy strains of a worn Benny Goodman record sounded from another room. *I shouldn't have brought him here.* Danielle stopped at her door, shame growing in her, not for the way she lived, but for the way she felt about it. *But I'm earning my way and taking care of my family.*

"Here's your last chance, Cameron. I wouldn't blame you if you left now. I'd understand." She bent her head, searching for her key.

"No, Dani, I'm here to stay, that I am." He gave her a quick grin. "Truth be known, lassie, this neighborhood is a far better place than the one I was born into back in the stinking slums of Dublin. I know you're doing the best you can. You have guts, Dani. Real courage. I admire that about you."

Danielle brought the key from her purse and held it up. "This is your final warning. You're about to meet the family."

When Danielle opened the door, she was shocked at the sight before her, a scene of such normalcy, such domesticity, that she almost cried out. Their tiny quarters sparkled, and Marie stood over the hot plate stirring what smelled like beef stew. Liliana was playing quietly in a corner, scrubbed and happy, with a pink ribbon in her hair. Jasmin was fast asleep; their neighbor, Anna, was napping in a chair.

For the first time since their arrival in America, Marie seemed normal. She had even applied makeup and arranged her hair in an upswept style.

Danielle recovered and performed the introductions. Marie was gracious and Liliana was a perfect angel. And they had no idea that Cameron was a celebrity.

"I'll make that arrangement while you're changing," he said to her. The call to his friend on the police force. She smiled at him and excused herself.

In the cramped confines of the dimly lit dressing area, Danielle turned her attention to her meager wardrobe. She'd learned that a well-fitted black dress could take her anywhere. But tonight she needed something spectacular. On a dressmaker form hung a sample dress for her new clothing line. She removed it and lifted it over her head, the golden satin slithering over her slim hips. The dress suited her well, skimming her frame and flaring dramatically. Delicate bronze embroidery trimmed the neckline, which draped across her collarbone. The dress plunged to her waist in the back.

Danielle had obtained a trunk full of clothing after cleaning storerooms for the owner of a thrift shop in the neighborhood. The fine-quality fabric had attracted her, so she redesigned several dresses. With funds running low, she'd also bartered perfume for several new bolts of fabric from a factory downtown, and experimented with combining new fabric with vintage accents.

Danielle ran her hands across the dress, adjusting it. *I wish Jon could see this.*

She brushed her hair, then pinned it back from her face. She had sold all their jewelry, so her ears and neck and wrists and fingers were bare. The effect was one of elegant simplicity. She looked in the mirror, heartened.

"I'm ready," she said, emerging from the dressing area.

Cameron was momentarily speechless. "Why, you're gorgeous."

Danielle kissed her family good-bye, marveling at Marie's miraculous turn, though she had grown accustomed to her mother's behavioral shifts. "I won't be late, Maman."

"It's all right, dear, you're in good hands with Jean-Claude." Marie smiled sweetly and a vague light shone in her eyes.

Danielle's heart sank.

"Who's Jean-Claude?" Cameron asked as they descended the staircase.

"My brother," Danielle replied curtly.

Cameron stopped, obviously confused. "But, isn't he . . ." His voice trailed off.

"Dead? Yes." Danielle grabbed the handrail for support. "My mother gets confused. That's why Anna is there to help."

They reached the bottom of the stairs and Cameron said, "For the record, I think you're doing one heck of a job." He kissed her forehead, and as he did, a smooth, woody scent of vetiver drew her in. She detected tonka bean and the sensual, animal aroma of civet. Guerlain's, she noted absentmindedly. *Jicky.* One of her favorites. He wore it well. *But he's not Jon,* she thought wistfully.

He pulled back from her. "In this light you look so much like me mum, like an old photograph of her before she married." His gaze fixed on a point beyond her. "Back when the bloom of youth was still fresh in her face, before the angry hands of me dad battered her cheekbones and broke her nose. Before he beat her to death one night." He blinked and shook his head, as though expunging the memory. "Yeah, she was a beauty then."

Stricken by his story, Danielle touched his face. "Cameron, I'm so sorry."

"Let's go, we're late as it is." As they pulled away, a police car pulled up, and an officer waved at Cameron.

Incredible, she thought. *How many times have I asked for help?*

The sun was setting in the western sky, casting a burnished brilliance over the horizon, like a shimmering scarlet cloth flung high across the cityscape. Cameron turned north on Beverly Drive into a neighborhood of mansions. They cruised the palm tree–lined road across Sunset Boulevard, and past the pink stucco Beverly Hills Hotel. The road curved beyond Pickfair, the estate of Mary Pickford and Douglas Fairbanks, as they climbed higher into the sunset-glazed hills.

There, perched on a promontory point overlooking the sprawling city, sat Lou Silverman's magnificent estate, a shimmering white vision veiled in the sun's crimson iridescence.

A pair of wrought iron filigree gates swung open. A guard waved them in after recognizing Cameron. Towering Italian cypress trees lined the drive, and the vista widened to reveal a sprawling Spanish-Mediterranean estate. A red-tiled roof, flaming pink bougainvillea, and royal blue tile punctuated the white stucco expanse. A pair of tennis courts and several cabanas dotted the landscape.

On the lawn, flowers bloomed in profusion, and trees heaved beneath the weight of oranges, lemons, and grapefruit. Danielle breathed in the scents of citrus, lilies, and honeysuckle—they reminded her of Bellerose.

Never had she seen such a magnificent estate in Los Angeles, so beautifully kept, so palatial. *Someday,* she thought, *maybe we'll live like this, Marie and the girls; we could have a garden, and Nicky could have a dog.* The harder she worked, the more her vision expanded. It was America, after all, the land of opportunity.

They stepped from the car and blinding white camera flashes popped in their faces. Cameron donned his famous grin and struck a well-practiced pose for a cadre of photographers. Danielle tried to remain poised, but the attention was nearly overwhelming. *So this is his world.*

A formally clad butler greeted them at the front door. The sound of an orchestra playing lively big band tunes filled the air.

Instantly, Danielle regretted her decision to accompany Cameron. There were so many people. And so many aromas jostling in her nose. Smoke, perfumes, cocktails, flowers, food. She spotted Cary Grant ahead of them, smelling of sandalwood. Near the bar was Ginger Rogers, in a white satin bias-cut gown that shimmered against her suntan, chatting with Charles Boyer, smartly attired in an ebony tuxedo. Danny Thomas waved to Cameron; Myrna Loy, wearing a sleek one-shoulder crimson gown and laced with rubies, kissed him on the cheek as they passed, while a young starlet drenched in Shalimar winked at him. From the dance floor, scents of civet, musk, and patchouli swirled in sensual rhythm.

"Relax," Cameron shouted above the din. "This is supposed to be fun."

"I haven't been to a social event in a long time, Cameron, not since, not since Max . . ." Her voice trailed off and she began to feel faint.

"Oh God, Dani, I didn't realize." Cameron pulled her into an alcove and hugged her tightly. "Tell you what, let's say hello to Mr. Silverman, and then we'll go. All I need to do is put in an appearance."

Danielle drew a breath to steady her nerves. "We can stay." She rested her head against his shoulder. He felt solid, reassuring. As Max had been. And Jon. She missed being with someone who cared about her well-being.

"There's the spirit. You know what they say about all work and no play." He glanced toward the rear door. "The patio isn't as crowded."

Cameron steered her outside, where a canopy of stars twinkled above the hills, and flickering silver candelabras illuminated dark corners like a Baroque theater set.

Danielle raised her nose to the air, drinking in the cool night air, detecting herbal aromas of lavender and rosemary.

"Stay here," he said, "I'll get drinks. Champagne okay?"

Danielle nodded. He *was* nice. As soon as he left her side, Danielle saw Hedda Hopper sailing toward her, iridescent peacock plumes bobbing from her hat. "Danielle, can you guess what I'm wearing?" She held out a wrist, and without waiting for an answer, she cooed, "Chimère, darling. What else?"

Danielle was glad to see her. "You must know everyone here, Hedda, but I hardly know a soul."

Hedda leaned close to her. "See that dark-haired woman standing near Lou Silverman? That's Erica Evans, Cameron's ex-wife."

Danielle followed her gaze to a beautiful woman attired in a slinky red evening dress that enhanced her voluptuous figure. "She looks Latin."

"She's from Mexico." Hedda arched a brow. "I happen to know her mother still works as a domestic there, cleaning houses."

A person did what they had to do, she'd learned. "How did Erica become an actress?"

"She ran away from home at fourteen, crossed the border at San Diego, and started singing in nightclubs. There she met an agent who changed her life. Juanita Juarez became Erica Evans, and after a nose job, two years of elocution and acting lessons, she landed her first movie role."

"She must have worked very hard."

Hedda gave a hearty chuckle. "On her back, some would say. You know, you should watch Cam around Erica." She kissed Danielle on the cheek. "Ta-ta, dearie, I must dash."

The party reached a fever pitch and Abigail stood next to Lou Silverman as he scanned the crowd. Lou's brightest star, Erica Evans, stood with them, the center of attention.

"Lou, I've been making the same plea for weeks now for you to help these orphaned children," Abigail said, drawing his attention away from the party scene.

Lou Silverman leaned against the railing. "Abigail, your energy and passion are a sight to behold."

At that moment, a director stopped to speak to Lou, diverting his attention.

Abigail watched Lou. She could imagine a man like this in her life, entertaining with him, strolling the terraced grounds with him, waking in bed with him. *What would it be like?* No, not a man *like* him. She thrilled to the sound of Lou's deep voice, the casual brush of his hand. If only she could give him what he had told her that he really wanted. *Children, a family.* She'd tried to deny her growing attraction to him, but the best she could do was to conceal her feelings from him. *Life simply wasn't fair.*

Lou adjusted the pristine white tie of his tuxedo and turned back to Abigail. "Now, what were you saying?"

Abigail gathered her thoughts. "You know all about the special benefit to introduce my new children's rescue program, but you have yet to accept or decline."

"Tell me again, Abigail. You have my full attention now."

Abigail plunged ahead, relating how she had spoken to Mrs. Roosevelt, the First Lady. She found herself chattering on out of nervousness, but she also enjoyed his undivided attention.

Erica interrupted. "Look, there's Cameron. Who's the woman with him?" she asked, envy oozing from her words.

Danielle watched Cameron return to her, bearing two flutes of champagne. He handed one to her, clinking her glass. "To the future. May your tomorrow be as bright as your eyes."

"Merci," she said, sipping. It was a fine French vintage.

"Feeling better?" Cameron asked, smiling.

Danielle nodded. She had to admit, the champagne was nice. She felt safe with him; in fact, she hadn't felt like this in ages.

"Let's celebrate your success tonight, Dani. I was mighty impressed with your debut today. I'm going to tell everyone I know about it. Ready to circulate?" He crooked his arm for her, and she slipped her hand through, resting it on his arm.

She smiled; Cameron was right. It was such a glamorous evening, just the thing to commemorate her accomplishment today, and the first time she'd celebrated anything in a long, long time.

"Why, Danielle, what a nice surprise to see you out." Abigail kissed Danielle on the cheek.

They spoke briefly, then Abigail said, "Did you hear that Jon is getting married?"

Had Danielle heard her correctly? *No, there must be a mistake,* she thought frantically. She tried to say something, to tell Abigail that she must be wrong, but when she opened her mouth she found that she couldn't get her words out.

Cameron grinned. "So he finally got the girl, huh?"

"Someone has to carry on the family line, you know." A shadow flashed across Abigail's face. "Cameron, you must remember Victoria."

Danielle fought to mask her devastation. "Strange," she managed to say, "Jon never mentioned her in his letters." *How could he do this without telling me? I told him I loved him.* She *had* rebuffed his offer, she admitted, but she had no idea he'd ask another woman to marry him. *But he's a man, a very handsome man, and—*

"Oh?" Abigail said. "He writes to you, does he? Well, I suppose he mightn't have mentioned it. It's just been assumed for years and years. They've always been promised or whatever. It's the way our families do things in England. Victoria wrote me about it, and Mother says it's all arranged."

"Well, give him my best." Danielle hoped she didn't sound as heartsick as she felt. *Why hadn't Jon told her?* Danielle hadn't confided in Abigail, because she was still presumed to be in mourning over Max.

Cameron draped his arm across Danielle's shoulders. "I'm glad Jon's love life is settled. Say hello to Mr. Silverman, Danielle."

She turned to Lou and found her voice. "Good evening, this is quite a party. Thank you for having us."

Lou nodded politely to Danielle. "Glad you're both here." He turned to Cameron, scrutinizing him. "You taking care of yourself?"

"Yes, sir, behaving myself, too, if that's what you mean."

"Good. Erica is still quite sold on you."

Erica cut in, her mouth set in a sensual pout. "Aren't you going to greet the guest of honor?"

Cameron laughed. "Of course I am, my Latin lassie. You're gorgeous tonight, Erica. But then, you always are." He bent to kiss her on the cheek.

Erica turned her cheek and caught him full on the lips. "For old times' sake, *mi amore*," she said seductively.

"Nice that you're on such good terms," Abigail observed wryly. "Most divorced couples hardly speak to one another."

Erica threw a wicked glance over her shoulder. "Why let a divorce ruin a perfectly good relationship?"

Cameron coughed. "You're in rare form tonight, Erica. But as I recall, you were the one who packed your bags and left."

Erica cast his words aside with a wave of her ruby-jeweled hand. "Details, details." Her gaze rested squarely on Danielle. "Who's the girl in the golden gown?"

Cameron introduced them. "I ran into Danielle today working at Bullock's Wilshire."

"Oh, a shop girl." Erica narrowed her eyes. "Nice dress. You should have borrowed jewelry, too."

"Sparkling eyes are more tantalizing than glittering stones," Danielle retorted with a smile. She'd just been kicked by Jon, she wasn't about to let a stranger do it, too.

Erica ignored her remark, but Cameron smothered a chuckle.

Lou spoke up. "As I recall, Danielle, the last time we met you were just starting your perfume company. Now I read about you all the time in Hedda's column." He turned to Cameron. "Danielle is a special lady. Take care of her."

"You needn't worry," Danielle said, still burning from Jon's dismissal. "He does."

"Really?" Erica flipped her jet black mane over her bare shoulder, the rich scent of Joy, bursting with jasmine and rose, emanating from her skin. "Just *how* good, Cam?"

"That's enough, Erica." Lou caught her arm.

Abigail cut in. "What a beautiful evening dress, Danielle, the color is magnificent with your hair. Where on earth did you find it? At Clara's?"

"No, it's one of my new designs."

"I love it, I've never seen anything like it. Let me see the back of it."

Danielle executed a graceful turn, the fluid satin rippling in golden waves about her legs, smiling through her disappointment over Jon. "We're already planning the first House of Bretancourt trunk show at Clara's. The focus is on enhancing a woman's natural figure, and combining sumptuous new fabrics with vintage accents."

"Erica, you'd look lovely in something like this," Cameron said.

Danielle imagined that Erica would rather rip the gown off her, but since Lou still had her firmly by the arm, Erica arranged a pleasant look on her face instead.

"Naturally, I'd love to attend," Erica gushed, her words dripping venom. "I always enjoy meeting new *dressmakers*."

"Danielle is much more than a dressmaker," Abigail said. "She could be the next great designer, like Chanel or Patou. Look at how successful her perfume line has become."

"I'll be sure to send you an invitation, Erica. You should bring your boyfriend, too," Danielle said, "so he can choose some dresses for you. Is he here tonight?"

Erica ignored her, and Danielle saw Cameron actually blush a little. *So, he lied to me about her having a new boyfriend,* she thought. *I wonder why?*

Then Danielle remembered that Lou had scouted designs at Clara's fashion show. "Mr. Silverman, I'd love to create special evening dresses and costumes for the studio," she added, filling the awkward silence.

"We have our own designers, but we also use stars from the world of couture."

"I assure you my designs are star-worthy. May I call tomorrow to discuss costuming for Erica's new movie?"

Erica looked like she wanted to scratch out Danielle's eyes.

A grin tugged at Lou's mouth. "Why not, we're always looking for new talent."

"I'll call first thing in the morning," Danielle replied. *And to hell with Jon,* she thought, though inside she was devastated.

When Lou left them to visit other guests, Abigail turned to Danielle. "Come with me to freshen up." They started off through the crowd, leaving Erica and Cameron alone.

Cameron glared at Erica. "What was all that about?"

"I don't know what you mean," she said, tossing her hair over her shoulder.

"You're such a bitch," he hissed as he grabbed her wrist and twisted it. "*Shop girl?* I'm glad Danielle gave it right back to you."

Erica grimaced. "Take your hands off me, Cameron Murphy. I'm *not* your wife, you can't pound me into submission anymore. Let go, what will everyone think?"

Cameron jerked on her wrist again, pulling her closer. "They'll think we're getting along just fine now."

"Not when I slap your face, you bastard," she hissed. A smile curved her full red lips.

He released her, shoving her away. "Stop being so dramatic, Erica. The cameras aren't rolling."

Erica stumbled, caught herself from falling. "And they won't ever roll for you again in this town unless you're nice to me." She rubbed her wrist. "I'm the only one who can save you."

Cameron spun on his heel to leave and saw Danielle motioning to him across the room.

Grinning broadly, he made his way to Danielle. "I've had enough of the party," Cameron said, making a face, "and enough of Erica. Let's get out of here."

"I don't think Erica has had enough of you, though," she said softly. "I think she's still in love with you."

He made no reply, steering her through the crowd and out the door.

They got into the Rolls-Royce and Cameron maneuvered through the gates and started down the hill. Before long, he pulled to the side of the road and turned off the engine. City lights sparkled beneath them, and to the west, the black velvet ocean stretched into infinity.

The night was still, the autumn breeze cool. Cameron slid his arm around Danielle. "I want you to understand, Dani. Erica and I loved one another very much. But we were like oil and water. Between my Irish temper and her Latin temper, it was pure combustion. Our marriage was like a prizefight—not at all like the relationship you and Max had."

"Don't think our marriage was perfect. Every relationship requires compromise. Do you mind if I ask why Erica left you?"

"Aye, that she did, and with good reason. I was wild in my younger days. Hollywood can be very alluring, Dani, but it's not real. Not like you." His hand rested on her bare skin, his fingers nestled in the small of her back. "I've tried to change, though not many people realize it."

Danielle stole a glance at Cameron, who looked like a little boy who needed to be loved. Her heart tightened as for a fleeting moment she thought of Nicky, and all her loved ones now lost to her. "Have you really changed, Cameron?"

"Sure an' I've changed. I've learned my lessons. I want to settle down, be a family man, work regularly."

"You? A family man?" She laughed. "I'm sorry, I just don't see that, Cameron."

"It's true, Dani. Sure, I'm a fun-loving guy. I think you like that about me." He tapped her nose. "I can make you laugh. But deep inside a man needs the love of a good woman. And I'll keep you safe; you'll never have to worry about protection with me around."

Cameron enfolded her in his arms. She was acutely aware of his hands on her skin. His touch was gentle and she closed her eyes, enjoying the warmth of his body and the sureness of his embrace and the effect of the champagne.

She missed the touch of a man. She ached for Jon, but knew now that their relationship would never be. Cameron's hand began to move, almost imperceptibly at first, caressing the nape of her neck, tracing her spine to the small of her back. Danielle quivered in his arms. *Just a moment more.* She could feel his muscles tighten under his shirt as she pressed her fingertips into his back.

"Oh, Dani," he whispered hoarsely. "I've longed for you from the minute I met you."

Though tempted, she pulled back. "We really mustn't."

Cameron laid his head on her chest, and she could feel the quickening of his heart. His hand brushed against her breast as he lifted his head. She stiffened under his touch. "Don't be afraid of me, Dani. I'll be gentle."

She relaxed against him, needing his reassurance, pushing away thoughts of Max, and Jon and his marriage. Cameron was here for her now.

"This is perfection," he murmured. "Utter heaven, with you in my arms. I adore you."

Danielle tilted her face to his. "Cameron, we should probably leave before . . ."

"Before what, before we both do something we'll enjoy?" Cameron brushed his lips against her face, his body tensing.

A warm, musky scent rose from his skin, and as Danielle breathed it in, her body naturally responded. Tonight, she needed comfort—comfort from the shock of Jon's marriage, comfort from a year of grief, comfort from the worry that she woke with every day for Nicky and Marie. Her lips found his and they kissed, tentatively at first, then with increasing fervor.

Cameron shifted from her lips to her neck, to her décolletage, and then paused. He framed her face in his hands and gazed into her eyes. "There's no turning back now, Dani."

Danielle averted her eyes. As she did, Cameron turned the key in the ignition. When the engine roared to life, Danielle knew Cameron wasn't taking her home, and her natural sense of propriety emerged. *Should I?* She glanced at him, considering.

After a short drive to Cameron's home in the flats of Beverly Hills, he guided her through the massive front door of his two-story brick Tudor-style home. He paused in the foyer, kissing her forehead, her eyelids, her cheeks, then finding her mouth, softly teasing and tantalizing with his tongue, taking his time. "Are you ready?" he whispered.

Danielle's heart beat wildly, and she gave in to Cameron's touch as their desire flamed. *Just for tonight,* she decided, relishing his touch. *No one has to know.* In truth, it was Jon she yearned for, but he had devastated her world, just when she had opened herself up to love again. *How could he have done such a thing?* she wondered, an ache growing in her chest. Cameron would soothe the wounds of her soul.

Then, in one swift motion, Cameron lifted her in his arms and carried her upstairs to his bedroom.

24

The poppy flower: A flower of eternal sleep, a narcotic to the wounded soul, a remembrance of the fallen soldier.

—DB

5 NOVEMBER, 1940 — LOS ANGELES, CALIFORNIA

"This dress is perfect for Erica Evans." Danielle swirled a crimson red dress around, her nerves fluttering along with it. The neckline dipped to a low V in front, and an even lower V in the back.

Lou Silverman leaned back in his chair at his desk, his hands steepled, the city view behind him. "Knowing Erica, she'd want the neckline even lower." He waved a hand to the rack Danielle had wheeled in, the clothes forming a Technicolor rainbow. "These samples speak for themselves. But can you produce to a deadline?"

"Of course, I have a dedicated staff." Danielle swallowed hard, and thought about Anna's teenage daughter, who had friends who sewed, and then there was Esmeralda at Clara's, who'd promised to help and bring in her friends, too, if needed. Danielle had used money from Clara's loan to rent another room in the Bradley Arms building on a week-to-week basis to store supplies, house her samples, and have space to work on her perfume and fashion projects. "No problem whatsoever," she added confidently. *Though it won't be easy.*

Lou rubbed his chin in thought. "I need costuming for *The Spanish Heiress*, Erica's new film. She's intimidated every designer we have on staff. Would you be up for the task?"

"Absolutely. I can start immediately."

"I admire your ambition, Danielle," he said. A grin spread across his face. "Come in tomorrow, nine o'clock, to begin. You'll meet with the director and his team, discuss his vision." Lou stood, signaling the end of the meeting. He strode to the door. "Need help with the rack?"

"Thank you," she said, barely able to conceal her excitement. "I can manage."

He opened the door for her, and then inclined his head. "By the way, do you make bespoke perfume?"

"I do."

A smile flitted across Lou's powerful face, and his steely blue eyes softened. "I'd like to surprise Abigail. Any idea what she likes?"

"She loves to grow roses and lilies." Danielle hadn't realized they had such a personal relationship. Or did they yet?

"Yes, that would suit her well."

After Danielle left Lou's office, she wheeled her sample rack into the elevator, and called a taxi from the lobby. She recalled how Lou and Abigail had looked at each other at the party. Now that she thought about it, the attraction was obvious.

She was elated to have the business, but she was nervous about production. Rapid growth was difficult to manage, because companies paid after products were delivered. In the case of retailers, it could be sixty or ninety days after the products were sold. She needed more funds faster to pay for supplies and inventory. It was an endless cycle. Would she ever get ahead?

15 NOVEMBER, 1940 — LOS ANGELES, CALIFORNIA

"Love me?" Cameron leaned against the doorjamb of her apartment and trailed his fingers along Danielle's neck, tickling her ears, tapping her nose. His famous grin lit his eyes, losing nothing in translation from the silver screen.

"This is terrible, how can you *do* this to me?" Danielle said, trying her best to admonish him, but failing. She laughed, relaxing in his arms.

After their intimate evening together after Lou's party, he'd sent her a diamond bracelet, but she'd promptly returned it to him. Today he'd arrived with a new dress and hat for Marie, a stuffed teddy bear and books for Liliana, and a new crib for Jasmin.

"Teddy!" Liliana screamed with delight, hugging the bear. "Books!" She fell to her knees, stroking the book covers with awe, as if they were made of gold.

Danielle's heart gave way—it was the first true happiness she'd seen on her niece's face in months. Even Marie's face was wreathed with smiles. She was adjusting her new hat in front of the mirror. Danielle sighed. How could she deny her family?

"Love me," he said again, and this time it wasn't a question, but a command, accompanied by a single red rose he plucked from his lapel.

Danielle accepted his offering, sniffing the flower out of habit. *Love him?* It was hard *not* to love his attention, his spontaneity, his infectious enthusiasm—and all the perks that came with being with a star. Wherever they went they received preferential treatment, and she met scores of celebrities and columnists curious about her perfume and fashion lines.

He kissed her deeply, and she felt the heat flaring within her. How long had it been since she'd felt this way? She was grieving for Max, aching for Jon, but the fates had intervened. Cameron was here for her, his arms tightening around her, offering himself to her, and, more important, offering his generosity to her family.

Should she be a fool?

"Have dinner with me tonight," he said urgently, framing her face in his broad hands. "I'm starting work on a new film next week, so I won't have much time for a while."

Danielle kissed him on the cheek. "I'll ask Anna if she can come over."

"And stay late," he murmured seductively in her ear.

Cameron had just left Danielle at her apartment and he was wide awake, although the sun wouldn't be up for hours. Craving the crisp night air, he had put the top down on his convertible. He loosened his collar and unbuttoned a couple of buttons on his starched white shirt.

Neon lights blinked comfortingly in the night. He liked cruising the nighttime streets of Los Angeles—the domain of runaways, grifters, pimps, and prostitutes. The kind of real people he'd grown up with.

He'd loved only one woman in his life—Erica, who shared his ignoble background—even though their explosive fights were Hollywood legend. He hated to admit it, but he was falling for Danielle. She was real wife material, and that scared the hell out of him.

Sure, he'd had plenty of experience with wives—someone else's, that is. He grinned at the thought. Lots of wives pursued him, but he preferred the challenge of seducing faithful wives against their best intentions. And the more high-born, the better. He thought of Jon's classy girlfriend back in England. Aristocratic, sure, but Victoria loved a good romp, too. He chuckled as he recalled their love-making. He liked nothing more than putting one over on Jon, a member of the lucky sperm club.

Was that why he wanted Danielle? In London, he'd watched the way Jon looked at her. If it weren't for Max, Jon would've made a move for Danielle. And now, with Max out of the way . . .

No, that wasn't it. Although he took pleasure in beating Jon whenever he could.

Lou Silverman thought highly of Danielle, too. A relationship with her might improve Cameron's career. Lou also had a good eye for women, although Abigail had never been his type. It would've been like sleeping with his sister, which was about the only class of women safe from his seduction.

He'd been with hundreds of women in his life. *And why not?* It wasn't as if any of them denied him. But Danielle was driving him to madness. He slowed to a stop at a red light, tapping the steering wheel in frustration.

Danielle had incandescent eyes that any silent screen actress would've killed for. She had a lyrical accent and slender, graceful hands that were so expressive when she spoke. She was sheer determination . . . and pure poetry in bed. She was a drug he couldn't seem to get enough of. It was a love high, and he needed his highs to feel alive. But if she *really* knew what he was about, she wouldn't have anything to do with him. Like Erica. Her rejection had nearly killed him.

He blew out a breath. He needed a drink. Or, God help him, something stronger.

Cameron wheeled a U-turn against the red light and sped downtown.

20 NOVEMBER, 1940 — LOS ANGELES, CALIFORNIA

"So where the hell is Cameron Murphy?" Lou Silverman barked into the phone on his desk.

"I don't know," Erica replied, her voice wavering across the wire. "But I'll find him."

"We were to have met at ten o'clock Monday morning. It's already

Wednesday. If this is any indication of his future behavior, I can't use Cameron in your picture."

"Please, Lou, give me twenty-four hours. I'll find him, and I swear to you, he'll never pull this stunt again. I'll stake my own salary on it, Lou."

"Hate to see you do that, Erica. But you're absolutely right, he'll never do this again, because if he does, he's finished, not just with me, but with every major studio. I'm doing you a favor now as it is." Lou paused, lowering his voice. "Don't let me down, Erica, or it's your contract we'll be discussing next."

"Once production begins," Erica said, sounding repentant, "I'll see to it personally that Cameron is on set every morning."

"You do that. Now find him."

Erica hung up the phone and quickly dialed another number. A man answered in Cantonese. "Sammy, it's Erica. I'm looking for Cameron."

"No, Cameron not here. Sorry."

"Wait, Sammy, don't hang up. Has he been there?"

The line was quiet for several seconds.

"Okay. He been here. Yesterday. You too late, Miss Erica."

"Do you know where he went?"

"I can't say on phone."

"I'll come there then. And don't run away," she hissed, "or I'll tell the police what I know." She slammed the phone down, her anger blazing.

Erica snatched her car keys and jumped into her Duesenberg roadster. Racing through town, tires screeching, she made it to Chinatown in twenty minutes. She slammed on the brakes in front of a dilapidated house with boarded windows. She ran to the rear of the house in her stiletto heels, and banged on the door.

The door swung open and a slight man cowered before her. She angled her fists on her hips and glared at him. "Where is he?"

"I write it down, okay?" Sammy scribbled an address on a scrap of paper. "Don't tell anyone I tell you. Very bad for me."

"Bad *joss*, huh?" Erica stormed out, cursing in Spanish. She scowled at the paper, immediately recognizing the address. Her shoulders slumped in dismay. *Damn Cameron a thousand times to hell.*

She didn't have far to go. Her next stop was in a grimy downtown industrial area near the railroad tracks. She parked, pounded on the door, and waited. No answer.

Looking from side to side, she tried the door. It was open. She stepped inside.

The air was sickly sweet and dense with smoke. She sniffed the air. Opium. She tiptoed through the hazy corridor until she reached a stained drapery. Shoving it aside, she let her eyes adjust to the darkness.

The putrid odor of human waste assaulted her nose. Her eyes burned from the malodorous mixture of smoke and stench. Blinking hard, she wiped her eyes, smearing her mascara, and pressed her white chiffon scarf over her nose and mouth to keep from gagging. Tattered cots lined the wall, but only one held a body.

A low moan emanated from the deathly white lips of the motionless figure. The man was clad in wrinkled pants, his chest bare, his hair matted. *Cameron.* Just like old times.

She hurried across the room. "Cameron, get up. Time to go," she whispered hoarsely. She rolled him over, and his head lolled listlessly off the bed. Startled, she pressed her fingers to his throat, found a faint pulse, and breathed a small sigh.

Hooking her arms under his, she heaved him off the bed and dragged him across the room. Erica was a tall woman with strength in her well-developed arms and shoulders, and she knew how to leverage her body. She had done this before.

Erica dragged him through the hallway and out the door. She propped him against the building and ran to the Duesenberg. Pulling the car onto the sidewalk, she pushed him into the passenger side and slammed the door.

In her rearview mirror, she could see two men running from the exit, shouting about money and shaking their fists.

Perspiration seeped through her hair and her silk blouse. She floored the accelerator.

A half hour later, ensconced in her Bel Air mansion, Erica gave her domestic staff the rest of the week off with pay. No telling who might wag their tongue to a tabloid newspaper.

When the help had gone, she dragged Cameron onto the rear porch and dropped him onto a lawn chaise.

When he regained consciousness, she screamed at him, "Don't ever do this to me again, or so help me, I'll kill you."

Several days later, Erica sat in her spacious, sun-drenched kitchen and stared at a cup of coffee, as upstairs Cameron dressed for his meeting with Lou Silverman. Erica had covered for Cameron during the horrible, gut-wrenching days it took for the opium to exit his system. He might have been the love of her life, but he put her through hell.

Yet on a good day, no one was more fun than Cameron Murphy. When he took her shopping for a new dress, he couldn't buy just one. Instead, he'd purchase a dozen dresses, with accessories to match, showering her with generosity. People flocked around him. His extravagance was legendary.

But so were his indiscretions. Erica gulped her coffee. They'd been thrown out of the finest hotels around the world for their violent arguments. She rubbed her thumb along the line of her jaw where Cameron had punched her one evening, shattering the bone. She'd confronted him, screaming, and biting his ear. They were on location, and production had stopped on the film. Of course, Lou had been livid.

Her makeup artist always managed to cover the scars left on her body by Cameron, but even now her left side was seldom filmed up close.

Cameron had soaring, jubilant heights one day, then black, bottomless depressions the next. She'd lived with the constant fear that he'd die of an overdose, or in an automobile accident, or that he'd be shot by a lover's husband. In the end, Erica was exhausted.

Even though she'd divorced him, she still dreamed he'd break free of his demons and return.

When Cameron's manager, Harry Nelson, told her that Cameron was broke, she had insisted that Cameron be given a part in her new movie. "He's just a drunken saloon singer," Lou had said. "Do you still love him that much?"

"Of course not," she'd smoothly lied. "But he's perfect for the part. Besides, you can get him at a good price."

Erica stared into the depths of her coffee cup, searching for answers in the murky blackness. What made him do these crazy things?

Cameron entered the kitchen, jolting her from her thoughts.

"How do I look?" he asked. He wore a cream linen jacket, dark sunglasses, and a hat tipped at a jaunty angle.

Erica couldn't help but smile. "You look like a star. Now, don't forget what I told you, and here—" She tossed him her keys. "Take my car."

"Thanks, Erica, I owe you one." His face lit up with a grin, his white teeth dazzling against his suntanned skin.

Erica scowled. "You owe me a lot more than one." She relented, giving him a kiss on the lips. "Get out of here, and don't wreck my car."

"*Hasta luego,* me darlin'." The screen door slammed behind him. Within minutes, Erica heard the throaty rumble of her Duesenberg roadster. She sighed. How long could she, should she, hold out hope?

———

Lou punched a button on his intercom. "Yes, Gladys?"

"Cameron Murphy is here. Can you see him now?"

"Send him in."

When Cameron entered his office, Lou made no motion to stand or acknowledge him.

Cameron crossed to Lou's massive desk, nervously turning his hat in his hand, his eyes downcast. "About my disappearance last week, Mr. Silverman. There was a death in my family back east. Pity my poor old aunt, God bless her soul."

Lou knew Cameron was lying. He leaned back in his chair, studying Cameron through narrowed eyes. He could smell a charlatan a mile away, and Cameron reeked of duplicity. "You understand the studio is taking a risk with you."

"Beg your pardon, sir, but I have millions of fans from my record sales and concert appearances. There's little risk."

"Only the financial risk of costly delays." Lou clipped his words. "And you haven't recorded a song in, what, three years?"

Cameron hung his head. "I appreciate your taking a chance on me. I won't let you down."

"I hope not. You wouldn't be here if it weren't for Erica." He smoothed his already impeccable silver hair and glared at Cameron. "Tell me how you plan to organize your life so that you'll be more responsible during our filming and contract period. Why should I put my studio resources behind you?"

"Well . . . well sir," Cameron stammered, "I'm getting married."

"Married?" Lou sat up, frowning. Would Erica make the same mistake twice? *I certainly hope not,* he thought, or there goes another star, just when she's on top.

"To Danielle Bretancourt, the perfumer and dress designer."

Lou tented his fingers, considering. No doubt she could keep Cameron in line, at least for the duration of filming. He recalled that when Danielle had asked about designing costumes, she had phoned him early the next morning as promised. And her designs were stunning. He didn't really see them together. *But who can ever tell about affairs of the heart?*

"Good move," Lou said. "Don't let her get away." He stood abruptly, signaling the completion of their meeting. "If what you say is true, then I have renewed confidence in your judgment. That is, *if* you marry Danielle, and *if* you can hold on to her."

"Absolutely, I couldn't agree more." Cameron shifted from one foot to the other.

"Have you chosen a date? Weddings are great publicity for the studio." Lou grasped his hand with an iron grip. "Don't let me down again, boy."

After Cameron scurried out the door, Lou turned to the window, gazing out across the city. *What makes women fall in love?*

A slow smile spread across his face. He made a note to call Abigail for dinner.

4 DECEMBER, 1940 — LOS ANGELES, CALIFORNIA

Sun streamed through the smudged windowpane in Danielle's apartment. She pressed her fingers lightly against the glass and watched her mother and Liliana two flights below on the street, strolling hand in hand to the corner market. Marie's mental condition had improved some, but she still had tremendous hurdles to overcome.

Danielle had visited with several doctors. They agreed that Marie needed a substantial period of rest in a controlled environment, and might benefit from recent advancements in psychotherapy and psychiatry.

Treatment would be expensive, and no matter how much she worked, there simply wasn't enough money. Danielle drummed her fingers on the glass, her frustration growing.

An enormous decision weighed on her mind.

Her girls also had needs. School, clothing, food.

Since Lou's party, she had been seeing Cameron, and he had been professing his undying devotion. Abigail had noticed, too, and Danielle confided her attraction for him to her friend.

Danielle also liked that Cameron was a hardworking professional. He'd disappeared for a few days after their last date, and she'd been worried, but when he resurfaced, he reassured her—he'd been studying and rehearsing for his new film part around the clock. And just yesterday, he had proposed marriage.

Although their lovemaking was extraordinarily passionate, when the sexual fog lifted, Danielle knew she didn't love him as she had loved Max, or even Jon. Could they grow into love?

Perhaps I owe it to Mother and the girls. They deserve a better life. Someday she would be able to provide for them, but when? Next year? Or would it take her three years, or five years? Those would be lost years for Marie. How could she justify that?

Time . . . how precious a gift. She thought of Nicky. Cameron would have the money to help her broaden her search. Surely she could find Nicky faster with his help.

Their safety was a concern, too. Even though her stalker had disappeared, Danielle had a strong feeling he would return. Cameron could provide a measure of protection.

Should I marry him?

Another question tugged at her heart. Danielle reached into the nightstand drawer and withdrew Jon's last letter. Curling her legs under her, she sat on the bed and began to read.

My dear Danielle,

Thank you for your last letter. Your words certainly keep this lonely sailor going.

We've scarcely a free moment these days. The night raids over London continue, with Nazi bombs raining down every night for nearly two months now, and Hitler seems intent on sinking every blessed vessel in the Royal Navy. I fear we can't hold out much longer without assistance from the Yanks. My heart bleeds for the poor young blokes on the front lines.

Last week I received a disturbing letter from my sister. Abigail wrote that you're seeing quite a lot of Cameron, that you're practically engaged. Why haven't you mentioned this in your letters? I was startled to learn you're contemplating marriage again so soon, particularly to Cameron. Think this through, I beg of you.

Danielle lowered his letter, thinking. Her relationship with Cameron *had* moved quickly. He was impetuous, accustomed to having his way, which was evident in everything he did, from his career to his passion for her body.

She lifted the letter again.

Abigail also wrote to say she told you of my engagement to Victoria, which is premature, to say the least. No engagement has been announced, and I don't intend to make any final decision until after the war. I hope you understand the reason for my hesitation.

It takes a long time to really know someone, Danielle. I wish I were there with you, to share our experiences and develop our friendship.

Give little Jasmin a kiss for me. Must sign off, on duty again soon.

Regards,

Jon

Danielle stared at the letter, trying to read between the lines. *To develop our friendship,* Jon had written. She remembered Grasse, how he had helped her through her grief over Max, helped her deliver

Jasmin. His offer for her to live with his family in England. *He told me he loved me. And now he writes about friendship?* A slow anger burned within her. Was he putting distance between them?

I've misjudged him. She wasn't the first woman to receive emotional letters from the front lines. Abigail told her he had proposed to Victoria. Danielle had rebuffed him when he asked her to come to England. But she could not have put her family in harm's way, not for the love of any man. *And rightly so,* she thought, growing more incensed. Nazi night raids by air were devastating London now.

If only Cameron were more like Jon. She missed the strength of Jon's embrace, the passion behind his kiss. She loved *who* he was—a man of integrity and honor. She remembered how gentle he was with Jasmin, how protective he was of Abigail. He was a charismatic leader; he cared deeply about his family and their business, its employees and passengers. Jon understood her passion for her work, and praised her talent.

Most of all, when she had shared her belief about Nicky, he didn't question her. He simply accepted her feeling as fact.

However, it was time she faced the truth, she realized, heartsick. She might have been a passing fancy for Jon, or maybe he had confused his feelings of sympathy for love. Abigail had told her that Jon and Victoria—and their families—had been planning their marriage for years. The Jon she knew was a man of his word; she had no doubt that he would keep his word and marry Victoria.

She reached into the nightstand for a pen and writing paper. She scratched a brief, hasty reply to Jon, sprayed it with perfume, then folded the letter and sealed it. It would probably be the last one she ever wrote to him.

The next morning, Danielle waited inside the doorway to her apartment building with an armload of dresses, not wanting Abigail to see the chaos in her apartment. She hoped Abigail would like the new slim silhouettes. Fabric was forecast to become scarce due to the war effort, even in America, so she'd tapered her patterns to skim the body. Her new designs were perfect for Abigail's athletic figure.

Danielle spotted Abigail pulling her car to the curb. She placed the garments carefully in the backseat of Abigail's Packard. "I can't wait to show you my latest work."

Abigail laughed. "I can't wait to try them on. I need something very special for this VIP luncheon."

Danielle swung her legs into the car. "Will Lou be there?"

Abigail smiled. "He seems to turn up wherever I go."

"Is it coincidence or something more?"

"No, it can never be anything more than it is." Abigail's voice was resolute, but her wistful expression belied her words.

Abigail drove to her home. She wheeled into the drive of the white stucco, red-tile-roofed bungalow, its palm trees rustling in the breeze. She opened the carved wooden door, slipped off her platform pumps after she crossed the threshold, and padded across golden oak hardwood floors, eager to begin trying on the clothes Danielle had made.

Danielle noticed a crystal vase of pink roses and stargazer lilies in the foyer. "Beautiful," she said, inhaling the sweet aroma.

"Aren't they? Lou sent those." Abigail was humming happily now.

Danielle tilted her head. "Any special occasion?"

"What? Oh, no, he's a sweetheart. Knows I simply adore flowers, especially these. I think he read my mind."

Danielle allowed herself a small smile, and then followed Abigail into her bedroom. She liked seeing her friends happy, especially Abigail, who was so thoughtful of everyone. Glancing around, Danielle said. "You've redecorated, I love it."

Mahogany English Hepplewhite furniture with straight, slender legs and decorative inlays anchored the room. A white cotton cutwork duvet and linen pillows created a relaxing ambiance. Danielle draped the clothes over the arm of a creamy chenille sofa. She held up a rich magenta-colored dress that mirrored the bougainvillea blooming in profusion outside the French doors. "This is my favorite for you."

"Mmm, this royal blue dress is drop dead gorgeous, too."

"This collection is rich jewel tones, which work beautifully with your creamy complexion. Try them on. I'll fit them to you when you're ready." Danielle reached into her bag and brought out an embroidered pouch. "I have a new perfume for you, too." She dabbed the elixir that Lou had ordered onto Abigail's outstretched wrist. The scent of roses and lilies emanated from her skin, and fit Abigail perfectly.

"This is heavenly," Abigail said, waving her wrist near her nose. "It's from Lou."

Abigail stared at her, and a slow smile spread across her face. "Well, I'll have to thank him." She picked up several dresses. "I love your designs, Danielle. You're going to be a mogul someday." Abigail began to unzip her dress, and then stopped. "How careless of me, I haven't offered you anything. Tea, coffee?"

Danielle waved her hand. "Don't bother, I know where everything is. I'll brew coffee while you change."

As Danielle was preparing coffee in the cheerful, Mexican-tiled kitchen, the telephone rang. Abigail called out, "Darling, will you answer that for me?"

Danielle picked up the receiver. "Hello?"

The line crackled, and she heard an operator's voice. "I have an international call for Abigail Newell-Grey. Do you accept?"

Danielle accepted the call. A man's deep voice boomed across the line.

"Is that you, Abigail? It's Jon, can you hear me?"

Danielle's chest tightened. "It's me, Danielle."

The line went quiet, and it seemed like an eternity before Jon answered. "Danielle, my God, it's great to hear your voice."

"Jon, where are you?"

"Can't really say, but I wanted to tell—that I plan—in a few— hello? Are you there?"

The line crackled. Danielle could hardly make out his words. "You're breaking up!"

"What?"

"Jon, I—I should congratulate you on your engagement." There was a long silence, as if he didn't know how to answer her.

"Listen, I don't have time. Danielle, I have missed you so much."

Danielle closed her eyes. *These were the words she had longed to hear.* But it was too late; he was engaged to be married. She opened her eyes and cleared her throat. "Jon, I want you to know—"

"Danielle, I'm—Angeles, want to speak—"

"What? Say that again?" The line sputtered. "I'll get Abigail."

"No, I— Danielle."

"Jon?" The line went dead. Danielle jiggled the telephone. "Operator, operator? Can you get that call back?"

Jon stood in a small town post office on a narrow lane, yelling into a phone. "I *have* to see you, Danielle. Can you hear me? I said I love you, and I *have* to see you. Wait for me!"

25

Tobacco, bitter in the mouth, obscures the truth with a plume of smoke, fire threatening from embers beneath the surface. Adds an irresistible air of mystery to the perfume composition.

—DB

7 DECEMBER, 1940 — WARSAW GHETTO, POLAND

"Where is he?" the guttural voice commanded.

Nicky knew to hide—all the children did—but this time the boots thudded through the icy flat and a viselike hand clamped around his ankle before he could dive from the window. The man hauled him back in, though Nicky struggled fiercely.

Nicky squeezed his eyes shut, but not before he recognized the man beneath the uniform.

The mother of the family he lived with was pleading, "He's just a boy, leave him alone. He was hungry, that's all, it won't happen again, I swear." She fell to her knees, grasping at Nicky.

With a powerful back-handed blow, she was flung to the floor, sobbing.

Nicky cringed, trying to make himself smaller, "No, please, no," he whimpered.

The next blow exploded against Nicky's skull, robbing his breath and sending waves of excruciating pain crashing through him. His sight blurred and the room wobbled around him. He sobbed a gargled plea, but the angry hands clamped around his throat, crushing, until his veins thrummed and bulged.

Darkness shuttered Nicky's eyes.

The mother screamed. Sharp, frigid fingers pressed his wrist, his throat. "Stop it, he's dead," she cried.

The boots cracked against the floorboards; the sound grew farther away.

"Shh, don't cry, don't move," the mother whispered.

The front door slammed, shaking the flat.

Heinrich was gone.

9 DECEMBER, 1940 — LOS ANGELES, CALIFORNIA

Danielle knelt on the black-and-white-checked linoleum floor in the studio fitting room, marking the hem of Erica's ball gown, an ivory duchess satin dress Danielle had designed for the new Silverman Studios film, *The Spanish Heiress*.

"Can't you hurry?" whined Erica.

"No, I can't." Danielle rocked back on her heels. "This is the dress Lou wants you to wear for the premiere, so it must be perfect. Now stand still." With deft fingers she measured, marked, and pinned. "Walk," she commanded.

Erica whirled, knocking Danielle over with the full skirt, the rich aroma of Caron's Tabac Blond rising in the warm room.

Danielle caught herself and grimaced. She would not let Erica ruin this opportunity for her with her petty actions. She needed this job, needed the money.

The actress had a well-earned reputation of being difficult. The first costume designer for the film had quit after one of Erica's tyrannical tizzy fits.

"Erica, I need to let the bodice out. Have you gained weight?"

The actress had strict orders to maintain her weight. If Erica gained weight, Danielle would have to refit the entire wardrobe. Not that Erica cared.

"Absolutely not." Erica sucked in her stomach. With her buxom, rounded figure, she had a tendency toward plumpness.

"I know you didn't gain ten pounds just by *looking* at that plate of enchiladas you ordered at lunch yesterday."

"How did you—" Erica stopped. "What would you know? You're too skinny, anyway."

"Breathe naturally, Erica. I've got to let this out. You're bulging over the top."

Erica smiled coquettishly. "Something you wouldn't know about, my sweet."

"It's not attractive in the back, trust me." She slit a seam, sniffing. "Tabac Blond is a lovely *parfum*, but are you bathing in it?"

Erica smirked. She clearly liked to annoy Danielle by dousing herself with a competitor's perfume. "Why don't you call it quits, Danielle? You're out of your league here in Hollywood. Everyone knows you're an amateur."

Danielle stood and walked around to face Erica. "I'm going to ignore that comment, but I won't ignore my responsibilities." She jabbed a finger in the air, punctuating her words. "Lou expects your clothes to be ready by the end of the week. You may have run off the last designer, but you won't get rid of me."

Erica folded her arms across her chest. "Oh, really. Let's take the gloves off, shall we?" Her lips curved into a wicked smile. "Lou told me you're marrying my husband."

"Cameron is no longer your husband," Danielle replied, though she still hadn't given him a reply.

"What does Cameron see in you?" Erica narrowed her eyes. "And that family of yours . . . I've heard you've got enough baggage to fill a railroad car."

"Leave my family out of it." Danielle picked up a pin and jabbed it into the side of Erica's bodice. *How dare she say that.*

"Ouch!" Erica glared haughtily. "Do you *really* know what you're getting into? Or are you marrying Cam for the fame and fortune? Because if you are, I feel honor-bound to tell you, there may be fame, but there's no more fortune, honey."

"Erica, we have work to do." *I will not allow her to intimidate me.* "Let's be civil."

"Okay, how about some friendly advice from the ex–Mrs. Murphy to the future ex–Mrs. Murphy." Erica's dark eyes flashed. "Cameron's a charmer, a seducer, a drunk, and a spendthrift, and those are his good points. You'll wind up hating him as much as you love him, and one day, you'll throw him out the door, or pack your bags, just as I did. Mark my words. And when you do, he'll run back to me. I know just how to lick his wounds."

What a jealous bitch. But then a small voice inside of her asked, *What if she's right?* Danielle's face grew hot. "I don't believe a word of it. I think you're envious."

"Of you? Don't make me laugh." Erica struggled out of the dress, tearing a side seam in the process. She threw it on the floor and stomped out of the fitting room in her underwear, grabbing her clothes as she left.

Danielle picked up Erica's dress, thinking about Cameron's proposal and Erica's so-called advice. The actress was clearly prone to dramatic exaggeration. Danielle knew he had a few minor faults, who didn't? *He told me he wants to change,* she thought, *and I can help him.*

Methodically, Danielle assembled her scissors, pins, and measuring tape. She needed to provide for her family. Cameron needed a wife to keep him grounded. *We'll help each other,* she thought. *And someday, we might even fall in love.* After all, their physical passion for each other was proof enough of their attraction and compatibility.

I must be practical. A vision of Jon appeared in her mind, and her heart tightened with yearning. *There's Nicky and my family to think about.* And then, although everything in her being warned against it, Danielle made a decision.

I will marry Cameron Murphy.

Moments later, Cameron appeared at the door, his mouth agape. "Erica stormed past me wearing practically nothing. What did you do to her?"

Danielle smiled. "She's heard of your proposal."

Cameron lifted her in his arms, smothering her face with kisses. "Just say yes, Dani. I've waited too long for a woman like you."

He *did* feel good, in a different way from Jon, or even Max, and her body began to respond with desire. "You win, Cameron. I'll be your wife."

Delight spread across Cameron's face. "Fantastic, I knew you'd come around, Dani. We've got to tell Silverman right away. He wants us to have a huge wedding. The studio will foot the bill, and then—"

"Absolutely not," Danielle interjected. How could she feign happiness at a large celebration while Nicky was still missing? "If we're going to do this, let's do it quickly. The justice of the peace is fine with me."

13 DECEMBER, 1940 — AIRSPACE OVER AMERICA

Jon tapped the pilot on the shoulder. "How much longer?" he yelled above the din of the small twin-engine airplane.

The pilot turned around, her short brown fringe sticking out from under her leather flight cap. "Two or three hours," she hollered. She pointed to a panoramic carved canyon below. "The Grand Canyon, a real beauty, aye? Used to fly this route for Hughes Aircraft."

"Glad you know the area," he shouted. Jon gazed out beyond white fluffy clouds into the endless blue sky. He'd hopped a Royal Air Force flight from England to Canada, ostensibly to inspect Newell–Grey ships docked in the Long Beach harbor of the Los Angeles basin, but it was Danielle he needed to see.

He remembered Libby's advice about Danielle. Though England was at war, he needed her now. *Tomorrow might never come.*

When he'd spoken to Danielle on the telephone, a sense of urgency had surged through him. The moment he'd heard her voice, he knew what he had to do. He'd understand if Danielle preferred to stay in Los Angeles, out of harm's way with the girls and her mother. All he knew was that he loved her, as he'd never loved Victoria.

He didn't care about heirs, he didn't care where they lived, he didn't care about anything but being with Danielle, however brief it might be. *I hope she feels the same about me.* They could be married before he returned.

He tapped the pilot on the shoulder again. "Can't this crate fly any faster?"

"Stop here, please," Jon told the taxicab driver.

The cabbie turned and raised a bushy brow. "You sure?"

Jon pulled Danielle's last letter from his shirt pocket. He checked the return address, and then glanced out the window. The apartment building across the street sported a crooked porch, peeling paint, and a rocky lawn where grass had been ground underfoot. "The Bradley Arms, this is it." He paid the cabbie and stepped from the car. And there, across the street, was Danielle.

His pulse quickened. Danielle stood on the landing, shifting a package from one hip to the other to open the front door. He rubbed the back of his neck as he watched her. What should he say? What would *she* say? What if she rejected him again? *That's why I'm here,* he reminded himself. How could she look into his eyes and not trust the depth of his love for her?

He held his breath. She looked beautiful in a fitted black suit that emphasized her narrow waist, skirted her slim hips, and revealed her long shapely legs. Her hair shone like burnished copper in the California sun. She wore it loose, and it skimmed her shoulders like a veil of heavy silk. How he ached to run his fingers through that hair, to touch her face, her lips, her throat, her thighs . . . he had to make love to her, or he would burst. *It won't be long now.*

The door was closing behind her. He strode across the street, climbed the front steps, and placed his hand on the grimy brass knob where her hand had been a moment ago; it seemed magnetized by her touch.

Inside, he inhaled the amazing wake of her perfume. She was walking up to the second floor, her hips swaying deliciously. He blinked in the dim light and found his voice. "Danielle!"

She froze at the top of the stairs, then whirled around. "Who is it?" A blaze of recognition illuminated her face. "Jon!" Her package tumbled to the floor and she gripped the rickety banister. "*Mon Dieu,* what are you doing here?"

Jon raced up the threadbare stairs two at a time, and then caught her in his arms, burying his face in her hair, reveling in her scent. He loved her perfume, and the sensual scent of warm skin that was her. She threw her arms around his neck and pressed her soft face to his, her breath warm on his cheek. He cradled her face in his hands and saw joy spread in her smile, a panacea to his wounded soul.

"I must be dreaming," she murmured, clinging to him. "I can't believe it's you."

"In the flesh." He tightened his grip and a warm glow spread through his body. He could feel her respond to him, just as she had in Grasse. "I told you on the telephone, I had to see you," he said, his voice hoarse from the airplane flight. Then he felt her arms go limp around his neck and her shoulders droop against his chest.

She pulled away slightly, her eyes downcast.

"Danielle?" With two fingers, he lifted her chin. Her lashes were like feathers against her smooth skin. Closing his eyes, he hungrily pressed his mouth to hers.

Again, she started to pull away, but he held her to him, caressing her back, her hair, her face. Slowly, her hesitation dissolved. She sank into his embrace as their kiss deepened. When he finally released her, he noticed her cheeks were damp with tears.

She rested her head against his chest. "Jon, why have you come?"

Her voice sounded strangely weak. He drew a deep breath. "I've missed you so much, Danielle." He heard her breath catch. "As I said on the telephone, I have only a few days here, but I, I thought . . ."

"I didn't hear you say that, Jon," she said softly. "The line went dead." Danielle raised her shimmering brilliant green eyes to him, lines of agony etched in her face. "What did you think, Jon? What?"

"It's what I *know*, Danielle. We belong together." He glanced around the dingy hallway, and guilt besieged him. Why hadn't Abigail told him about Danielle's circumstances? He kissed her again, softly this time. "I love you, Danielle. I don't want to wait until the war is over. Come back to England with me, marry me, let me take care of you. Or stay in Los Angeles, you'll be safer here, I realize." He glanced at their surroundings. "But you don't belong here."

Danielle moaned. Perplexed, Jon lifted her face to his. "What's wrong?"

She lifted her left hand. A diamond band glinted sharply against a stream of light overhead. *No, no, no . . .* Jon could practically feel the fire emanate from it, striking his eyes, searing his soul.

"I was married two days ago."

Jon staggered back as if he'd been hit. His head swirled. Danielle leaned over the banister, her pale face contorted in anguish, her body shaking with silent sobs.

Seeing her, feeling her, and not having her . . . the searing pain within him was worse than he'd ever imagined.

"In your letter, you said you planned to marry Victoria," she said through her tears.

He drew his hands across his face. *"Didn't you read my letter? Didn't you understand why I was stalling my engagement? Because of you, Danielle. Because I love you."*

"I read your letter," she said, her voice rising. "You said you wanted to be friends, Jon. *Friends.* After all we've been through? I couldn't believe it. I loved you, Jon, I told you that I did. But now, *c'est fini.*"

"Then you *do* love me?" Despite a surge of hope, tension gathered in his shoulders, knotted the muscles of his neck.

She dropped her head back and sighed. "Yes, yes, I love you, Jon. But I'm *married* to Cameron Murphy."

Instant rage boiled within him. "Why would you *do* such a stupid thing?"

Danielle whirled around, anger snapping in her eyes. "Stupid? Stupid is waiting for a fool on a ship who can't make up his mind."

Jon threw his hands up. "I don't believe it, of all people on earth, you married Cam? Do you know what kind of man he is? My God, he's a drunk, a spendthrift, sleeps with a different woman every night."

"No, he's changed, Cameron's a good, kind man. He's committed to me. He protects me and my family."

"What about your daughter? You want Jasmin to be raised by Cameron Murphy?"

"This is none of your business." Danielle's resolve hardened. "I made the best decision I could under the circumstances. He's good to the girls; he's teaching Liliana how to sing."

"What, for her supper?" Jon banged the wall with his hand, frustration welling within him. "All he'll teach them is how to drink themselves under the table."

"How can you speak about him like that? I thought he was your friend."

"Who knows him better? Believe me, Danielle. You've made a huge mistake."

"How dare you judge me." She took a step back. "He'll take care of us, protect us. And don't you dare blame me for this. You're engaged to Victoria." Danielle stooped to pick up the package she'd dropped. She drew herself up and glared at him, her eyes steeled with determination. "We have nothing else to discuss." She turned and slammed the door.

"Danielle, Danielle!" Jon hammered on the door, but she didn't answer. She had effectively sliced him out of her life.

Angry at himself for waiting too long, for not being able to express himself to her sooner, Jon turned and left, his heart a heavy stone in his chest.

How could I have been so stupid? He walked through the city streets for a while, not knowing or caring where he was, blinded by emotion. He was devastated, he'd never known such heartbreak, such intense, palpable pain. *My God, how could this have happened? Why?*

Danielle leaned into the door, tears of anger and frustration streaming from her eyes. She slid to the floor, her heart breaking into a thousand pieces. As the full force of her feelings rushed through her, she realized her horrible mistake. She had never stopped loving Jon.

Oh, what have I done? Why wasn't Jon clearer in his letters? Why had he misled her? Or had she been too swift to marry? And Cameron— she couldn't believe what Jon had said about him. Cameron made her laugh, he was there to help her, he was an incredible lover.

Wasn't that enough? How dare Jon criticize her when he had led her to believe he was getting married.

Danielle wiped her eyes and pushed herself from the door. Moving boxes lined the walls. She had already started to pack their few belongings. She flexed her jaw. She'd show Jon. And Erica. *God help me, I'll make a go of this marriage.*

26

The gardenia is an enigma, its petals dusted with the creamy white purity of innocence, but its aroma is wildly seductive. How appropriate; for in the language of flowers, the gift of gardenias conveys the message of secret love.

—DB

16 January, 1941 — Beverly Hills, California

Danielle and Cameron were married at the Beverly Hills municipal office—she in her royal blue crepe dress, Cameron in a white wool sports jacket—after which they motored off, waving from his convertible to a gathering of press and friends. The next week she moved her family into his home in time to celebrate Christmas. Danielle also arranged a Hanukkah celebration for Marie, pleased her family was comfortable honoring both faiths.

Cameron had left early for a morning call at Silverman Studios, so Danielle rose to begin preparations for a cocktail party she was planning.

Brushing her hair, she let it fall softly to her shoulders, then applied red lip rouge and a light veil of Chimère. Peering in the mirror, she noticed a bruise on her shoulder where Cameron had grabbed her the night before. They'd had an argument, but it was nothing, she told herself, embarrassment—and concern—flushing her cheeks. *How could this have happened?* They'd been married barely six weeks.

We're still adjusting, she told herself, *that's the way Cameron is, passionate in everything he does.*

The truth was, Cameron desperately wanted a son. She had flatly refused. *I can't, not until Nicky comes home.*

Although she had been devastated after seeing Jon, Danielle managed to convince herself that she was happy with her marriage. Cameron's passion continued, and overall, life was vastly improved for her family.

Cameron's home in Beverly Hills was a classic Tudor-style home on shady, tree-lined Maple Drive. There was even a two-bedroom guest house on the rear of the property—perfect for Marie and a live-in companion to look after her until her mother could take care of herself again. She'd arranged a treatment program for Marie at a nearby hospital, in hopes that she would respond without the need of long-term hospitalization. After mere weeks, Danielle saw marked improvement in Marie.

Shortly after Danielle and her family moved in, there had been a mysterious break-in, but nothing was stolen. At her frantic insistence, Cameron ordered a high brick wall with barbed wire erected around the entire corner lot. Beverly Hills had an excellent police force, too, which kept a watchful eye on resident celebrities.

She reached across her vanity to remove fallen leaves from a bouquet of roses from the garden. Next to Marie's bungalow, she had planted more rosebushes, jasmine, and gardenia, reminiscent of her uncle's farm in Grasse, and Sofia's garden in Poland.

Her thoughts drifted to Nicky; he occupied her dreams with increasing frequency. With the help of Cameron's attorney, who had guided her to new information sources, she had reached out to more people who might help her find Nicky.

She slipped a satin dressing gown over her nightgown, wincing as she rotated her sore shoulder into the sleeve.

She walked through the hallway and paused to look into the bedrooms where Liliana and Jasmin slept. At Cameron's urging, Danielle had taken the girls shopping, filling their rooms with toys and stuffed animals and new clothes to make up for the hardships they'd endured. But when Liliana pleaded for a stuffed monkey, Danielle firmly forbade it. It reminded her too much of the monkey she'd made for Nicky.

Danielle redecorated to suit her young family, disposing of all reminders of the vivacious Erica. "Send the bills to Harry Nelson," Cameron had told her, explaining that his business manager handled all expenditures.

Though she still adhered to a full work schedule, Danielle's early mornings were spent reviewing menus with the cook and giving instructions to the housekeeper, the nanny, and the gardener. She had inherited Cameron's staff, except for the new nanny, and although they were courteous, she could tell they weren't pleased that their workload had increased. She made her way downstairs to the kitchen. Scanning supplies in the walk-in pantry, she realized she needed to make a list. She opened a cupboard drawer where she'd seen the cook retrieve pencils and paper.

She found a pad, but no pencil. Shuffling through the drawer, she pulled it out a little farther. Beneath a place mat, she spied the edge of a folder.

She slid it out and opened it.

The folder contained receipts for household bills. One on top was marked "Overdue." Frowning, she flipped through them, growing angrier as she did. Every invoice was long past due.

The cook blustered in, plump and round-faced, her thick hair wrapped in a bun, her cheeks pink from exertion.

Danielle waved a fistful of delinquent grocery bills. "Why haven't these been paid? They're all past due. Six months and longer," she exclaimed, rifling through them. "Do Cameron and Mr. Nelson know about this?"

"Of course," the cook said indignantly. "Mr. Nelson is taking care of them."

"Is he paying them?"

"No, but I can still charge food on the account."

Danielle pressed her lips together. "Are there other outstanding household bills?"

The cook flushed crimson red. Danielle was mortified. "Put all the unpaid bills on the dining room table."

She marched to the phone and dialed the number of Cameron's business manager. "Good morning, Harry. I need to speak with you right away. Will you come by this morning?"

Harry yawned. "Don't you ever sleep, Danielle?"

"Hardly, Harry, it's a waste of time." She motioned to the cook. "We'll have a pot of fresh coffee."

Danielle changed into a black sweater and slacks. An hour later, she greeted Harry.

She opened a pair of ebony-stained doors to the mahogany dining table, where stacks of paper were arranged. Morning sunlight spilled into the room, glancing off the Waterford crystal chandelier.

Danielle tapped a stack of receipts. "The cook tells me the grocer hasn't been paid in more than a year. Is this true?"

Harry sipped his coffee and raised a brow. "It is, but—"

Danielle forged on, gesturing. "And these are for household repairs, laundry, and milk delivery. How can this be?"

"I thought I'd wait until you were settled." Harry hesitated. "It's time you knew that Cameron owes a little . . . well, there's no other way of putting it . . . he's seriously in debt."

"How much?"

He cleared his throat. "Three hundred fifty thousand, more or less."

Danielle gripped the edge of the table. *Three hundred fifty thousand dollars.* How could he owe that much? *Why, this is utterly unfathomable.* Her face burned with anger and shame.

"Why didn't Cameron tell me?" she demanded. And then she remembered, with a sickening feeling, that Jon and Erica had both warned her. Now she felt guilty for the money she'd spent redecorating. "What about this house?"

"I carry the mortgage on this house, and most of the debt he owes to me."

"Why doesn't he pay it?" she snapped. She couldn't imagine owing that much money and continuing to live in a grand style. She was ashamed for their lifestyle. Champagne, caviar, filet mignon. They couldn't even pay the grocer.

Harry shrugged. "Because he doesn't have to, I suppose. Look, I'm guilty, too. People like me make it easy for celebrities, just to count them as clients and brag about it." He grinned sheepishly. "Cameron has earning potential, especially with you behind him. You're a smart businesswoman. Look at what you're doing with the line of bank credit I arranged for you. Even if he doesn't earn money, you can repay his debts. The only serious problem is the tax lien."

Danielle jumped up, seething with rage over Cameron's irresponsible behavior.

She stopped, and then started to laugh. The irony of it was that if she was truthful with herself, she had married Cameron, in part, for his money. *And out of fear.* Cameron wasn't just broke, but so deeply in debt it might take years to pay back. And because they were married, creditors would look to her for repayment. *How did I miss that?* She began to laugh and sob, alternating hysterically.

Harry rose to help her back to the table, clearly concerned. "Sit down, you're upset."

"Of course I am," she snapped. She sank onto a chair, tears streaking her face.

Harry stood behind her, an awkward hand on her shoulder as her strong facade cracked. "You need some time. I'll come back later," Harry said, excusing himself.

Danielle climbed the stairs to her room and locked the door behind her. She and Max had spent years scraping by to rebuild the factory. Debt had hung over their heads, but they had repaid it. And now, here she was, in worse financial shape than ever.

It was one thing to be poor, to own or owe nothing. But it was worse to live a lie, to labor under a mountain of debt. How could she hold her head up when she knew the gardener's children needed new shoes, while they lived lavishly but couldn't pay his wages?

I can't face these problems, she thought, panicking. And just when she thought that help was available for Nicky and Marie. She shook her head, realizing her entire life with Cameron was based on deception—hers, his, what did it matter? *My life is a lie.*

Did everyone know it, except her?

From Europe . . . Max, Nicky, my family . . . the Nazis . . . to this. Memories of the torpedoed ship, the smell of dead bodies in the sea, smoke from burned-out homes in Poland, the stink of alcohol and oud wood on Heinrich, dried blood on her hands, the stench of dying irises . . . the horror of it all came flooding back. It was too, too much.

Her marriage to Cameron was the last insult. She had given up Jon—a man she loved—in order to provide for her family's desperate needs. *How can I possibly live like this?*

Her entire existence was crashing down around her, and she was powerless. Sobbing, she flung herself on the bed, wishing again that she had died, too.

Finally, when she had no more tears to shed, she stared numbly at the ceiling. She could follow Jean-Claude's solution . . . or find other options. Then she thought about Jasmin, Liliana, Marie, and Nicky, and was ashamed of her cowardice.

I can't let them down.

Cameron didn't come home that night, or the next, and Danielle guessed that Harry had told him of her discovery. When Cameron finally called, he said they'd been filming on the set through the night. She knew he was lying.

She spent the weekend tallying figures, working desperately on a plan. On Sunday morning, Danielle dialed Harry's number. "I know it's early again, but I have an idea," she said. "Can you come over now?"

When Harry arrived, she handed him a handful of demand notices. "I insist that these hard-working people be paid immediately. I'll have money by the end of the week."

She set her mouth in a resolute line. She had to raise money, and if it meant selling some of Cameron's antiques or paintings, or the Oriental rugs she'd purchased, that's what she would do. People talked, and she would have none of it. Not while she was trying to build a respectable business.

Danielle asked about the expansion of her House of Bretancourt clothing line. "In view of all these debts, is the financing still viable?"

He shrugged. "I'll see."

She went on to explain the introduction of two new fragrances for spring, Jour de Bretancourt and Nuit de Bretancourt, perfumes designed to be worn for day and evening, respectively. As she spoke, she began to feel more confident. "Just as one changes clothes, so should one change fragrance to fit the occasion, the season, and the time of day."

"That's an intriguing concept, Danielle. But will American women understand?"

"They will once I explain it." She quoted a figure, which also included her new Fleurs line of single-impression floral fragrances. "That's how much I'll need. See if it can be arranged."

Harry scribbled a note. "Sounds aggressive, Danielle."

"We have to be, don't we? Now, let's talk about Cameron. He has to go back to work."

"The major music labels won't touch him. He's cost them money, and in this town, you're only as good as your last project. Despite that, his fans still love him."

Danielle frowned in thought. "Could we start our own music production company?" She'd never sold music, but she had learned how to start a business.

"Yeah, but it will take at least a year for Cameron to develop a new body of material."

"Too long." Danielle rubbed her forehead.

"There is one new song," Harry said slowly. "He wrote it for Erica, but it's a hit, I'm sure, if you wouldn't mind."

"I don't care, as long as it sells millions." She drummed her fingers on the table. She remembered a beautiful singer at the studio, Pauline d'Amore, for whom she'd designed a dress for a nightclub scene. "What about duets with other famous singers?" she said, thinking aloud. "Cameron could reprise his old hits. Everyone knows the music, so we could produce it quickly. We'd lead with the new song."

"Might work." Harry rubbed his chin. "But Cameron has a poor reputation."

"Leave that to me." She planned to start with Lou Silverman, and every singer he had under contract. "Please draw up documents of incorporation for a new production company. Put it in my name. I don't want him to have access to the money."

When Harry looked up at her in question, she explained, "I'm using my money. I'll pay his debts, including his debt to you. He'll have a contract with the firm, but I'll manage the business. And Harry, I'd like you to serve on the board."

"With pleasure. You're one hell of a woman, Danielle."

28 JANUARY, 1941 — BEVERLY HILLS, CALIFORNIA

"Jon is *married*?" The words sliced through Danielle's heart with a sweep as broad as a scythe.

Abigail stood on Danielle's front steps in a soft robin's egg blue day suit of Danielle's design, clutching a wrinkled telegram. "We were surprised, too. My brother, he's always so impetuous, but we had no idea he was planning on taking the plunge so soon."

Danielle cast her eyes down and nodded in numb agreement, blood thrumming in her ears. Jon's last visit reeled through her mind like a Shakespearean tragedy. *How could he?* Obviously he'd married Victoria on the rebound. But wasn't that what was planned, before he and Danielle had met? *Isn't it only right?* Her limbs began to shake involuntarily. She reached for the stone door frame to steady herself. "I'm afraid I don't feel well, Abigail. Let's have lunch another time. So, so sorry."

Danielle closed the door and climbed the stairs to her bedroom, clinging to the banister for support. She locked the door behind her, threw off the taupe jacket to her slim suit, and flung herself onto the bed, pounding her linen pillows with her fists.

She'd traded her happiness for her family's comfort. And yet, if she was honest with herself, she would do it again if she had to.

Her head throbbed with frustration as she grieved for love's lost opportunity. Angry at herself, she screamed into her pillow, again and again, until the room spun around her and she fell asleep from exhaustion.

27

The orchid, queen of exoticism, a mute observer slow to reveal the mysteries of her petals. Would that I had such patience, too.

—DB

1 March, 1941 — Beverly Hills, California

A week later, Abigail had just stepped into her high-heeled satin pumps when two sharp knocks sounded at the door of her Beverly Hills bungalow. Recognizing Lou's signal, she strode to meet him, kissing him on the cheek. He smelled deliciously of Bay Rum cologne, and his impeccably styled silver hair shone against the midnight black of his tuxedo.

"Good evening, Abigail. Hmm, marvelous perfume. One of Danielle's?"

"It's Joie de Bretancourt. Tell me, what do you think of the dress?" She whirled around in her navy silk Bretancourt evening dress, unusual in its sleek simplicity, and the perfect backdrop for her silvery South Seas pearls.

"Stunning," Lou replied. "The mayor couldn't have chosen a more beautiful, talented woman to honor tonight. Beverly Hills Woman of the Year, but in my opinion, you're Woman of the Century. You've earned it."

His approval meant a great deal to her. She hugged his neck, letting her hand linger on his shoulder. "You look quite handsome, too, as always."

Lou cleared his throat. "Don't get me started, Abigail, I don't think I could resist you tonight. You really don't know the impact you have on me, do you?"

"Silly man, always teasing me." She laughed to mask her feelings. There was nothing she'd like more than to give in to his flirtations, but Lou wanted a family. She had seen another doctor about her condition, but the diagnosis was always the same. *Impossible.* Against her will, she had fallen in love with Lou. She couldn't even bring herself to tell him why she resisted his advances. *Once he knows, he'll move on to the next woman.* She picked up her clutch purse.

Lou turned her face to his. "I'm not teasing you, Abigail. Don't you know you mean the world to me?"

Abigail gazed at him. "But I—"

Cradling her face in his hands, Lou silenced her with a kiss. Abigail responded, twining her arms around him, her emotional wall crumbling at last. His kiss was incredible—powerful, passionate, demanding—all she'd ever dreamed it would be.

"Well then," she sputtered, flustered. "Shall we be on our way?"

Lou's blue eyes blazed with admiration. "If we must. Your public awaits." With a wink, he offered his arm and she hooked her arm into the crook of his elbow. They slid into the back of Lou's black limousine, and Lou draped his arm across her shoulder.

Abigail regained her composure and smiled shyly up at him. Their relationship had changed in an instant. She decided to enjoy the moment, because once he knew her truth, it would be over. *I will remember this as my one perfect evening.*

As they rode to the mayor's home, Abigail tore her thoughts from Lou's passionate kiss to reflect on her work for Operation Orphan Rescue, the charity she'd founded, and for which she was being honored tonight. It was nice to be recognized, but that was hardly the reason behind her efforts. After every battle, orphaned children were left behind.

"You should also receive an award, too," Abigail said to Lou. "The money you've given, the documentary your studio made on the children from Europe and Asia . . . honestly, I couldn't have done it without you."

Lou smiled. "Seeing children placed with loving families—that's my reward."

"It's incredible the donations that have been pouring in since the film has been running." Abigail thought of the orphans as *her* children, replacements for the babies she could never have.

The limousine turned into the driveway of the mayor's Beverly Hills home. Flickering lanterns lined the pathway to the Japanese-style home, its roof edges gracefully upturned. They strolled past a rippling koi pond. As they walked, Abigail noticed someone in the shadows, darting between the lanterns. *Must be a server,* she thought idly.

Guests milled about, and Abigail recognized one of her father's friends, an American who owned a smaller, rival shipping firm.

"Congratulations on your honor, Abigail," he said. "How is your father?"

"He's a tough old buzzard, but this war is really taking a toll on him."

A sympathetic look crossed the man's face. "I'm awfully sorry about the ships he's lost."

"We've all lost them," Abigail said, remembering. German forces sank two fine Newell-Grey ships that had been put into His Majesty's service. She hated to think of the waste incurred, and more than that, the lives lost.

"And your mother, is Harriet still in London?" he asked.

"Indeed, she won't leave my father's side, despite the Nazi air strikes." Abigail and Lou moved on and continued toward the tennis court. She caught her breath in surprise. An enormous tent had been erected over the court like a draped pagoda. They walked inside, where the Asian theme continued, with pale celadon green fabric lining the interior, an enormous golden Buddha at the entryway, and gaily colored lanterns illuminating each table.

"How exquisite," Abigail said, taking in the scene. An orchestra played on a stage, and urns of exotic orchids and fragrant jasmine enhanced the ambiance.

Danielle and Cameron appeared and Abigail hugged them both. "So glad you're here. And look, here's Clara." They turned to greet her and Abigail added, "Clara, you look marvelous. What a perfect dress for the occasion."

Clara wore a sleek red cheongsam, with red enameled chopsticks in her platinum up-sweep. "Danielle designed it for me. It's part of her new Chinese collection."

Abigail turned to Danielle, who wore a similar tunic and pants outfit in emerald green. *Quite daring,* she thought, to wear pants to a formal event, but Danielle carried it off with great aplomb. "Looks like you're starting yet another trend tonight."

Danielle laughed. "It's good for business. Speaking of which, you remember Harry Nelson."

"I'm so happy to see you again," Abigail said. "Congratulations on your success with National Music."

Harry laughed. "Danielle was the brains behind it all."

"Yeah, I jus' sing," Cameron cut in, slurring his words. "Shut up and sing, that's all they say."

Abigail saw Danielle shoot a sharp glance at Harry, who grabbed Cameron by the arm and guided him away.

At least Harry was swift, Danielle thought, watching the scene unfold. She didn't want any more wild stories leaking to the press. *Why can't he behave, just once?* Cameron's new album was scheduled for release in a few weeks. And she'd hate for him to spoil tonight's special honor for Abigail.

Worse, the mayor wanted Cameron to sing after dinner. *He'll be in no shape to sing tonight,* she thought ruefully. *All he has to do is sing and flash his million-dollar grin. Is that so much to ask?*

As she looked around, she noticed a man loitering near the lanterns. As she watched him, the short hairs on her neck prickled with unease. *Who is he?* When he caught her looking at him, he dashed through a hedge on the back of the property. Although she hadn't been followed since she and Cameron married, at times she'd had a sense that she was being watched again. She told Harry right away when he returned. "We should call the police," she said, her anxiety rising.

"Relax, Danielle, it was probably a fan or paparazzi. Lots of celebrities here tonight. Nothing to worry about, I'm sure."

He's right, she thought, calming down. That was a long time ago.

They were interrupted by the sound of her mother's lilting laugh filtering across the crowd. Marie was speaking animatedly with a group of friends. Her blond hair was styled and she wore one of Danielle's chic ebony dresses with high-heeled pumps. Danielle was pleased to see her enjoying herself again.

Marie had made tremendous strides under the care of Dr. Genet, a French doctor living in Los Angeles. Survivors of tragedy were his specialty. She had blossomed under his care. Even her voice had regained its lovely harmonious quality.

Danielle couldn't forget that it was Cameron who'd made Marie's initial treatment possible. Danielle checked her anger against her husband. For all his faults, he was generous to her and Marie and the girls. *Had it not been for Cameron . . .* She glanced at him again. She owed him a great deal. He had opened doors for her, and she would never forget it. However, that didn't excuse his behavior. Cameron must agree to professional counseling. She couldn't live like this any longer.

Abigail, who had excused herself when Harry had led Cameron away, now swept up behind Danielle, concern evident on her face. "Will Cameron be all right?"

Danielle nodded. "He's had a fair amount to drink, but Harry will see to him."

"Cameron has a good heart, and he needs you now."

She lowered her eyes. "It's not that easy, Abigail."

Abigail quickly changed the subject. "Did I tell you that I received a letter from Jon?"

"No, but I hope he and Victoria are happy." Danielle didn't want to hear about him.

"I doubt it. Last I heard, she's visiting friends in Acapulco. Wherever the fashionable place to be is, that's where Victoria can be found."

"I am truly sorry for him, Abigail. It's no wonder you shy away from marriage. Jon and Victoria, Cameron and me. We don't exactly inspire a sprint to the marriage altar."

"We were brought up believing in fairy tale marriages. But it's not reality. Not in today's world."

Danielle couldn't help herself. "And Jon? How is he doing?"

Abigail drew a sharp breath. "I can't say, I really mustn't say, Danielle." Her voice cracked.

Alarmed by her reaction, Danielle asked, "Abigail, what's wrong? Is Jon all right?"

Frowning, Abigail looked over her shoulder. "He made me promise not to tell you. Oh, Danielle, really, this isn't the time or place."

Danielle clutched her arm. "Has Jon been wounded?" A thousand terrible images rushed through her mind.

"No, nothing like that." Abigail sighed. "Victoria is pregnant."

Danielle caught her breath. Had she heard right? Yet she'd known it was inevitable. The family wanted heirs to the business. "I don't understand, what's wrong with that?"

"*Everything.*" Abigail's face crumpled into a frown. "She's too far along; it's *not* his child."

28

Wildflowers, the orphans of nature, flourish where they will—
until the curious gardener, or perfumer, reins in their adventur-
ous seeds.

—DB

26 MARCH, 1941 — BEVERLY HILLS, CALIFORNIA

Danielle parked her Delahaye automobile in front of a modest red-
brick church. She paused for a moment, her hand on the key. *This
could be the day,* she thought. The attached playground was deserted
as she made her way to the side door and went inside.

The children of the Prince of Peace orphanage had breakfast
from six to seven o'clock. On the next block, in the Temple Em-
manuel orphanage, breakfast was served from six-thirty to seven-
thirty. A quick walk through both to check on any new boys who
might have arrived, and she could still be at her desk by seven
o'clock. She made a point to visit all the orphanages in Los Angeles
County.

She'd had a sketch artist make copies of Nicky's photograph, ag-
ing him two years. She sent these copies to orphanages and relief
agencies on the East Coast and in England. The last letter she had
received from Philippe said that he was closing the chateau and
joining the free French efforts, but he had written that he was still
looking for Nicky, too.

Unfortunately, this morning was no different from other visits.

Danielle swept through the dining hall, but she saw no child who even remotely resembled Nicky. But her dreams of him had become increasingly vivid. What else could she do? To return to Poland was impossible now.

She shifted the Delahaye into gear and wheeled onto the street, heading for her office. She relished the early morning solitude that allowed her to work uninterrupted. Her new office was her cocoon, which she had decorated to her exacting standards before she'd discovered Cameron's financial condition.

A coffee urn, ready to brew, stood on a red lacquered Chinese table in the corner. She flipped a switch to start the coffee. Humming a soft tune, she snipped a few wilted flowers from a native California wildflower arrangement, which graced a low table in front of a brocade sofa. After pouring coffee, she seated herself at her Louis XIV inlaid desk.

She glanced at the clock. She and Harry had a meeting with her banker today, and she had to complete her review of the finances. Her father had brought work home from the bank sometimes, and he had taught her how to read financial statements. By the time her secretary and staff arrived at nine o'clock, she would have completed reviewing projections for the next fiscal year for Bretancourt Holdings. As she reviewed the documents, she noted items to discuss with Harry over lunch.

Harry was a board member of Bretancourt Holdings. He would think her projections aggressive, but she was determined. She welcomed his advice, as well as his ability to handle Cameron's increasingly difficult spells. She'd even started seeing a psychologist to try to understand Cameron's mood swings.

Danielle recalled the mayor's function honoring Abigail, when Cameron had actually passed out onstage. The gossip columnists had gone wild with the story. She had been so embarrassed, and the resulting publicity had been a nightmare.

Her mind drifted. With a sigh, she put down her pen and opened her desk drawer, extracting a letter she'd received from Jon. He had started writing to her again. She opened the letter; it was short, as his letters usually were now, and with no mention of Victoria's pregnancy. She could tell he was deeply troubled. Most likely, he would claim Victoria's child as his own. It was, after all, the honorable thing to do. *If only things were different.*

She heard a bang and footsteps in the hall outside her locked door. She stiffened. No one else ever arrived this early. The doorknob jiggled. Her heart raced. Was it the man she'd seen at the party?

The door burst open with a kick, slamming against the wall with such force that paintings rattled on their hooks. Cameron staggered in, his fine evening clothes wrinkled, his face blotched and unshaven. His eyes held a dark, wild expression.

"Knew I'd find you here," he said, slurring his words. "Look at you," he sneered, gesturing toward the financial statements on her desk. "Always countin' your money. You never quit, do you?"

"It's your living, too," she said pointedly.

Cameron grinned. "We share the wealth, do we? Tha's not the way I see it. You control the money, you wear the pants in this family. Hell, ever'body knows that. You don't even want to give me a son, do ya, Dani?"

Danielle clenched her jaw. "You have no business here. Go home, sleep it off."

"I got a problem." He lurched menacingly toward her. "You hired Buck Jones to watch me, didn't you?"

"Buck Jones will manage the tour." Her fingers tightened on the edge of her desk. After Cameron's recent drunken mishaps, she and Harry had retained Buck Jones, a seasoned manager.

"Why the hell do I need him?" He leaned closer and slammed his fist on her desk, rattling its contents.

He stank of alcohol and smoke. Danielle stood up. "His job is to control the tour."

"The tour? You want him controllin' *me*, right, Dani?" His face contorted and his bloodshot eyes bulged.

"You have a contract to fulfill, Cameron."

"To hell with the contract. I'm the star, I say he's out."

Cameron cursed, snatched a crystal vase from her desk, and hurled it against the wall. Shards shot through the air like projectiles.

"Stop it, the board decided on Buck Jones," she said, hands on her hips. "Under your contract with National Music you have no right to dispute the decision."

He whirled around, jerked a thumb at his chest. "You think *you* can call the shots?" His face darkened. "I don't think so." He clenched his hands into fists and started around the desk.

Her heart racing, Danielle realized she was cornered. "We'll talk about this later, when you're sober."

"We're through talkin'."

She tried to run, but he grabbed her by the arms. "Cameron, don't!" She arched instinctively, twisting her face from him. A blow exploded against her cheek. She hit the floor with her palms, screaming, glass from the vase slicing her hands and forearms as she careened across the polished parquet floor. Quickly, she rolled onto her side, blood splattering her white silk blouse.

Cameron charged toward her again.

Danielle spied the silver letter opener that had been knocked from the desk. Kicking him away, she lunged for it.

Cameron grabbed her legs and dragged her toward him. He straddled her and pinned her to the floor. His eyes were raw and savage, her blood seemed to feed his frenzy.

Danielle tried to struggle from his grasp. *Mon Dieu,* she thought, *he's going to kill me.*

He gripped her neck and raised a hand to strike her.

She stretched her fingers for the letter opener, found it, and jabbed in defense.

The letter opener pierced his hand and protruded through his palm. Cameron roared with anger, clutching his hand, blood gushing from his wound.

Just then, Harry raced through the door. "My God, what's going on?" Harry pulled Danielle free with one hand, and shoved Cameron off with the other.

"Call the police," Harry shouted, fighting to restrain Cameron, but the drunken actor jerked away and ran from the office.

"Let him go," Danielle cried. "He's completely crazed."

Cameron disappeared, blood trailing behind him in the hall.

Harry pulled a handkerchief from his pocket and wiped Cameron's blood from Danielle's face. "I'll make the call."

Danielle collapsed into a chair. Gritting her teeth, she began to pick shards from the palms of her hands.

After Harry finished the call, Danielle said, "I've never been so glad to see you. What brought you here at this hour?"

"Erica phoned me. Cameron was at her house ranting and raving about you and Buck Jones. She became frightened for you. I had an idea he might come here."

A police siren sounded outside. They watched as the police apprehended Cameron. Harry turned back to Danielle and pressed his handkerchief to her hands to stem the bleeding.

"He doesn't deserve you, that bastard." Removing the handkerchief, he inspected her injuries. "You need stitches. We'd better go to the hospital." He grabbed a tea towel by the coffee urn and wrapped her hands. "Why don't you divorce him?"

She was quiet for a moment. "I spoke to a doctor about having him committed to an institution for help with his addictions. Cameron opened his home and his heart to my family after we'd been devastated. Now he needs help. Cameron's not a monster, he's an addict. But this is no way for any of us to live." She grimaced, keeping pressure on the deepest wounds on her hands.

He nodded. "We'll have to cancel the tour and the new record."

Danielle gazed from the window as they turned into the hospital parking lot of Cedars of Lebanon.

"When do you plan to commit him?" Harry asked, easing the car into a parking space.

"Soon. But even if he can't do the tour, at least he can finish the voice tracks for the new record. Don't you agree?"

"No, not at all. Delaying committing him puts you at risk, and for what? A few bucks? What would you be worth dead?"

Danielle shot a sidelong glance at him. "You wouldn't be so quick to say that if you'd ever been poor. Cancel the tour, but I will do everything in my power to deliver that album."

After Danielle had been stitched and bandaged at the hospital, Harry drove her to the Beverly Hills Police Station, where Cameron was being held.

Chief of Police Dave Walsh, a beefy, leathery-faced man, waved them into his office. Harry had telephoned Danielle's attorney, Otto Koenig, who was waiting for them there, a trim sentinel in his pinstriped suit and burgundy tie.

Walsh leaned back in his chair, shrewdly studying Danielle through a haze of cigarette smoke. "I'm told you don't want to press charges."

"That's right." Danielle sat rigid in her chair, her freshly bandaged hands folded in her lap. Her white silk blouse bore bloodstains and she knew her face was bruised and swollen. "You may release Cameron into my custody."

"We can charge your husband with attempted murder." Walsh held up a plastic bag containing her silver letter opener smeared with Cameron's blood. "It appears you might have acted in self-defense."

She sucked in her breath at his brutally honest words. *Attempted murder.* "Can't you simply release him into my custody?" Her neck crawled with tension. Cameron had crossed the line; it wouldn't be easy to sweep away this incident. She couldn't afford the publicity, not with the planned record release. Furthermore, she'd signed a deal with Lou Silverman to use the new recordings in an upcoming movie starring Erica Evans. *A month, that's all we need to finish the recordings.*

"You allege your husband attacked you this morning," Walsh said with an unrelenting stare. "Next time, Harry here might not be around to save you."

Danielle was torn. If Cameron didn't fulfill his contracted appearance obligations on the last tour, she'd be left with the debts. She owed a great deal of money for Cameron's recent indiscretions—from her personal and business funds—much, much more than Harry realized. *Without the album,* she thought, *my business will be bankrupt.*

Harry stroked his chin. "Look, Walsh," he began in a conciliatory manner, "none of us wants to see this in the newspapers."

Walsh narrowed his steely gray eyes. Leaning across his immaculate desk, he jabbed an accusatory finger at Danielle. "There'll be plenty of publicity when you're wheeled out in a body bag." He leveled his gaze at her. "One day, you won't make it out alive. Then where will your family be?"

Danielle shook her head. "No charges."

Walsh shook his head in return. "All right, then. The district attorney is in the next office. We're prepared to press charges against you for attempted murder."

Danielle gasped. "Against me?"

Harry leapt to his feet. "This is outrageous."

Otto Koenig stepped forward. "This charge won't stand up in court. I'd never have imagined such deplorable tactics from you."

Harry turned to her. "Danielle, he's dead serious. You've got to do something about Cameron. The recordings aren't worth it."

She stared at her bandaged hands, her mind clicking. She desperately needed Cameron to complete the recordings. *And the publicity.* The headlines alone would decimate his career and National Music. Furthermore, her business relationship with Lou Silverman would undoubtedly suffer. Her head pounded. The thought of bankruptcy sickened her.

Walsh barked an order into his intercom. He swung back to Danielle. "We're placing you under arrest, Danielle. My officers are on their way."

Danielle shifted uneasily. Clearly, Walsh wanted to make a point, but at her expense? How far was she willing to go to protect Cameron and her investments? She couldn't subject her family to another disaster. Cameron was a threat to everything that she held dear. And yet, she owed him for their lives, too. *What can I do?*

She had an idea. Mindful of her bandaged hands, she pushed herself up by her elbows, meeting Walsh's glare. "I have a deal for you."

"I propose the deals, Danielle."

A sharp knock sounded, and two uniformed police officers stepped in.

Otto swung around. "Come on, Walsh, at least listen to her before you arrest her. Have some respect for my client."

Walsh glared at the attorney. "When she shows respect for the laws of this country."

"She does," said Otto. "She's perfectly within her rights."

"Let's hear it, then," Walsh said, motioning to Danielle.

"I have a plan that should be satisfactory to all concerned," she started. "First, no charges."

Walsh began to protest, but Danielle held up a bandaged hand. "I'm willing to commit Cameron to a sanitarium, effective immediately, and grant full authority to the medical staff to determine his eventual release. Otherwise," she added, offering her wrists to the officers, "you may arrest me now."

Walsh raised his brows, considering, and then nodded. "You've got a deal."

"There's one condition," she said, lifting her chin. "Cameron's music is terribly important to him, and to his recovery. As part of his treatment, Cameron will be allowed to express himself creatively through his music. Even if it means releasing him periodically to Harry Nelson's custody to record music."

"You'll have to clear this with his doctors," Walsh said, "but as far as I'm concerned, we'll release him as soon as you have a judge's order to commit." He motioned to the officers to depart.

Otto was right behind them. "I'll have the order right away." He raced from the office.

Danielle breathed a sigh of relief, then bowed her head, inspecting the bandages on her hands. *How did our marriage come to this?*

29

The gardener coaxes seeds from the earth, lavishing attention on their every fragile leaf, their magnificent blossoms. How fragile, how fleeting—this beauty, this love. Only the perfumer can capture, extend nature's response. Oh, that we could grasp real love so.

—DB

5 April, 1941 — Beverly Hills, California

Wearing gloves over the fresh scars on her hands for protection, Danielle stepped on the shovel with her espadrille slip-on, driving the blade into the soil. Pausing, she craned her head toward the sky, confirming that the rosebushes would have sufficient sunlight in the spot she'd chosen in the rear yard for the new garden.

"I wanted to see you before Lou and I left for San Francisco," Abigail said. "I wish I could help you," she added, glancing helplessly at the white sundress she wore.

"I'm glad you came by, but don't you dare get a speck of dirt on my creation." Danielle rested her chin on the wooden shovel handle, catching her breath. "With the press lurking around looking for a story about Cameron, I've hardly been out."

"This will blow over. Next week there'll be a new sensational story and the reporters will be on to that."

"I hope so." Frowning, Danielle thought about her options as she dug holes for the rosebushes. "I have some decisions to make."

"It's been rough on Cameron, too," Abigail said softly. "I visited him yesterday."

"And how was he?" Danielle knelt in her dungarees to position the new rosebushes.

"Charming as ever." Abigail perched on a wrought iron garden bench. "What color are your roses?"

"Crimson, apricot, lavender, pink, and yellow." Hands on her hips, Danielle stood back to consider her handiwork. "Some will have thorns, even though the blossoms are beautiful."

While Abigail watched, Danielle dragged her shovel along the footpath to furrow the soil, and then sprinkled in seeds for snowy white and purple alyssum. She topped the seeds off with loose soil, and hosed the new plantings with water. After Cameron's damaging behavior, Danielle was trying to bring beauty and tranquillity back into their home.

"Will you give him another chance?"

Danielle blew out a breath. "No one realizes how many I've given him already. His mood swings wildly between euphoria and depression. It's been exhausting for all of us."

"It's good that he's receiving treatment," Abigail said. "Committing him to the sanitarium must have been hard for you, but it was correct."

"I know, but how can I ever trust him again?" Danielle pressed the back of her gloved hand to her forehead. The police chief's words had shocked her into reality. "Philandering was one thing—*attempted murder* is quite another."

Abigail blinked and shook her head. "You can't put yourself or your family in danger."

"No, I refuse," Danielle said with force. She'd been through enough in the past year. "My mother and Liliana were devastated over this. We're all in counseling now. It helps, but it doesn't solve Cameron's psychological problems."

Danielle deposited her tools and gloves in the garage, and then reemerged. She drew a breath and took stock of the pleasant, orderly yard. Through a window she could see her mother with the girls sitting inside the kitchen, smiling and laughing. This was the life they deserved, not the terror that Cameron had inflicted upon them.

She sat next to Abigail on the bench. "Like some roses, Cameron will always have thorns."

"That's true. Then, is it over?" Abigail asked.

Danielle brushed bits of dirt from her scarred hands. "I plan to divorce him upon his release."

22 APRIL, 1941 — BEVERLY HILLS, CALIFORNIA

"*Merci,* Danielle," the young woman said as Danielle placed an armload of fragrant white lilies next to the blush pink roses and purple hydrangeas she had already chosen. "You always choose my best flowers."

Danielle smiled at her friend, the owner of the Flower Pot in Beverly Hills. "And you always have the best flowers in town, Mimi."

"*Mais oui,* my brother sent some potted gardenias from the farm, too. They're heavy with buds, perfect for your boudoir. Did you see them? They're in the front of the shop."

Danielle meandered through a brilliant maze of cut flowers, charming topiaries, and magnificent floral arrangements. The scents that swirled through the air lifted her spirits. She drank in the aromas wafting through the air, closing her eyes as she leaned into an exotic flower or plant to breathe in its scent. *I could almost be in Grasse.*

She rubbed the glossy green leaves of a gardenia, touched the moist earth in the pot, and let her fingers trail along a fresh white flower bursting from a tightly swirled bud.

Perhaps I'll capture this aroma, she thought. *Cool greens combined with sweet gardenia, the moist earth, the warmth of the sun—it would be perfect for this season. Maybe a new line of garden-inspired perfumes—*

"Danielle?"

Am I hearing things? She heard someone call her name. And not just anyone, but it sounded just like— And that scent . . . the patchouli, the hint of rose . . . it was Spanish Leather and the scent of his warm skin . . . *oh, mon Dieu!* She felt a hand on her shoulder, and a quiver coursed through her.

"Danielle."

Slowly she swung around. The shop seemed to fall away. She blinked, staring at a handsome man holding a bouquet of roses. "*Jon?*"

"It must be kismet." A wondrous smile spread across his face. "I stopped to buy flowers for Abigail, and here you are." He touched her shoulder and caught her hand, drawing her to him, intensifying his delicious scent.

"I can't believe it, what brings you here?" Her heart beat wildly, and she was certain he could see it beneath her blouse.

"I had to attend to some business with ships in the Long Beach harbor. I didn't have much notice. So I thought I'd surprise Abigail."

Danielle laughed nervously. "Oh, you would have. But she's not here. She's in San Francisco with Lou. He has a film shooting on location."

He ran a hand through his thick hair, releasing a faint scent of the sea. "Ah, once again, I should have called ahead."

He smiled wistfully at her, his warm eyes crinkling at the corners. She remembered how one side of his mouth tugged more than the other, and the cleft in his chin seemed more pronounced. His face was leaner, but his chest was broad, and he looked more muscular. *He's even more magnificent than I remembered.*

"Then our meeting really is kismet," he murmured. His deep baritone voice was charged with emotion. "You look different, Danielle, you've bloomed, just like these flowers. How long has it been since that day outside your apartment?"

Danielle's cheeks grew warm, and she moistened her lips to speak. *Before Cameron,* she thought with a jolt.

"Here, I'll get these for you." Jon paid for her flowers and scooped them into his arms.

She said, "I'm parked in the back, follow me." As he held the door for her, she glanced over her shoulder and noticed his gaze lingering on her body. She laughed nervously. "I'm in the Delahaye."

Jon walked to the car and let out a low whistle. "What a beauty—the car, too," he added, looking appraisingly at Danielle.

"Jon, you're being naughty. And I'm supposed to be mad at you." She unlocked the doors.

"At me? Why?"

"Well, why shouldn't I be? You show up again with no notice at all."

"Danielle, let's not waste time on the past." Taking the keys from her, he opened the car and placed the flowers inside. "I didn't call you, or anyone, because I didn't know how much time I would have. As it is, I only have a few hours, and I don't know when I'll return." A serious look shadowed his face for an instant. He took her hands in his. "But I'm here now, and it's a beautiful day. May we enjoy it together?"

She smiled up at him. "Come with me to the house. My mother and the girls are visiting friends in San Diego. And you know where Cameron is. I wrote to you about that."

He nodded. "Is he any better?"

"He's taking this opportunity to work on new songs, and is looking forward to coming home soon." She paused, and then sighed deeply. That was her standard answer to the press. *Why should I lie to*

Jon? "Actually, he was released from the sanitarium to work on his new album, but he had a horrible relapse within days and returned. But let's not talk about Cameron." She put on her new aviator sunglasses. "Want to drive?"

At her direction they took the long way home so that he could experience the fine, sleek automobile. Jon drove south and turned east on Wilshire Boulevard, relishing the feel of the car at his command. With the demands of his wartime service, there had been few moments truly to enjoy life, especially with a woman he found so fascinating. In truth, there had never been anyone like Danielle in his life.

Danielle. This was not the woman he'd left in France, not the woman he'd last seen in Los Angeles. Had he thought she would remain unchanged after all she'd endured?

He recalled the last time he'd seen her in Los Angeles, right after she'd married Cameron. Could he really blame her for that? She'd been so emotionally scarred and painfully poor when she'd first arrived in Los Angeles; he knew that now, but he hadn't realized the extent of her suffering at the time. Abigail told him that Danielle had confided in her that she'd also had a man stalking her. When Jon heard that, he chastised himself for failing to take care of her. And then Cameron had come along, offering relief from her hardships. Jon only wished he had been the one.

Turning onto La Cienega, he glanced at Danielle, hardly believing that she actually sat beside him on this glorious sunny day. Even in her casual white shirt and cotton pants, she was clearly an independent woman in charge of her destiny. She was so . . . He paused, searching for words. *So sophisticated, so self-assured.* He could still feel the spark of electricity between them.

She lifted a slender hand to smooth her hair, and as she did he noticed several angry pink scars.

"What happened to your hand?"

"Oh, I forgot my gloves." Danielle hesitated, looking down at her hands. "It was Cameron, that last fight we had." She lifted her hands and turned them over gracefully. "They're healing."

"I wish I'd been there." He watched her from the corner of his eye as he drove. Her every movement transfixed him; she was graceful and refined, as elegant as always. He turned onto Sunset Boulevard and they wound through the neighborhood.

"So you approve of my choice of car?" she asked brightly, changing the subject.

"What's not to love?" He grinned. "I've always thought this was one of the most gorgeous cars ever built. I met René Dreyfus, the auto racer, not long after he won the Million Franc race in thirty-eight in his Delahaye." He laughed. "What a great victory over the Nazis *that* was."

"The greatest victory is yet to come," she said with a world-weary smile.

"Yes, it is, though at what price remains to be seen," he agreed, turning serious. "Have you heard anything more about Nicky?"

"No," she said, nervously tugging a lock of hair. "Do you believe he's still alive?"

"I've always trusted your intuition. If you feel he's alive, then he is."

She smiled gratefully at him. "Turn here, and we're home."

He eased the car into the driveway of the walled Tudor-style home and turned off the ignition. As he did, he glanced at her and she caught his eye with a soulful gaze. In that moment it seemed as if they had the power to look deep within each other, to the place where they harbored no secrets and their desires were laid bare. It was then that Jon knew that they had never really left each other.

"I'm so glad to see you," she said huskily, touching his hand.

As he curled his fingers around hers and she responded in kind, a rush of desire coursed through him. "I've thought about calling you so many times." He kissed her cheek, marveling at the softness of her skin, and the subtle perfume that wafted about her hair and neck. She seemed flustered, and he pulled back. "Let's put those flowers in some water, shall we?"

He gathered the flowers. She led him to the side entry and into the kitchen.

Jon looked around, taking in the comfortable surroundings, photographs of Danielle and the girls, potted palms, and fresh oranges on the kitchen table. He stood behind her, so close he could feel the warmth from her skin. "Are you happy here, Danielle?"

"I have so much to be thankful for." Danielle picked up a pair of scissors and began furiously snipping the flower stems. "My family is together, my business is thriving."

"That's not what I asked."

She sighed. "I know what you meant."

"We have just a few hours, Danielle."

"I'm very aware of that." *Snip, snip.* She tossed discarded leaves in the trash bin.

Jon watched her for a moment. Her wavy hair flowed around her shoulders, her face angled from him.

"Danielle?" He touched her arm, and when she looked up at him, he saw that her brilliant green eyes glistened with tears. It tore at his heart.

She brushed her eyes and waved him away. "I'm just being silly."

"No, you're not. Come here." He wrapped his arms around her and her body relaxed into his. *God, she feels so good.*

"I don't have much time for myself anymore. This is a rare day."

"You're still a woman with feelings." He tilted her chin up and looked into her eyes. "And I still have feelings for you, Danielle, I always have, from the first moment we met. There was a time, right after Max died, when I should have spoken up, told you how I felt, but I thought it was too soon for you. And then when I did . . . what a disaster. I've made so many mistakes with you."

She laughed softly. "And now it's too late for us. We're both married."

"It doesn't change the way we feel about each other. I know what you don't say in your letters. And I've always known that when I saw you again—"

"Shhh." She pulled away, her hand lingering on his face. "Let's just enjoy the day," she said, as he turned into her hand, kissing her palm. "I have a bottle of champagne in the refrigerator. It's been there a long time, waiting for a special occasion."

"I'll get it," he said, and kissed her lightly before he released her.

"And I'll get the flutes from the bar."

Danielle made her way through the living room. She knew what she felt for Jon, she knew what she wanted, but wanting didn't make it so. And yet, if there was one lesson learned, it was to seize the moment and whatever joy might come your way. *What if Jon never returned from war?* How would she feel if she never saw him again?

How would she feel if she did?

Her attorney had already drawn up her divorce papers. But Jon was still married. Victoria was expecting a baby. *And I shouldn't be thinking this way.*

She chose two tall flutes from the bar and returned to the kitchen.

Jon had opened the champagne and filled the flutes. "To us," he said, kissing her.

Just one day, she thought. There was no harm in that, was there?

He listened as Danielle told him about Liliana and Jasmin, and Marie's fortunate recovery. They talked about Abigail's work with orphans, and Jon's parents, but when she asked about his war experience, Danielle saw that Jon was troubled.

"It's been tougher than anything I'd ever imagined," he told her. "Victoria doesn't want to hear any of it, but I know you understand. She hates the amount of time I'm away, but I have my orders. She doesn't grasp the demands of military life. Or doesn't want to." He shrugged. "She has a lot of friends who keep her company, though."

"And the baby?"

"So Abigail told you all about it." Jon shook his head. "It's strange, you'd think Victoria would appreciate the fact that I plan to accept her illegitimate child as my own. But not her."

Danielle brushed a petal from his hair. "And how are you holding up?"

"Not bad, considering it's been a walk through hell." He turned up a corner of his mouth. "You know, most everything can be rebuilt or replaced. But not what really matters."

He placed his hand over her heart. "Family, friends, love, and health. I've seen destruction and heartache; bravery and heroism; the best in men, and the utter worst. I've lived three lifetimes since the war began. Am I weary? Sometimes I'm way past that. But the men and women I've worked with are among the finest I'll ever know. We fight for freedom, and we earn our victories."

Danielle listened quietly. "What do you plan to do after the war?"

"This war still needs to be won. Beyond that, I'm not sure." He looked at her and smiled. "Now, I want to hear more about your life."

"I'd like to show you something special," she said, taking his hand. She led him to the rear of the house and opened the door to a large room. "This is where I work at home when inspiration strikes. I like to dabble after everyone is asleep, when I have time to think and imagine and create."

He peered in. "This is amazing." The room was tidy, but her creativity was evident. On one side sat a perfumer's organ, with neat rows of amber bottles, and across from it was a drafting table with her fashion sketches and fabric swatches. A pair of comfortable brocade chairs, a stack of books, a vase of flowers, beautifully framed impressionist paintings, and a phonograph added to the ambiance.

Jon seemed genuinely interested in everything she was doing, unlike Max or Cameron. He picked up a platinum lighter from her desk, studying the Art Deco styling. "This was Max's, wasn't it?"

She nodded, touched that he remembered. "I had it made for him by Cartier in Paris. He couldn't risk taking French items into Poland or Germany."

While they talked, she opened a set of glass doors to the backyard, where a swimming pool sparkled in the sunlight and a soft breeze billowed the canvas drapes of an open-air pool house.

"You described this to me in a letter. It's exactly the way I imagined it." He paused at the perfume organ. "This is where you blend your perfumes?"

"Many of them. Here's one I've been working on." She picked up an amber bottle, opened it, dipped a slender white blotter strip into it, and waved it. "What do you think?"

He took her wrist, guided the strip under his nose, and closed his eyes, inhaling. "It's fresh, very modern, smells like California in the summer."

He has a good nose, she thought, acutely aware of his hand on her wrist. "That's California orange blossoms, with a fresh accord reminiscent of the Pacific Ocean."

"It's spot on, Danielle." He took the blotter strip from her, trailed it along her throat, and leaned closer to smell her neck. "A great perfumer once told me that it's better to experience scent on skin." He nuzzled her neck. "Remember when you told me that?"

Danielle let her head fall back, exposing her throat to him, and savoring the warmth of his touch. "It was in Grasse, after Jasmin was born. I was so glad you were there. I don't know what I would have done without you."

Jon slipped his hand under her hair and held her neck, his lips brushing hers as he spoke. "Do you remember the first time we kissed?"

"How could I have forgotten?" she murmured, tasting his lips with her tongue.

He picked up the perfume bottle, poured a small amount of perfume into his palm and, unbuttoning the top button of her shirt, pressed the fragrant oil into the skin of her chest between her breasts. A small moan escaped her lips as he bent to her, intent on experiencing the aroma as it emanated from the gentle curve of her breast, warmed by his touch.

He slipped another button free, trailing the perfume on her skin with his fingers, past her lace brassiere, and onto her firm, flat stomach, pausing to caress her skin with his lips and fingertips.

At once he stopped, and cradled her face in his hands, his eyes dark with desire, implicitly asking her permission to continue.

"Take me outside," she whispered. *Not in the bed I shared with Cameron,* she thought. He lifted her easily in his arms. "To the cabana," she added, leaning against his chest and feeling the beating of his heart.

Jon carried her outside to a slate-floored room with a stone fireplace. He placed her on a wide chaise lounge, and Danielle lay with her hair fanned out beneath her. Jon propped himself up on one arm next to her and gazed at her. "You're the most beautiful woman I've ever known, Danielle. We're meant to be together, you know that."

"I know, Jon, I know," she murmured, pulling him close and unbuttoning his shirt. He bent to kiss her and she met his lips again, gently, then more passionately, as their desire flamed against the cool spring breeze.

"I want to make love to you, more than anything I've ever wanted to do. You are my heart, my soul. I love you, Danielle."

A thought welled from deep inside of her: *I love this man . . . I always have.* She ran her hands through his hair and pressed him toward her, then hesitated, checking her desire. She knew what she wanted, *but should she?*

He brushed his lips against hers. "I once promised Max I would look after you. Will you let me?"

Jon's words hung in the air as she met his intense gaze. "But there are others . . ."

"Who don't have to figure in our future."

Danielle sucked her breath in. *Do I dare hope?* "Until then, let's just lay together, Jon, there's no harm in that."

The minutes turned into an hour, and then another, and as the sun set, Jon rose and started a fire in the fireplace. Danielle lit citrus-scented candles. Jon brought champagne and cheese and fruit from the house, and they laughed and drank and ate, then caressed one another again, enjoying each other's touch.

Finally, the champagne unleashed their inhibitions, and Danielle opened herself to Jon, who hesitated only for a moment before entering her with an ease and naturalness that surprised them both at first. They fell into rhythm with each other's body; their scents mingled, merged, and exploded with passion, and they knew no boundaries between them.

Danielle was transported on wave after wave of pure joy, pure love, pure feelings.

Later, as they lay by the flickering fire, she was simply happy. *I feel truly, deliciously loved.* This day was a gift. She knew he would be leaving soon, and prayed for his safety. In war, lives were changed in an instant. And then, there was Victoria.

If only . . . She stopped herself, not daring to spoil their one night of pleasure. Tonight would have to be enough for them. Forever.

Then Jon was covering her with a blanket and kissing her—kissing her face, her lips, her hair, and she must have dozed off, for when she awoke, he was gone.

30

Marcel Proust wrote in *Time Regained*: "An hour is not merely an hour, it is a vase filled with perfumes, sounds, projects, and climates." Every hour my nose is filled with nature's fresh perfume.

—DB

3 May, 1941 — Beverly Hills, California

Shrugging out of her persimmon-colored jacket and removing her matching hat, Danielle spied the mail on the floor, where it had fallen through the chute by the front door. She scooped up the envelopes and walked to the kitchen. An oversize letter caught her eye. Curious, she tore it open and withdrew a folded newspaper clipping. A moment later, she gasped.

A photograph of her speaking at a women's fashion show at Bullock's Wilshire had been cut from a newspaper.

Written in large red block letters across the photo was the word *Jude*. "Jew" in German. A series of numbers were printed beneath the word on four lines. *Numbers?* A pattern emerged; she sucked in her breath and flung the clipping as if it were ablaze.

When she had returned to Poland to search for Nicky, she had seen the word splashed in red paint across storefronts and homes, with windows broken and doors nailed shut. She had also seen it in Paris after the Nazi invasion.

She pressed her hand to her mouth, horrified. *Not here, not again.* With Cameron away in rehabilitation, he was no longer there to protect them. A chill crept over her. *Someone must know this. But who?*

Danielle turned and raced upstairs, her heart pounding. She burst into the nursery play room, startling the children and their nanny. "Get them away from the window right now!" she screamed. "Stay together."

"What's wrong, what's happened?"

"Do as I say." Danielle ran outside, looking from side to side, and raced toward Marie's bungalow. She burst in without knocking. "Maman, come with me, right now." Danielle explained as they ran back into the house. She locked the doors behind them, and drew the drapes.

Danielle *knew* she had seen someone lurking around her. She remembered the man at the mayor's party for Abigail. She shouldn't have ignored her feeling; she'd known something was wrong then. And now that person knew where she and her family lived. Fear struck her, but she had to think clearly.

She picked up the telephone and dialed a number. "Mr. Dave Walsh, Chief of Police, please."

Within minutes a patrol car pulled up in front of the house. Danielle met the officers at the door, and they followed her into the kitchen.

"Maybe it's an ugly joke," the officer said.

"It's a *death threat*," she said, pointing to the photo. "Look at these numbers." She was nearly hysterical now.

The detective studied the clipping, stroking his chin. "Do they mean something to you?"

"They're birth dates," she said, gesturing to each line. "The first three that are crossed out are the birth dates of my late husband, his mother, and our son. My husband was murdered in Poland, and our son and my mother-in-law are missing."

"The last one isn't crossed out."

Danielle stared at him. "That's *my* birth date."

The detective whipped out a notepad. "You're going to need protection. Now, tell me everything."

Later that morning, Cameron Murphy's rich baritone rang out, resonating with the rounded warmth of a well-aged cognac. The time he had spent in the sanitarium had been good for him. He knew he sounded better than he had in years, but there was still something missing.

The young sound engineer gave two thumbs-up through the glass window that separated them. They were all working overtime this Saturday to finish the vocals.

"That's great, Cam," Harry said through a microphone. He sat next to the engineer at the control board. Next to him was Danielle, who nodded her approval. "Okay, let's do the third number now."

"Sure, old man." Cameron grinned and continued his masterful vocals, gliding through one love song after another, the words of each ballad flowing like a slow rippling stream. He was in good form, but he knew his voice lacked its old soulful connection. He completed a song, and then motioned for more water.

He had to admit, his treatment had benefited him in every way—physically, mentally, and emotionally. But Cameron wasn't one for a mundane, workaday existence. *Not like Danielle,* he thought, pitying her. He realized that his actions had inflicted extreme suffering on Danielle and the girls. On Erica and Harry and Lou, too. On every friend he'd ever had, and for that he was genuinely sorry.

But he missed the excitement of living on the edge. He thrived on the heightened reality produced by drugs and alcohol. The passion it brought to his work was electrifying. How could he explain this to anyone? How could he exist, and still write great music, without it? The answer was simple. He couldn't. *Sobriety isn't all it's cracked up to be.* But he had devised a plan to escape it all. His eyes slid over to an electrical extension cord; he figured he could lift it without anyone noticing. This tune was his swan song.

Cameron finished his water. Motioning to Harry, he began his final vocals.

When Danielle had called Harry and told him about the terrifying letter, he insisted on picking her up and bringing her to the last vocal session. She was so worried about her family, and asked that the first available officers be assigned to their protection. They had waited until the police arrived before leaving.

Now Danielle sat in the soundproofed engineering booth, listening as Cameron sang the last tune of the session, "Perfumed Letters," one he'd written for her during his confinement. The title referred to letters she'd written to him before he was well enough to receive her visits. It was a ballad of star-crossed lovers.

She listened to him spin the tale, then the haunting finale: *"And in my still hands they'll find, yellowed with time, perfumed letters from my love, my love for all time."* What a beautiful arrangement, she thought, blinking back tears. *It's sure to be a hit.*

And then she thought of Jon, and all the letters he had written her, too. *Just one delicious day,* she remembered.

She dragged her attention back to Cameron, feeling guilty about her plans. She hadn't told him about the divorce. She'd been supportive of him, though she was careful not to encourage him romantically. But their marriage was over. Otto Koenig had already drafted the legal documents.

She planned to vacate the house and relinquish the deed to Cameron. After all, it had been his home when they'd met, though judging from the strong, increasing sales of the duets album, which had been a smash hit, it would soon be paid off. Harry had carried Cameron's debts for a long time, and had called in years of favors to put the album production on a fast track. "I'll take only what I've personally developed and built," she had instructed Otto.

Once the divorce documents were signed, she planned to return to England to continue her search for Nicky. Refugees were pouring out of Poland and other countries, and all of Danielle's contacts were searching for Nicky. She *knew* he was there, somewhere.

Cameron's final vocals hung magically in the air, and a hush gathered in the room. Harry tapped the microphone. "That's a wrap. It was absolutely perfect, Cam." Harry glanced at his watch, put his hand on her shoulder. "Danielle, I'll call the police, see if they have any leads yet. Don't go outside without me, I'll be right back."

"Thanks, Harry." She passed a hand over her face, mired in anxiety.

Danielle watched as Cameron gathered his sheet music. He shoved it into a large leather valise and then stooped to pick up an electrical extension cord.

He's made remarkable progress, she thought guiltily. The medical staff had approved of Danielle's unusual conditions for his admission, probably due to his celebrity status. Nonetheless, it had given Cameron hope and purpose, a *raison d'être.*

An attendant arrived to escort Cameron from the recording studio to the sanitarium. According to the provisions, he was to be escorted at all times. The medical staff concurred that the recording sessions had been of enormous benefit to Cameron's recovery. He was on suicide watch in the beginning, but once he began to respond, the fine part of the old Cameron had emerged, almost as charming and fun-loving as ever. Danielle fervently hoped that the end of his confinement was near, and that this time, he'd make it. He had a good heart, and she wished him only the best.

Cameron poked his head through the door. "Hey, Emerald Eyes, how's Dani mine?"

Danielle smiled at his nickname for her. He'd also written and recorded a song entitled "Emerald Eyes." She believed it was another sure hit. "Fine," she said cordially, rising. "You sounded marvelous, Cameron."

He responded with a roguish grin. "Just wanted to say good-bye. Got a moment?"

"Of course, what's on your mind?" *He's in unusually good spirits,* she thought, happy for his progress. The sound engineer excused himself, closing the door behind him.

"Awful business with that stalker again this morning, Dani. Wish I'd been there to take care of him."

"I appreciate that. The police sent surveillance units to the house."

Cameron dropped his valise, caught her in his arms, and pressed her to him. "I wanted to tell me darlin', me favorite girl, that I love her dearly."

She hesitated, uncomfortable in his embrace, then said guardedly, "And I've loved you, too, Cameron. In my way."

A trace of disappointment flashed across his face, but he gave her a smile. "Sure, and it's good to hear those words from your lips, Dani. You're a beautiful lady, and I thank you for what you've done for me. Give my love to the girls, to Liliana and Jasmin, and to your lovely mum, too. Now I understand what Marie went through with her treatment. What a grand lady she is."

"I'll give them your love." *It's the old, good Cameron again.* When he'd began his decline, descending into his dark abyss, it was the girls he would first appeal to after an absence, tail between his legs, with gifts and surprises, until Danielle finally absolved him. Not surprisingly, the girls missed him. When he was sober, he lit up the room with his funny quips and antics; he was certainly more fun than she'd been, what with her mountain of responsibilities. But his dark side had troubled all of them.

"You won't forget, will you?" He released her, but still held her hands, gently stroking them. "I've always loved you, Dani, to the best of my ability. As much as I could love anyone." His dark eyes searched her face. "You understand, don't you?"

"Perfectly." *He must know about the divorce,* she thought, *or at least suspects. This is his good-bye.* Wistfulness overtook her, sorrow for all that had passed between them, for all that had gone so wretchedly wrong. She gave him a light kiss on the cheek.

Cameron responded with a flare of passion, kissing her on the lips, then slowly retreated, releasing first one hand, then the other. He picked up his valise, opened the door, and turned back to her, giving her one last smile, his famous smile, the grin that could light up a movie screen like fireworks, sending mothers and daughters swooning at his songs. And then he was gone.

Guilt slashed her heart as she watched him go, the sanitarium attendant close at his heels. *But I'm doing what's best for both of us.* She had never shared with him the kind of feelings she had for Jon. And yet, Jon wasn't the reason she was divorcing Cameron. She was doing it for the protection of her family. The police chief's words had jerked her back to reality. *Attempted murder.* She no longer deluded herself. Cameron might have killed her.

Harry appeared at the door. "Are you all right?"

"I'll be fine." She watched Cameron disappear around a corner. A strange mixture of longing and remorse gripped her. *Could I have loved him after all?*

"Ready when you are," Harry said gently. "I spoke to the police. They'll still have protection at your house when we arrive."

"Thanks for driving me here. Let's go." She cleared her prickly throat. Walking through the empty parking lot, she spied a man loitering. Her pulse quickened, and then she realized he wasn't the one she'd seen before. Nevertheless, when Harry put his arm around her, she was grateful.

Harry asked, "Anything wrong?"

She shrugged, trying to calm her nerves. "Cameron and I said good-bye. Somehow, I think he knows of my plans for the divorce."

At that moment, a gunshot rang out, and a patch of pavement exploded near Danielle. She screamed, and Harry shoved her behind his car. The man took off and Harry raced after him.

"Harry, no!" Stricken with terror, Danielle huddled against a tire, her heart pounding, her breath coming in short rasps. *Where can I go?* The parking lot was a wide expanse. There was nowhere else to hide.

Shortly, Harry called to her, panting, "Danielle, are you okay?"

"Yes, I'm here."

"I lost him, but stay there, I'll try around back."

"Harry, the keys!" But he was gone.

Every synapse in her system flared in full alert. She turned and saw the man creeping alongside the building in back of her. His gun was sighted on her.

Thinking quickly, Danielle rolled under the car to the other side. Peering out, she watched him advancing. *This is a professional,* she realized, breathing hard. She squinted, and her world tilted. She recognized the man's movements, his posture, the cut of his hair. *Mon Dieu, this is a Nazi.*

She pressed against the hubcap, trying to make herself small. If she ran, he'd pick her off as if this were target practice. Harry, too.

From the street she heard the shrill squeal of tires, followed by the thunderous impact of metal on metal. At the same time, Cameron emerged from the side door of the building, unheard against the din of the accident. The sanatarium escort was right behind him.

Cameron hesitated when he saw Danielle crouching by the car. Frantically she motioned him away, pointing to the edge of the building. The attendant backed through the doorway, but not Cameron. Her fears, the break-in, the stalking, the threats—he knew everything, he'd been by her side through it all. *No, Cameron, go away.*

From her corner vantage point, she could see both sides of the building. Cameron dropped his valise and slinked along the building perpendicular to the assassin. *Don't do this.* She reared up to deflect attention from Cameron.

When she did, she heard the killer chuckle as he rounded the corner.

At the edge of the building, Cameron met him with a hard chop to his forearms, but the man retained his grasp on the gun, staggering back, falling to one elbow on the ground, and firing. Off balance as he was, the bullet glanced off the building.

Danielle yelled and ran toward them. Still on the ground, the assassin had a clear shot at her. He raised the gun, steadied it, and took aim.

Danielle dove onto the scorching pavement. But Cameron lunged a split second before the man acted.

"No, Cameron, no!" She screamed as the gun exploded; Cameron fell on top of the man, and then rolled off with a thud.

Harry charged up behind them and kicked the gun away. Behind them, a police car had pulled over. Hearing gunshots and screams, a pair of officers ran to assist Harry, subduing the assassin and cuffing him on the ground.

Her heart bursting, Danielle tore across the lot to Cameron and sank to her knees beside him. Thick blood pumped from his chest and she pressed her hand against the wound, trying to stem the flow. "What have you done? I told you to go away." She bent over, kissed his forehead.

Cameron smiled up at her, his lazy, charming smile that crinkled the edges of his eyes. "Did it for you, Dani, my lovely lassie." And then his eyes glazed over, his golden voice silenced for all time.

31

Consider the relationship of odors, one to another. A perfume is
a symphony, the sum of the parts, where the whole is far greater
than the individual. And yet, excellence stems from individual
effort. The artist intuitively understands this circular relationship, and therefore selects only the best ingredients.

—DB

5 MAY, 1941 — POLAND

Nick swatted the little boy's hand. "Don't eat that." The spider scurried away. The boy couldn't have been more than five years old.

Before they had moved on, the older boys had taught Nick what
was edible and what made one ill.

Nick plucked a handful of grubs from a felled log, mashed them,
and wrapped them in a leaf. "Here, eat this."

He swung around. They'd been drinking water from the lake.
He remembered someone being afraid of the water—a woman—
she couldn't swim. Could he?

Random memories sometimes floated back to him; he had lost
part of his memory after being beaten in the ghetto. The mother
had written his name down for him: Nicky Holtzman. For some
reason, that didn't seem quite right. Besides, he was Nick now that
he was older.

Nick's eyes shot around to make sure they were alone. He shimmied out of filthy clothes and hid the bundle behind a stack of

rocks. He stuck a toe into the lapping water's edge. He stumbled in, not as strong as he used to be, before the incessant gnawing in his concave stomach had taken over.

Holding his breath, he waved his arms and paddled his feet. His muscle memory gained control, and soon he was gliding through the cool water. The weightless freedom revived him.

He dove under the surface, and then opened his eyes to an unknown world. Hundreds of small, silvery fish darted around him, while larger fish hulked nearby, inspecting this new creature. Nick hung motionless in the water, thinking. The older boys had told him Japanese kids actually ate raw fish.

They'd eat tonight, he decided.

9 MAY, 1941 — LOS ANGELES, CALIFORNIA

Sitting in her office, Abigail picked up a stack of new files that Danielle had reviewed for her. It was a heart-wrenching task, reading the children's brief biographies, their diaries of anguish and suffering and loss, each one an unwilling witness to death and destruction. Abigail and Danielle always hoped a trace of Nicky might emerge.

Her heart tightened for her friend. Danielle was grieving over Cameron—they all were. Danielle had promised a sum of her future earnings to her charity in Cameron's memory to help fund more placements. It seemed to help ease the pain of Cameron's death.

She glanced at a clock on her desk; Lou would be here in an hour for their lunch date. She sighed, their relationship gnawing at her conscience. Every time she planned to tell him about her inability to have children, she lost her nerve.

After their first kiss, she meant to tell him her secret the next day. But as soon as she woke, the flowers she loved began to arrive at her home, then her office. He showered her with such attention and passion—more than she'd ever known. She knew she should tell him the truth, even if it meant breaking his heart as well as her own.

Abigail dragged her attention back to her task. In front of her loomed yet another tall stack of slender files of new candidates, of children available for adoption. She picked up the first file and clicked her tongue after reading the sad contents. Every child deserved a family. *Maybe Nicky's will be in this stack.*

As she sorted through the files, she made notes of each child's age, native country, language, and religion. She noted whether the child had siblings, for whenever possible, they tried to keep them together. They'd recently been able to place a family of six youngsters with three brothers and their respective wives, all of whom lived within a two-mile radius. Each couple had adopted two children. It was a miracle, and she'd cried when the children met their new families.

When she opened another file, her heart lurched. *Triplets.* Eight-year-olds. Almost impossible to place; she'd need another miracle. Most adoptive parents wanted babies, and hardly anyone would take three children. They would probably remain in an orphanage. She sighed and studied their photos. One girl, two boys. Alexandra, Aaron, and Aristotle. A lump formed in her throat. They looked so precious.

Birthplace: Russia. She smiled. Lou was from Russia. She'd mention the triplets to Lou at lunch. Perhaps he'd know of a family who might be interested.

Lou Silverman parked his car outside Abigail's office. He rested his hand on the steering wheel for a moment, thinking. For a man accustomed to making decisions, there was one decision he'd been hesitant about making for several weeks now. Not because he wasn't sure of it, but because it was so vitally important that he wanted to make sure he chose exactly the right time to execute it. He knew the answer he wanted, but he wasn't at all sure that it would be the one he received. He was as nervous as a teenager.

Lou walked into Abigail's office. "How's my favorite lady? Ready for lunch?"

"Sure, but there's something I want you to see first. Do you have a moment?" Abigail gave him a kiss, her velvet brown eyes dancing with excitement.

"For you, all the time in the world. What's on your mind?" He cast an appreciative gaze in her direction. She wore a sleek beige dress, nipped at the waist and lean in the hips, with beige platform pumps.

"I have a challenge." Abigail perched on a corner of her desk, swinging a trim leg well toned from swimming. She opened a file. "We have a set of Russian triplets to place. Aren't they darling? I thought you might know of a family."

Lou looked at the photos. "Cute kids," he said, instantly drawn to them. A plan began to form in his mind. *This could be perfect.* "Actually, I might."

"Lou, that's marvelous. They're already here, at our downtown children's home. We can see them anytime." Abigail was beaming. "In fact, we could go today. And you can see the work that's been done at the home, thanks to you."

Lou grinned. "Get your coat, gorgeous. I brought the convertible."

When Abigail and Lou arrived downtown, they could see eager faces peering from the windows. Abigail smiled and waved.

"What a welcoming committee." Lou turned his gaze to Abigail. When she was with her orphans, her entire persona changed. *This is the woman I love,* he thought. The mantle of the ambitious fund-raiser gave way to her maternal instincts, which sent her doting and laughing and clucking and pampering. She truly loved the children, and they loved her right back.

"Come on," she said, pulling him by the hand. "Remember, every child gets a hug. They need love, they need to be held and made to feel secure and valued. And wait until you see your studio crew's handiwork. The children adore their new rooms."

The bright red door flew open and a plump woman stood beaming in the doorway. "Welcome," she called out.

"Mrs. B.," Abigail exclaimed, and flung her arms around her. Beatrice Bonnecker was a big-hearted Austrian woman who held a degree in child psychology, and spoke seven languages fluently, which endeared her to the children. Nothing was more comforting to a frightened child in a strange country than to hear the familiar sound of his or her native tongue.

Mrs. B. greeted Lou with a brisk handshake. "Have we got a lot to show you, Mr. Lou, *ja*, you'll be as happy as the children."

"I like it already, Mrs. B.," Lou said. "Red was a fine choice for the front door. Cheerful and welcoming, a true reflection of you."

Abigail was on her knees now, greeting each child. "Hello, Leon, how you've grown. And Marisa, what a pretty pink ribbon in your hair. Tito, what a nice haircut, how grown-up you look. Hello, Henri, and Maria and Katia. Gerard, why the sad face? I've got a hug for you. Oh, I love you all." She hugged several children at once.

Love and admiration welled in Lou's heart. *What a wonderful woman she is,* he thought. *But will she have me?* He knelt and chatted with several of the boys who gravitated toward him.

When Abigail stood, her smart beige dress and coat were covered with tiny handprints, but she didn't seem to care. "Where are the triplets, Mrs. B.?"

"In the art room. They love the watercolors."

"We'll see them now, and I'll show our Lou what we've done with the home."

Mrs. B. smiled with pride. "Your stylish friend, Miss Bretancourt, certainly liked it."

Abigail and Lou stopped and looked at each other. "Danielle Bretancourt was here?"

"*Ja*, she comes here often. I thought you knew. She told me she lost her little boy, Nicky. Gave me a nice drawing of him. She hopes to find him someday."

Lou threw a worried glance at Abigail and dropped his voice to a whisper. "I thought he'd died."

Abigail answered quietly, "A mother never gives up hope."

Mrs. B. nodded in agreement. "Now, if you'll excuse me, I'm needed in the kitchen. I hope you'll join us for lunch."

Walking through the hallway, Abigail and Lou paused at the first door, where a sun-filled room was painted lemon yellow and giant cushy cubes of bright green and red and blue were stacked in the center like a pyramid. Thick blue mats for acrobatics were arranged around the cubes, and matching pillows were stacked to the side near a blackboard and a well-stocked bookshelf.

"This is the indoor playroom and reading room," Abigail explained. "The children learn English through storytelling and pictures, and Mrs. B. uses the blackboard to go over new words and sounds."

"And my staff did all this?"

"This and more. Follow me," she said with a wink.

They wound through the house, examining one room after another. The rambling old home had once been a rundown boardinghouse. Abigail had bought it at a good price, and with the aid of Lou's staff and volunteers, she'd transformed it.

Abigail opened the door to the art room. There sat three redheaded, freckled eight-year-olds, two boys and one girl, cloaked in smocks, intent on their artwork. A volunteer worked with them. "Try the blue," the woman was saying, pointing to the blue paint, and repeating, "blue, blue."

"Bel-u," they repeated.

"Very good," she said, clapping her hands.

"Good," they repeated, laughing and clapping, blue paint spattering from their fingers.

"Oh, Miss Abigail, I'm afraid you're blue, too. I'm terribly sorry." The volunteer was clearly mortified.

Abigail looked down. Sure enough, her beige woolen dress was now splattered with fine blue drops, and Lou had blue splatters across his white starched shirt and burgundy tie. "It's okay," Abigail said, smiling. "I rather like it. Greatly improves our image, I believe."

The children, at first afraid for their transgression, broke into wide smiles.

Abigail said, "We came to see Alexandra, Aaron, and Aristotle. We'll take over, if you'd like to go to lunch. I wanted Mr. Silverman to meet them. He's also from Russia."

The volunteer left, and Lou removed his dark suit jacket and perched on a stool next to the children. They turned their faces up to him expectantly. *What precious children,* he thought. Speaking in his native tongue, he said to them, "Hello, how are you?"

At the sound, their eyes widened with delight. All at once, they began to chatter.

Their happy voices tugged on his heartstrings. Lou laughed and looked up at Abigail. "I think we understand each other perfectly."

Lou spoke to them and then translated for Abigail. She knew a few Russian words, too. "Ask them if they have other brothers or sisters." They shook their heads no.

They played with the children all afternoon and when it was time for them to go, Abigail and Lou hugged each one. Lou closed the door behind them and slipped his jacket back on. He checked his watch, his heart quickening. *The timing is perfect.* "We have some time before dinner. Shall we take a drive up Mulholland? We can watch the sunset." Lou folded down the convertible top on his ruby red roadster and helped her in.

Abigail drew a silk scarf from her purse and tied it over her hair. She turned eagerly to Lou. "Do you think your friends will like the triplets? Who are they?"

"They're a great couple."

"I'd like to meet them sometime."

Lou draped his arm casually over the back of the seat, and Abigail moved closer. She asked, "What does he do for a living?"

He tapped her nose. "Has anyone ever told you that you ask too many questions? I said they *might* be interested, Abigail." But these were the things he loved about her. *Her enthusiasm, her tenacity.* He steered the car up around the curves. "Look at that view."

He touched her hand in a familiar gesture as they drove. "Let's watch the sunset from here," he said, maneuvering the car off the road.

The sun was setting over the Pacific Ocean, burnishing the sky with coppery, shimmering shades in the encroaching twilight. Abigail leaned comfortably into Lou.

He gazed out, admiring the watercolor sky. His mind was far, far away. He reached into his pocket, playing with the velvet box he'd carried for so long. He'd never done this before. *I'm ready, but is she?* he wondered. "What a sky, Abigail. Isn't it marvelous?"

"When can I meet them?"

This wasn't going as he'd planned. She was still stuck on the topic of the children. He stroked his chin. "How about tonight?"

"Tonight?" she exclaimed. "Why, I'm a mess. Did you have this planned all along?"

Lou grinned, glad he'd interrupted her flow of questions. "No, this is one of those pure coincidences, Abigail."

"Really, Lou, you should have warned me. Look at my dress."

"You didn't mind before; besides, you look lovely. They'll understand. We have a reservation pretty soon at Braga's." It was a casual Italian café with a lively atmosphere. *Maybe it's better there,* he thought. *Less formal.*

"Well then, what are we waiting for?" she said. "I'm starving. Let's go."

Lou had to laugh at the situation. The romantic moment he'd planned to perfection had passed. *Love is seldom what you expect,* he thought, glancing at Abigail. His friends had always assumed he'd fall in love with one of the young starlets at his studio. But it was Abigail who'd captured his heart. Reluctantly, he turned the key in the ignition and shifted the car into drive.

They walked into the café, and Lou motioned to the maître'd, who greeted them and sat them at a red-checked, cloth-covered table for four.

When they sat down, Abigail asked, "What type of work did you say he did?"

"I didn't say." A thousand questions, she had. He could hardly get a word in. *This isn't going well.* Feeling anxious, he excused himself to speak to the chef, an old friend who knew Lou's favorite dishes.

When Lou returned to the table, Abigail said, "I wonder what's keeping them?" A waiter delivered a bottle of wine and a basket of bread. She removed the napkin covering the bread and reached for a breadstick.

Abigail gasped. Encircling a crusty garlic breadstick was a glittering diamond ring.

Lou took her hand, his eyes shining. "Marry me, Abigail," he said, his heart welling with passion, and then he kissed her. *There, finally.*

Abigail didn't respond. Instead, she pulled away. Then, pressing her hand to her mouth, she stood and raced from the table.

Lou covered his eyes with his hands, his shoulders sagging. *What happened?* He heard the front door of the restaurant slam. *Did I read her wrong?*

He thought for a moment. *I won't take no for an answer, not without a good explanation.* He stood up and strode to the door, aware of other diners watching him, but not caring. *I can't let her go that easily.*

Abigail was standing outside, sobbing.

Loud wrapped his arms around her. "What's this all about?" he asked.

"I love you, Lou," she said, sniffing. "I know you're going to say it doesn't matter, but I know it does. I know what you want. All men do."

Lou tilted his head, confused. "Are you talking about sex?"

She looked up at him. "What? No, no, of course not. I like sex."

A couple passed them on their way into the restaurant and stared at them with interest. The wife nudged her husband. "Open the door."

Abigail's face colored. "Oh no, I didn't mean that."

"I'd rather hoped you did," Lou said, sighing. *Just when I thought the night couldn't get any worse . . .*

"Well, I do, actually." She looked up at him with wet eyelashes, sniffing. "It's a splendid offer, Lou, and if I were a normal woman, I'd accept."

"But you're not normal, are you?"

Abigail shook her head.

"Tell me what's wrong, sweetheart."

"When I was young, I fell from a horse. I was badly injured." Her voice cracked. "I can't have children, Lou. There, now you know." She squeezed her eyes shut, tears spilling onto her cheeks.

"Shhh," he said, stroking her hair. *This explains a lot.* Now he understood her compassion for the orphaned children. "I have loved you from the first moment we met," he whispered. "That won't stop me. It's *you* I want, I want us to spend our lives together." He found her mouth, kissing her through her tears.

She kissed him back, then said, "Are you sure you don't mind not having children?"

Lou wiped tears from her cheeks. "You know the couple I mentioned to you?"

She started to speak, and then a look of joyous comprehension spread across her face. "That's us?"

Now he couldn't speak. He tightened his embrace, and Abigail began to laugh. "We'll make a perfect family," she said, smothering his face with kisses. "Oh, Lou, of course I'll marry you."

32

Perfume, like a lover, can never be fully possessed. Desire—
abated for a few hours of pleasure—returns evermore.

—DB

12 MAY, 1941 — SAN FERNANDO VALLEY, CALIFORNIA

Danielle left the orphanage in the San Fernando Valley and wove
through the blossom-laden orange and lemon groves that surrounded
it. Squinting into the setting sun, she wished she had left earlier, but
she'd wanted to meet all the new children.

The narrow road over the Santa Monica Mountains into Beverly
Hills was difficult enough to navigate in the daytime. Cameron had
always warned her against this drive at night.

Poor, dear Cameron, she thought, a lump rising in her throat. He'd
given his life to save her. A sob of guilt and grief escaped her lips.
Her family was devastated, too. None of them had slept much since
the incident.

Cameron's fans had held a candlelight vigil outside their home
the night he died. At the funeral, thousands had waited outside the
small chapel. His singles "Perfumed Letters" and "Emerald Eyes"
held the top two positions on the popular music charts. She choked
again. These were the last songs he wrote for her. Found in his room
at the sanatarium, Hedda Hopper reported, were a handful of sweetly
perfumed letters from his wife, yellowed with age. *Maybe it was his
way of making things up to me.*

She had a measure of relief that the police had caught the man who had been stalking her, and they confirmed his former Nazi party affiliation. Furthermore, he was already wanted for murder in New York.

Danielle drew a breath and turned onto Coldwater Canyon Road to begin a series of fishhook switchbacks that led into the mountain pass. The steep hill, known for its dangerous landslides, was covered with native brush, lantana, and purple *delosperma*.

Her Delahaye was being repaired, so she was driving Cameron's white Rolls-Royce. She turned the wheel out of the first curve and came upon a road repair crew removing fallen boulders. The road narrowed to one lane. She stopped to allow an oncoming car to pass. As she waited, she glanced in her rearview mirror and saw a man in the car behind her, the brim of his hat pulled low on his forehead. She wondered about him, feeling uneasy. *But they caught the man who tried to kill me.*

After the car passed, she eased into the single lane. She noticed the car behind her was getting dangerously close. She touched her brakes in warning.

He didn't let up, and instead tapped the rear of her car with his bumper. *What's he doing?* Danielle sped up. He pulled alongside of her in the closed lane, his wheels kicking up gravel from freshly laid pavement, pinging her window.

Fear flooded her. *Is this another assassin?* She thought about her family. *I've got to get home.*

She glanced over and saw the glint of a gun barrel pointed at her. *No, not again.* Horrified, Danielle pressed the accelerator and the powerful car thrust ahead. The other car mirrored her actions, pulled ahead of her, and screeched to a stop.

Her heart in her throat, Danielle stomped on the brakes, barely missing a rear end collision. Her mind raced. She threw the car into reverse, squealing the car around. He drove on, roared around a curve. *This is the only way home.* Danielle swept her hands across her face, trembling, waiting for him to disappear.

When she was sure he was gone, she shifted the car into gear and gunned the engine. She raced past Mulholland Drive at the crest of the mountain and began the descent.

She maneuvered through a sharp switchback, and then all at once, bright lights blinded her in the review mirror as a car bore down upon her. She peered down a steep mountain incline on one side and a soaring wall of rock on the other. *He means to kill me.* Sweat trickled down her temple.

Thinking fast, she gripped the burl wood steering wheel and whipped the car around the curve, building speed. She prayed there wasn't another car coming around the bend. The man sped up, too, then smacked her rear bumper with such force it snapped her head back.

She jerked the wheel, tires squealing, and saw the car behind her fishtail, felt its immense weight on her bumper, heard it grate against the rock mountain wall, saw rocks begin to tumble. *Mon Dieu,* she thought, panicking, *the bumpers are stuck.* The next curve lay ahead, and she was losing control of her car.

A shot rang out and her rear window exploded, the bullet whizzing past her head, shattering the dashboard.

Terrified, she yanked the wheel into another curve. The tires hit gravel at the edge of the road.

Steeling her nerves, she aimed straight into the next curve. She opened her door, sucked in a breath, and jumped, rolling as she hit the pavement, screaming as the blacktop scraped skin from her arm, the second car's engine roaring near her ear. Her head hit the road with a resounding thud. Out of control, she skidded until her body lodged against a pile of rocks.

Metal upon metal screeched like animals in the night and a man's shriek pierced the blackness. Clouds of dust and dirt sprayed into her eyes and nose and mouth. Taillights hurtled over the edge of the curve, followed by the sound of cars smashing down the mountainside.

She struggled to lift her arm, wipe her eyes. *Blood.* Then the world began to spin around her, and everything went black.

Danielle didn't know how much time had passed when she heard a faint voice reaching out to her. "Ma'am, we're moving you, on three. Now one, two, three."

Pain shot through her, but she was too weak to cry out. Darkness clouded her vision.

The next time Danielle woke, she opened her eyes to blurry whiteness. Her entire body was throbbing in agony.

Marie rose from a chair and hurried toward her. "You're going to be all right, *ma chère*." She kissed her cheek. "Another motorist spotted you by the side of the road. Oh, my poor darling."

The door to her hospital room swung open. A man walked in and flashed his badge. "I'm the detective on the case," he said. "You're one lucky woman. That was quite a risk you took, but it saved your life."

"Who—did this?" She touched her jaw, wincing as she discovered a bandaged lump.

"We found his body in the rental car," he said. "Searched his apartment and discovered a stash of newspaper clippings about you. We confirmed his identify. Another Nazi. Ma'am, do you know who is so intent on killing you?"

33

Perfume is a journal of life's emotions, recalling the scent of desire, of fear, of sadness, of elation. Perfume lodges in the memory, never to be forgotten.

—DB

20 MAY, 1941 — BEVERLY HILLS, CALIFORNIA

After Danielle was released from the hospital, she returned home, intent on spending time with her family as they healed from Cameron's death.

At night, Danielle slept fitfully. She dreamed of being chased, of screeching wheels, waking upon impact drenched in sweat and panting with fear. Cameron's killer was in jail, her stalker was dead, but the incidents haunted her still. She wondered, *Are we really safe?*

Creating a studio at home allowed Danielle to stay abreast of her rapidly growing business while she recovered. Harry visited daily, and she hired an experienced woman to sell the line, delegating the task to her of traveling to sell to new markets.

Danielle worked in the studio blending perfumes, sketching designs, and selecting fabrics for her winter collection. She had time to think about Cameron, their tumultuous marriage, and the impact on her family. Still, she had no regrets. Except for Jon. And Nicky was never far from her mind.

While Danielle was recovering, Jasmin took her first baby steps, cheered on by the family. The little girl seemed oblivious to the tragedies that marked her first year of life. Her wide green eyes sparkled with curiosity and her gleeful giggles brightened the house like a rainbow. Playing with Jasmin and watching her daily progress helped them all cope with their losses.

One day Abigail visited, carrying a stunning arrangement of white orchids. "Just what I needed to lift my spirits," Danielle exclaimed. She placed it on a round table by the curved entryway staircase. The white orchids complemented the antique cherry wood table and the silk Persian rug. "Orchids are so graceful, the flowers last such a long time."

"How are you feeling?" Abigail asked, concerned.

"Better, the concussion has healed, and the doctor said my scarring should be minimal." Her voice dropped a notch. "We all miss Cameron, but the outpouring of love from his fans has helped."

Jasmin tugged on her linen skirt, and Danielle hoisted her to her hip. "Jasmin has three new baby teeth," Danielle announced, smoothing her daughter's strawberry blond curls. "She adores the avocados, grapefruit, and mandarin oranges from the yard."

Abigail gave Jasmin a kiss, and as she did, Danielle noticed Abigail seemed especially radiant. It wasn't her rosy pink spring dress, or her new straw hat adorned with tiny rosebuds, but something else that lit Abigail's face. "Would you like to sit in the garden and talk? I have fresh lemonade for us."

The nanny came to look after Jasmin and Liliana, while Danielle and Abigail sat on the patio with tall glasses of cool lemonade. The sweet scent of sun-warmed orange blossoms from the garden's orange trees swirled around them. Danielle's new rosebushes were sprinkled with tight buds.

"So, Miss Cheshire Cat, what's your secret?" Danielle asked.

Abigail's eyes widened. "Oh, Danielle, Lou and I can't hide it any longer, we're getting married. And we're going to be parents."

"What? Why, you're . . ."

Abigail laughed into her hand. "Oh no, darling. We're adopting triplets, two boys and a girl, adorable eight-year-old orphans from Russia. And I want you to be my matron of honor." Abigail's face shimmered with happiness.

"I'd be delighted," Danielle said, hugging her.

"And would you design my wedding dress?" Abigail asked, holding her breath in anticipation.

"Ideas are already dancing in my mind. Have you set a date yet?"

"We've decided on the fifth of July. Will that give you enough time? It's also the only time that Jon and Victoria can visit."

Jon, here. With Victoria. At that, Danielle's world shifted on its axis. She nodded in numb agreement. Abigail continued to chatter about details of the wedding. Danielle listened, unable to speak for the lump in her throat. She ached as she recalled the tautness of Jon's skin under her touch, the warmth of his breath between her breasts, the beat of his heart against hers.

How can I stop caring about him?

29 JUNE, 1941 — BEVERLY HILLS, CALIFORNIA

Danielle glanced nervously at the calendar in her home office. The past few weeks she had worked feverishly on Abigail's wedding gown, and had also created a new perfume for her. She had designed the House of Bretancourt *prêt-à-porter* collection for autumn, blended perfumes to match, ordered fabric and notions, and balanced her financial accounts.

No matter how much she occupied her mind, the date she dreaded would soon arrive, and she would be face-to-face with Jon and his wife. *I'll be perfectly cordial,* she thought, anxiously practicing her responses.

Jon and Victoria, his parents, and the Leibowitzes were making the journey from England. After they had arrived in New York on a Newell-Grey ship from England, Lou arranged first class train ac-commodations to Los Angeles. Jon was granted travel time in order to assess Newell-Grey ships in the Long Beach harbor that might be outfitted for military use.

That wasn't her only worry. She studied the messages she was preparing to wire to orphanages, embassies, and relief agencies be-fore her visit to London. She planned to leave soon after the wed-ding. She had heard relief organizations were rescuing children from war zones. So far, there had been no sign of Nicky, but she felt she had to be there.

Liliana bounded into Danielle's office clutching her fashion sketches. "What do you think of these?"

Danielle studied them. "Why, they're excellent." Liliana was ma-ture for her age, and had real artistic flair for drawing and painting. Jasmin toddled after her, the nanny racing behind them. Jasmin was a spunky ball of fire, always in motion.

Danielle knelt to hug them. *Seeing my family happy and healthy is all that matters,* she thought, embracing the girls. *And finding their brother.* "I love you both so much. I hope you're having fun today."

A knock sounded on the front door. Danielle closed her perfume journal and ledgers and answered the door.

"Hello, darling," Abigail said gaily. "I can't wait to see the new wedding gown, and I hope you don't mind that I brought my *family* along." Abigail grinned as she used her favorite new word.

Liliana had befriended the eight-year-old triplets, Alexandra, Aaron, and Ari. Lou had legally adopted the three children, and Abigail had essentially become their mother. Soon that would be legal, too.

Lou held up a bottle of fine French champagne. "We thought we'd kick off the celebration."

"My favorite," Danielle said. "Come in," she added, and asked the cook to bring glasses and hors d'oeuvres.

Marie joined them in the airy living room, her silvery blond hair perfectly coiffed, a pastel green dress of Danielle's design skimming her figure. "I think everyone is eager to celebrate this wedding. And someday soon, I hope, an end to the war."

"Hear, hear." Lou turned serious and raised his glass. "To the brave men and women at the front lines."

They all raised their glasses. Marie cleared her throat and held her glass high. "And to those who've gone on before us, may they watch after us," she said solemnly, then added with a lilting laugh, "and may we never cease to amuse them."

"Hear, hear," they chorused again and clinked their champagne flutes in remembrance, murmuring their names.

"And for Nicky," Marie added quietly. Danielle kissed her mother on the cheek.

Marie said gently, "I've lost a son, too, *ma chère*."

"But Nicky is still alive," Danielle murmured. She understood her mother was only trying to comfort her. "I can feel him." The sympathetic look in her mother's eyes told her everything. *She's lost hope.*

Marie patted her hand and changed the subject. "I look forward to meeting your brother, Abigail. I've heard so many wonderful things about Jon."

Abigail giggled. The excitement and the champagne had clearly gone to her head. "Wait until you meet Victoria," she said, waggling her eyebrows. "Honestly, I'm surprised she's coming."

Lou gave her arm a squeeze. "I'm sure you'll make his wife welcome, Abigail."

"I hardly need to try," Abigail declared. "Victoria makes herself welcome wherever she goes. Especially with the men," she added, *sotto voce.*

Danielle saw Marie glance at her under her lashes. "Abigail, I have your dress upstairs. I'd love for you to try it on."

Lou grinned. "I'd like to see it, too."

"Not until the wedding," Abigail said. "It's bad luck."

1 JULY, 1941 — BEVERLY HILLS, CALIFORNIA

Danielle stood in front of her wardrobe trying to decide what to wear. Abigail had made her promise that she'd come to the train station to welcome her parents. At the time it had seemed impossible to say no to Abigail—perhaps it was the champagne—and now she regretted it.

Danielle threw off her dressing gown and pulled on a pair of black summer wool trousers, along with an ivory silk blouse and jacket. She applied her favorite perfume, Chimère, drawing the crystal stopper behind her ears, down her throat, on the back of her neck, and inside of her wrists. With a deft hand, she secured her long auburn hair in a chic updo, anchoring it with two tortoiseshell combs. After adding discreet emerald earrings, a delicate emerald and platinum tasseled necklace, and an ivory and emerald–colored silk scarf, she was ready.

She stepped into her pumps and turned, checking her image in the mirror. She thought of the words that a journalist once used to describe her: *modern and accomplished.* She leaned into the mirror, touched faint lines around her eyes. *And twice-widowed.*

Marie was giving final instructions to the nanny for the girls. "Let's go, Maman," Danielle said, false enthusiasm masking her nerves.

They met Abigail, Lou, and the triplets at Union Station in downtown Los Angeles. Everyone was in high spirits as they walked through the ornate, dome-ceilinged station to the platform.

They didn't have long to wait. A train slowed, nearing the platform. Passengers stood at the windows, waving merrily to the crowd. People called out as they spied friends and family.

Danielle stood back from the crowd. *Is he here?* she wondered.

The train halted, doors opened, and passengers stepped out. Danielle pressed her lips together, her heartbeat quickening. There, by the first class car, stood Jon. His sun-bleached chestnut hair framed his rugged face. He stood erect, with an officer's posture, his broad chest filling out his suit.

Her skin warmed in remembrance of their last day together. She'd never regretted their stolen day. *It's all I'll ever have of him,* she thought, aching for his touch.

Danielle slid her eyes to the woman next to him. *Victoria.* Blond and willowy, she stood apart from Jon. Danielle tried not to feel envy, but she couldn't help herself.

Victoria was a beautiful woman. *She's dressed in Mainbocher's latest suit,* Danielle noted, recognizing the American designer's work. And thickening noticeably around the middle.

How could Victoria have treated Jon so badly?

Jon gazed out over the platform, searching. *Where is she?*

"I'm hot," Victoria whined. "Can't they hurry up?"

"Be patient, and remember your promise." Jon regarded his wife with disdain. "I will not allow gossip to ruin Abigail's wedding."

Victoria flicked a speck from her collar. "I'll be glad when this is all over, and you'll finally sign the papers."

He sighed. "My solicitor will have them for you immediately."

She smiled victoriously.

He'd resolved not to let Victoria spoil the day, but she was trying his patience. Jon was pleased for his sister and couldn't wait to meet her fiancé and children. But first, he had something terribly important to settle.

"Everyone here is so rude to me." Victoria was pouting now, her huge aquamarine eyes filled with accusation.

Why she was pouting, he didn't know. No doubt, her mood had something to do with the surreptitious phone call to her married lover he'd overheard her make before they left London. At least the bloke's wife had finally agreed to give him a divorce. Victoria had actually tried to pin her mistake on Jon, saying it was *his* fault she'd slept with the man, that she'd done it on the rebound from Jon, so she was justified in marrying him.

Jon shrugged. It was over. He'd stopped caring, stopped trying to pacify her.

The only woman I want is here in Los Angeles.

He bit his lip and frowned. He hated to think of it . . . that awful day at Danielle's apartment . . . but if Danielle hadn't married Cameron, he certainly would *not* have married Victoria.

He scanned the platform for the one touchstone he held to. *The one who still holds my heart.* He had relived the afternoon they'd spent together so often that her every word, her every movement, and her incredible scent were seared into his memory.

He pushed his hand impatiently through his hair. *Where the devil is she?*

And would she still feel the same for him?

Abigail whirled around, her face flushed with excitement. "Look who's here."

Danielle stiffened, bracing herself. This was the moment she'd been dreading.

"My parents, look right there, and the Leibowitzes," Abigail added, pointing and waving. "And there, right in front, see? Jon and Victoria."

Danielle lifted her hand, nodding to the Leibowitzes, her old friends, and Harriett and Nathan Newell-Grey, Abigail's parents. She kept her eyes carefully averted from Jon.

Abigail and Lou and the redheaded triplets were swept into a sea of open arms. Danielle saw Jon and Victoria greet them, and then she watched as Victoria stalked off by herself, although Jon barely seemed to notice her leave. *Interesting,* Danielle thought, wondering what they were arguing about. She couldn't help the tiny flicker of hope that crossed her mind.

Danielle greeted Abigail's parents with warmth, recalling their kindness to her and Max. As she hugged Libby, the woman's soft Floris lavender fragrance brought back a flood of memories about London. She introduced Marie to Libby, and soon they were chatting like old friends.

Danielle was startled to feel a hand on her shoulder. Without turning, she felt the hand press and squeeze her shoulder. She inhaled deeply, detecting a trace of the incredible scent of his skin, musky and virile. His natural scent was layered with leathery notes, sensual patchouli with a touch of carnal rose. She would replicate this scent, improve upon it for him. She closed her eyes and she was back in his arms, dancing in New York City.

"Hello, beautiful."

Danielle took another breath and turned. She found herself staring into Jon's liquid brown eyes. *I was so wrong . . . I have never stopped loving this man.* Words caught in her throat as she strived to compose herself. "Hello, Jon."

They stood in silence for an awkward moment. Their families were talking and exclaiming over the children. His hand lingered against her cheek as he lifted it from her shoulder; the memory of those hands caressing her skin burned in her mind.

"I'm glad you came," he said, his voice husky.

"I came for Abigail." Danielle flushed, overcome with emotion.

Jon's eyes roamed over her face, her figure. "It's awfully good to see you. You look marvelous, Danielle."

"So do you." She glanced away, aware that her heart was pounding wildly.

He brushed a wisp of hair from her forehead. "My darling Danielle," he said, lowering his voice. "We have to talk. How's tonight, after dinner?"

Danielle shook her head. "I can't," she murmured.

"I *must* see you," he whispered, urgency rising in his voice. "You know we need to talk."

She shook her head. "It would be wrong for us to continue our—our friendship. It's over." *There. I've said it,* she thought, though it was as if a piece of her soul had shriveled and died.

Jon leaned in; his breath was warm on her neck. "It's not over, Danielle," he whispered, his voice gentle yet firm. "It will never be over between us."

34

On a frigid night of an Italian winter, crimson flows through the veins of nature's sweet orange, staining its flesh. Cold-pressing releases its addictive oil: tangy, warm, balsamic. Blends well with frankincense, cedar, and clove. And always transports me to Italy.

—DB

2 JULY, 1941 — BEVERLY HILLS, CALIFORNIA

The next morning dawned crisp and clear, the sky a vivid cerulean blue, heralding a perfect summer day in Southern California, even though the forecast had called for rain.

Danielle yawned and stretched before the window. Thoughts of Jon had kept her up half the night. *But Jon is married . . . happily or otherwise, it doesn't matter. It's over.*

She tore her thoughts from Jon. Today she had a busy schedule. She and Marie were taking the girls shopping at Bullock's Wilshire department store. Danielle had also planned a meeting with the store's executive buyers responsible for her *parfum* and *prêt-à-porter* lines.

Abigail and Lou would be married the day after Independence Day. Although Lou had joked about it, he was eager to trade his independence for Abigail and the triplets. This was Danielle's first celebration of the American holiday, and it held special significance for her.

After the wedding, she planned to travel to London, where she had scheduled appointments with embassies, orphanages, and relief agencies to continue her search for Nicky.

She bathed quickly and dressed in a slim black skirt suit piped with white, added a red silk rose on her lapel, and applied the latest perfume she'd created for summer—d'Orange Sanguine, a tangy, radiant melding of blood orange and cedar wood. She hurried downstairs to meet her mother and the girls.

Danielle handed her mother a small amber bottle. "I thought of you, Maman, for a *parfum* in my *collections de parfum d'été*. I call it La Violette; it's fresh and powdery, lovely for summer. It reminds me of our holiday in Italy a few years ago."

Marie removed the cap and sniffed with her eyes closed. "Ooh la la, deliciously feminine. I detect an undercurrent of basil, *n'est-ce pas?*" She touched a few drops to her wrists and neck.

"For me, too," Liliana said, offering a slender wrist to her grand-mother.

Marie laughed. "*Naturellement.*" She put a single drop on Liliana's wrist, and the little girl waved it under her nose, breathing in the scent with a happy smile, her eyes fluttering. Jasmin clapped her hands and squealed with delight.

"Another generation of perfumers," Marie remarked, and kissed her granddaughters.

Danielle met Libby at the entrance to the Beverly Hills Hotel on Sunset Boulevard, where the wedding party was staying. Danielle drove the short distance to Bullock's Wilshire, arriving under the porte cochere where valets in fine livery assisted Libby, Marie, and the girls. They swept into the store and went to the shoe salon, where they bought several pairs of shoes. By the time they rode the elevator to the top floor to the desert-themed tearoom, they were all exhausted but happy.

Danielle enjoyed catching up with Libby. Liliana enjoyed her first tea, complete with thin cucumber sandwiches, crusty scones with Devonshire cream and strawberry jam, and fragrant Earl Grey and Darjeeling teas. Libby pronounced it nearly as fine an afternoon tea as in London.

Danielle left them to finish their tea while she met with the buyers. The executives showed her the design for the new Parfums Bretancourt section in the *parfumerie*. Next they went to the evening wear salon, where she met salespeople and discussed an upcoming fashion show.

When she returned to the tearoom, she sucked in her breath. Jon was sitting at their table. *I can't do this,* she thought, panicking. She was turning to leave when Libby spotted her and called out.

Jon's eyes lingered on Danielle as she sat down. He turned his attention to Jasmin and Liliana, asking Liliana what she'd bought and how she liked California. Danielle marveled at the ease with which he spoke to her daughters. The girls seemed to like him and she relaxed a little.

When the conversation lulled, Libby said, "What are you shopping for, Jon?"

"I had to have a new suit for Abigail's wedding."

"Well, I'll say, you've filled out in all the right places. What muscles," Libby said, squeezing his arm.

Liliana made a muscle of her own, which sent both girls into gales of laughter.

"Feisty, aren't they?" Jon said, winking at Danielle.

"Like their mother," Marie said, smiling. "You were a stubborn little girl. You had definite ideas, even then." She turned to Jon. "I'm so proud of my daughter. She's become quite a trendsetter in America."

"Indeed she has." Jon leaned back and crossed his long legs, his eyes dancing as a smile played on his mouth. "I saw your new evening dresses here. They're stunning."

"Shopping for your wife?" As soon as the words left her lips, Danielle regretted it. *Why did I say that?*

"Abigail told me I should see your work," Jon said smoothly. He glanced at his watch. "I must hurry to pick up my suit, though." He hesitated, looked directly at her. "I'd sure appreciate a woman's advice on the accessories. Danielle, would you mind accompanying me?"

Libby was quick to answer. "An excellent idea. We'll take a taxi back, Danielle. You don't mind, do you, Marie?"

"Not at all," Marie responded. "I can manage the girls."

Danielle was nervous at the thought of being alone with Jon. In her heart she wanted nothing more than to be with him, but her head warned her otherwise.

She accompanied Jon to the men's department, where they assembled his attire for the wedding. Jon had also ordered additional suits, and Danielle laughed as Jon tried to pair ridiculous ties and shirts. "You know better than that," she said, relaxing a little. She brushed her hair over her shoulder and smiled at him.

"Hold it right there," he said. "That's the way you looked when we ran into one another at the flower shop. The way I always remember you."

She shook her head as the smile faded from her lips.

"Danielle, I'm sorry if I said something wrong. But you must admit, fate intervened today to bring us together."

"Fate? Really?"

He shrugged and pushed his hand through his thick hair. "Libby might have mentioned that she was meeting you here today."

When they emerged from Bullock's Wilshire, the forecast had materialized in rain; by the time they arrived at the Beverly Hills Hotel, the summer storm was in full force. With water flowing down from the hills, Sunset Boulevard had turned into a treacherous waterway.

Danielle peered up at the grand, peachy pink hotel with a wry smile. "Perhaps there's room at the inn."

They raced through the rain with Jon's packages, laughing as they nearly bumped into Claudette Colbert, one of Danielle's favorite actresses and clients.

"How about dinner?" Jon suggested to Danielle.

"Here? What about Victoria?"

"She's locked herself in her own suite; I really have to talk to you about her. I've heard the Polo Lounge here is excellent. Please say you'll have dinner with me, Danielle. We need to speak."

"I'll call my mother first to make sure everything is fine at home."

When Danielle called her from the lobby, Marie assured her they were fine. "I'll kiss the girls for you," Marie said, then added pointedly, "and I won't wait up."

A few minutes later, Danielle and Jon were ushered into the chic pink-and-green Polo Lounge, and seated in a curved leather booth surrounded by celebrities, potted palms, and polo accoutrements. Jon ordered a bottle of Chassagne Montrachet, one of his favorite white wines. As they dined and chatted, Danielle found it hard to imagine that this was all they would ever have together. But that was the reality; she had to be honest with him. *No matter how much it hurts.*

When Jon made a toast to new beginnings, Danielle flushed and put her glass down.

"I must admit, I dreaded your visit. But now I know, feeling this happiness, but knowing it can never be—this is what I really dreaded."

Jon looked shocked. "You can't mean that, we're so right together."

"But we're *not* together. You're married, Jon." She lowered her eyes, her heart shattering. "You *must* leave me alone."

Jon laced his fingers through hers and said, "I have something very important to tell you."

Danielle raised her eyes to him, her lashes damp. *What could he possibly say that would make a difference?*

"Victoria and I have a deal. She asked me for a divorce, and I agreed on the condition that we wouldn't announce it until after Abigail's wedding. I don't want the gossip mill to ruin my sister's happy day."

Danielle let his words sink in, her pulse hammering in her head. *He'll be free,* she thought, hardly daring to hope. "What will Victoria do?"

"She's going to marry her baby's father. His wife is granting him a divorce. It's going to be quite the scandal in London, I assure you." He kissed her, and gazed into her eyes. "I want to be with you, Danielle. And I meant what I said about helping you find Nicky. I still believe."

These were the words she had longed to hear, but never thought possible. She had shared precious parts of her life with Jon—Max's death, Jasmin's birth, her search for Nicky, her most private passions. Could they build a life together?

Jon wiped a tear from her cheek. "Will you think about it?"

When they finished dinner, torrents of rain were still sheeting across the streets. Jon withdrew his room key from his pocket. "Give me a few more minutes," he said, his voice gravelly with desire. "I can't let you go, not yet."

As soon as he shut the door to his private suite, they found themselves in each other's arms, drinking in the intoxicating scent of one another. When their lips met, Danielle's resolve evaporated. Her purse dropped to the floor.

"Danielle, I have dreamt of this moment for so long," he whispered.

"So have I, my darling."

He tilted her chin and cradled her face in his broad hands. "The night is ours," he said, his voice thick with emotion. In one fluid motion, he lifted her and carried her to his bed.

Danielle had only one thought: *We are meant to be.* Slowly and deliberately, they undressed each other, exploring the deepest pleasures of one another's bodies. Danielle caressed Jon's chest, his back, his thighs, remembering the feel of his skin on hers, tracing scars where he had been wounded. She kissed each scar, and he moaned in response.

After they made love, Jon stroked damp tendrils from her forehead and kissed her softly. "Don't ever desert me, Danielle."

"Never," she murmured. Her strong will had softened, become pliable in his hands.

Over and over, they promised their undying love, until finally, as dawn crept through the windows, Jon fell into the deadened sleep of the exhausted.

Quietly, Danielle dressed and returned home. But as she closed the door to her bedroom, doubt crept into her mind. They had so many obstacles that could not be overcome in one night of passion.

She thought of his family, and hers, and the war raging around the world. They'd be separated until the war was over—if he survived. Were these problems insurmountable? Was their happiness really too much to hope for?

Would her heart be broken again?

She covered her face with her hands. *Oh, what have I done?*

35

An independent woman selects her own perfume—scents to accent her style, her personality, her ambition.

—DB

4 JULY, 1941 — BEVERLY HILLS, CALIFORNIA

By the next morning, the summer storm had swept across the southland, disappearing into the east. It was such a clear evening that Danielle took her family and the entire wedding party—except for Victoria—to a summer concert at the Hollywood Bowl, a concave hillside amphitheater.

The Los Angeles Philharmonic performed stirring patriotic American songs, and Danielle and Jon were enraptured. Liliana and Jasmin were awestruck by sparkling fireworks bursting above the arched stage, while Jon's mother, Harriett, craned her neck to see the Hollywood stars: Charlie Chaplin, Edward G. Robinson, and Igor Stravinsky in one box, and in another, Jeanette MacDonald and Deanna Durbin.

When the show was over, members of the press asked Danielle, Lou, and Abigail to pose for photos, then peppered them with questions: "Where is the wedding? Who is wearing your designs? Any new perfumes? Where is the honeymoon?"

"You'll get used to this," Lou said to Abigail. They laughed and shared details about their upcoming wedding with the reporters.

Danielle added that she was traveling to London soon, and asked everyone for their support of the war for freedom in Europe.

Early the next evening, Abigail stood perfectly still while Danielle fastened the twenty pearl buttons lining the back of her wedding dress. "This is a dream I thought would never come true, Danielle."

Strains of laughter floated up the staircase at Danielle's home. Candles flickered in the windows, brilliant beacons for the guests who were beginning to arrive at Danielle's home.

"There, now turn around," Danielle said, "let me see how it falls on you."

Abigail swirled in front of the mirror, her face glowing. "It's utterly gorgeous," she breathed.

"You're a beautiful bride," Danielle said, happy for her friend. "And the design is yours alone. No one else could do it justice."

Danielle had fashioned the exquisitely simple dress to showcase Abigail's svelte figure. The ivory satin, off-the-shoulder gown had a tasteful décolleté, and the fitted bodice featured tiny pleats nipped into a slim fitted waist. It was the perfect frame for the heirloom Edwardian jewelry she wore, treasured family pieces of diamonds and pearls Harriett had brought from London. As Abigail turned, the expertly draped train swished gracefully behind her.

Danielle lifted a delicate veil above Abigail's sleek coiffure and secured it with two antique hairpins. "Don't forget your perfume." She picked up a crystal bottle of fragrance she'd blended especially for Abigail's wedding.

As she trailed the perfume along the nape of Abigail's long neck, the sweet floral aroma of jasmine, lily, and orange blossom transported her to Grasse. Memories misted her vision.

Danielle gazed at Abigail. "You're absolutely stunning."

Abigail's eyes began to fill. Danielle whipped out a lace handkerchief to dab Abigail's eyes, and then her own. "We'll have none of that, this is a happy occasion."

A tap sounded at the door and Abigail's father joined them. A smile lit his face. "My dear daughter, how lovely you look."

Abigail smiled, her brown eyes glistening. "Have all the guests arrived?"

Nathan Newell-Grey nodded. "All present and accounted for. Are you ready?"

"I am. Danielle, you're first." Abigail hugged Danielle, then turned to her father, who held his hands out to her.

Danielle glanced down from the top of the stairs. The intoxicating aroma of white lilies and tuberose perfumed the air, reminding her of her own wedding to Max. She blinked against her memories. Today, it was Abigail's turn at happiness.

A pianist played in one corner of the living room, candles provided subtle illumination, and fresh green garlands lined the banister. Six rows of chairs were arranged for the intimate ceremony. A soft evening breeze carried the scent of orange blossoms from the garden through open French doors.

Danielle descended the staircase, her emerald green silk dress trailing on the steps behind her. Walking past the guests, she nodded to the Newell-Greys and the triplets. Behind them were the Leibowitzes, Marie with Jasmin and Liliana, and a few other close friends. Victoria sat in the second row, her face a brittle mask of boredom.

Lou stood beaming next to the minister. Jon, his best man, waited next to him. As matron of honor, Danielle took her place across from Jon. She acknowledged him, careful not to let her gaze linger, but she could feel the spark of connection between them. A moment later, Abigail made a grand entrance on the arm of her father amid hushed murmurs of approval.

As Abigail took her place beside Lou, Danielle was aware of Jon's unwavering eyes on her.

The simple exchange of vows proceeded, and before long, the minister announced, "You may kiss the bride."

"At last." Lou's bright blue eyes twinkled as he lifted Abigail's veil and they kissed. A happy chorus of cheers and well wishes filled the room.

After the ceremony, Danielle joined her family. "I don't think I've ever seen a more beautiful wedding," she said to Marie, "or two people more suited to one another."

Marie smiled at her. "*L'amour.* You can always see it in the eyes."

After photographs were taken, they spilled onto the rear lawn, where linen-covered tables laden with crystal and silver were arranged. But Victoria called a cab and left before dinner was served.

As Danielle watched Victoria leave, Marie caught her daughter's eye. "Life is short, darling." Marie lowered her voice. "Victoria is gone. You and Jon shouldn't suffer."

Danielle opened her mouth to protest, but Marie put her hand on her daughter's arm. "You're wise enough now to follow your heart."

My darling," Jon murmured, opening the door to his hotel suite. "I didn't think you'd come tonight, it's so late."

"How could I stay away?" She sank into his warm embrace. "You've become a habit I can't bear to break. And we haven't much more time together."

Jon pressed Danielle against his muscular frame, his hands sliding along the length of her body, caressing every curve, his lips teasing her bare shoulder, the length of her neck, the line of her jaw.

She tilted her head and their lips met in a deep, satisfying kiss.

———

On the outskirts of Los Angeles, a lean, battle-hardened man sat in a cheap boarding room with newspapers fanned out on the bed in front of him. Methodically he sharpened his scissors, then sliced an article free and added it to a notebook. To anyone observing him, they would think he had a keen interest in fashion and perfumery.

His men in America had failed him. But he would not.

36

How to convey the effervescence of champagne in perfume?
The secret is in the imagination.

—DB

Jon wheeled Danielle's Duesenberg onto Santa Monica Boulevard. They'd spent the morning meeting with a relief worker who had returned from Europe, but there were no new leads for Nicky. Their search for one little boy was miniscule in comparison to the war's scale of disaster. "You're the only one who truly believes me," Danielle said, thinking about her son.

"Your mother and Abigail support you."

"They support me, but they don't really believe. My mother even suggested that we have a memorial for Nicky." She shook her head. "I know she means well, she thinks it would give me peace and closure, but, Jon, I *know* he's alive, I can feel it. I'm not crazy."

"I don't think you are," he said, hugging her to him.

Danielle was shocked as Jon had described the enormity of the devastation that had taken place since she had left Europe. It was one thing to read about it, yet another to witness it. Nazi air raids over England had abated as Hitler turned his focus east, but tens of thousands of lives had been lost and homes and businesses destroyed in London, Liverpool, Birmingham, Plymouth, Southampton, and other cities. The death toll in Europe had climbed much, much higher. The war was far from over.

"Finding Nicky may seem hopeless, Jon, but I can't help my feeling."

He put his arm around her shoulder. "We'll keep looking," he said, his voice husky.

As they neared a church, Danielle asked Jon to stop. "Let's go inside."

They entered and knelt before a bank of votive candles. Reaching into her purse, Danielle withdrew the platinum lighter that had been Max's. She flicked it, and touched the flame to the candles, reciting the names of her family members who had perished. "And for Nicky," she said. "I still believe."

"For Nicky," Jon intoned.

Later that evening, after they had spent the afternoon with their families, Danielle and Jon opened the door to his hotel suite, where a crackling fire and champagne, caviar, and lox greeted them in the sitting room. Jon drew her to him. "I thought you'd like this after such a long day."

"You read my mind," Danielle said, kissing him. *This is a special man,* she thought. *I'm a lucky woman.*

"There's a new life ahead for all of us," he said earnestly. "Nicky is out there, Danielle. My own belief, like yours, is growing stronger every day."

"We'll find him together," she said.

Jon's eyes crinkled at the corners and his lips tugged into a crooked smile. He motioned toward the champagne. "Let's celebrate our future tonight."

"Veuve Clicquot, my favorite," she said. "Named after the French widow Clicquot."

"Who, like you, took the helm of the family business and charted a successful course."

Danielle gazed at him. *This is why I love this man.* Not many people understood this side of her. "I like a man who knows his history, especially about the historically rare female entrepreneur."

"And I admire women like you who are making history." He slid a finger under her chin and kissed her. "You know you're the only woman I've ever really loved." He cradled her face in his hands and kissed her again with ardor.

They settled on the sofa in front of the fire, and Jon poured the pale golden liquid into two crystal flutes.

"Here's to the beginning of the rest of our lives," he said, lifting his glass. "And to finding Nicky."

"*Salut,* my darling, thank you." She clinked his glass. "To the best years of our lives."

He kissed her again, then drew away and slipped a hand into his pocket. "I found something I believe you've misplaced. Close your eyes."

Danielle did so, wondering what he had. She heard a click.

"You can open them now."

In his hands sparkled a fiery emerald so vivid, intense, and *familiar* that she gasped. She pressed her hand to her mouth, stunned. *But how can this be?*

Jon took her right hand and slipped the ring onto her finger. "Abigail told me you'd sold your wedding ring to fund your business. Max once said the ring had belonged to his mother, and that it had been in her family for years. I thought you might like to wear it again in her honor."

"I can hardly believe it." Tears welled in her eyes and Danielle blinked, touching the ring with reverence. Sofia had once worn it, pledged her love to her husband with it, as Danielle had promised herself to Max with it. And the money it had brought not only helped her family endure a horrendous time, but also facilitated her business. As poignant as the ring's history was, having it again gave her a measure of solace. "How did you find it?"

"It wasn't easy. I rang up a jeweler I know here in Los Angeles and told him I was looking for a large Victorian-style emerald ring, one that had been sold recently. I sent him a photograph I had from the ship when we first met and you were wearing the ring. It took time, but my man came through. When I arrived, and matched the photo to it, I bought it straightaway."

Her eyes brimmed with tears. "Jon, it's perfect," she said, choking through her words. "I'm amazed, I can't begin to thank you enough. It's all I have left of Sofia, except for my memories." She ran a finger across the magnificent emerald, remembering Sofia and Max. *And Nicky.* She raised her eyes to Jon and reached up to kiss him.

Jon kissed her back. "There's something else, too."

He brought out a small suede box and removed an intricate fili-greed ring encrusted with diamonds, which surrounded a breath-taking center diamond. He took her left hand and held the ring poised before her third finger. "And this one is a symbol for our lives together. Will you wear it as my wife?"

Overwhelmed, a sob caught in her throat. She hesitated, fully aware of the enormity of such a pledge. She considered the trage-dies they had endured, the misunderstandings that had transpired. Did they have a chance for happiness?

Jon's expectant face glowed in the flickering firelight, his eyes urging her acceptance.

"I will," she said solemnly, then threw her arms around him.

"At last, it's official." Jon slipped the ring on her finger, his face flush with desire. With one easy motion, he swept her into his arms and carried her to bed, where they made love until the darkest hours before dawn.

As tendrils of dawn slowly illuminated the suite, Danielle snuggled into the crook of his arm, her wavy hair fanned across his chest, wishing the night would never end.

Jon ran his fingers through her hair, while she played with the cleft in his chin. "You know, I've always thought that was sexy," she murmured.

"You're the sexy one," he said, kissing her playfully on her forehead, nose, and chin. "But let's be serious." He leaned up to face her. "We'll have to wait until my divorce is final to marry. You could come to London, but I'd rather you stay here, out of harm's way."

Danielle's happiness was crushed as she contemplated their reality. Could she subject her girls and her mother to danger? *No, never again.* If she were childless, she'd be at his side in a moment—or as close as she could be.

She chewed her lip, thinking. They could commit to each other, but when would they ever be together? She thought about her ancestors—every generation had fought for their principles, or for peace. Today, it was their turn. It was dedicated men and women like Jon who would win the war and return peace to their world. She must support his service, and do what she could, too.

"I'll stay here," she said. "We'll work out the future."

But she'd learned there were no guarantees in life, no promise of roses.

37

Sandalwood, a stalwart of the perfumer's palette. Impervious to termites, matured more than thirty years. A superb fixative, an anchor. Stable, rich, smooth. Important qualities—desirable in men as well.

—DB

8 JULY, 1941 — LOS ANGELES, CALIFORNIA

Jon's leave was nearly over. He and his father were touring the Long Beach harbor this morning, checking on ships docked there that could be converted to military use. As for Victoria, the hotel manager said she had checked out and left for Acapulco. She didn't even say good-bye. Danielle promised to gather everyone for supper at her home that evening after she concluded her business.

"It's wonderful to have you here with us, Madame Bretancourt," the marketing director from Bullock's Wilshire said. "Follow me, let's start in the new ballroom."

"I'm thrilled that you're including my new evening gowns in the fashion show," Danielle said to the woman. The show was a fundraiser for Abigail's charity. Danielle and two other fashion designers were scheduled to speak at the event at the Beverly Wilshire Hotel.

"The ladies insisted on it," the woman replied. "They love the clothes you've designed for film stars. And I love this cranberry silk dress you're wearing, it drapes so beautifully on you. One of your own designs, I assume?"

Danielle smiled and nodded. It was humbling, really. She'd worked hard, and was simply glad that her work was well received. The show was planned for the next day, but she wanted to inspect the clothes and the perfume display. Bullock's Wilshire had agreed to take her entire line, and the event had been publicized in the newspapers for weeks.

They toured the backstage area, and Danielle examined the dazzling array of evening gowns that would be modeled the next day. "Everything looks to be in order," she said, straightening a few dresses on padded hangers.

They returned to the Italian Renaissance–styled ballroom. Danielle thought the Tuscan stone and white Carrara marble would be a perfect backdrop for her fashions.

"And here's your perfume display. We're still setting up," the woman said, gingerly stepping over a cord. "Mind the electrical extensions." She flipped a light switch, and gestured to a grouping of red velvet–draped tables and gilded chairs. Danielle's products were artfully arranged on tables around several enormous crystal bottles she'd had made especially for the occasion. "These are the most exquisite flacons I've ever seen," the woman added, reverently gliding her fingers over the curved bottles.

Each one was filled with one of Danielle's new perfumes and would be auctioned to raise money. Her inspiration came from Max's bottle designs from years ago. In her way, this was an honor to his memory. The last time she'd seen him was in England. She sighed. *When he was on his way to find our son.*

An aide interrupted them. "Pardon me, ma'am, but you have an urgent call."

"Go ahead," Danielle said. "I'll wait here."

"So sorry, do you mind? Last-minute emergencies." The woman and her aide hurried away, leaving Danielle alone in the half-lit room.

She inspected the runway where the models would walk, and

estimated the number of chairs in the audience. *This is quite the event,* she thought, pleased.

She leaned over to straighten the bottles and noticed smudges on the fine crystal. She put her purse down and opened it to retrieve a polishing cloth especially for removing fingerprints.

Humming to herself, Danielle began to polish the huge flacons, intent on shining each bottle to sparkling perfection. She had stepped back to admire the effect when she detected an unusual odor. *That smells like . . .*

Oud wood.

She froze for a moment, and then reached into her purse, ostensibly to exchange polishing cloths. She knelt to rub a smudge from the bottom of a tall bottle, surreptitiously observing the reflection in the crystal as she did. *What shall I do?* she thought, panicking.

A lean, hardened figure behind her came into focus. Terrified, she hardly dared to breathe.

Then she heard the click of a gun's trigger being cocked. A man's throaty laughter sent chills through her. "At last," he said, "we meet again."

Heinrich. Her heart pounded. She swung her head around on her shoulder.

He had a gruesome grin on his lips. A disfiguring scar ran the length of his face.

"What do you want, Heinrich?"

He laughed again. "Turn around so I can see you."

Slowly, she complied, crumpling the cloth and its contents into her pocket.

"Look at you, so glamorous, aren't you? How convenient that the newspapers publicize your exploits." He withdrew a clutch of articles from his coat pocket, crushed them, and let them fall to the floor. "Made it easy to find you this time."

"You sent those men to kill me, didn't you?"

Heinrich's smile vanished. "You're such a nuisance."

She saw his eyes blazing into her, and he advanced toward her, his gun pointed at her head. She breathed through her nose, trying to calm her fear. Perspiration gathered on her torso. "A gun? I thought you'd be more original, Heinrich."

He started to laugh again. "It was good enough for Max, and good enough for Sofia."

She waited. *He didn't mention Nicky.* "Why bother with me?"

His face twisted into an expression of cold hatred. "The day you joined our family, you destroyed it. And when you returned to Poland, your appearance—and your escape—destroyed my rise in the party. I had a future ahead of me until you showed up." He touched the scar on his face. "No matter how many of your kind I killed, *you* still have to pay."

With trained precision, Heinrich took aim.

Danielle flung herself to the floor. The bullet ripped through the air, demolishing a chair behind her.

Heinrich began to advance. "You'll die just like Max and Sofia did," he snarled. He marched forward.

The toe of his boot caught on an electrical cord, and as he tried to keep from slipping, his focus cracked for a second. In that moment, Danielle sprang up and heaved a large crystal flacon at him. He tried to dodge it, but the bottle smashed on his forehead, the scent of Chimère exploding into the air, perfume drenching his hair and clothes, and shards of crystal slicing his skin.

Cursing, he aimed again. Acting swiftly, Danielle flung a perfume bottle at the gun, and it clattered to the floor on impact, trailing the scent of blood orange in its wake.

"You *bitch*," he yelled, and dove for the gun.

Danielle pulled the stopper from another giant flacon and hurled it, thoroughly dousing him. The amber-colored liquid puddled around him, sandalwood fumes rising from his skin. He scrambled for the gun and rolled over to shoot.

Danielle tugged Max's platinum lighter from her pocket, flicked it, held it to the polishing cloth, and cast the flaming cloth onto him.

Instantly, the alcohol in the perfume ignited, engulfing his clothes, his hair, and his skin in flames. Shrieks of agony erupted from his mouth, echoing off the walls.

Squinting in revulsion, she watched the fire dance over him, the putrid smell of burning hair and flesh assaulting her nose. She covered her nose and backed away, turning from him, horrified at the sight. Behind her, a gunshot blasted, the bullet ricocheting from a pipe overhead. She screamed.

Someone grabbed her shoulder. "Are you all right?"

She looked back into the face of a police officer. "I think so."

Another officer knocked the gun from Heinrich's grasp, stomping out the flames with his boots. Heinrich clutched his chest with a blackened hand, and with one anguished, excruciating wail, he was gone.

Danielle stood outside watching as Heinrich's covered body was removed from the hotel ballroom. She breathed through a handkerchief pressed to her nose and mouth.

A white car from the Beverly Hills Hotel screeched to a stop in front of her. The marketing director had called Jon for her. He emerged from the backseat and raced toward her. "Oh, God, Danielle, I'm so glad you're all right," he said, wrapping his arms around her.

In the safety of his arms, she began sobbing, releasing pent-up tension. Worried, she turned her face up to his. "Where's Maman?"

"She's with the girls. They're safe, the police are at the house." He brushed tears from her cheeks and smothered her face with kisses. "What happened, darling?"

"It was horrible, he tried to kill me." She told him about Heinrich, and as she spoke, she relived the incident, choking on her words. The stench of his incinerated flesh clung to her clothes. *I need a bath,* she thought, desperate to cleanse herself of Heinrich and his hatred.

In the car, exhausted after the police had questioned her, she leaned her head against Jon's broad chest, and he stroked her hair as he drove her home in her car.

"He didn't kill Nicky," she said.

"How do you know?"

"He confessed, no, he *gloated* about killing Max and Sofia. He said nothing about Nicky. I *know* he's still alive, somewhere."

He kissed her. "We'll keep looking for Nicky, I promise. Nothing will stop us now."

The next morning, Jon sat at a desk in his suite drumming his fingers. He was on the phone to Pan American Airways. "Yes, two tickets. As soon as possible. Southampton? Yes, thank you."

He hung up the phone and turned to Danielle. "I hope you're not afraid to fly. We have a few flights to take, but we'll get to London as fast as we can."

38

Philosopher Jean-Jacques Rousseau wrote: "Smell is the sense of the imagination." How my imagination sustains me, conjuring scents from the past for comfort, when there is little peace in my soul.

—DB

18 July, 1941 — Southampton, England

Nick stepped off the bus onto the dock with the other children, and hoisted his knapsack over his skinny shoulder. Tall for his age, he would be nine years old this year. In his mind, he was almost an adult.

Nick knew a lot for his age. He knew which berries you could eat and which ones would make you sick. He could spot leaves that would make you itch like the devil, and he knew how to fashion traps for squirrels and rabbits. He had learned how to trade things, like food and tools and cigarettes, and he could communicate in several languages. He could even become invisible if he had to.

Most of all, he knew how to get things done. Nick was a natural leader, and all the other kids looked up to him.

But there was one thing that Nick didn't know. He glanced around to make sure no one was watching him; he reached inside of his jacket to retrieve his most prized possession. Opening a smudged envelope, he withdrew an old photograph. He touched the face of the woman, whose hair was swept up into a pretty style. The man who stood next to her seemed to be in love with her. There was an older woman, too, who stood so straight, but she looked kind. He turned it over. It was blank on the back.

Nick didn't know who he really was.

He'd forgotten a lot after he'd been beaten in the Warsaw ghetto, before he'd escaped. Occasionally, a memory came back.

These people, were they his family? Or some other child's family? If he belonged to them, why hadn't they found him yet?

The nuns had told him that the picture had been in his pocket when he'd arrived at the convent, starving, his feet bleeding. They'd taken it for safekeeping.

He knew his name was Nick. His surname, Holtzman, was written on a piece of paper. Outside that, he thought, *who am I?*

The nuns tried to find his family. In the end, he'd been placed in hiding with one family, then another one, until he escaped again. A group of Catholic volunteers took pity on him; they scraped together money to smuggle him out and send him away to a better life. The orphanage in London was kinder, but bombs shook the city almost every night.

Now he was on his way to Australia. He'd heard of the wide open spaces, the big sun, and kangaroos that had pouches for their babies, so they'd never lose them.

Who had lost him?

He had a vague recollection, not actually a memory, but a feeling. A feeling of being held and kissed, a feeling of being loved. He kicked the ground, sending pebbles scattering.

It was an incredible feeling, one he would never forget.

Some of the other kids had been found, or sent to live with distant relatives. A few of the little ones had been adopted. He waited, but no one ever came for him.

He knew it was time to make a life for himself. Glancing over his shoulder, he saw children from the orphanage forming a line. He hung back, watching.

Australia. The nuns had told him there was a lot of opportunity there for someone like him, for boys who were willing to work hard. *Someone without a family*—that's what they really meant. *What will it feel like,* he thought, *to be free?*

He knew he should go, but something was holding him back.

"I hear you're leaving for Australia tomorrow."

Startled, Nick swung around. He didn't like people sneaking up on him, and he'd been so deep in thought that he hadn't heard the woman approach.

"Yeah," he said.

"That's exciting. You're a lucky boy," the woman said.

"Guess so." Once he left, he'd be on his own. There was no chance that anyone would ever find him. His chest tightened at the thought.

"My name is Irina," she said, holding out her hand.

He shook her hand. "Nick Holtzman."

"You can study, learn a trade in Australia. The orphanage is close to the ocean. Do you know how to swim?"

"A little." Last year, he'd found a net, repaired it, and learned to dive into the lake and catch fish. The kids ate well that summer.

"What's that you have?" The woman gestured to the photograph. "Mind if I look at it?"

He shrugged and handed it to her.

"Is this your family?" Irina asked softly.

Is it? "Yeah, I think so."

"She's very attractive." She studied the black-and-white photograph. "You have her eyes, you know."

Nick's heart quickened. "Do I?"

"You sure do, I'd recognize those eyes anywhere." Returning

the photograph, she said, "It's nice that you have this, it's a real treasure."

Nick smiled, a little embarrassed. He slid it back into the envelope, taking care to make sure it wasn't bent.

"Ready to join the group now?"

Nick shrugged, started off, and soon fell in line with the other children.

18 JULY, 1941 — LONDON, ENGLAND

"That's right, Nicolas von Hoffman." Danielle clutched the phone, waiting for a reply. "Can you check again?" she asked. After a moment, she shook her head at Jon. Dejected, she returned the receiver to the cradle. Libby had told them to call Irina, a woman from Poland who was working with a resistance group.

Danielle sank her face into her hands, and Jon began to knead the tension from her shoulders. Nothing was working out for them, it seemed. But she would not give up until she found Nicky. *Or until I know the truth.*

Since arriving in London, her presentiment had never been keener. An extreme sense of urgency gripped her. "I must visit Libby's friend."

"That's quite a drive, Danielle. Can't you call again?"

"No, I must speak to Irina in person." She couldn't explain why.

Jon stared at her, and finally nodded. "I know that look in your eyes, my dear." He checked his watch. "We could go tomorrow, or leave now and find an inn, see her first thing in the morning."

"No time like the present," Danielle said. "I'll get my bag."

19 JULY, 1941 — SOUTHAMPTON, ENGLAND

The next day, Irina walked into her office at the children's relief agency. Originally from Poland, she had married an Englishman.

She had been a social worker with a Catholic church in Warsaw before the war. After the victors had taken over, she'd become involved with the Resistance, helping smuggle out children.

The number of displaced children was overwhelming. It was her job to help find orphanages or families who would take them, wherever that might be. She sat at her desk and opened her engagement book. It looked to be a busy day.

She opened her office door and called to her assistant for a file she needed.

Her assistant crossed to her office. "There's a couple from London who drove to see you. It's Mrs. Bretancourt, she said she spoke with you yesterday."

While her assistant looked for the file, Irina glanced at Danielle, who sat motionless in the waiting room, her eyes closed. Her lips were moving slightly, as in prayer.

When her assistant returned with the file, Irina said, "Tell them I'll be with them as soon as I can."

As they waited, Danielle grew more and more anxious.

"Are you all right, darling?" Jon put his arm around her. "Why, you're shivering. Are you cold?"

"Just nervous."

Presently, Irina invited them into her office. As Irina greeted her, Danielle noticed the woman looked at her with a strange expression. They exchanged pleasantries, and then Danielle began. "As I mentioned on the phone, we're trying to locate my son. Yesterday you said that you didn't know of anything, but I felt we should come here anyway." She reached into her purse. "In 1939, my son was six years old. I had an artist in Los Angeles prepare a sketch of how he might look today."

As Irina took the drawing she said, "There's something quite familiar about you, Danielle." She inclined her head. "You have the most amazing eyes." She studied the sketch for a moment, drawing her brows together. "What did you say his name was?"

"Nicolas von Hoffman."

"Could it be Holtzman?"

Danielle and Jon exchanged a look. "Anything is possible," Jon said.

Irina stared at Danielle. "Does he have your eyes?"

When Danielle gasped, Irina said, "You must go to the dock right away. There's a ship leaving for Australia this morning, but you have to hurry. I met a boy yesterday, and he showed me an old photograph." She paused. "There was a woman in it, and I'd swear it was you."

Danielle and Jon rushed to the docks. An ocean liner loomed ahead of them, its gangplank being retracted.

As Jon helped Danielle out of the car, he looked down at her shoes. "Can you run in those heels?"

She yanked them off and they raced after the great ship.

"Hold up," Jon yelled, waving. "I need to speak to the captain."

"Please wait," Danielle screamed. "There's someone on board we must see."

"Should've been here earlier. We're casting off, Captain's order," came the reply.

A row of children lined the railing, watching with fascination as the enormous vessel began to heave away from the dock.

"No, wait," Danielle screamed. "I'm looking for my son. My son is on board!" She waved her arms. *What can I do?* She yelled, "Nicky, Nicky! Nicolas von Hoffman, Nicolas von Hoffman!"

Jon joined in. "Stop the ship," he shouted. And then, "Nick, Nick Holtzman, your mother's here!"

The children began pointing to her and chattering, but the ship kept easing away. Danielle fell to her knees on the pavement, tears misting her eyes. Desperation seized her, and she cried out again, "Nicky, Nicolas von Hoffman!"

On board the ship, Nick heard a commotion, and joined the other children at the rail. "What's going on?" Tenting his hand against the sun, he peered out and spied a woman and a man, shouting. He leaned over to get a better look.

"Nicky, Nicky!"

An old memory surged to the surface. *The woman . . . I know that accent, it's French.* He climbed up on the rail and waved, tentatively at first.

Danielle saw a boy waving at them. "Jon, it's him, I *know* it." She stood and raced to the edge of the dock. "Nicky, it's *me*, your *mother*."

That voice . . . He remembered something about the way she spoke, and then he recognized her. *It's the lady in my photograph!*

A crew member behind him was watching the exchange,

"Maman?" he said tentatively, and then, when the woman began jumping up and down, he yelled, "Maman!" He waved back wildly.

"Nicky," she cried, clutching Jon's arm. "How do we get them to return?"

The boy disappeared from the rail. Danielle screamed, "Nicky!" When he didn't reappear, she dropped to her knees again, sobbing. Jon knelt down, his arms around her. The ship was moving farther out; she could hardly discern faces anymore. "Why won't they come back?"

"We can radio a message. We'll try to catch them, go aboard, or go to Australia. We'll find him, I promise."

Inconsolable, she sobbed Nicky's name over and over, her heart splintering with grief. *We were so close, so close . . .*

Jon looked up at the ship again, and saw a crew member gesturing to him. "Wait a minute," he said. "My God, I think they're coming back."

They watched as the great ship edged closer in its return. It seemed to take forever.

Finally, the gangplank was lowered again.

Danielle's heart was in her throat when the captain and a young boy rushed down the gangplank.

"Maman, you came for me!" Nick flung his arms around her, tears of joy streaming from his eyes.

"Oh, Nicky, it's *you*," Danielle cried joyfully, burying her nose in his hair, drinking in his scent, her cheeks glistening with tears. *It's really you,* she thought, murmuring her thanks to God. *At last, at last, how long I have waited, how many tears I have shed.*

The captain handed a photograph to Jon. "He showed me this."

Jon looked at it and nodded. "Danielle, this is you and Max," he said, amazement in his voice. "Here, look."

As she did, memories flooded back. "And that's Sofia."

Nicky caught his breath. "Is that my father in the photograph?"

Danielle looked at him, pain in her eyes. "Yes, my darling boy, that's your father and his mother. You were so young then."

"Are they here, too?" he asked, hope rising in his voice.

"No, I'm sorry," she said, her voice cracking. "But I promise, you'll never be alone again."

Epilogue

Perfume is the essence of beauty, the heart of illusion, the soul of desire. It is my past, my present, my future.

—DB

Danielle stood at the bedroom window gazing over fields of flowers, their shaded hues emerging in the waning moonlight, their sweet scents mingling in the early predawn air. Her nose tingled, juxtaposing the fresh aroma of dew-laden grass with musky warmth from their night of lovemaking. An idea for a new perfume danced in her mind.

Jon stood behind her, his arms wrapped around her, nuzzling her neck. *This is a perfect moment,* she thought, resting her head against his chest and breathing in the beloved spring aromas of the Grasse countryside. *How many years I've waited for this.*

After Danielle left for America, Philippe had shuttered Bellerose, the Bretancourt family chateau, and joined the Free French forces. With renewed vigor, he had rallied supporters in Africa and fought for the liberation of Paris.

It had been a year since the war had mercifully come to an end in a victory for the Allies. Jon had remained in England, assisting with the transport of thousands of troops, the majority of them destined for America. After his service to his country, his father had asked for his aid in the refurbishment of Newell-Grey ships converted to military use.

How Danielle had loved seeing newsreel images of French tanks passing under the Arc de Triomphe in Paris. Charles de Gaulle had organized the Resistance fighters into the French Forces of the Interior, which rose up against the German garrison in Paris. The Free French Army of Liberation and the United States' 4th Infantry Division had joined in, and now freedom was restored to her beloved homeland. And thankfully, to her immense relief, Philippe and Yvette had survived the liberation.

This is our homecoming to Bellerose, Danielle thought, her heart brimming with conflicting emotions. Gratitude for those who had survived the war, grief for those who had not. She ran her hand along Jon's neck, caressing his skin, releasing the scent she had fallen in love with the moment she'd met him. And now, it had finally come to this, a new chapter in their lives. They'd waited years for this, never knowing if it would come to pass.

And so Danielle had brought her family back to France. They had arrived two weeks ago, meeting Jon and Philippe in Paris to celebrate the first Victory Day. They continued on to Grasse to help Philippe reopen Bellerose and prepare for the first harvest since the end of the war. Danielle and Jon would return to Los Angeles with Marie and the children at the end of the summer, but for now, Bellerose was their sanctuary.

How the next generation had grown—Liliana and Nick, as he preferred to be called, were thirteen years old, and Jasmin had just turned six. Danielle and Philippe were tutoring them in perfumery. Jasmin already showed a natural talent in aroma identification, while Liliana loved to design and sew her own clothes. Nick was a born leader. He loved nothing more than listening to Jon and Philippe talk about their wartime adventures for hours on end. But Danielle and Nick had a special bond, never to be broken again.

Jon dragged his lips along her neck. "Back at hard labor again today, my love?" he asked, only half jesting.

"What do you think?" she replied, stretching her limbs. "While you're leading the troops, I'm feeding them." Danielle and Marie had been cleaning and restocking the kitchen, and preparing for the upcoming celebration. Meanwhile, Jon and Philippe had led the charge on the property, clearing rubble, pruning and planting, replacing broken windows, and repairing fixtures. More than five years of accumulated dust, pests and rodents, and overgrown fields had to be cleared.

"You have more help, what with Abigail here," Jon said. He kissed her bare shoulder, and then reluctantly pulled on his work trousers and a worn shirt. He swept a hand down Danielle's nude back. "I could stay here all day with you, just the two of us."

"Soon, darling," she said, pressing against him. But there was work to be done. The rebuilding of a business, an economy, a country. The rebuilding of lives. Many would never be the same. Millions had died or disappeared, the damaged remaining to reconstruct what they could.

"I'll have coffee ready for you." With a wink, Jon tossed a cotton dress to her on his way out of the bedroom. He banged on another bedroom door on his way downstairs. "Nick-o, time to rise."

Several neighbors had lent a hand with the larger tasks, and Jon and Philippe and Nick returned the favor. Neighbors often gathered their fresh produce and came together for a feast, al fresco, under an arbor covered in a canopy of white climbing roses, overlooking the lights of the village. And to their delight, Philippe had found their wine cellar untouched. The dusty bottles of wine and cognac had aged remarkably well.

Danielle buttoned her dress and brushed her hair; she pinned waves back from her face and touched a fresh verbena eau de cologne to her skin, a simple formula from her old perfume journal. She smiled; Liliana and Jasmin had helped her blend it.

It was the children's first visit to France in many years, too. None of them had remembered the buttery croissants, beribboned hills, or balmy Mediterranean nights sweetened by fields of flowers.

"This is where you learned to blend perfume?" Liliana had asked, wide-eyed, when they reopened the laboratory. Danielle found her old notebooks full of formulas, trials, errors and successes, and shared them with the children. She also presented them with blank moleskin journals of their own to record their tests, impressions, and thoughts.

But their most important event was this weekend.

Guests were arriving already: Harriet and Nathan Newell-Grey; Libby and Herb Leibowitz from London; Yvette Baudin from Paris; Abigail and Lou, along with Alexandra, Aaron, and Ari from Los Angeles; as well as Clara and Harry, who'd married last year. Other friends from England and France were coming, too. There would soon be dining and dancing and revelry lasting until long after midnight. Bellerose had blossomed again, full of life and laughter, just the way she'd remembered when she was a young girl.

And tomorrow afternoon, Danielle and Jon would be married at Bellerose.

Danielle wore a simple bias-cut gown of the palest blush silk—one of her own designs—with white roses and jasmine braided into her thick auburn hair swept up from the nape of her neck, onto which she'd applied a new perfume she'd blended with a corresponding harmony just for the wedding. She carried the flowers of Bellerose: mimosa, rose, jasmine, violet, and orange blossom, twined into a voluptuous bouquet that spilled from her hand.

Jon stood before her, his velvety brown eyes sparkling with flecks of gold. She drank in the delicious, virile smell of him, loving how the scent of his skin melded with the perfume she had blended for him for this day—blood orange and orange blossom, patchouli and sandalwood, cinnamon and clove. She had devised a salty note, too, and added the sea's airy freshness.

Their family, children, and friends were gathered around, joining them in their long-awaited celebration of commitment.

Danielle lifted her face into a balmy breeze that carried the scent of orange blossoms. Jon smoothed a wisp of hair from her forehead. "What are you thinking, my beautiful woman?"

She smiled at him as they joined hands. "That I want to capture this moment forever."

Author's Note

Chapter 1. The prime minister's radio address is a transcript of British Prime Minister Chamberlain's radio address. To hear the actual speech, search the Internet for the audio of the British Declaration of War Radio Broadcast, September 3, 1939.

The Perfumes:

The fictional perfume, Chimère, is based on a perfume created for me by perfumer Marvel Fields, then of Mane USA. It was called Fabulous by Jan Moran® Beverly Hills, and was sold in boutiques. It exists today only in my private reserve.

Other perfumes, including d'Orange Sanguine and La Violette, are based on an artisan perfume line I developed. The Joie de Bretancourt, Jour de Bretancourt, and Nuit de Bretancourt perfumes are entirely fictional. For a list of referenced historical perfumes, visit www.janmoran.com.

Discussion Questions

1. In the beginning of the story, Danielle is constrained by societal values, but as the story progresses, she shuns convention. Why do you think her beliefs and behavior changed?

2. Women's career roles in history underwent seismic shifts during World War II. Do you think that Danielle's motivation for business was external, internal, or both? Why?

3. How would today's modern communications of mobile phones, e-mail, and satellite media have changed this story? The relationship between Danielle and Jon? The war itself?

4. Danielle experienced many scenes through her sense of smell. What are your favorite olfactory observations in this story?

5. How does Danielle's keen sense of smell add to setting and characterization?

6. Danielle and Max make the distinction between Germany and the Nazi party. How does this conflict affect their relationship? How do politics affect other relationships in the families?

7. When Danielle is launching her perfume line at Bullock's Wilshire in Los Angeles, she realizes she feels like an American.

What do you think she meant by that? Do you have any stories of immigration in your own family?

8. Do you know what year women in your country gained the right to vote? The right to own property? Can you imagine how having new access to these rights might have motivated women? Why or why not?

9. Danielle never gives up hope of finding her son, and senses that he still lives. Do you think parents have a sixth sense about the well-being of their children?

10. As an entrepreneur, what were Danielle's challenges and keys to success? Do you have any entrepreneurial ambitions, or have you ever started a new venture? Do you know where you might find business advice in your community or network?

Visit www.janmoran.com to discover more details about this book, learn about Jan's upcoming new books, and follow Jan's blog. Please join the reader's club list, too!